Books By Kevin Lee

- **TRIO Book One 'H*E*R*O*E*S**
- **TRIO Book Two 'Dark Dragon's Dawn'**
- **TRIO Book Three 'Ascension'**

Forthcoming;

- **FUTURE SCAN (2011)**
- **TRIO Book Four 'Retribution' (2012 - 2013)**

Other Books

- The Black Wolf 'Metal Monsters of Doom' (Co-writer)
- The Black Wolf 2 'The Demon Door' (Co-writer)

Forthcoming;

- The Black Wolf 3 (Untitled) (2011) (Co-writer)
- Churchill (Untitled) (2011) (Co-writer)

Enjoy the next adventure!

Trio: Book Three

'Ascension'

by

Kevin Lee

authorHOUSE®

AuthorHouse™
1663 Liberty Drive
Bloomington, IN 47403
www.authorhouse.com
Phone: 1-800-839-8640

©2011 Kevin Lee. All rights reserved.

No part of this book may be reproduced, stored in a retrieval system, or transmitted by any means without the written permission of the author.

First published by AuthorHouse 1/18/2011

ISBN: 978-1-4520-8394-0 (sc)
ISBN: 978-1-4567-1028-6 (e)

Printed in the United States of America

Any people depicted in stock imagery provided by Thinkstock are models, and such images are being used for illustrative purposes only.
Certain stock imagery © Thinkstock.

This book is printed on acid-free paper.

Because of the dynamic nature of the Internet, any Web addresses or links contained in this book may have changed since publication and may no longer be valid. The views expressed in this work are solely those of the author and do not necessarily reflect the views of the publisher, and the publisher hereby disclaims any responsibility for them.

Acknowledgments

As ***TRIO Book Three*** comes to a wrap and brings to a conclusion the initial trilogy I have to say thanks to a number of people who have helped bring this series of books to fruition.

First and foremost, to those who have read, are reading or who would like to read the series, my deep felt thanks for all your comments, good, and bad because without you the reader, there would be a story but no one to read it! Your enthusiasm for the books has driven me to strive for a higher bar of excellence with each new adventure! I hope I can keep you hooked with further new adventures like my favorite authors have kept me intrigued over the years. Thank you, one and all.

A big thank you to **Ryan Crouse** who's artistic talents as the 'map maker' for books two and three are greatly appreciated and for working with me to design my website and bring it to life! www.kevinleeauthor.ca.

A great appreciation and thanks to the artist **Joewie Aderes** from Edmonton AB for his fantastic artwork that graces the cover of TRIO Book Three 'Ascension'! A tremendous talent that you will see for a long long time in the realm of fantasy!

And an enormous thank you to my mom, Hazel, who has been there to support and tolerate me with all my antics over the years, thanks Mom!

On a final note, it has been a thrill to see my ideas come to life in ***TRIO*** and my other co-writing projects and I appreciate you letting me into your imagination, once again thank you.

DREAM OF AN ADVENTURE,
AND YOU MAY FIND YOURSELF LIVING IT
AFTER ALL, **ANYTHING** IS POSSIBLE!

Forest Swamp
Elf Archers
Helana's Army
Battle At The Falls

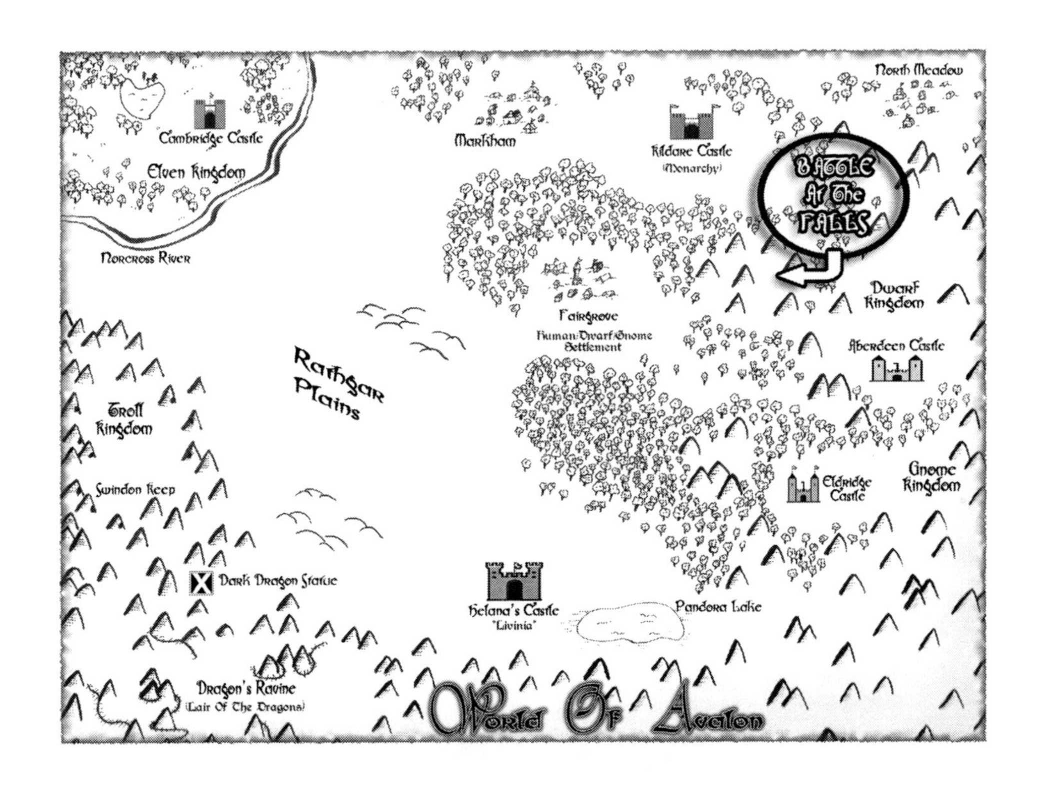
World Of Avalon
Cambridge Castle
Elven Kingdom
Norcross River
Markham
Kildare Castle
(Monarchy)
Battle At The Falls
North Meadow
Dwarf Kingdom
Fairgrove
Human/Dwarf/Gnome Settlement
Aberdeen Castle
Rathgar Plains
Troll Kingdom
Swindon Keep
Eldridge Castle
Gnome Kingdom
Dark Dragon Statue
Helana's Castle
"Livinia"
Pandora Lake
Dragon's Ravine
(Lair Of The Dragons)

Prologue

He awoke with a start, and sat upright in bed with a scream. His breathing was hard, and sweat covered his entire body. The bell chimed in the distance. Big Ben struck two in the morning, the sound echoing in through the open window. Wiping his face with the edge of the cotton blanket, he slowly calmed himself with several deep breaths. The vision was so vivid, so haunting. For the past few nights the same scene unfolded in his dreams. It had been a long time since anything of this magnitude had come to him in his sleep. In fact, the closest one he could recall dated back to the days of prosecution against those who had practiced magic. Footsteps on the stairs made him look towards the bedroom door. A moment later it opened and the shadow of a figure stood in the weak light of the hallway.

"Sir, are you all right?"

It was his young female apprentice. Even though her voice was just a whisper, he could tell she was concerned.

"Not to worry my dear. I'm quite all right. It was only a dream."

"Another? Was it the same one sir?"

"Yes, yes it was." He was considerably calmer now and

got out of bed to fetch himself the glass of water that rested on his table across the room. "You needn't worry about me Falon. You can return to your room."

"Sir," she started, and he immediately knew she was about to ask him about the dream. "It has been four nights in a row. How does one interpret that?"

He knew what the vision was about, but thought better that she not know its magnitude until he deemed it was time. His answer was simple.

"All I can tell you right now my dear, is that within the next few days we'll be having company."

"Company?" Now she was confused. "Who?"

"I'm not sure to be honest, but they will be coming for our assistance. We'd best prepare ourselves for a journey."

"A journey? To where sir?" Falon was curious now. As much as she respected her teacher, it annoyed her that he was so vague at times. All he did was smile.

"Someplace where you'll get to use your new talents. I'm sure you will find it," he paused, "very intriguing."

TRIO

Book Three

The spell had been cast by wizard and princess, and had banished the witch Helana with her demons supposedly, forever. That was what the spell had dictated.

Tasha gripped the staff firmly, and began to speak the words needed to finish what Malcolm had started.
"DARKNESS IS WHAT MAKES YOU! DARKNESS IS WHAT SHALL BREAK YOU! INTO PERPETUAL NIGHT YOU SHALL BE SENT, WITH THE DEMON LORD MAGIC SPENT! TO NEVERMORE SEE DAY OR LIGHT, FOREVER MORE SEALED WITHIN! SO MOTE IT BE!"

'ASCENSION'

Chapter One

Malcolm Weelder reached down and grabbed a handful of soil. He knelt as he let the dirt fall between his fingers. It was dry, and had the texture of fine sand. A glance around the landscape confirmed his thoughts. The land was like a desert. Nothing grew out here, not even a meager shred of grass. Only rocks, dead trees, and patches of brown, withered shrubbery jutted out here and there. Something was wrong. He and the elves had been using their magic abilities to slowly restore all the lands ravaged by Helana. In every place, but here, Helana's old stronghold did the magic not work. Despite all their efforts, nothing changed.

Tony Merello, and Zach Thomas wandered over to rejoin the wizard from their little assignment Malcolm had asked of them. They had tagged along to give Malcolm a hand with investigating the land surrounding Helana's old castle. Apparently the wizard had wanted both of their opinions on whatever it was he was surveying.

The youngest of the three, Tony, had only bad memories of the place. He figured it was about time to return and put it behind him, once and for all. The last real vision he had of this dried out, barren landscape was of some creature impaling him with a sword. It was more of a blurred memory, but it was still there. On the occasional night he dreamed about the battle, and it felt like he was reliving his death all over. Around him the war raged, swords clanged against the other and he could see the monster, his opponent right in front of him. So real were the dreams he awoke screaming and clenching his abdomen as if the sword has just cut in. Mia would wake with him on those nights and she could see the anguish in his face, and wished there was something she could do to make the dreams go away. Tony was glad she couldn't. He wanted to overcome his vision on his own, without the use of magic. Since his return had been brought about by magic for which he was grateful, he thought that his mistrust of the practice would have eased. It did not. His home had been the streets, and even after his rebirth Tony still had faith in overcoming obstacles by ordinary means, and not by magic. Zach could never figure out why Tony acted that way, but who was he to argue. By coming here, to the place of his death, Tony wanted to face his past.

Zach didn't care for the place either. The battle against Helana had been a hard fought struggle and it was something none of them cared to relive. He knew why Tony had come, despite Malcolm's urging. He had heard about the dreams from Mia. Zach gave the kid credit for traveling with them. Coming to the place where you had died was something he himself would have rather avoided. Many had perished in the war against the witch. There was Tasha's family prior to their arrival on Avalon and countless others throughout the lands at the hands of Helana's assassins. The whole region looked worse now than at that final battle. Whatever it was that Malcolm was seeking answers to, it must be important. Both Zach and Tony shuffled up next to the kneeling wizard.

"Hey Malcolm, what's the story?" Tony asked.

Without turning to look at him, the wizard replied in quiet voice. "The magic is not healing the land as it should."

"No shit," cracked Zach. He kicked the dirt and a puff of dust blew away in the breeze. "I'd say it hasn't done a damn thing. There's nothing living out here except us. Boy, I think this place has gotten uglier since we were here last."

Malcolm glanced over at Zach. "What of the condition of the castle?"

Zach looked at Tony, "should I tell him or would you like the honor?"

"Go ahead."

"Well, those vines that covered it have pretty much fallen away and that swamp behind it has just about turned into a dust bowl. Only things still growing in the swamp are a few old marsh grasses. Other than that…"

He was interrupted abruptly by Malcolm at that point. "And what of the castle itself?"

"Relax, I was just about to get to that. The castle seems to be in pretty good shape actually, if you can describe that creation that way."

Tony spoke up "It's kinda weird how everything around here is dead or dyin, and that misshapen hunk of rock looks as it did at the battle."

"Yeah," continued Zach, "hardly a sign of any breakdown from the lousy weather out here. No wear and tear on the walls, gate, oh yeah, and that canyon surrounding it seems to be actually getting narrower."

The wizard stood and started off towards the castle, "come, I must see for myself."

"Hey Malcolm, what's the problem?" Tony asked as he walked after him.

"I cannot say until I've seen the castle."

Zach trailed behind the two. He'd rather be off with his dwarf friends Axel and Ruskin taking part in the festivities at Kildare Castle, than out here trudging through the parched sand. He was also a little curious to see how Riane was doing in the first Unified Games. It was something Neil had come up with to bring all the races together for some friendly competition and hopefully, some fun! Riane was the Elf Captain, and Zach's 'girlfriend', in a manner of speaking. Until him, Tony and Malcolm finished their survey of this miserable wasteland he'd have to wait to see how things were going.

The three of them approached the edge of the canyon surrounding 'Livinia' castle. Malcolm looked the structure over and then removed a small sphere from inside his robe. He held it up and let it float just in front of them. It turned pitch black within moments, and then abruptly exploded. All three jumped back in shock from the blast. Nobody said anything, each were too stunned at the sudden event. The only sound was that of the wind blowing over the land and the dust it moved.

It was Zach who the silence first. "What the hell just happened?"

Malcolm looked up at the castle and shuddered. A blast of arctic air swept over the threesome and Malcolm drew his robes in close around him for protection. Tony and Zach could see their breath form a fog as they exhaled. Clouds moved across the sky to hide the sun and the abstruse mass of rock cast a shadow over the canyon and over them. The air changed once again and the stench of rotting plants and carcasses burned their nostrils. The odor caused all three to cough and gag.

"Geez," gasped Tony covering his face with his arm, "smells worse than the city dump on a hot summer day."

"Malcolm, you never answered my question. What the hell just happened?"

The wizard's eyes went wide and the look of absolute horror came across his face. "There is an evil presence amongst us here, more powerful than I have ever felt before. Something is happening here."

"That," coughed Zach, "we could tell. So what is it?"

"I can't describe what I feel, except that we are all in danger."

Tony pointed at Malcolm's staff. "Can't you just use the amulets to get rid of whatever it is?"

"I cannot use the magic against something on which I am unable to focus. Even if I could find the source, there is no guarantee the amulets can stop it."

A brisk breeze swirled around the trio and the stench vanished, allowing them to breathe without coughing. Malcolm went to the edge of the canyon and gazed up and down the walls of the ravine. It was as Zach and Tony had said. The gap was narrowing. The stones almost looked as if they were 'growing' new stone upon old stone. There was definitely something out of order.

"So, what the hell do we do now?" asked Zach. He took in a deep breath and wiped the tears from his eyes. "Thank goodness for that fresh wind. I couldn't take much more of that smell."

Malcolm turned away from the ravine and began to walk off. "In response to your question Mr. Thomas, we leave. I must return to Cambridge and consult with the elves. There is not much time before whatever this evil is, enters our world."

"Enters our world? Then it's not here yet?" checked Zach. He looked back at the castle and then back at the wizard.

"Enters our world?" he repeated. Zach glanced over at Tony and he just shrugged. Zach ran after the wizard with Tony right behind him. "So then, any thoughts on where this so called EVIL might be coming from?"

"I have merely a theory."

"Care to share it with us?" Tony urged.

Malcolm stopped abruptly and turned to face the other two. "I believe," Malcolm nodded towards the castle, "That Helana may have found a way to free herself from her prison."

Both of their jaws dropped, and Zach spoke up. "I thought that spell you used to put her away was unbreakable?"

"So did I, Mr. Thomas, so did I. Quickly, stand next to me. I will transport first to Kildare where you must speak with the King and Queen about what we have discovered. I must go to the elves, and after speaking with Xanthus I will rejoin you at Kildare."

"The King! You know, I'm never gonna get used to Neil being called the 'King'," remarked Zach. He moved to stand next to Malcolm and Tony did the same.

"Makes two of us, okay wiz, ready whenever you are!"

Malcolm held his staff out in front of him and spoke the spell in a slow steady voice. The staff glowed with a white light that then surrounded the trio and in a flash, they vanished. For the length of time it takes to blink, they re-appeared in the throne chamber of Kildare castle. Zach gazed around the room and sighed.

"Whew, made it in one piece."

"Prefer to use horses?" Tony teased.

"Nope."

"I will take my leave and I will return as soon as I can."

"Later Malcolm," Zach nodded.

The wizard disappeared in a flash of light and the two

of them went in search of the King and Queen. Judging by the amount of noise filtering in from outside they assumed that the two were likely out on the terrace watching the festivities in the courtyard below. It was the first day of the Unified games and all the races were involved in a series of sporting events to see who stood out in both ability, and determination. The cheer of the crowd roared in through the open terrace doors and both smiled. It sounded as though everyone was quite excited and getting into the spirit of the event. Tony stopped and motioned for Zach to go first.

"After you, mister second in command."

Zach gave him a light smack on the head, "and don't you forget it." He then proceeded to grab Tony in a headlock and dragged him out onto the terrace. Each saw the royal company immediately.

"Hey your kingship!" bellowed Zach. "How goes things?'

Neil turned upon hearing Zach's yell. "It goes well, and stop calling me your kingship. My name is Neil."

"Yeah yeah, sure sure your kingship. Who's winning down there?"

Zach leaned over the railing and the view below was quite interesting. Two riders were racing their horses around a series of barrels trying to see who could out maneuver the other and cross the finish line first. An enormous crowd of elves, humans, dwarves and gnomes lined the walls of the castle encircling the courtyard. Each had their own favorite and the cheers were quite deafening.

"Looks like our barrel racing from our rodeo's back home," Zach observed.

Neil grinned. "That's where I got the idea from."

The Queen, Tasha, added with her friendly smile. "It's quite entertaining. Oh Zach, you'll be glad to know that so far, Riane is in first place overall."

"Your queenship was there any doubt!"

"I think you are a little bit too overconfident old man. There's still a lot of competition to come," Tony ribbed. He slapped Zach across the back and chuckled.

"I'm sure she'll win. I've got a bottle of elf brandy that says so."

"You know you aren't allowed to do any betting, especially with the dwarves," Neil reminded him.

"I know that," Zach replied, "this is just a friendly bet, with Thatcher, a gnome."

"I can't believe Thatcher would bet on anything with you," Tasha said. "What does he get if he wins the bet?"

"A bottle of that goo that gnomes drink."

"Who did Thatcher bet on?" Neil queried.

Zach looked back down into the courtyard, trying to locate someone in particular. He found his target in short order and pointed out a rather tall, behemoth of a man they all knew too well. Jacinto stood a good two feet above them and the arms the size of Zach's chest, or so it seemed. Jacinto perhaps had the size advantage over the elf captain Riane, but the smaller woman was a lot more adept at horseback riding. So, Zach figured the elf, which he cared very much for, would come out on top at the end of the tournament.

"Jacinto?" Neil Pointed.

"The one and only."

"Do I hear the mention of my good friend Jacinto amongst the group?" Thatcher beamed as stood in the terrace doorway. He walked out to join them, a glass of the 'goo' Zach had just mentioned, in his hand.

"We were just talking about how Riane is going to whip Jacinto's butt," Zach cracked.

Thatcher sighed and adjusted his glasses. "His butt?" Thatcher shook his head. "Maybe she will, maybe she won't.

I only took your foolish bet since you could not find anyone else to partake in the silly thing."

Neil glanced over at his friend. "Is that so?"

Zach blushed. "Um, well, you know, I, I, um. I just thought Riane was going to win and I just wanted to, you know, share my enthusiasm."

"Nice try at covering your ass," Tony kidded.

"Shut up kid, you aren't helping my cause here."

"You know gambling is off limits to you Zach. You nearly drove the entire dwarf nation into a gambling frenzy after you taught Axel and Ruskin to play poker," Neil stated.

"You know I didn't mean to do any harm. How would I know the little twerps would take such a liking to the game!"

Thatcher came to his rescue. "Never fear my lord I have no desire to teach the fine art of BETTING to any of my fellow gnomes. I only did this to appease Mr. Thomas's faith in the woman he loves."

Zach pointed at the gnome and nodded. "Yeah, what he just said."

"Okay, I'll let it go this time. And Thatcher, just call me Neil, please? No need to be so formal."

Very well," Thatcher snickered. He leaned in close to Tasha, "still a little uneasy with his title after all this time is he my lady?"

Tasha put her arm around Neil's waist and smiled at her husband. "I'm trying my best to make him feel comfortable with it. He'll come around eventually." She looked back to Zach and Tony, "By the way, how was your expedition with Malcolm? Is he with you?"

"He had to go off to see the elves about something, but he said he'd back as soon as possible. As for our little jaunt, well, it was pretty interesting," Zach said.

"How so?" Neil inquired.

Tony picked up where Zach had left off. "We went out there, and found a lot of nothing. No life anywhere. No grass no trees just dust and rock. And a real wicked smell that made us all sick. Boy, did it ever spook Malcolm."

"You should have seen him, all jittery and that globe he always uses for whatever magic trick he does just exploded after turning pitch black. It scared the hell out of me."

"What did Malcolm say about it all?" Neil had learned to trust the wizard's opinion, and judgment. The older man had not only won his respect but he valued him as a good friend too. If something upset Malcolm, it must have been significant.

"You sure you wanta know?" Tony asked.

"It would help," Neil urged.

Zach and Tony looked at one another and then Zach filled in the blanks. "He made some sort of reference to a very strong evil presence, and that, well, he said Helana may have found a way to escape from her prison."

"Is that possible?" exclaimed Tasha, shocked.

"He made it seem so. You'll have to ask the wiz when he gets back. He knows a lot more than we do. We're just the messengers," Tony said.

"Helana? Free? The thought alone makes me fear for what could very well happen. Until we hear from Malcolm with all the details I think we should just continue with our business as usual," said Tasha. Neil nodded in agreement. There was nothing they could do until hearing from the wizard.

"My queen, are you up for a little mingling with our subjects in the courtyard? I think we've spent enough time up here and away from all of the action." Neil held out his arm and Tasha put hers through his, and they started for the stairs. He glanced back at the rest, "Care to join us guys?"

Zach shrugged. "Why not, it'll be fun to annoy Axel for a bit."

"Adeena does that enough already, kinda hard to top her," Tony jested.

"Mmmm, yes, th' fairy does it quite well. However, at present she is busy with Shar at Eldridge. That leaves you to do yer best," kidded Thatcher.

"Well then, we can't pass up on the opportunity, can we kid?" Zach grinned and pointed at Neil. "Lead on your kingship."

"To the courtyard!" piped Tony.

Another cheer floated over the courtyard as the barrel race came to a conclusion and the participants lined up to find out who had claimed first in the latest challenge. The committee of five appointed by Neil and Tasha to anoint the winners, and maintain the rules of the challenges, consisted of a dwarf, a gnome, one of the royal guard captains, an elf from the elf council and Riley, a man whom Neil had come to trust since their encounter with the Dark Dragon. Riley also promised to not show any favoritism towards Jacinto regardless of how many threats the larger man gestured towards him. That alone made him worthy of the appointment!

As the company entered the courtyard, they arrived in time to see Riley place the gold medal around Riane's neck as the winner of the race. Jacinto was given an honorable mention with a close second place finish. Riane saw Zach and waved happily, Zach returned the wave. Neil and Tasha proceeded to mingle and visit with as many of the spectators as possible. Tony wandered off to find something to eat and Zach worked his way over to visit with Riane. Thatcher opted to follow after Tony and try to find some more of his favorite liquid refreshment. His glass was nearly empty!

Chapter Two

At the elf castle, Cambridge, Malcolm was hurriedly researching the book of magic that was kept within the safe confines of the council chamber. Within its pages were all the spells known to exist. The book had been compiled by an unknown master wizard century ago and had been sent with the races when they had crossed over to their New World from the old. It was in this very same book that Malcolm found the spell that had enabled him to return to the Old World, and locate the three who could help them with their crisis with Helana. The book also aided in the resurrection of Tony, and the final destruction of the Dark Dragon. Now, the wizard hoped it would contain some of the answers he was seeking regarding the evil recognized at Helana's old fortress.

Malcolm turned the frail, brittle, and yellow pages carefully, studying them thoroughly before moving onto the next one. He was so focused on the book that he failed to notice the elf king enter the room and approach.

"Malcolm," Xanthus spoke up. His voice caught the wizard by surprise and he looked up sharply from the book. "Sorry old friend, I did not mean to startle you."

"Quite all right my lord. I was so caught up in my reading that I did not even hear you come in. I'm sorry for the lack of advance notice of my visit, but I felt it was too urgent to wait."

"What is it you wish to discuss?"

Malcolm stepped out from behind the book. "Earlier, I was at Livinia to see why our efforts to heal the land around it were failing. During my investigation I came across the presence of an evil so dark that it destroyed my orb within moments of exposure."

"What sort of malevolent force would cause such a thing? I have never heard of an orb being destroyed before. To do such a thing would require a power stronger than you or I, and to my knowledge, there is no such power here." The elf king put his hand to his chin and thought more about what Malcolm had just said. "What do you think it is?"

"I have only a theory my lord."

"And that is?"

The wizard drew in a breath and let it out slow. "That Helana, however absurd and impossible it may sound, perhaps, has found a way out of her prison."

"But, how Malcolm? The spell that banished her is impenetrable from the other side. Only we have the capability to release her if we so choose."

"She was always creative as my student, and would often bend a spell or alter it to suit her needs. The threat of her return is all too real and I'm afraid of what she's done to bring about her escape. She may put us all in extreme danger."

Xanthus nodded quickly in agreement. "I concur. Whatever she has done will undoubtedly make her an abomination perhaps more powerful than any magic we may possess. We must alert the king and queen and move them here to Cambridge immediately. Do you have a concept as to how long we may have before this evil presents itself?"

Malcolm shook his head. "Unfortunately, I cannot tell. We must also consider other options of stopping this presence if our magic is not enough, or fails."

"What would you suggest?"

"I think we should seek out the master wizard who found this world for us. His abilities and his power may be the only thing capable of preventing the spread of this particular darkness. Therefore we must move quickly before our chance to cross back over to the Old World is unattainable."

"The master mage," whispered Xanthus. "Question is my friend, could he still be alive? After all this time?"

Malcolm held up an envelope, and walked around from behind the book. He handed it to the elf king and smiled. "This letter accompanied the book when we first crossed over to our new home. It is from the master wizard himself."

Xanthus had an obvious expression of shock on his face. "Really?"

"Go on, read it. You may find it quite interesting."

The elf king unfolded the ancient parchment and read the following.

TO SCHREDRICK, OR ANY OF HIS SUCCESSOR'S:

As you begin a new life in your new home, I do hope that the transition goes well. It will not be easy to forget where you came from, so might I suggest you name your new home after a place that will be a constant reminder of where you originated. I have given instructions to the elves to be the official guardian of the book entrusted with you Schredrick(or to those who succeed him) as a precautionary measure. It is necessary to keep the book from those who may seek the incantations within and may use them for their own personal agenda's. Do not doubt evil, it is forever present and always seeking ways to undo what is good and just. It is my hope that perhaps one day your New World may be free of such darkness, but only time will dictate such.

In closing, I say to whoever reads this, that if a time should ever arise that the darkness threatens and is more powerful than even the elves, then seek me out on the Old World. I will always be around if I am needed. Where, I cannot say, for as time goes on I may relocate for several reasons, including my own safety. These are dangerous times for those like me that practice magic. Again, find me if the need presents itself and I will join you in your time of need. I do hope that day never arrives then I shall know all of those who crossed are well and the magic is prospering.

Sincerely,

The signature was too faded to read, but Xanthus knew it was from the master wizard. He looked up from the letter and smiled. "Incredible. Alive? Even after all this time?"

"We have to believe he is but, the difficulty lies in finding him. As the letter states, he will relocate."

"Then, how will we find him? We have no way of knowing where to begin the search on the Old World. Even the spell that will take you there is limited in its ability to seek him out considering that he does not want to be found. No doubt his magic will keep anyone from finding him."

"I agree my lord. We will need to locate him by ordinary means, free of magic." Malcolm smiled then, like someone who had the winning hand in a game of poker. "I do believe I know the perfect person for the task."

Shar and Adeena where occupied elsewhere. The gnome castle of Eldridge played host to the two. Both had been sent by Malcolm to help negotiate a minor dispute between the gnomes, and the dwarves over some land both claimed as their own. Their negotiations had almost concluded when Malcolm made a sudden appearance in their room. His abrupt materialization shocked the duo and Shar almost cast a spell at him because of it. Once calm had prevailed again, both realized that if Malcolm had gone out of his way to see them, then the matter must be of vital importance.

"Sir, you really must learn to be a little more discreet when you appear. Perhaps outside the door and then knocking?" Shar teased.

He smiled. "Sorry my dear. I will keep that in mind for the next time."

"What brings you out to see us sir wizard? We've almost finished up here," said Adeena. She flew over to Malcolm and gave him a hug.

"Thank you my dear." He nodded to the fairy and then looked at them both. "I am here to bring you a warning."

"Go on then," urged Shar. She sat on the bed and Adeena floated over to do the same.

"Earlier today, I, Zach and Tony paid a visit to Livinia. I've detected an extremely powerful dark magic and it is growing in strength with each passing moment."

"What is the source of the darkness?" wondered Shar.

"Undetermined as yet, though, I must admit, I have never encountered anything of this magnitude ever before. I do have a theory, and have told Xanthus of it. He concurs with me that all the races be warned." Malcolm paused, and then continued. "I believe Helana has somehow found a way to break free from her prison."

"How can that be? The spell you and Tasha used can only be countered from this side of the void, not from within. In order for her to do such a thing would require, well, nothing short of a trick to fool the incantation itself," remarked Shar, stunned on hearing the possibility of the witch's return.

"Perhaps, or something more."

"More? If that is true, then there will be no telling what has been done and that may upset the balance of the magic," Shar commented.

"Indeed it may. I need you to warn the gnome council, and have them put Eldridge on the alert, quite possibly prepare for an evacuation."

"Evacuation?" questioned Shar. "Is the magic that strong?"

Malcolm nodded. "It is. Until it shows itself I cannot determine its full strength. Use what I have taught you and perhaps you can get a grasp of the magic. I am still quite tired from our encounter with the Dark Dragon."

Shar nodded. "I will try. If I may ask sir, why did you not stay in the druid sleep for a while longer?"

"Duty calls my dear. I shall 'catch up' if you will, once we have this matter at Livinia settled."

"What about the amulet things? Can't they do anything?" Adeena wondered.

"They can help to a certain extent. For how long, I do not know. It is best to prepare for the worst, just in case. If this magic continues to strengthen they may be of no use to us. We best be cautious."

"Are you sure you don't want me there at Kildare? Together we might be able to determine the source of this darkness at Livinia with more ease?"

Malcolm waved her off. "Me, Xanthus and Tasha can manage nicely, but thank you anyway. I need the both of you there. I am about to meet with everyone at Kildare, and once that is over, I will return to inform you of our next course of action. I am sorry that I cannot be more helpful at this point."

"That's all right Malcolm. I will do what I can here."

"Adeena, you do what you can to assist Shar."

The little sprite nodded, "yes sir. I will."

"Then I will take my leave of you now." Malcolm spoke the spell, and vanished in a flash of white light.

Adeena put her head in her hands. "Oh goody. We get stuck here with the gnomes while they're off havin all the fun."

"Come now Adeena, don't pout. You know that is not true. Let's go and talk with the council. Afterwards, why don't we go for a stroll along the outer wall?"

Adeena sat up and opened her wings. "I guess so, after you my mage." She lifted herself off the ground, and hovered.

"I am a mage in training only." Shar corrected her with a smile.

"And that must make me a mage in training assistant!"

Shar made a motion with her hand, and out of nowhere, the image of the dwarf Ruskin appeared on the bed. "There you go my assistant. It is a servant just for you."

Adeena laughed and flew over to the illusion. "If only it were real and if both he AND Axel were at my service."

"My my, aren't we a little on the greedy side?"

"I can dream can't I?" Adeena floated to the door and held it open. "After you."

The two suns began their descent, signaling the

conclusion to the first day of the unified games. The King and Queen ordered the lighting of the castle torches to officially end the festivities. A loud cheer from all of the participants, as well as from all those who attended to watch and cheer on their favorite reverberated throughout Kildare castle. It gave Neil and Tasha the confidence that the races were finally on the road to recovering from the damage done from past disagreements. At least most were.

"Yer too big for me! Why don't ya race against somebody yer own size!" Axel jested as he ambled alongside the much taller Jacinto.

"Not my problem you are too short to hold up a blade!"

"Who ya callin short? Ya troll!"

"Now now brother, he did beat ya fair an' square! As ol'Zach would say!" chuckled Ruskin. He patted his brother on the back in comfort.

Axel gave his brother a shove and pulled out his battle-axe. "I'll shave ya closer than that wee bit of a fairy did, yer rat of a dwarf!"

Zach saw the commotion and after grinning at first, opted to run interference and keep the peace. He ran up behind Axel and grabbed the axe out of Axel's uplifted arms.

"Now guys, lets try to get along. Your family!"

"What be it of yer concern? We dwarves always fight betweenst one anuther!" growled Axel.

"Then fight without something sharp, or you might cut yourself."

"Or worse, cut me!" Jacinto mocked.

Ruskin pointed to a group of competitors across the courtyard. "Look at it this way, the elf woman is still the leader, and she did beat the troll."

Axel thought about that for a second and laughed in

agreement. "Yer right! The elf IS better than the troll! Still, I hate losin."

"You'll be a lot shorter you stubborn dwarf if you keep callin me a troll!" threatened Jacinto. He clenched a fist to emphasize his point.

"Yer wishin yer was as short as us! Come, how about we buy ya some ale? Then we need not talk about winnin, or losin!" offered Ruskin. He put on a smile. "Would ya like to play poker there my big friend? Give me brother a chance ta win?"

"Hey, hey, hey, no poker allowed at these games," reminded Zach. "Or at least wait until Neil goes to bed so I can join you."

"Yer a cheater. Yer not allowed," Axel scoffed.

Jacinto laughed and slapped Zach across the back. "I don't think you cheat my friend. I will play if my friend can play."

Ruskin shrugged. "Sure, but yer bringin yer own ale to show us ya won't be cheatin."

Zach nodded. "That I can do. Where's the game?"

"In my tent. Tis a way off from the castle and your friend the King won't find ya! When the moons reach the top of the sky then?" said Jacinto. The group agreed, and that was that. "Then I must go eat, beating dwarves makes me hungry!" The big man wandered off, laughing as he strolled.

"Troll," Axel mumbled under his breath.

"If it'll make you guys feel any better, Riane is sure to win the tournament. That should give you a little satisfaction."

"Ya think so?" Axel grunted. He snatched his axe from Zach and stuffed it in its case behind his back. "Then Zach m'boy, yer ill in th'head. She be an elf, an tha's worse'n him." He stomped off, and Ruskin just shrugged at Zach.

He then trailed after his brother, leaving Zach to stand there and scratch his head.

"Isn't he ever happy?" He wandered off to the stables to find Tony and Riane, but they came across him first. Both had a look of concern and that usually meant bad news wasn't far behind.

"What's up? You two look like you've just been told you haven't won the lottery."

"Excuse me?" Riane asked, curious.

"Um, never mind, not important. Bad news?" Zach wondered.

Tony shrugged. "We don't know yet. Malcolm just showed up, and he wants to meet with all of us immediately. He ain't lookin too good."

"If he's not doing well then it must be bad. Lead on kid." First he leaned over to give Riane a kiss, and she reciprocated with a hug too. "Congrats on the day you've had! Number one so far, good stuff."

"Thank you, but it is a lot of work. The others are very good as well. Who knows, perhaps tomorrow will be harder and someone else will be number one."

"Don't talk like that! Just keep thinking that you're the best and before you know it you'll be holding up that first prize!"

Riane put her arms around his waist, and smiled. "I will try. Would you care to join me at the elves supper this evening?"

Zach thought about the card game for a second and made some lame and weak attempt to get out of going with her. "Are you sure it's okay if a non elf sits in on something like that? Won't they be offended or something?"

She shook her head. "No, not at all. They know of us, and they approve of you."

He sighed, "How nice to know."

Tony leaned into his ear and whispered, "Guess you won't make that poker game after all." In doing so, he forgot that the elves are considerably more adept at hearing.

"Poker game? You know the King has forbidden any such gambling at these games. Remember the ruckus you caused amongst the dwarves?"

"I know! I know!" he tried to defend himself. "It was just going to be a fun game tonight, no money or anything like that."

Riane took her arms away and stormed off. "Then you go and play your silly little game!"

"Riane!" He called after her, but it was for naught. She disappeared into the castle, leaving them far behind.

Zach turned on Tony. "Thanks you idiot! You know elves have really good hearing! Really really good hearing! And how'd you hear about the game anyway?"

"I ran into Axel and Ruskin a few minutes ago, before I met up with Riane. They invited me over to play too."

"You did that on purpose then! Just to make her mad at me!"

"No I didn't!" Tony replied quickly. "I totally forgot about how well they hear, really! Hey, the last thing I wanta do is screw things up between you two." Tony grinned, "It is fun to watch you two argue though. Those elves have quite the temper."

"Shut up kid. It's even harder to try and make up with them too! I wish you and that scout lady would get into a fight. Then I could get a laugh or two."

Tony's smile faded away. "Hey, I'm sorry, okay. You and Riane go well together. I know it wasn't easy for the elves to accept you as her mate."

Zach cut him off. "NOT, I repeat, NOT her mate!" He waved his finger in the air. "I'm seeing her, not her mate, got that!"

"You know the elves mate with one elf, er, person in your case for life."

"I've heard that before, but I AM NOT her mate! So stop saying that!" Zach started back towards the castle. "Didn't you say Malcolm wanted to see us right away?"

Tony ran after him, "Uh huh. It must be pretty big if he wants us all in there."

"Every time he does this we end up in some deep shit. I hope that isn't the case this time. By the way, where is the scout lady these days?"

"Her name is Mia. She's somewhere to the east doing her usual guarding thing with the unicorns. Hey dude, I do hope you and Riane can patch things up."

"Yeah sure, whatever. Next time, just don't mention poker, or worse, bring up my bet with Thatcher! If she finds out about that, she'll skewer me with her sword."

"Now that's somethin I'd pay money to see!"

"Shut up kid."

Chapter Three

Desolation, and nothing but. That was all there was within the radius of Helana's old castle, Livinia. No life whatsoever, no vegetation, no animal, and no moisture. It never rained near Livinia, there was only a continual shroud of gray cloud. The wind blew silent over the landscape; the dust moved by the breeze carried the only sound. Malcolm, Zach and Tony had found no sign of the healing process that the wizard and the elves initiated not along after the witch's imprisonment. Livinia looked, and bore the semblance of death. It appeared as though the grim reaper himself had made a permanent home. The gorge surrounding the keep was created to keep everybody and everything out. Perhaps even to signify what was kept inside. Helana had been banished to the dark void with the demons she had used as her servants. Malcolm and Tasha had cast the spell that had put an end to her reign and her threat to the races of Avalon. Helana was gone, though nothing Malcolm or the elves did could heal the wretched land she claimed as her own. It was as if she was still draining its life force somehow, some way.

A lone pebble shook, and then fell. It tumbled down

the canyon wall ricocheting off other stones as it did. Each bounce brought a hollow echo that carried through the gorge. From the bowels of the earth beneath Livinia, a low rumble began. Other stones started to fall, creating a domino effect. The sound of it all grew with each new stone adding onto the other. Within the castle itself, in Helana's throne chamber, a sharp cracking noise reverberated off the walls. Then a crack that had been nothing more than a sliver began to move outward from the center of the room. Through the breach, a red mist and light escaped, and though weak, a chorus of hideous shrieks mixed in with the rumbling. It had begun.

The western mountain range that bordered the Rathgar Plains was the home of the trolls. Very rarely did they venture out of the safe haven that the rock and mists provided. Many had migrated to the southern expanse where Rakia, a former apprentice of Helana's, had used them and their strength to carve out her own castle from the stone of the mountain itself. Her own kingdom was built right into the mountains but had fallen back into ruin after Rakia had awakened the Dark Dragon and had failed to maintain control over the beast. The Dark Dragon had its own nefarious intentions, and had become the master over the dragons and Rakia's own forces. In the end both had perished. Rakia had given her own life force to aid Malcolm in the destruction of the Dark Dragon and because of that had been put into a long deep druid sleep in an attempt to heal her. The trolls that had survived the ordeal migrated back to Swindon Keep and since their return the trolls had not been seen outside of Swindon. They opted to keep to themselves, and did not associate with any of the other races. Trolls as a rule, were not a very pleasant race, thus those from the other races had no difficulty in leaving the trolls to their own business.

A group of five trolls returning from their duties of the day had just come within sight of the familiar walkway up to Swindon Keep when the lead troll came to an abrupt halt. The heavy mist that shrouded the mountains had begun to swirl. It was quite breezy and cold but the mist never moved as it was now. It was cause for curiosity, much to the chagrin of the other trolls behind. One of them gave the leader a shove.

In a deep guttural voice, "What make you stop? Keep on!"

"Be quiet, something move ahead."

Another of the trolls squinted at the mist, and then lifted his bulky, hairy arm. "There."

The mist swirled and a voice spoke to them. "My trolls, the time is near."

The lead troll spoke up. "Who there?"

Again the mist whirled and the voice answered, "I am the one you once served and shall do so again!"

"We serve Gartog! He our king!"

The voice grew in intensity. "Gartog serves me! He knows that all too well! Tell him the true queen returns and that I require the service of the trolls once again!"

A troll fears nothing. They are huge, bulky creatures whose strength is that of twenty men. In battle it would take a small army of men, or elves to bring one down. That was what made them such a formidable foe. However, this voice made them cower, and they agreed to what it asked.

"We tell Gartog, we tell him!" nodded the lead troll.

As fast as the mist had begun to swirl, it returned to its usual sedate form and the wind disappeared. The trolls scurried along the walkway anxious to tell their king what they had seen and heard.

Swindon Keep was built inside the mountains. There were various entrances on several levels of the mountainside.

Paths or walkways connected all the entrances and within the mountain itself, the myriad of tunnels joined at intersections. Swindon Keep was a maze. That made it easy to defend from the outside, and inside.

Inside the largest cave carved out of the mountain, the so-called 'dining' area for the trolls, Gartog gnawed away on some sort raw meat that resembled the hind end of a goat. The appearance of five brethren, apparently nervous about something, upset his stomach and that in turn angered him.

"What you want? I eating!" he bellowed as he pointed at the remains of the carcass in front of him.

All five bowed, apologizing as they did. The first troll spoke up with the news and held his arms ready to fend off any attack from Gartog's food that he may abruptly begin throwing.

"We heard voice in mist, say we must tell you what it say to us!"

Gartog's interest suddenly peaked, "voice in mist? What is say?"

"Voice said it true queen, need us go to her."

"True Queen?" Gartog had to think about that for a moment, but the sudden appearance of a wall of mist blowing into the room distracted all. The five trolls moved to the side of the room nervously, trying their best to stay out of its way.

The mist had no definite shape, but it whirled around the room, and then around the trolls. The voice the five had heard reverberated off the walls.

"You know who I am Gartog! You joined me once before to fight the elves! Now I need your help again to finally rid this land of those vile creatures!"

Gartog fell to the ground in absolute fear. He bowed to the mist.

"True Queen, I did not know you were alive! Ask what you want."

"Go to Livinia! The time for my return is almost here!"

"We will go, we go now!"

"I promise you Gartog, I will not fail this time. You and your fellow trolls will be duly rewarded! Go to my castle at once!"

The voice faded, and the mist dissipated as fast as it had come. Gartog was standing up quickly and a sense of urgency was evident in his order.

"Go get others! We go to the true queen! Get others now!"

The five trolls rambled out of the room, almost tripping over one another in their haste. Gartog sat down in front of his food and ripped off a leg. He was going to need a full stomach for the journey. It might be quite some time before he would be able to enjoy another good meal. Gartog shook his head in shock. The true queen was about to return. How? Those made the troll scratch his head. After a minute he gave up trying to solve the riddle and took a bite out of the goat leg to quench his appetite. Eat first and think later. No point in trying to think on an empty stomach!

The entire group had convened in the throne room of Kildare Castle awaiting the return of Malcolm from his visit with Shar. He appeared suddenly in a flash of white light, and promptly apologized for keeping them waiting. Everyone moved to the adjoining council chamber and Malcolm took the seat at the head table to rest. He looked very weary, and took a deep breath as he placed his hands on the table.

"Are you all right Malcolm?" Tasha was concerned and sat down next to him.

Malcolm smiled weakly, and nodded. "I am quite fine, just a little tired from traveling so much in one day. It does tend to put a bit of a strain on my magic."

She knew he was lying. As a little girl, she had often caught her teacher in little white lies. A few times he had tried to fool her with small pranks.

"There must be something else Malcolm? I've never seen you so uptight and nervous. What's really bothering you?"

"Hmm, you always were too observant for your own good," he smirked. "If you must know, something is creating a great deal of stress on my magic. It feels as if I am somehow being drained of its power."

"Could that be as a direct result of what you may have discovered at Livinia? Could it be Helana?" asked Neil.

The wizard nodded. "I do believe so. All the more reason I must not waste any time in preparing for the worst. First, my queen, you and the king must be moved to Cambridge immediately. Within the safe confines of the elf boundary can Xanthus and I be assured of your safety, at least in the short term. Second, the games must be postponed and everyone is to return to their home and wait for word from the elf king, their respective leader, or myself. If what I fear is true, and Helana is about to return to this world, she will undoubtedly begin her rampage all over again. This time, I fear it may be even more destructive than before. Thirdly, my magic, and the elves can only withstand the onslaught of this dark force for a period of time. After which, we may be vulnerable."

Tony was a little confused. "Excuse me wiz, but what about those amulets?" He pointed to the staff. We went through a lot a year and a half ago to get them back. They worked once, why can't they work again?"

I do not know how to explain it Mr. Merello. Until Helana, or whatever this entity is that threatens, comes to be, the amulets can do nothing. I feel, as does Xanthus, the dark magic pulling and drawing power from the lands. Once it enters our world, then we can ascertain the exact danger we are up against."

"Okay, got that. So when this dark magic, as you call it, comes around, you can figure out what it is, and then you can use the amulets, right?"

Malcolm sighed. "We can only hope so Mr. Merello. We can depend on the amulets to protect us, but as I mentioned earlier, possibly for only a short time. The entity I sense is not Helana entirely. It is somehow different."

Zach threw his arms up. "Great, this is just great! All we really know then is that we could really be in some deep deep …."

Riane cut him off, "Zach, control yourself! Malcolm and my father are doing the best that they can right now."

"You think Helana has done something to allow her escape, don't you? Something that may have changed who she is?" Tasha asked.

"There is that danger," nodded Malcolm. "If that is so, then we really do not know what we are facing."

Tasha put her arm around Malcolm. "When do we leave for Cambridge?"

"As soon as you are ready my queen."

Neil was already moving towards the door. "I will go and get a courier dispatched to all attending the games and have them alerted to return home immediately, and that the games are temporarily postponed."

"Be sure to tell them nothing more, no need to start a panic. That may very well take care of it," warned Malcolm.

"I will go and pack what we need. I will see you in our room after you are done my love," said Tasha. Neil nodded and left the room. "How much time do we have before whatever it is you sense, enters our world?"

Malcolm shook his head. "I cannot be specific, only that the strain is growing with each passing minute. We may have only a few hours, at best."

"May I help you pack Tasha?" Riane offered.

"Thank you Riane, I could use some assistance. We will move as fast as we can Malcolm."

"The sooner you are within Cambridge's walls, the better I will feel my lady."

It was a slow process for those at Kildare as they prepared to leave. Once word of the postponement had been sounded it was almost an hour since the courier had been dispatched. Almost two hours later and the first of those camped on the fields outside Kildare were finally showing signs of packing up. Neil saw the lack luster and lazy attitudes and feared the end result, but he could do nothing to kick it into a higher gear. The attack of the Dark Dragon still lingered in the minds of many so he would do nothing to start another panic. He kept his fingers crossed that nothing of catastrophic nature would happen. For once, he hoped Malcolm was wrong.

In Livinia the crack in the throne room floor was no longer just a splinter. It had spread like a spider's web to cover the expanse of the floor. In its center, the crevice started to expand and the howls from within grew louder. The rumble beneath Livinia moved outward and away from the castle, slowly stretching and reaching out to the rest of the land.

The gnome castle of Eldridge was the first to experience the vibration and the land began to quiver and shake. On the catwalk Shar grabbed onto the railing and held on tight, as the castle seemed to move beneath her. Gnomes were falling and yelling all around her, shouting in confusion at the bizarre occurrence. Adeena flew erratically, and lost her ability to stay in the air. She crashed to the ground in a heap. Objects crashed every which way. Some of the smaller walls and parts of the railing shattered and the sound of cracking stone echoed throughout the castle.

"Shar! What's happening?" screamed Adeena. She had crawled up into a ball and hid beneath one of the gnome benches alongside the railing.

"I don't know! Just hold onto something! It should pass soon enough!"

The quake continued outward, stretching itself to the dwarves in Aberdeen. A dwarf, Davgar, was just returning from an exceedingly long binge with a few fellow dwarves when the shaking began. He thought it was just a part of his imagination at first. Soon enough he realized the noise, and rather excessive movement of the ground wasn't because he was too intoxicated, but that it was indeed an earthquake beneath his feet! He latched onto the nearest post he could find, and held on for dear life.

"By a troll's ugly face! That be th' last time I guzzle down a'hole keg of ale by myself!"

The settlements of Fairgrove, North Meadow, and Markham followed by Kildare castle felt the wrath of the quake next. As soon as it struck the monarchy's home, Malcolm fell to the floor, overcome by a wave of nausea. He gripped his stomach, and struggled to keep himself from retching. The evil he felt then was more than he had ever detected before. This was not Helana, but yet there was still a part of her within the dark force. The time to move the

King and Queen to Cambridge was almost up. The entity he sensed was about to enter their world.

The quake stopped at the edge of the elf land, right at the shoreline of the Norcross River, which bordered their haven. Still, the elf king Xanthus felt the malevolent force. How strong it was! He hoped, and wished that his old friend Malcolm was fine. Only the wizard had the capability to transfer the King and Queen to Cambridge. If he was unable to do so, and with Shar off at Eldridge, the monarchy was at risk of being destroyed by this darkness. Xanthus walked outside to stand on the terrace adjoining his room. Looking up at the sky, he saw nothing but clouds. Their gray mass hid the sky from view, and he wondered if he would ever see the stars, the suns, or the moons again. This sight was not a good omen.

The quake came to stop and Malcolm was doing his best to stand. Zach ran over to assist him.

"Are you okay? You aren't looking so good."

He took a deep breath, and sighed. "You are correct in your observation Mr. Thomas. Thank you for your help."

"Whoa, now that was quite the quake! Huh Zach? Man, I haven't felt one like that in years! Musta been about sixteen, back when I was in L.A.," said Tony.

"Sure kid and I don't care to feel another anytime soon. That's got to be a first for this place, well, for as long as I've been here anyway."

"It was a warning to me," murmured Malcolm. "Mr. Thomas, there is one thing I forgot to mention earlier."

"Oh? And what would that be?"

"I need you to find someone who can help us. In my readings from the book of magic, I came across a letter near the back, stuffed between the final two pages."

Zach shrugged, "Yeah, your point?"

"It stated that if ever a time arrived that the magic's would fail to keep the land safe, that if the amulets and the elves magic was not strong enough, we should then call upon the one who can aid us in our time of need." Malcolm sat down, still weak from the quake.

"And who might that be? Some elf hidden away in a mountain cave someplace guarded over by some renegade faeries or something?"

"Why don't you stop interrupting the man and let the guy finish his story," Tony nagged.

"As I was saying," Malcolm smiled, "there is one person who can help us stop this evil." He was once again interrupted as the Queen and Riane entered the room, followed only seconds later by Neil.

"We're ready to go Malcolm. Everything we'll need is packed. Anytime you're strong enough to invoke the spell we can go to Cambridge," Tasha smiled. "I assume that tremor was only a sign of things to come?"

"Quite correct my lady," Malcolm nodded with a weak smile.

"As I have said many times, I had a good teacher."

Malcolm looked over at Neil. "How is everyone proceeding with their packing elsewhere?"

"Slow, very slow. Though, that quake might just help speed them up. I have told the royal guard to stay behind, but at the first sign of trouble they are to leave immediately."

"It might be best if they were to depart for Cambridge as well. We cannot risk leaving anyone here unprotected," Malcolm said.

"Do you think it necessary?" Neil asked.

"I do."

"I assume you will be coming with us as well?" Neil nodded at Zach and Tony.

"Well what do you think your kingship?" Zach quipped.

"Actually Malcolm here was just about to tell me about something he needs me to do, before you barged in."

"I need to speak with the honor guard anyway, I'll have them start out for Cambridge immediately," said Tony. He was out the door and gone from view.

Zach was about to speak up, but Neil grinned and cut him off. "I will attend to the Royal Guard buddy; you can let Malcolm finish his conversation with you."

Malcolm began to speak, but then grimaced and placed his hands on the table to steady his dizziness. Another wave of nausea began to wash over him. Tasha felt uneasy, and had to lean on Neil for support. Riane covered her ears with her hands as a high pitched ringing began to irritate her hearing. The rest watched as the three showed the obvious discomfort. What was happening now?

In the gnome castle, Shar looked up at the sky and noticed the lightening strikes in the distance to the south. The clouds grew darker, and thunder rolled over the landscape. She sensed the air going cold, and tried to fend it off by pulling her cloak in tighter. Her fairy friend Adeena was worse off. She sat on the edge of the railing along the rampart, extremely agitated, nervous, looking this way and that as if she felt a thousand eyes were all watching her at once. Both looked at the other, scared of what they felt, and unsure of what to do about it.

Shar put her arm around Adeena, "Easy my friend, this too will pass."

"It better Shar, but I don't like what I feel. What's happening? I'm scared and it takes a lot to scare me!"

"I know, me as well."

The cracks in the floor of Helana's keep, Livinia, split open and a giant fireball exploded upward. Black lightening struck out from within the opening, scorching the walls of the castle. Outside Livinia, jagged rock thrust itself through the canyon walls and the rumbling began again.

The spiked rock formed a bridge, scraggy, uneven and ugly. Another blast of fire and lightening spewed from the depths of the pit in the throne room and out through the broken ceiling and towards the sky. The clouds turned pitch black, and the darkness spread, reaching out to the rest of the land. A form rose from the pit, and its arms reached up to grasp the new found freedom.

"FREE! I AM FREE!" Helana's scream resounded off the walls of her old home. She floated out of the pit to stand on solid ground once again. Though it was Helana, it was also someone, or SOMETHING more. Her eyes were blood red, and she stood now at almost seven feet tall! A good foot or so more than before her imprisonment! Her hands resembled claws more so than fingers and her teeth were as sharp as an imps and looked just as terrifying! It walked over to stand on the weather worn terrace, and gazed at the land below.

"Avalon, your true queen has come home." The voice was a deep hiss, and full of hatred.

Chapter Four

Malcolm fell to the floor; the pain was just too much for him to bear. Zach was at his side moments later. Again, he helped the elder man stand and the wizard leaned on him for a little extra support. Tasha had almost fainted, and Neil held her up as her legs gave way. Riane had screamed as the ringing in her ears reached a feverish pitch and then it began to subside as fast as it had come. After seeing to it that Malcolm was seated at the table he ran over to Riane to see if she was all right. She gave him a hug, tears streaming down her cheeks from the ordeal.

"Oh Zach, the pain, it was almost more than I could take," she whimpered.

"Is it still there?"

Riane shook her head. "No, it is gone now." She looked over at Tasha, and the Queen was beginning to get her own strength back. "My lady?"

"I will be fine Riane, but for a brief moment I felt as if all my strength was being drained from me. Thank you for holding on my love," she smiled at Neil.

"It was the least I could do," he smiled back.

Malcolm looked up at the group and spoke in a monotone

voice. "The evil is here now, amongst us. It is far more powerful than I had anticipated earlier. If it affects all three of us, then we have little time." His voice changed to one of urgency. "Gather everything for the trip to Cambridge and when Tony returns we must leave immediately!"

"I will quickly attend to the Royal Guard. Once they have seen to it that everyone has embarked for their home I'll have them join us at Cambridge," said Neil. "Tasha, go through everything and make sure we have what we need, I'll be back as quick as I can!"

Neil gave her a quick kiss on the cheek and ran from the room. Both Tasha and Riane went through all their gear to double-check everything. Zach sat down next to Malcolm and looked the wizard head on.

"Who am I supposed to find wizard? From what I've seen so far, we're going to need this person."

Malcolm patted him on the shoulder. "I will talk with you in private at Cambridge. Find Axel, Ruskin and Thatcher. Have them meet us at Cambridge as well. Go quickly."

Zach nodded. "Consider it done." He left the room in haste and Malcolm sat back in his chair. Tasha and Riane joined him once they were sure everything was in order for the trip to the elves. Tasha took Malcolm's hand and smiled at her old friend.

"Malcolm, can you determine what this force is, now that it is here?"

He shook his head, "not quite my dear. Though I do believe Helana has a hand in it. How much she is involved, I am unsure."

"Once we are at Cambridge will we be able to find out more? Can my father help us?" Riane asked.

"I am sure we will and your father will undoubtedly aid

us in that venture. Perhaps together with the amulets we can get to the source of this disturbance."

"How is your strength?" Tasha wondered.

"It is slowly coming back. I should be able to invoke the spell to get us to Cambridge as soon as the rest return."

Helana strode through her once well kept throne room. She kicked several pieces of debris out of the way and looked around. It had not been that long though her time in the abyss had felt like she had been away for an eternity. The pain, the misery and the fear had compounded the duration of her suffering. There had not been a moment that Helana wasn't scheming a way out of her prison. When the solution had been found it had come at a high price. She would dwell on that at a later time; it was time to see if her powers were as strong as expected. It was time to pay a visit to an old friend.

Zach had retrieved his two dwarf friends along with Thatcher and returned to the throne room to make their final arrangements with the rest of the company. Tony was waiting and Neil had made his way back as well. All were present and accounted for.

"Any time you're strong enough to get us to Cambridge we're ready to go Malcolm," Tasha nodded.

"All the guests and all of our guards will be gone within the next few hours. Kildare will be completely abandoned by nightfall," assured Neil.

"What be the rush?" Axel asked. "This wouldna be about th'ground shakin earlier would it?"

Malcolm nodded. "Yes it is Axel. You and your brother may want to return to Aberdeen and help prepare the dwarves for any sort of threat, and you may want to go home to assist the gnomes Thatcher."

"Aye, thank you fer the advice my friend. However, I will be of better use here with you an' the others. Shar and Adeena can take care of my fellow gnomes better than I," said Thatcher.

"I should go with Axe and Ruskin, I might be able to lend a hand," Tony offered.

"If yer able to keep up with us, yer welcome to tag along," teased Ruskin.

"And you Zach? Are yer comin too?" Axel checked.

"Not this trip guys. Malcolm here has something else for me to do once we get our King and Queen here to Cambridge."

Malcolm stood and walked around to the dwarves. "Safe trip my friends. I will keep in touch and alert you of any danger to Aberdeen."

"Well then, c'mon boy, let's get ridin before it gets too dark out," Axel urged taking the lead to the door.

He, Ruskin and Tony got three steps before a blue cloud appeared and whirled across the room! It sent the company scattering away from it and spun itself to face the wizard Malcolm. A screeching wind sailed around the room and from within the oscillating cloud out stepped a creature that at first was unrecognized. Malcolm soon realized whom it was he was facing.

"Helana, what, what have you done?" Malcolm held his staff in front for protection and the amulets flared to life.

"You remember me, I am honored." Helana smiled an evil grin and her eyes glared red.

"That's Helana?" questioned Zach. "It hardly even looks like her anymore."

"She's done something to herself," Tasha whispered.

Helana heard the Queen all too well and turned to face her. "Observant, good to see you are still the good little student princess."

"Tis Queen now ya hag!" snarled Axel. He withdrew his ax and held it ready.

"Queen?" Helana walked closer to Tasha. "Queen?" She looked over at Neil and saw the royal cloak on his shoulder. "And you must be the King. Well well, I see you decided to stay and make this world your home. How unfortunate. This time I will be sure to make you wish you had left. But then, what would that matter? I'll just destroy your old home this time and you won't have anywhere to run."

"Helana, you have broken all that is bound by magic! You cannot let this continue, end whatever it is you have done or else nothing can be saved, yourself included!" warned Malcolm firmly.

"No Malcolm, I will not. Even if I wished it to be it cannot be undone. This is who I am now! Look at me closely wizard! This is who will destroy you and every elf that infests MY KINGDOM!"

"You've joined with the demon haven't you?" Malcolm shook his head in disgust. "That was how you were able to escape your imprisonment. You have no idea of what you've done."

"Oh yes I have old man, my power is beyond what you and the elves can fight against. It will continue to grow and yours will fade! Once I have taken the throne of Avalon I will cross over to the Old World and make them all bow down to me! ME! And there is nothing you can do to stop me."

"Your power is not yet strong enough witch, and therefore I will do everything in my ability to stop you. That is my promise! NOW BE GONE!" Malcolm held the staff fronts and center and spoke the words he needed. *"All the powers drawn by the stones joined as one, earth, air, fire and water! Called are thee and thy knowledge! Return to your keep you will go! A sasha A lortag!"*

The amulets exploded with white light and a beam struck out at Helana. The witch held her hands up to deflect the magic, but failed. It got through her defenses and encircled Helana. It engulfed her and sent her flying back wards into the spinning blue cloud! In an explosion of sound and wailing wind the cloud imploded and vanished.

Malcolm closed his eyes and leaned against the table for support. Neil, Tasha and the others were there to assist the wizard. He motioned that he was fine and took in a deep breath.

"We must leave for Cambridge now. She will be only temporarily winded. Tony, Axel, Ruskin, ride hard to Aberdeen and watch yourselves. Come, the time to go is now."

"See you soon guys. Be careful," Zach nodded. He shook their hands and quickly moved to stand beside Malcolm and the rest.

"We will be in contact, safe journey," Malcolm smiled. A few carefully spoken words and the company disappeared in a flash of light.

"Come on then, I don' wanta be here if th'witch comes back!" Axel urged leading the way.

"Aye, she'd be in a sour mood!" Ruskin added.

"And then some," Tony whispered in agreement. In short order all three were on their horses and riding eastward towards the mountains and forest that preceded Aberdeen. There were only a few guards still left in Kildare but soon even those would be traveling the route to Cambridge. Once more, Kildare was abandoned.

The blue cloud appeared in the disheveled throne room of Livinia and Helana was thrown from it. She was flung onto the floor and the cloud exploded and shattered! Its remnants fell to the ground in a million tiny fragments.

Helana propped herself up with her arms and screamed with all the anger she possessed. The walls of Livinia shook from the volume. Her power was not yet up to the task of a confrontation with the wizard, or the elves for that matter. Still, she knew the wizard was scared and that made her feel a little better, albeit it was only a small consolation.

Slowly Helana stood and composed herself. The element of surprise was no longer hers hence the only option now was to prepare to wage her all out war against the races of Avalon. Her armies must take the forefront now and they would crush all those who stood in her way to the throne of not only one, but two worlds.

Chapter Five

Cambridge castle, a haven for the royal family in times when Kildare could not give them the protection they required was about to be one again. The elf kingdom was warded by a special magic endowed only to the elves and the Norcross River marked the border. Once those who had crossed to the elf side of the riverbank safely were they then provided some defense, but not complete safety. Every kind of magic has its limits and the elves were no exception to that rule. Border patrols kept watch on the river all hours of the day as a precaution, but even the patrols were not foolproof. As the past had shown, there are always 'kinks' in any armory. Still, the elves provided shelter in the interim. Cambridge would be safer than Kildare for the present, but if Helana's magic strengthened, as Malcolm knew it would, even the elves would not be safe.

Xanthus burst into the council chamber, arms open to welcome his guests and the relief that the royal couple were safe showed very plainly in his facial expressions. He gave Tasha a hug and shook Neil's hand.

"I am glad to see all of you safe. After the ear piercing tone, I was deeply concerned."

Malcolm bowed to Xanthus. "We almost did not get away."

"Is that so?"

"Yes sir, we had a visit from an old friend," said Neil.

Xanthus was curious. "An, old friend?"

"Friend would be over exaggerating considerably," Malcolm chortled. "As I thought, Helana is the root of the evil and was rather bold in stating such in appearing to us at Kildare castle. She thought her power to be stronger than it was and it's a good thing it wasn't. I sent her back to her old home rather abruptly. No doubt she is angrier than ever."

"I think we may safely say she is extremely upset with us," said Tasha. She could not help but snicker at the comment and the rest did too.

"We can joke about it now, but it will not take long for her magic to grow and ours to fade. We will have to work quickly and prepare for the worst," said Malcolm.

"Agreed. I will have my guards show you to your quarters. You could use some rest I'm sure, you perhaps more so, my old friend. You're beginning to look a little weathered, as it were," teased Xanthus.

Malcolm smiled. "You make a good point, and who am I to argue with the king of the elves."

Xanthus burst into laughter and patted Malcolm on the back. "That never stopped you before."

"Thank you for providing a home away from our own," said Tasha with a bow.

"Tut, tut my dear, think nothing of it." Xanthus smiled at her and then nodded at his guards who promptly stood ready to lead their guests to their rooms.

"I will see you all in a few hours," said Malcolm with a nod.

Each were led to their own rooms and most were prompt to get some rest, others though, found sleep hard to come by and opted instead to wander and hope that in time exhaustion would over take them. The circumstances surrounding their flight were rather vague with the appearance of a considerably altered Helana providing their most solid reason for fleeing.

Zach had found the kitchen area and had poured himself a cup of elf brandy to help him relax. Everything had happened so fast his mind was all over the place, and for him, being unable to sleep was a serious matter. He could fall asleep virtually anytime, anyplace, even on the hard ground these days. The wizard had started to tell him something and had failed to finish. It ate at him like a hunger pang from lack of food for several days. Nothing bothered him more than someone not finishing a sentence and veering off on another tangent. What the hell was Malcolm going to tell him?

Zach winced after swallowing a mouthful of brandy and looked down at the cup. "Rather bitter batch. Didn't think they could make it that way. Oh well, learn somethin new every day."

A voice from the shadows made him turn abruptly. "Talking to yourself again I see."

"Damn you, stop doing that! I would think that since being made king you'd stop sneakin around."

Neil stepped forward and smiled. "Now where would the fun be in that?"

"Grab a stool and some brandy bud, this jug's got a kick," motioned Zach.

"More so than dwarf ale?"

"Wellllll, not quite."

"Works for me." Neil grabbed a mug and poured some of the brandy. "So what the hell are you doing up? If I thought anyone would be sleeping, it would be you."

"You'd think." Zach shrugged. "Just a lot on my mind.

One minute we're over at Kildare, next we're back here at the elves and some ugly lookin witch is out to get us. What the hell is with this place? Can't we ever get by without some hag startin up a storm?"

Neil laughed lightly and sipped his brandy. He sat down at the table and shrugged. "I'm afraid I don't have an answer for you."

"I hope Tony is all right out there. We're here, protected somewhat, he's not."

"He's with Axe and Ruskin. He'll be fine. You've hung out with them and survived, so he should be doubly safe."

"Funny," retorted Zach.

"Once every one has had the chance to get some rest, we'll be able to sort this all out and figure out which way we're going with everything."

"Hope so," Zach burped. "Excuse me. If what's her name is as all powerful as Malcolm keeps saying, this is going to get messy real quickly."

"I know," Neil agreed. He downed his brandy and stood back up. "I'm going to try and catch some shut eye, you should do the same."

"I will, after one more cup of this tang," he quipped. "It'll make me drowsy enough I won't have much say in th'matter," he slurred in a bad dwarf accent. Both laughed a little and Neil left the room. Zach poured a little more elf brandy into his mug and let out a sigh. He looked at the bottle and his reflection on the side.

"Why do I have this gut feeling I'm about to go on a trip someplace?" he wondered.

In a sheltered grove at the edge of the mountain range bordering the dwarf kingdom and human settlements, two dwarves and a man were doing their best to sort out the mess they were suddenly thrust into. Ruskin, Axel and Tony were just finishing up their meal prepared by Ruskin and had gotten their fire to a nice comfortable blaze. Tony had propped himself up against a tree and had a cup of dwarf ale in hand. The two dwarves had their own mugs full to overflowing and were conversing freely as the ale took hold.

"Never shoulda trusted that wizard's magic, best ta have just used a good ax on th' witch!" blurted Ruskin.

"Aye cut her ta pieces an'be done with'er."

"I never thought I would see the day I would actually agree with you two," Tony chuckled. "But your argument makes perfect sense."

"Tis th'ale," Axel smirked, "makes th'dwarves think better."

"Well I wouldn't go that far," Tony laughed.

"Watch it boy, we've had ta teach Zach a thing or two, we might have ta do th'same to you," Axel winked.

"I'll stay on this side of the fire, you guys stay over there and I'll keep my yap shut," Tony joked.

"He's learnin much faster than Zach ever did," Ruskin snickered as he looked at Axel.

"Aye, that he is. Zach never did learn did he?"

"I don't think he did." Each burst into a fit of laughter and Tony couldn't help but laugh along.

The three kept the conversation light and as the night slid by and the wildlife of the dark even grew quiet Axel took the first watch. The fire cast flickering shadows over the overhanging branches and the leaves rustled from the rising heat. Tony and Ruskin lay down to catch some sleep and Axel wandered off to find a higher level of ground to keep his eye on things.

He found a dead tree stump on the top of a small hill and parked himself beside it. Axel had a good view of the entire surrounding area and he propped his ax next to the stump. Sitting there, he gave the valley a good look over and then tipped back his ale, finishing it and then letting loose a burp. Axle chuckled and wiped his beard.

"Ahhh, nothin beats good ale on a warm night." He looked back up at the sky, took notice of the lack of stars and then back down at the forest. "Cept maybe another mug of good ale." He dug out his flask and filled the mug half full. It was his watch, so it was best to go easy on the brew or he'd fall asleep a might fast! Last thing he wanted to do was give the boy a good reason to poke fun at him. Axel settled in and stared out at the trees below. Nothing moved but an odd branch stirred by the night's breeze. He snorted. It was the calm before the storm. He felt it in his bones. There was big storm coming indeed.

Shar stared at the dark sky, the faint outline of the moons barely showing through the overcast, and she drew her cloak in close. Adeena wandered out on the balcony to stand next to her but said nothing. Both knew something was terribly wrong but were not sure what it was. They had heard nothing from Malcolm as yet. Shar would give the wizard, her teacher, until dawn. If she had no news by then she would make the effort to contact him. There was a dark force unleashed, that much she knew, and she had to risk the contact to have some idea of what was going on. They could not proceed with any sort of action until knowing the situation.

It was Adeena who whispered her thoughts out loud first. "I don't like this Shar. I'm feeling as though I've been hit by an invisible hand full across my body."

"When day breaks, I will take the chance to contact Malcolm. Not until then." Shar did not take her gaze away from the dark outlying lands and the few torches still lit below in Eldridge.

"Is there a reason we're waiting?"

Shar looked down and smiled at her. "Be patient, we'll know what's up soon enough."

"You're sounding more and more like Malcolm all the time, it's beginning to annoy me."

"Am I now?" Shar snickered. "Well he is my teacher."

"So stop learning," snorted Adeena. "I liked you better when all you did was make illusions."

Shar turned to face her. "Unlike you my fairy friend, I have to grow up at some time." She laughed lightly and patted Adeena on the shoulder. "I am still the same person I've just got things I need to learn."

"Why?"

"Because little one, my gifts are greater than I thought. I am learning to use all of my abilities so that I can keep troublesome little faeries like you, out of trouble." Shar grinned and waited for the reaction she knew she'd get.

"Hey!" Adeena frowned. "I am not that misbehaved." The fairy crossed her arms like a spoiled little child pouting after not getting their way.

"I know you aren't, I am only teasing."

"Well cut it out. It's bad enough to put up with the moles bad sense of humor I don't want to put up with yours as well."

"I'll try to behave, and I won't tell Axel and Ruskin you called them moles."

"Oh I don't care, I can dish it right back at'em as fast as they insult me," Adeena grinned.

"You've been hanging around Tony to long," Shar teased. "He's beginning to rub off on you."

"He's fun when he wants to be, still kinda keeps to himself or he's off with that unicorn lady."

Shar returned her gaze to the land below their balcony and nodded. "I know. He's chosen his path, I've chosen mine." She looked down at Adeena. "The two of them go well together."

Adeena nodded in agreement. "They do. Are you sure we have to wait until dawn?"

"Yes, we do. Go get some sleep it'll help the night pass quicker."

"Fine, it seems I have no choice. Good night Shar." Adeena stomped off inside and Shar smiled, watching her go. So childish after all the years but that was what made Adeena so unique. She was a true faerie who had found a home away from her own realm and someone who had become a good friend. Shar wanted to rest but she was too agitated and confused to even try sleeping. She needed information and the swifter morning arrived the sooner she would get through to Malcolm. Then perhaps the chance to rest would present itself.

A rustling of the underbrush made Mia stop where she was and hold her position, as she listened for any further movement. The unicorn watcher could feel her heart beat in her chest, and its beating throbbed in her neck, and hands. Her legs tensed ready to launch at whatever moved towards her. A twig cracked and Mia knelt even lower to try and get a look through the thinner part of the shrubbery. She squinted but saw nothing at first and then a few branches began to get shoved aside. Mia withdrew her dagger and held it ready. Her legs ached from the tension and from kneeling but she would not give in to the pain. Another bush shook and Mia felt her heart beat faster.

A small deer stepped free of the brush and shook its head to get the twigs and leaves off its head. Mia smiled and fell to her knees, relieved it was nothing more than a small animal that had lost its way.

"You had me scared little one, go on," Mia waved to

her left. "Your herd is over that way, not that far. You'll find them soon enough."

The deer bobbed its head as though it understood her word for word and moved off to the watchers left. Mia ushered it along and once she was confident the animal was on the right course she returned her attention to her own flock. She had been trailing the unicorns' eastward for several days now and they had just passed the outer edges of the North Meadow settlement. The human hunters knew better than to even attempt to take the life of a unicorn but it was her duty to keep them safe and she never took that chance. That 'duty' had been bestowed upon her by her father and his father unto him, her grandfather Seth before him. Mia Oravek was the unicorn watcher and it was her guardianship that kept the magical creatures out of harms way.

The quake earlier that day had caused her some concern but after it had subsided she had found the unicorns safe and all accounted for. Mia had returned to trailing behind the herd as per her usual tracking. With North Meadow safely behind them, the threat of any human hunting expedition would be rare. She knew where they were migrating too, and wondered why they had chosen to do so earlier than their usual seasonal transmigration. Mia would have asked the stallion if it was possible, but she was the one who had to be contacted before such a meeting. So, she waited for her chance to ask about the altered trek northeast. It may, or may not happen but there was nothing Mia could do.

As if her thoughts had been read, a voice in her head brought her mind back from its wanderings. "Mia, meet me at the pine forest beginnings."

Nodding in understanding, but there was no one to see. Mia always had to smile after doing so because it was just a reflex action to answering the request. She raced through the underbrush, selecting each step with care as she wove between each tree, and each limb with precision. It did not take her long to reach the edge of the tree line at the base of the rising hills. The territory in question was known as the Valhan Range or to those who traversed the area, 'Valhan Haven' due most in part to the many valleys and caves that provided sanctuary. Though high in elevation, they did not come close to the actual mountain range just a short distance to the south leading to the dwarf and gnome kingdoms. They did however provide an ample haven for the unicorns. The forest lining the hills was lush, thicketed with pine over the entire expanse. Unless those who entered were experienced hikers or guides, it would not take a great deal to find oneself lost within. That was why the unicorns migrated here, for absolute privacy.

Mia surveyed the area carefully, looking for the stallion. She could not see him but she knew by instinct that he waited, hidden by the forest. Mia stepped into the clearing and knelt down, waiting. The watcher knew the unicorn would make its appearance when it was ready. She did not have to bide her time for long. The stallion stepped through the trees with grace so quietly that the branches barely stirred. Mia could never understand how an animal that size could be so discreet. The stallion never gave her a straight answer.

"I am here at your beckoning," bowed Mia.

"I have a request of you."

"What is it you wish?"

"I need you to travel south. Find any that will listen, tell them there is a dark threat coming from the deep south. It is an evil that threatens us all."

"The quake earlier that was what that was all about wasn't it?"

"Yes. Something has come into our world. I can feel it

all around us. There is a danger to all. There will be a war soon."

"A war?"

"A war of magic's is soon to begin, you need to warn the monarchy and assist in any way you can."

"But I am a mere watcher, not a warrior of magic. What can I do besides warn the others?"

"I don't have those answers, but others may. We are going further into the Valhan where we will be safe. Find us again when the time arrives. Your duty to us is forgiven for now."

Mia bowed again and looked back up at the stallion. "I will return when the storm has passed."

"Until then my lady, take care." The stallion bobbed its head and then turned, vanishing back into the forest.

Mia breathed the night air in deep, letting her lungs fill with its taste and then slowly exhaling. She would go to North Meadow first and talk to the one man she knew there, Jacinto, and then find a horse. Jacinto would get her message to the king and queen and perhaps she would hear news of Tony and his location. From there she would travel south to the dwarves to deliver the message again. At that point she would make a decision as to whether she would continue on to the gnomes or have one of the dwarves carry it on so she could travel on to Fairgrove. Mia's course of action was set. With one good gulp of moist mountain air she turned and sprinted west through the forest to North Meadow. If all went well, she would be there just before dawn or just as the two suns began their ascent.

Helana stepped into her courtyard as she finalized her survey of the old keep. It had held up reasonably well since her banishment into the demon realm. She was somewhat surprised that Malcolm had not destroyed it all together.

Typical, she thought to herself. So much was he like his old teacher Schredrick. Wizards thought it best to leave around a reminder of those that had crossed their paths and what the consequences were. Helana always thought that to be a weakness. Why leave mementos? They could always backfire. Helana took one final look around and then decided it was time to get down to business and begin amassing her army for the assault on Avalon.

Helana spread her arms wide and shouted to the sky, "BRING FORTH MY GENERALS OF DARKNESS! OPEN THEIR GATE AND LET THEM STEP FORTH BEFORE ME! I COMMAND IT TO BE SO! A'LA LORTAY!"

The ground shook and cracked in the midst of the courtyard. It began to fall away into the pit that began to take shape. From the depths of the darkness a wail of screams exploded into the night and slowly shadowy forms stepped up into view. Tall, gangly demons moved out of the opening to stand before Helana. More than twenty clambered out and then the gate closed and left no more than a crack where it had been.

Helana looked over those that would begin it all, the wraith. They would find her the mercenaries and filth of this world to do her bidding and guide the trolls to her. Once that was accomplished, she would bring the demons out of their well to follow her commands and to keep the men and trolls in line.

"What isssssss thy bidding masssssster?"

"Go out and find me those who hate as I do. You," she pointed to one half of the gathering, "send them here, tell them anything they want to hear and they will follow their greed. Once I have them gathered I will cast my own controlling web over them. You," she motioned to the remaining half, "make sure the trolls find their way here and 'push' them if you have to. I want to march on the gnomes within the next few days. Go and bring me my army."

The wraith's changed shape before her, sprouting wings and adapting their form to that of airborne creatures. Elongated necks, their eyes changing color to a bright yellow and narrowing almost birdlike. Their arms became shorter and more clawed and their legs bent lower, muscles thickening. When the transformation was complete they lifted themselves into the sky and began the task commanded of them.

Helana watched them vanish into the cloud and turned to go back inside. Another day to draw more energy from the lands would give her the strength to begin the march of the demon legions from what had been her prison. A few more days and the most massive army to ever walk on this world would be hers to guide. Helana climbed the stairs to the rampart, her one thought was focused on seeing Malcolm crumble beneath her and knowing then the balance of power would be at her fingertips to do with as she pleased. There could be nothing less, for she had sacrificed everything to achieve just that.

Chapter Six

Zach stood on the bulwark of Cambridge sipping his tea. On a day that sleeping in should have been a given it was anything but. The fact he knew Malcolm wanted to talk to him about something was the one determining factor to his not sleeping. For that, he hated the wizard. He took another sip and let out a sigh, smacking his lips as he did.

"This stuff keeps tasting better all the time."

"Which is why I drink it," said Malcolm. Zach turned his head to see the wizard standing next to him. "Good morning."

"Tell me what's good about it?"

"Well, I am feeling somewhat better. And you are up long before the others, a first I must say." Malcolm chuckled and took a sip of his own tea.

Zach smirked. "Yeah, well don't get too used to it. So, yesterday, you were about to tell me about something you needed me to do?"

"Anxious, aren't we? I've hardly been able to have a taste of my tea."

"I hate to wait and worse, I hate unfinished sentences.

So finish what you were going to tell me and let my mind relax already."

Malcolm smiled. "As you wish. Come, let us sit down and I will tell you everything."

"If you make it quick I might be able to get a snooze in before the others wake up."

Malcolm sat down at a small table with two chairs just outside the doorway to the council chambers. Zach could've sworn they weren't there a second ago and started to say as much.

The wizard cut him off. "You think correctly, now, sit and enjoy the suns rise."

"What sunrise? Nothing but cloud and gray sky for as far as the eye can see."

"The night is fading even though we may not see the suns Mr. Thomas. That in itself is reassuring."

"I want to know what's going on Malcolm, have you talked to Neil yet?" Zach tipped his cup back and sat back in his chair.

"Not as yet. I will before long."

"Back at Kildare, that was Helana, wasn't it?"

"Yes, and no. She is no longer who she was. Helana was always one to mold a spell to her liking so that it suited her, and she has done so again in order to free herself of her prison. She has become one with the demon Valgor with whom she had associated before. The two are now one. Her power is growing at an alarming rate and if I am not mistaken, she has already begun to mass her own forces to march on the rest of the lands. She will not waste any time and will move quickly to destroy everything in her path. Helana has broken all laws of magic in doing what she has done and has tipped the balance in her favor. My magic will dwindle, even with the amulets and in time she will be strong enough to abolish me, and," Malcolm motioned around him, "the elves."

"That would be bad," said Zach.

"Very bad."

"Then what do you need me to do?"

Malcolm dug into his robes, looking for something. Zach finished off his tea and placed the cup on the table. Malcolm found what he was seeking and withdrew a rolled up scroll. He placed it on the table, his left hand resting on it protectively.

"What's that?"

"Something important that I need you to deliver."

"A delivery? You want me to deliver this? Why? And to who?"

"A detective to the core I see," Malcolm commented.

Zach shrugged. "Can't help it."

"This was written by someone long ago, and he will be very hard to find. That is why I need your abilities to track him down."

"Where is he? You do know I can only do so much here. The tracker these days is Tony. He's learned a lot from that unicorn lady. I guess I could get Axel and Ruskin to guide me where I need to go and I'll wing it from there."

"They will be no use to you where you need to go Mr. Thomas."

"Why is that? You mean to tell me there's someplace around here they've never been? I find that hard to believe."

"That is because you will not be looking anywhere near here."

Zach was confused now. What was the wizard talking about? And just where was it he had to go? He sat up in his chair and looked right at Malcolm.

"Then where am I going?"

Malcolm smiled and winked. "I need you to go back to your world Mr. Thomas."

Zach sat back stunned at what he had just heard. He said nothing for a time, letting what the wizard had said take a hold in his mind. Zach had never fathomed the idea of ever going back to his old home, but now Malcolm was asking him to do just that.

"Say again."

"You must deliver this to him on your world, where he still lives, somewhere."

"Somewhere, that's being a little vague don't you think?"

"That is why I need you to go. Only you and your detective skills will work there. Axel and Ruskin cannot help you this time."

"Oh shit," Zach sighed. "I wouldn't even know where to start. You do know that the 'old world' as you keep calling it is rather large! It'll be like trying to find a needle in a haystack!"

"A needle, haystack?" questioned Malcolm.

Zach waved it off. "Never mind. It'll be hard, that's what it means."

"I can only tell you what I know. The rest will be up to you."

"Uh huh. And when am I supposed to go home to do this little job of yours?"

"Tonight."

"Tonight! You sure aren't one to give somebody a lot of notice, are you?" Zach joked.

Malcolm snickered, "bad habit I've developed over the years."

"Well," Zach sat back and saw his cup was full of fresh, steaming tea. Malcolm winked back at him. "Uh, yeah. So, tell me what you do know and I'll go from there."

"Very well."

Malcolm spent the next hour or so talking about who the letter had to go to and between a few curious questions he fielded from Zach managed to give him a sort of starting point in his search. The two went through a couple cups of tea before the wizard felt confident enough that Zach understood what was required of him and the time limit in which to do it.

Zach couldn't believe what was being explained to him not to mention he had to do it in a certain time frame or else this world, and his own would be lost to Helana and her legions. No pressure to get the letter delivered, not at all. The sarcasm in his mind filtered out into words, by accident.

"Talk about mission impossible. Tommy couldn't even pull this one off."

"Who?"

Zach looked at Malcolm and chuckled. "Uh, nobody. Just thinking out loud."

"Get what you need ready by this evening. Xanthus and I will open the portal to get you home. One thing you must remember, Helana will know what we've done and will do everything to close the portal back to this world. Unless you find who this belongs to," Malcolm held the scroll up, "You will not be able to return. I will not have the sufficient magic to bring you back. There will be no talisman this time."

"Then I've got a lot of work ahead of me." Zach took the scroll and held it tight. "I'll do everything absolutely possible to deliver this. You just make sure I've got a world to come back to."

"I will do everything possible to make that so."

"Then we both have a task to fulfill. If I see Neil, I'll have him join you. Keep the tea warm," Zach winked. He stood up and looked around the courtyard. The elves were changing their guard and he watched with a renewed curiosity more for the sake of taking it in one last time. There may be the chance he might not ever see it again.

"Tell the king and queen to both join me. They're up and walking through the castle, I'll have an extra cup ready for the queen."

Zach looked down at him. "And you know this how?"

"Magic," Malcolm shrugged. "I think."

Zach laughed and started inside. "I'll tell'em where you are. See you later crazy man."

Malcolm smiled and lifted his cup of tea. "Crazy? Well, perhaps a touch."

Mia was pushing her horse as fast at it could climb the mountain trail. She had met up with Jacinto just before daybreak and the large man assured her he would get a message to the king and queen and would take care of getting a messenger to Fairgrove. Mia thanked him for saving her a trip and had asked about Tony, but Jacinto had heard nothing. He gladly parted with one of his finer horses and the watcher accepted with a promise to take care of the animal.

Thus far the trail had been quiet. Very little wildlife of any kind crossed her path. She felt a fear within the forest, and through the mountains. It was as if the animals knew something was coming and were already going into hiding. Here she was, riding right towards the oncoming shadow. Mia calculated she would reach Aberdeen by nightfall if she pushed on without stopping too many times and if the trail didn't slow them down.

At some point it would level off and make the ride that much easier on both her and the horse. When the road started downhill again, she knew that Aberdeen wouldn't be too far off. Mia hoped the dwarves were receptive to a tracker's advice! All of her previous experience with the dwarves found them to be stubborn and closed-minded. With any luck, they would be half gorged on ale and a bit more friendly by nightfall. Mia grinned at the thought and urged her ride forward.

Shar had waited all night, and still no word from Malcolm. Now she felt she had to take the risk to contact him and get word of what was happening. Shar closed the drapes in the windows and then made sure the door was secure. She had no need of unwanted visitors while she attempted to converse with Malcolm. When she was certain the door couldn't be opened by anyone from outside, she moved to the center of the room and sat on the floor.

"What is it you would like me to do?" Adeena asked.

Shar smiled. "Stay by the door. It is locked, but someone may have a key. To be safe, make sure no one enters."

"I am but your meek little servant," giggled Adeena. Shar snickered and waited until the fairy had taken up residence in front of the door. She crossed her legs and reached into her cloak to withdraw an orb. Carefully, Shar placed it directly in front of her and then crossed her arms. She inhaled slowly and then let her breath ease out of her to bring herself to a completely calm state. As her body became tranquil and her mind focused, the words to the magic Shar required came from her lips.

"Find my teacher quick and true. Send my spirit secret and safe. Make this journey shrouded so, one step there my soul must go. Orta, la sorta, so mote it be."

Shar's head fell to her chest. She became aware that a part of her was now floating freely and Shar saw her own body, motionless below her. Then she was moving as the magic took hold and Shar felt herself flying over land, over trees and through clouds. She could feel no breeze yet she was cognizant of its sensations as her spirit raced over the lands to find Malcolm. Trees were but a blur, the clouds were like a fog and there was no sound around her. For what seemed like only a mere moment of travel she suddenly came to a pause and felt herself beginning to key in on where the magic had been guided. Shar could feel the magic drawing her down and a castle came into view.

Malcolm put his cup down and turned about in his chair. The magic alerted him to a presence immediately but he could feel no threat. He stood and waited for the spell to take shape. Malcolm smiled as he recognized Shar's form.

Shar could feel herself 'take hold' and she saw Malcolm standing before her with a grin on his face. The wizard did not appear angered at her use of the spell but she had learned from many lessons that he rarely showed his true emotion.

"Sir, it is good to see you."

"Likewise Shar. If I were to muster a guess, you must have begun to worry since our last conversation."

"Yes, you guess correctly. I've felt the darkness and since I had not heard from you I felt it necessary to take the risk of the spell to find you."

"I am sorry Shar. My magic has been 'tested' as it were since we talked. While I would normally frown on casting this particular spell since there is a danger but it is warranted this time. We must be quick though, so I will give you as much information as I can."

"Is it as bad as I fear?"

"Even more so." Malcolm sat down once again and Shar's image sat in the adjacent chair. "Helana has found her way out of her prison, and she has twisted the magic to suit her needs and by doing so has upset the very balance of it. She has made her presence known and her strength is growing at a phenomenal rate and as you know, mine weakens."

"Guardian of the lands seems to have its faults."

Malcolm chuckled. "Yes, it does. Though never forget, there are more advantages than faults."

"Sorry sir," Shar apologized. She felt a little foolish for making such a remark. Ever since she had taken up studying with Malcolm she knew full well what he meant.

The elder wizard went about explaining what he knew as he had earlier with Zach. Shar would intervene at every pause to ask her own questions to make sure she understood fully what was transpiring. Even though Shar was not really there, her image acted as though it was her conscious self with expressions of disbelief, anger, and fear all coming across. When the knowledge was shared, and all the questions asked, the two mages sat there for a moment, Malcolm to gauge Shar and how she was absorbing the information he had just given her and Shar trying to sort out all that was in her mind.

"What are we to do?" her thoughts coming to words.

"I have already spoken to Zach on what I need him to do. I will be speaking with the king and queen shortly on what I need from them. You and Adeena are to prepare the gnomes for a possible retreat back towards Cambridge. If Helana moves on the gnomes, and I believe she is already preparing to do so, there is no way they can hold the gates of Eldridge for any period of time."

"You think it is that serious?"

"I do." Malcolm sighed and sat back in his chair. "I do not know if we will be able to communicate after this for any period of time. Tony has gone to the dwarves with Axle and Ruskin. You will find him there. In case my theory holds true, you are to warn them for their own possible retreat, regardless of how stubborn they are. Helana's army will not stop until she has crushed everything in her path."

"I will deliver the message sir."

"Good. Now you had better return to your body before

Helana gets wary of what we are doing. In the future, be very careful of your magic and how you use it. She does not know of what you are capable. Once you use any magic on her, or her army, she will know and the element of surprise and any edge you may have, will quickly vanish."

Shar nodded. "I understand sir. Good luck and I hope to see you soon."

"Thank you Shar. Be careful, the days ahead are going to be full of many unknowns. Be prepared for the worst."

"If I have learned one thing from your teachings, it is to do just that." Shar smiled and her image stood. "I will take my leave. You better be prepared too." She warned.

Malcolm chuckled. "Hmm, to hear my own words on advice from a student, this would be a first for me. It is a nice change."

"Good words sir. Take care." Shar's image wavered and vanished.

"She is learning quickly," Malcolm nodded.

Shar opened her eyes and lifted her head. Adeena was sitting in front of her, head resting in her hands. The little fairy smiled and sat up straight.

"Well?"

"I found Malcolm, and we had a very interesting conversation."

"Do tell," urged the fairy. Her curious nature was coming to the forefront and Shar smiled.

"In due time little one, come, we need to speak with the council." Shar stood up and stretched to get the stiffness from her body.

"The council? What for?"

"All in due course. Do be patient."

"Oh that's easy for you to say," Adeena frowned. "You go off into a daze, I have to sit here and be absolutely bored wondering what or if you've been able to find out any information and now you tell me to wait even longer?"

"Correct."

"You are starting to act even more like Malcolm. I don't like it."

Shar laughed lightly and then stopped at the door and looked down at Adeena. "The news I have is not good Adeena and its best if I say it with everyone in the room at the same time. There is a lot to be done in a short time, and I don't want to have to repeat myself."

Adeena sighed. "All right, I'll wait. Can you tell me at least if it's bad, or real bad?"

"It is not good," replied Shar. She opened the door and with Adeena at her side, strode down the hall to find the council and its members.

Tony, Axel and Ruskin rode into the courtyard of Aberdeen around midday and were greeted by a number of dwarves who seemed a little surprised at seeing their brethren and without Zach riding with them.

"What brings ya back so soon, ya get lost? And without Zach I see, ya lose th'joker finally?" cracked Ricker as he leaned over the railing of the catwalk.

"Just fer now, he's busy elsewhere, but we did find a lost boy on th'trail," joked Axel.

"Lost boy?" questioned Tony. "Watch your words or I'll have to knock ya down with my sword."

"ooooooooo, a boy that be speakin brave for bein amidst us dwarves," Ricker chuckled. "I like that. Does th'boy like ale?"

"He will," Ruskin chortled.

"Good ta hear, c'mon in to th'hall, food's still warm an' there be plenty of ale ta wash it down," winked Ricker.

"Oh joy," Tony remarked sarcastically.

Axel shouted up at Ricker, "Can ya find th' chief an' th'council? We need ta speak ta them!"

"I'll go find'em. Go on in, ya know th'way." Ricker ambled off down the catwalk to do what they asked and the three handed their horses over to a few other dwarves and found their way into the hall to find some sort of nourishment. The kitchen staff were quick to urge them to find a seat and promptly served up some of the regular cuisine. Food was always ready in the dwarf kitchen since the dwarves liked to snack on a regular basis. It went hand in hand with regular tipping back of the ale over the course of a day, and night.

Tony winced at the aroma and realized what was placed in front of him was something that he had tried back at Neil and Tasha's wedding. He picked up his fork and with a little hesitation, managed to get a mouthful in without gagging.

Axel laughed lightly and winked. "The haggis not agree'in with you today boy?"

"It was," Tony swallowed and coughed. "Hard to stomach the first time I tried it, it's not going down any better the second time."

"Bring over something a tad easier on th'boys gut!" laughed Ruskin. "A loaf of bread a bit more ta yer likin?"

"How the hell does Zach put up with you two?"

Axel merely shrugged. "Not a clue, not my problem though is it?" He laughed again and stuffed another helping of Haggis into his mouth.

"I'll eat this stuff thanks," Tony waved off the bread. "If these two can eat it, so can I."

"It'll make ya grow up big an'strong," teased Ruskin.

"Just like you two?" cracked Tony. He winked and laughed at the two dwarves.

"Oh that be a good one, he got ya there boys," snickered

Ricker. The dwarf had just entered the room and sat himself down next to Tony.

"An' who asked you anyways? So, what is th'word on the council?" asked Ruskin.

"Th' council be busy at th'moment. We may have ta wait til later this day, they be in no rush ta see ya."

"Then ya go an'tell them we have important news, this cannot wait fer too long," warned Axel.

"Really now, well, guess I'll go an'pass th'news on ta them, again. Not promising anythin, they be in no rush at th'best o'times."

"Tell'em I'll kick th'door in if they make me wait too long," snorted Axel.

"Aye, I'll tell'em." Ricker vanished again and the three went back to their meal without any further interruptions.

Ricker found them a little later and informed them it would be early evening before they would be seen. It did not sit well with Tony, or either dwarf for that matter, and he could not believe the council would put off anything that would be important. Ricker said the dispute with the gnomes was their main topic of concern these days and everything else was considered secondary. Axel and Ruskin muttered some things under their breath but gave up for the time being and ambled off to find something to keep them occupied. Tony ventured off in another direction. He had seen very little of Aberdeen during his time on this world so he opted to give himself a tour of the place. There was no better time than the present after all he might not get another chance.

The suns were settling closer to the horizon to signal an end to their day as Mia Oravek rode out of the forest to see the outline of Aberdeen castle against the mountains into which it was carved into. She had not been here in some time and she hoped her visit wouldn't be a bother to the dwarves. From her recollection in her past travels with her father, the dwarves were never really receptive to outsiders, especially humans. Mia hoped the dwarves had already begun to get into their ale which was the one thing she knew was consistent at meal time. With any luck they would have tipped back a few mugs by the time she arrived at the gate. That in turn would make her entry into Aberdeen considerably easier. After that, somehow find a way to meet with the council. As she gave her ride a prod to move forward she sighed and thought 'one thing at a time'. First to get in, then she'd deal with the dwarves once she was inside.

At the gate she shouted up at the sentry to get his attention. The dwarf stuck his head out of a hole next to the gate and looked down at the stranger on the horse.

"Who be you an'what be yer business?"

"I am not important, but the news I bring for your council is, I have urgent need to speak with them!"

"Is that right! Well what news be that important?"

"I am to speak to the council in person, not some messenger barely sober at his post," she retorted.

"A wee bit of a big mouth on ya!"

"Let me in or else I will have the wizard Malcolm deal with you personally!" It never hurt to put a little fear in someone if it was for a good cause, or in this case, to contend with a dwarf too intent on being unruly. She had no patience this evening.

"Well why you didn't say so in th'first place, anyone a friend of th'wizard be a friend of ours! Enter!"

The gate to Aberdeen began to open and as soon as there was enough room Mia slipped through and into the courtyard of the castle. She dismounted and took a look around the yard, surveying her surroundings. A few dwarves sat on the catwalk staring down at her, their crossbows aimed at her. A couple more stood near the gate, with axes drawn and ready. She smiled and nodded to the dwarves.

"I am unarmed friends."

"An' what is so important that you need ta see th'council?" grunted one dwarf."

"I bear news with regards to a threat to your lands, and to the rest of our homes."

"Is that so?"

Mia recognized the voice immediately and turned to see Axel and Ruskin strutting across the courtyard. "Well, I thought I would not have to see either of you two anytime soon. I see you have not cleaned up since I last saw you," she teased.

"An' yer still bargin in where ya shouldn't be," quipped Axel.

"Nice to see you as well," she replied.

"A message ya say, for th'council, sounds like we have th'same business here this day," said Ruskin.

"You as well?" she asked.

"Aye, we do. All three of us," replied Ruskin.

"Three?"

"Yes, that includes me stranger." Tony stepped out of the shadows and Mia smiled at the unexpected surprise! She tossed the reins of her ride to a nearby dwarf and ran up to Tony. She gave him a big hug and he returned the embrace.

"Enough! Th'two of ya can catch up later," scowled Axel. "We need ta get up to th'council. I've had enough waitin fer one day."

"I agree. We've been hanging out here all afternoon and we're getting nowhere standing around. Axel, Ruskin, feel free to lead the way," urged Tony.

"So why are you here?" wondered Mia.

"I'll explain on the way to the council," he smiled. The company made their way down a series of hallways until they came to a door guarded by two other dwarves and where Ricker was waiting.

"I knew ya would be along shortly, figured I'd wait ta lend a hand," winked Ricker.

"Enough waitin, we need ta speak to th'council. No is not an answer we want ta be hearin, understand me?" Axel stated to one of the guards.

"I'll pass your request on Axe, but they be a might stubborn as late," replied Angus.

"Just deliver my message Angus, Feel free ta throw in Malcolm's name if ya wish," suggested Axel. He looked at Mia. "It worked for ya, might work fer me."

"It might," chuckled Mia. The guard Angus vanished inside the council chamber and the other guard moved in closer to the door to see if he could hear anything.

"What ya hear Nab? Anythin?" asked Ruskin.

"Not much, some arguing, but hey, that be normal," he chortled. "I think he's comin." Nab stepped back to his normal spot and waited for Angus to emerge. Angus stepped out of the council chamber and grumbled under his breath.

"Ya can go in Axe, but I'm warnin ya, they are not in a cheery mood."

"I can handle them, not ta worry," he replied. Axel led the company into the room and as Angus had mentioned, the council did not appear to welcome the visit. The chief walked up to Axel and shook the dwarf's hand grudgingly.

"So Axel, what it is that has yer bangin at th'door when we're busy with other matters?"

"I don't think a fight with th'gnomes is worth th'headache yer givin yerselves, but then, that be me."

"Tis none of yer concern then is it?"

"Aye, maybe, but th'news I bring is of concern to ya, and to th'rest of ya as well."

"And what be this news then?" grunted one of the council.

"Fife, mind yer tongue," snapped Ruskin. "We don't nag ya unless we need ta, ya should know that by now. There is a danger ta all of us, an' we need ta be ready fer what's comin."

"An' that would be?" asked the chief.

"Helana has escaped from her prison, an'she's none to happy bout it! She is likely puttin' her army tagether, an' you best be ready fer it!" said Axel. His tone was determined and the council took notice.

"Helana?" whispered the chief.

"Aye, th'witch is free, an'she's not like before, she an'th'demon have become one, that's what's been goin on th'last day or so, the sky, th'land shakin, an'all. She's dangerous, an'we need ta be ready," Axel further explained.

"It can't be true, tis impossible," snorted Fife.

"It's true, and you had better believe him because we've seen her, up close and personal. She's not who she used to be, and she's powerful, so much so that Malcolm is seriously scared of what she can do. You had better take Axel's advice, and be ready for anything, and if I can say so, be ready to get the hell out of here because if she comes here she isn't going to spare anyone, or anything. She'll level this place with you in it if she has to," said Tony.

Mia added her own thoughts. "I come on behalf of the unicorn stallion who has also felt the danger, and if he is able to sense what is happening, then we must take every precaution. If they say the threat is real, do not take it lightly."

"You have seen th'witch?" asked Fife.

"Aye, we have, an'we barely got through it. Th'wizard used them amulets ta send her on her way, but he said it may not work th'next time. I think we'd best figure out a way ta protect Aberdeen, an' if it means we leave, then we leave," said Ruskin.

"It can't come to that, ta leave? We have enough strength ta stop her, an'we can fight'er off," said another council member.

"Ya might at first, but I don't think we can hold'er off fer long. An then what?" asked Ruskin.

"What of th'gnomes, surely they are preparing ta fight?" said the chief.

Tony shrugged. "I don't know what they're going to do, but Shar is there and she's been told or will be told by Malcolm to evacuate Eldridge. If he is that scared for them then you need to be prepared to move as well. Fight if you want, but I'd suggest do so only to delay her so you can get Aberdeen emptied out."

"I don't know ya well young lad, tis Zach we're used ta listenin to but since he ain't here, I have no choice but ta listen ta Axe and Ruskin. Are ya sure th'witch is free, an' putting tagether an army?" Checked the chief.

"She is free and you can bet she's getting her army prepped to march. Think about what she had planned before, now take that and add in the fact she's much much stronger now. There is likely no end to what she can or what she could do. We're all in danger," assured Tony.

Down south in the gnome's home of Eldridge, Shar was having a similar conversation with the gnome council. She, like Axel and Tony were having a tough time convincing the council the threat was all too real from Helana.

"We are to take th'word of a mage that Helana is free,

an' out to do us harm?" commented Royan, the chief of the gnome council.

"Yes sir, you must. Have you not seen the change in the land? The sky, the quakes? Malcolm has told me that Helana is free from her prison and is more determined than ever to subdue the races and do away with them if necessary."

"I need more proof of such if we are ta even think we need ta move th'lot of us out! What ya ask is not an easy task!"

"I understand that. Therefore it is necessary to begin at once, it will only be a matter of days before Helana shows up on your doorstep, and trust me, if she has become one with the demon who she was in legion with before, then her powers will be more than your army can handle," Shar said with conviction. She was determined to get these stubborn people to listen. "Your squabble with the dwarves will seem like a light dinner after she gets through with this place. Do not take her lightly Royan, it is time to get your people on the move."

"I will take yer advice to a few of my fellow gnomes an' see what they have ta say on th'matter. Thatcher isn't here to put his take on it, but we will have ta make do without the lad."

Adeena who had sat quietly off to the side had had enough of this gnome. "You silly little man!"

Royan looked at the fairy and frowned. "What is that ya say?"

"You silly little man, you heard what I said. This is no time to sit around and do nothing! If Malcolm can take Shar and make her his student, then you can be assured that he knows what he's doing. So if she says that there is danger, and that Helana is free, then you best pay attention! She was nasty before and if she's out again, then she's probably even meaner! And with demon power now? I'm a fairy and

I'm scared of what she can do with that, so you best be scared to!"

Royan was a bit taken aback by the fairy and crossed his arms, his eyes locked on Adeena. After a moment he nodded and sighed. "Very well little one, if yer sayin that the threat be real, then I'll take yer word." He looked up at Shar. "My apologies Shar, sometimes we forget what be needin ta be taken seriously. Even gnomes can be scolded by a wee fairy ta wake us up."

"She has no hesitation is speaking her mind when she wants to," Shar smiled. "It seems to be a fault of hers."

Royan laughed. "A fault eh? Tis a good fault I might say. I will talk with th'rest of th'council immediately."

"Thank you sir," Shar nodded. Royan left the room and Shar faced Adeena. The fairy shrugged with a smile.

"Sorry Shar, but he was annoying me."

"That's okay, this time your impatience paid off. Thank you," Shar answered. Adeena was all smiles then and bowed.

"Only to do my duty as required my lady."

Shar laughed and the two of them started out to the hall. "I hope all is going well with the rest, the next few days are going to be hectic."

"I would like to think 'chaotic' would be a better word of choice," Adeena commented.

"Chaotic," whispered Shar. "Yes, a better choice."

Chapter Seven

Zach pulled his old shirt on and adjusted it accordingly. He looked at himself and laughed lightly. He thought he would never be wearing this shirt ever again. After his, Neil's and Tony's arrival on this new world of Avalon their clothing had been replaced with garb more reflective of their new home. Now as he looked down at his old jeans and shirt, and boots, he had forgotten what they had felt like. Strangely enough, he felt like he had just stepped back into a life he had pretty much forgotten about. A knock at the door altered his thoughts and he shouted out to whoever was waiting on the other side.

"It's open!"

Neil entered the room and his friend even managed to chuckle at the sight of him. Zach threw his old jacket on the bed and went about gathering up a few of his other things for the trip that he was about to embark.

"Well don't you look a little out of place," Neil quipped.

"Yeah yeah, feels weird too. Never thought I'd hear myself say those words but hey, a guy has to do what he has to do."

Neil walked over and sat down on the edge of the bed. "Malcolm told me what he's asked of you. Are you sure you can do this?"

"I don't really have a choice do I? They need me to do this because if I don't, Helana might just kick our ass to smithereens."

"We don't know what she can do yet. If we can get all the races together we might be able to fend her off and stop her."

"You really think that's possible? I mean, really? Look at Malcolm, he's wearing out fast and he was just able to get rid of that hag. What if the amulets don't stop her next time? I have to do this Neil, if I don't we might lose everything we've come to like about this place."

Neil stood up and walked over to the terrace and stared out. "You're right. I wish I was going with you though."

"You have to stay here and keep this place around long enough for me to finish what I have to do. Think you can manage without me?" Zach joked. "I know it'll be hard since I tend to do all the work most of the time."

"Yeah right!" Neil laughed. "I have to spend most of the time cleaning up after you and your dwarf buddies, the three of you are walking disasters!"

"Whatever," snickered Zach. "I'll work as fast as I can, but it won't be easy."

"Next to impossible I would think," added Neil.

"I'll just have to drop in on my old boss and see if he'll let me use some of their resources. I know he'll just love to see me again," he cracked.

Neil wandered back over to Zach and pulled out an envelope from his pocket. He gave it to Zach and his friend looked at him for an explanation.

"Inside is some money and my credit card to help you out at first and there is a letter to my old partner at my law firm. He will get you access to whatever money you may need and anything else for that matter. The credit card should still work. It doesn't expire for another year yet. It will be up to you to make sure you can convince him that the letter is authentic."

"Oh hell, that won't be easy. He's a lawyer!" Zach chuckled and Neil couldn't help himself but laugh along. "I'll do what I can, but it'll be the letter itself that will have to convince him it's not something I put together."

"I think it should, but just in case, use that charm of yours and make Riordan pay attention."

"What's his first name?"

"Matt. He likes doughnuts, just in case you need to bribe him."

"And I thought us cops were the only ones who ate them."

"Sorry, but it's quite the delicacy with us lawyers too."

"That credit card better work!"

"It will. I asked Malcolm to make sure it does."

"Ah, nothing a little magic can't fix, huh?"

The two shared another laugh together and Zach continued to throw the rest of his gear into his old gym bag. It was the same bag that had accompanied him to this world and now it would do the same going back. There was a tinge of fear, and sadness at the same time within him. Going home was something he never thought would ever happen. This world, Avalon, had become his new home and leaving it at a time when he thought he should be staying to assist in some way just didn't feel right. He stuffed his last bit of clothing into the bag and zipped it shut.

"Done, now all I have to do is wait until they're ready to do whatever it is Malcolm needs to do."

Neil faced his friend. "They're ready anytime you are. I was told to come and get you."

"Well why didn't you say so?"

"Because I wanted to have the chance to talk to you before you left."

"I am coming back you know, and I won't be alone."

Neil smiled and nodded. "I know you'll be back. You have to, who are Axel and Ruskin going to drink their ale with otherwise?"

"Well, you could always take my place," he winked.

"I don't think so, I can't handle that ale in the quantities they consume it," Neil cracked. Zach grabbed his gym bag and took another look around the room. This world, these people, races were about to be left behind.

"Let's go, the longer I take to get back, uh, home, I guess, the longer it takes for me to get my job done."

Malcolm stared out at the sky from the terrace adjacent to the elf council chamber and watched the ever darkening sky to the south. He could feel the evil coalescing and the energy it was drawing from the land, and in turn, from him. Never in his years on this world had he ever felt a dark shadow with such ever growing strength. Helana had violated every known condition of magic, and in turn would lose herself because of it. The demon side would eventually consume what was left of her and she would become the entity in whole, with an insurmountable power to destroy. Her threat of crossing over to the old world was all too real and well within her or its ability once her strength had reached its zenith. He let out a deep sigh and heard footsteps come to a stop behind him. Malcolm turned to see Riane standing there.

"Sir, may I speak with you?"

"Of course Riane, what is on your mind?"

"Tasha tells me you are sending Zach back to his world, and I would like to accompany him."

Malcolm had to admit to himself that he didn't see that one coming and the surprise he showed was quite real. "Is that so? You do understand that as an elf, but more importantly, being from here, you will find it a very harsh world, and you will very likely be quite confused as to what you will see."

"I understand that sir, but he might need my help at some point. At least I will be there to assist if he requires it."

"Are you quite sure? I know you would like to be there at his side, but did you perhaps think that you might be more of a hindrance than a benefit? He might find himself too busy to assist you in adapting to your new surroundings."

"Not to worry sir, I am very capable of adapting to whatever I may face on the old world. I would like to go. Please sir, do let me travel with him."

Malcolm smiled and motioned for her to follow him. She fell in beside him and he sighed.

"You love him dearly don't you my dear?"

"Yes, I do sir."

"Then who am I to stop you from keeping him out of trouble," Malcolm chuckled. "But, we're going to have to do something about your appearance. The sight of an elf in their midst will likely start a panic, so, we are going to have to fix that."

"What is it you will do? A spell?"

"Of course my dear, My, my, Zach will be surprised now won't he?" Malcolm could not help but smile, like a child about to pull a mischievous prank. They came up to the book of magic nestled on its stand and he opened its pages. He found the incantation he needed to use and whispered it to himself to be sure he understood the words. Malcolm looked at Riane and motioned for her to stand in front of him.

"The spell is quite simple really. It will hide your actual

appearance as an elf and instead show you as one of them, a normal human woman. Are you ready?"

"Will I feel anything?"

"Only a slight tingling sensation, nothing more," he assured her. "My lady, are you sure you want to do this?" he checked.

"I do," she nodded.

"Very well," Malcolm smiled back at her. He called on the magic required to transform Riane. With a simple flick of his wrist after reciting the words, a ball of white light floated out toward the elf and vanished inside of her. Riane began to pulsate with a white glow moments later and Malcolm watched as the magic took hold.

Zach and Neil strode down the hall, not saying a whole lot, since neither knew what to say at this juncture. Zach was leaving and he did not know what he would return to, and Neil was unsure if his friend could actually accomplish the monumental task asked of him by Malcolm. It was only a day ago that they were just having a good time watching the unified games at Kildare, now in the blink of an eye it had all changed. They were now scrambling to fight off a new threat from an old nemesis who had become more of a danger than they had ever thought possible. Once more the trio was being split up to accomplish the task of stopping an encroaching storm. A storm not related to the weather, but a demon storm! One that would could carry ramifications back to their own world if their tasks fell short.

"Can you bring me something back from your trip?" wondered Neil.

"Uh, sure, what do you want?"

"A chocolate bar, any kind, doesn't really matter which one."

Zach looked at him incredulously. "A chocolate bar?"

"Yeah, I'd kill to sink my teeth into some chocolate."

"You're kidding?"

"No, I'm not," chuckled Neil. "What?"

"I never took you for one to like candy, but hey, who am I to deny you your chocolate addiction. Sure, I think I can manage to bring one back. Hey, I'll bring a couple, and then you can stop bugging me about betting with the gang."

"I'll give you a bit of a reprieve, deal?"

Zach laughed and shook his friends hand as they entered the elf council chamber. "Sure, deal. I guess it'll have to do."

Zach and Neil came into a room full of people there to see Zach off and it took Zach by surprise. He expected there to be only a couple of people there due to Malcolm's usual quiet way of doing things. The entire elf council was there, Malcolm of course, Tasha, Thatcher, Xanthus the elf king, and a bunch of other elves he assumed were part of the guard detachment. There were a few others he didn't recognize but the one person he expected to see there wasn't to be seen. He showed his disappointment openly.

"Riane not around?" he asked.

"Oh, she's around," Malcolm smiled.

"Where?"

"My my, aren't we the one who can't see clearly today." The voice Zach recognized immediately. He smiled and turned to face what he thought would be the woman he cared for, but instead saw a stranger. "Uh, and you are?"

"Look closer Mr. Thomas," urged Malcolm with a wink as he stood next the woman.

Even Neil had to look twice to realize who it was. "Wow, you had me fooled to."

"Riane?" checked Zach. Her features were now human and he soon realized it was indeed the elf Riane. "What the?"

Riane's elf features were completely gone! Her hair had a bit of curl to it now, still blonde, but no longer the straight blonde hair that made her distinctly elf. That included her arced eyebrows, now gone, and her ears which had the appearance of any other human. Even her face had a touch more 'roundness' to it and he had to admit, Riane made an extremely attractive looking human! He looked at Malcolm for an explanation.

"A simple spell, she will need to look more like yourself if she is to accompany you."

"Huh? What? Would somebody like to fill me in here?"

Riane merely grinned and came up closer to him. "It is I, but now, I am human, for now. At least I look that way. If you think I'd let you go off alone then you are sadly mistaken. Without Axel and Ruskin around to keep you safe, the job now falls to me."

Zach looked her over from top to bottom and shook his head. "No way, you won't last a day back where I come from. There is way too much you won't understand."

"Oh come on Zach, I will be fine. Trust me; I am more adept than you may think." Riane gave him a kiss and he sighed.

"You've made up your mind I'm guessing and there's nothing I can do or say that will change it huh?"

"None at all. You are stuck with me."

"Well I can think of worse people to be stuck with, Axel and Ruskin come to mind first, but hey, you are much cuter," he twinkled.

"You two be sure to come back safe and sound," urged Tasha.

"We will my lady. I will see to it," assured Riane.

"My lady, ya make a fine addition to th' humans! Zach m'boy, ya better keep an eye on this one," Thatcher hinted.

He whistled and snickered. Riane blushed and played with her hair and then she caught herself realizing what she was doing.

"A human reaction my dear," said Malcolm. "There will undoubtedly be a few other things you may, uh, react to differently. It is part of the magic. Not only will you look human, but you will feel a little differently, so don't be too alarmed if you do things you may not normally do."

"Maybe I'll have to watch her closer then, but it'll be worth keeping an eye on her."

Tasha gave Riane a hug and did the same to Zach. "Good luck to both of you. I hope to see you again soon."

"We'll be back soon enough, and I promise we won't be empty handed," stated Zach confidently.

"And don't forget my chocolate," joshed Neil as he shook Zach's hand.

"Yeah, yeah," he laughed.

Malcolm waited until all had said their good-bye's and when he had the chance, he motioned to Zach and the two moved off to the side to talk privately. The wizard held out his hand and Zach shook it. Neither had to say anything, both understood with a simple nod.

"You have the letter?" checked Malcolm.

"Yes sir, I do." Zach patted his bag and nodded. "It's safe and sound, along with Neil's letter to his old business partner. Apparently I won't have to worry about money or anything as long as his partner believes the letter is for real. If he doesn't well, I could always bribe him with doughnuts." Zach grinned as Malcolm looked at him, rather surprised.

Zach explained further, "It's a food us cops, and apparently lawyers, eat often."

"I see." Malcolm shrugged and continued. "As I said before, once you have crossed over, you will be unable to return without assistance. Helana will undoubtedly know what has happened once we send you through and with her powers increasing by the minute she will be able to close that door for good. If you succeed, and only then, will you be able to cross back. Mr. Thomas, I hope we see each other again." Malcolm shook his hand again and Zach nodded.

"You will. Keep the witch at bay as best you can, and watch over the others, especially those two," he nodded towards Neil and Tasha. "They're the most important people to get the races together for this one."

"I agree, and I will do my best. Well my good man, Are you ready?"

Zach sighed. "I guess, can't be much more ready than this. Let's get it over with."

"Very well, please, stand over near the terrace doorway."

Zach shook Neil's hand one more. "I'll be back as soon as I can. You have my word."

"I'll have some of that dwarf ale ready for you," promised Neil. Tasha gave him one last hug.

"Thank you for doing this Zach. You don't know how much we appreciate it," said Tasha as she wiped a tear away.

"See you both soon. Well, now that you're human Miss Riane, shall we?" Zach offered his hand to her and she accepted. Both took position near the terrace doorway and Malcolm moved to stand behind the book of magic. Xanthus, the elf king, took his position next to the wizard to aid in the casting of the incantation.

"This time Mr. Thomas, do try and stay on the path in front of you," teased Malcolm.

"I'll do my best," laughed Zach.

Wizard and Elf King began to speak the words to open the portal to the old world once more. First, Malcolm would say the phrase, and then Xanthus would repeat it. As the spell continued the vortex that had opened a year and a half ago to allow the wizard to cross over the first time began to reappear. Zach and Riane stood, waiting for the two to finish and await their cue to enter. All watched as the magic of the vortex grew in strength and began to coalesce before them a 'doorway' of sorts. The mist drifted inward as it took shape signaling that it was nearly complete.

Helana looked abruptly to the north as she detected the magic being invoked. What was her old teacher up to now? She moved out of her gate to stand on the bridge and tried to get a sense of the spell. Helana uttered a few words and her eyes glared angrily. It was a portal spell. He was opening a door to go somewhere, but where? What would he accomplish by doing such a thing? Too many questions flowed through her mind and Helana frowned in frustration. She felt the magic come to a zenith and suddenly she realized what the wizard was doing.

"As this world opens the door to the old, take the travelers, one to home, the other as guardian, give safe passage as required by thee, open this door as requested by me! So mote it be!" Malcolm read the last phrase with emphasis and Xanthus followed suit. The vortex took full form and Zach stared into the abyss. He looked over to Malcolm and the wizard nodded. It was time to go.

Helana began to speak her own words to counteract the magic Malcolm had just cast. Her eyes, full of hatred and contempt, focused on the sky to the northland and her lips said the words to stop the magic of the portal spell. From what she could determine the portal was opened back to the old world. The question she could not answer was 'why'? Was he going there, or was he sending someone else? Or something? The only thing she wanted to do was to shut the 'door' that was there, for good.

The vortex began to fluctuate just as Zach and Riane neared its entrance. Both stopped and looked back at Malcolm to see what was going on. The wizard recognized the interference immediately.

"Hurry! Enter before it begins to close! Helana has already started her own magic to close the door! Quickly now!" Malcolm urged nervously.

Not needing to be told twice Zach and Riane raced into the vortex without any hesitation and without a look back. Neil, Tasha, Thatcher and the rest watched as the two vanished into the mist and the vortex began to close. A few seconds later it collapsed onto itself and the magic shattered amidst thunder.

"Malcolm, Malcolm, Malcolm, Just what do you think you are trying to do!" The voice reverberated off the walls in the elf council chamber.

Malcolm looked around the room in disbelief. He knew Helana wasn't there, but if she was capable of casting her voice within elf territory, then her power was already growing exponentially.

"I am merely doing what I need to."

"Open a door to the old world? And just what do you hope to achieve? There is nothing you can do to stop me, and you will know that soon enough."

"Never assume anything Helana," Malcolm warned.

"Always the hopeful one! Tis a shame. I will see you all soon enough and when I do, I promise you will wish otherwise." The voice trailed off in an echo. The crowd stood there, stunned and wondering if Zach and Riane had made it through the portal successfully.

"Did they make it, ya think?" wondered Thatcher aloud.

"I'm afraid we will only find that out in due time," Malcolm sighed. "She was much quicker to react than I had anticipated."

"Quite, this threat of hers will come to pass far too soon to our liking," added Xanthus.

"We need to talk about our options. Can we convene the council this afternoon?" Neil asked.

"I can have everyone here in short order," Xanthus said.

"The sooner we can establish our method of defense against Helana, the better," added Tasha. "We have much work to do and so far she has us at a disadvantage. It is time we turned this around on her."

"Agreed! The longer we do nothing, the more confidence she will have. We cannot sit idly by and let her get organized while we sit and wait. We must start to do the same!" said Malcolm. "We need to be ready for anything in case Zach has difficulty finishing what he has to do."

"Let's do it then," Neil nodded with conviction. He was not going to let his new home be destroyed without a fight. Tasha gave him a smile. The two of them had accomplished too much to have it all go to waste. There was still so much to do but if Neil knew anything about history, it was those races still uncertain about the new monarchy who would no doubt be turning to them to lead during this crisis and that is exactly what he and Tasha intended to do. Helana would be up against a determined and united Avalon. Of that much he was certain.

Helana stood outside her castle for a few moments and then strode back into her courtyard. Several wraiths stood there, waiting for her orders. She had been about to send them off until the interruption from Malcolm and company. Now she was composed and ready to get her minions off on their assignment.

"You three, go to the eastern lands and to the gnomes first. Tell me everything about the layout of the land outside their castle. I have been away for a time; they may have done something to enhance their defenses. Investigate everything, and then travel up north to the dwarves and do the same. I intend to march as soon as the trolls arrive, if all goes well, within the next few days. Now go, and don't overlook anything, understand?"

The wraith nodded and began their morphing to the winged creatures required for the charge by Helana. Arms stretched to form wings, legs shortened and necks became elongated as the transformation became complete. Each lifted off into the sky and the journey to the north eastern range and the home of gnomes was underway.

Helana watched them go and her face twisted into its evil grin as her plans were all going ahead smoothly. Soon all she needed would be in place. The other wraith would have the trolls well on their way to her domain, and the others should have the mercenaries rounded up in short order. Perhaps she should drop in and see how the trolls were progressing. Helana uttered a few words and she vanished in a whirlwind of sand and thunder.

The wraith herding the trolls became aware of their visitor the moment the blast of wind and sand appeared. The trolls did not understand until the wind had calmed and Helana stepped forth. The trolls cowered at the sight before them the half human half demon creature was a formidable vision. Helana faced the trolls and sought out their leader. She found him, the one troll brave enough to not hide behind another.

"Hello Gartog, it has been some time."

Gartog stared at her, and slowly realized it was the witch he had crossed paths with before. Though, this version of her was twisted and frightening.

"You true queen? You not look same."

"Is that so? Well, the change is for the better, trust me on that. How much longer before I see you at my gates?"

"We sssssshould be there sssssoon, maybe thisssss night," hissed one wraith.

"Good. Gartog, get your kind to move faster. Push them until you get to my castle. They can rest once they get there," urged Helana. "We have places to go, and kingdoms to crush." Helana scowled and the trolls cowered more. "I will reward you with anything you could ever want. Just get them moving!"

"Will move faster, have food to eat, we be hungry," replied the Troll.

"I'll have it ready, don't you worry Gartog." Helana looked at her wraiths and they merely nodded. A few words spoken and she vanished in another whirlwind of sand and thunder.

"Letsssssssssss move," screeched one wraith. The march to Livinia was reinstated and the trolls grudgingly quickened their pace at the behest of the demon queen.

Helana reappeared in her throne room and a sudden pain struck her in the abdomen. She fell to her knees and felt the pain sear through her entire body. Her eyes flared red, and then yellow as the demon within began to fight for more control. Helana concentrated on maintaining domination but felt a 'piece' of her fall to the demon. In the process, her features altered ever so slightly. Helana's chin stretched outward fractionally and the teeth grew followed by the hairline on her forehead receding marginally which now gave Helana a much longer looking face that began to lean towards the demon more than her own. The pain faded as she subdued the demon back within her but she was less of who she was before. It would continue thus she knew. It was a part of the 'cost' of doing what she had done to gain her freedom from the abyss. Malcolm had guessed what the consequences were and for that, she did give her old teacher credit. At some point in time the demon would be the dominating persona and her human side would be a mere fragment, lost forever. There could be no undoing what she had done and this Malcolm knew as well. It only made the wizard fear her more because there was no telling into what she would evolve. Helana stood and breathed in the air. 'No matter' she thought to herself. Everything was beginning to take shape! The last few pieces of the puzzle she would add upon the arrival of those the wraith would lead here. Then Avalon would bow down to her, or fall to the wayside.

Chapter Eight

Tony stood on the catwalk of the Dwarf castle and watched the dwarves prepping their defenses for the imminent assault from Helana. He had this feeling of impending doom and that nothing the dwarves would do or prepare for would be enough to stop the witch. Mia joined him and she put her arm around him. She leaned on him and he felt her breathing hard.

"Anxious too?"

She chuckled. "Yes, these dwarves are a rather angry bunch sometimes."

"Yup, always lookin for a fight," he laughed.

"Axel and Ruskin are looking for you. Guess why? They've been put in charge of organizing the evacuation if necessary. They want some help from us."

"Oh, great."

The sarcasm was rather evident in his tone and Mia merely smiled and poked him in fun. "Now now, they don't really know how to do that kinda thing. You know them pretty well, I'm sure they'd rather be using their axe to kill something rather than run from it."

"That much is true. Well, guess we better get them

pointed in the right direction, as it were," he grinned. "I would hate to have them run into a wall or something."

"That's not nice," she laughed.

Tony shrugged. "Just trying to live up to Zach's antics. He always liked to taunt them, so, I'm only doing my best to keep up the tradition."

"I think the two of them have their own head-aches without you adding to it."

"Ohhhhh, all right, I'll be nice. Come on then, let's go see what they need help with," said Tony as he led the way back into the castle.

The two of them were able to find Axel and Ruskin talking up a storm with several other dwarves and pointing repeatedly down the hall. Upon joining them both look relieved and let out rather large sighs of relief.

"The lad can explain things better, can't ya boy?" asked Ruskin.

"Well that depends on the question?"

"We've been tellin'em that ta get out faster we need to have'em all lined up, not in groups, they'd be pluggin th'hole up!" said Axel.

"Uh, okay. Makes sense, I guess. What hole are you talking about?" asked Tony, really confused at this point.

"It be our way outta th'mountain, a cave, tunnel, or th'like through th'mountain to th'other side," explained Axel.

Tony began to understand what the argument was about at that point and looked at Mia shaking his head.

"This isn't gonna be easy," he chuckled.

"Aye, it will be, if they go down in order, an'not in a hurry scurry way," grunted Ruskin.

"Then you are going to have to keep them from seein Helana's army, and have them all ready and in line before they do get here, cause if you don't, then all hell's gonna break loose," said Tony.

"That won't be an easy task, yer askin a lot," added Ruskin

"All you can do is try," assured Mia.

"When were you planning on beginning the evacuation?" checked Tony.

"Soon, if we can get th'rest to get movin!" snarled Axel looking over at the other dwarves who merely scowled in return.

"We be tryin to get'em ta move, but they don't seem ta understand that if th'gnomes do th'same, they'll be here an' it'll be that much more of a head-ache," said Ruskin. "Which is what will happen ya toads," he snapped.

"We don't know they be comin this way," said one of the other dwarves, Iver.

"That's true, but in case they do, I think you should listen to your guys here. If the gnomes do go through the mountains to get away, then it is likely they will head this way," said Tony.

Mia added her own agreement to Tony's comment. "It would only make sense to do so. The mountains provide cover and the forests add to that. To attempt to go over the plains would make them an easy target for Helana."

"Fine," muttered Iver, throwing his arms up in defeat. "I'll start sendin word ta get'em all movin. I think we should organize ta th' northwest up near th' falls. In case we need ta fight back."

"I agree with ya on that point Iver, pass it on ta th'rest," nodded Axel.

"What do you need from us Axe?" asked Tony.

"Just ta help us keep them from goin all over th'place, we keep'em busy an'movin, they won't be carin bout what's goin on outside th'walls."

"I think we can manage that. We'll go and grab our gear and meet back here shortly," said Mia. "Then we can start organizing the groups."

"Good idea, see you guys shortly," nodded Tony.

The gnomes had begun their own organizational evacuation and much like the dwarves, the gnomes had a lot of questions as to why it was happening and the answers they were getting were a little too vague for their satisfaction. Shar was getting a little frustrated with it all and Adeena had just flown off to get away from it altogether. The young mage got tired after a time and left the explaining to the council who were doing their best to accommodate. Shar strolled to the outer rampart and felt the wind on her face. It cooled her and made the stress of the day fade away. Her skin tingled at its touch and she felt the magic inside her begin to listen to the elements. She felt a surge of fear flowing on the wind and her eyes opened wide. There was something nearby, something evil. Shar looked over the surrounding landscape trying to locate the source. She could have easily used a simple spell but she did not need Helana or whatever it was to know about her or her abilities at this time, and Malcolm had warned her to keep her magic to a minimum in case she ever had to confront the witch. That way the element of surprise would be in her favor with the hope the demon witch would underestimate her capabilities.

The wind changed direction, as if to give her guidance in her search, and Shar paid attention to where it changed. Instead of flowing down it changed to an upward draft and she shifted her gaze to the forest below. Her eyes scanned the trees slowly, trying to see any change at all in its appearance. Then she saw the wraith, partially hidden amidst the forest greenery. The creature was looking the castle over and seemed to be studying the outlying land around it. It only took Shar a few moments to understand what was going on. It was 'looking things over' for Helana. That made sense. She had been imprisoned for some time, and what better way to know your enemy than to study them and see if anything had changed. Shar watched it until it decided it had seen enough and then vanished back into the cover of the woods. If there was one wraith here, then no doubt there would be others out to be Helana's eyes and find out whatever it was she wanted to know. The wraith confirmed what Malcolm had thought, that Helana was on the verge of an outright assault on the races of Avalon. It would only be a matter of time before the witch would be on the doorstep of the gnomes. Shar turned and strode back into the castle. The gnomes would have to speed up their evacuation and put aside their questions until a later time. A tiny surge of panic rose within her and Shar did her best to put it down. If she had to, she would tell the populace the truth. That would likely cause the panic she dearly wanted to avoid but if they persisted on asking, she would tell and live with the consequences.

Neil looked the map over that was laid across table in the elf council chamber and was amazed at how large Avalon really was. There were so many areas he had never thought existed and there were still areas waiting to be 'found' explained Malcolm. Races still unknown to all could very well be living amidst them in the land but 'undiscovered' at this point in time. He would have to make it a point to try and do a little exploring in the future. So much to see, and so many places to visit!

The immediate area the group was focused on was the northern regions where most of the different elf races had settled. The tree elves had settled in the thick forest regions to the north east while others had found a home in the ice plains directly to the north and some had set up shop in the desert regions between the forests and ice. The group had decided to dispatch couriers to each one to explain the situation and to call on their aid during this crisis.

"With all of our forces alone, we can present a formidable opponent for Helana's army," stated Xanthus. "If you include the humans, dwarves and gnomes, we should be able to show her we will not surrender easily."

"Which brings us to another matter," started Malcolm. "There will be refugees from all looking for sanctuary here on elf lands. We will have to be ready with supplies," he finished.

"I thought you might say that old friend, we can send small groups out to collect what we need since we still have time before the worst of it. I already have Vasillis attending to that," said Xanthus.

"Can I make a suggestion?" wondered Neil.

"By all means," smiled Malcolm.

"We seem to be talking a lot about making our stand here, and so on, but what about taking the fight to her? Why wait for her to get here? Let's go and see if we can make a difference out there, away from here, and use this," Neil motioned with hands in a circular motion, "as our last stand if it's necessary."

"We can be no match for what she will have out there," said one of the elf captains, Keiran. "If we take our full force out to meet her, we run the risk of failing completely, leaving no one to make our stand here."

"I'm not saying take everyone but take the best of the best. I have my royal guard, men who have been trained by yourselves, and you have your elite elf forces. The dwarves, likely the same and I'm guessing the gnomes do as well. I know Jacinto has his own best men at his disposal when he needs them. So why not go out and give her a taste of her own medicine? We might not stop her, but we can make her think twice about her plans. At the very least, it will give those back here enough time to really mount an even better defense," said Neil.

"The risk is high for those who would do this," said Malcolm.

"There is risk in everything we do, but we need to give her a reason to reconsider," replied Neil.

"The idea does have merit," agreed one elf, Taith.

"How fast can we get a force together?" asked Neil.

"A couple days, at least," said Taith.

"If we push ourselves we might be able to get to the dwarves before the witch, but the gnomes I'm afraid are on their own. It will be impossible to get to them before she does," said Taith. He looked at Thatcher and then the group and pointed to the map. "We have the forest to use as cover, and the river will help. If we have to retreat, we can backtrack through the region just north of Fairgrove. That way we will be less in the open. Our best place for a surprise attack will be just west of the dwarves, near the falls."

"Aye, my brethren will be with th'dwarves, they can lend in th'attack. If Aberdeen falls an' th' dwarves are on th'move, you will find them at th'falls with us gnomes. It has always been th'place to meet. If you be plannin to strike, there be th'place," said Thatcher, agreeing with the elf.

"After that, we might be able to do more near the valleys to the west of there, but after that, she will have a straight path to us here at Cambridge," stated Taith.

"She'll make a stop at Kildare first," muttered Neil.

"It is out of the way, why would she?" asked Keiran.

"Because it is the one place she wants more than the destruction of the elves, she wishes to be queen. She will, as Neil says, stop there first. She will not be able to help herself," said Malcolm.

"That will give us more time to reconvene back here at Cambridge with the rest of the forces," nodded Taith.

"We will discuss the final stand once the other elves have arrived. We will need to change the message for our couriers somewhat, and have those dispatched within the hour," said Xanthus. "Let us hope that they respond quickly and with any luck we will be able to do as Taith says, move out within a couple days to meet the witch."

"It will done your highness," nodded Taith. "Keiran and I will begin to organize our forces here as soon as the couriers are on their way. If we can leave shortly after the others arrive, then we get a jump on our plan."

"I'll go and get my own royal guard prepped, we can be ready pretty quick," said Neil.

"We?" Malcolm asked his eyebrow arced curiously.

"Yes, we, I intend to go as well."

"Sir, might you reconsider? The risk as Malcolm mentioned will be even greater for you since you are the king of this land," reminded Taith.

"I don't care, I'm going. There is no way I am going to sit here and wait for her to show up," Neil said defiantly.

"And I will be going with him as well," piped up Tasha as she entered the room.

"My queen, I cannot allow such," Malcolm shook his head in disagreement.

"I will be going with him and there is nothing you can say or do will stop us, we work together, and we will do so until we are both too feeble to ride a horse," said Tasha. She looked at Neil and he merely smiled back.

"Very well, I know better than to argue the point, but you will have certain magic's at your disposal to give you a little extra protection, that I will insist upon," said Malcolm.

"You do what you have to Malcolm, but I will be leading

this expedition, and I'll do everything I can to give Helana a severe head-ache," assured Neil.

"Be careful Malcolm, if you use too much magic, Helana will know something is up. We can ill afford to draw more attention to us, keep the talismans to a minimum. If she does not know we are a part of it, then she has no reason to single us out," warned Tasha.

"The lady makes a point," Neil admitted.

Malcolm chuckled and shrugged, "point made and understood, from both of you. I will keep it simple, so don't do anything foolish." He pointed at both with a wave of his finger in warning and both nodded obediently. "Good, now I will take my leave so I can conjure up what I need. Everyone," Malcolm took a look around the room at everyone, "let us make haste and keep this meeting to ourselves. No one can know of our plans, except those of us who make them. She will have spies and demons amidst us, among the populace, anyone who can listen could be a spy. Be wary and keep your thoughts to one self. I can feel her power and the evil within her strengthening quicker than I thought possible. Let us hope we can together stop her."

"Aye sir, agreed," Thatcher concurred.

"Then let us prepare and give the witch a homecoming she will never forget!" Xanthus said.

"Well put sir," Malcolm nodded.

Upon the completed notes from Xanthus to all of the elf tribes of the northlands the couriers were dispatched immediately. Atop the rampart of Cambridge, Neil and Tasha watched the riders veer off in different directions at top flight. Another two riders broke off in the direction of the villages of Markham and North Meadow. Jacinto resided in North Meadow and would no doubt bring the citizens of Markham with him when traveling to Cambridge. Unlike North Meadow, Markham lay directly in the path of Helana and her forthcoming army. Already Xanthus had his elves preparing tents for the refugees that would be arriving and seeking their protection. The elf captain Vasilis had departed earlier with several others to journey to the major trade center of Avalon, Fairgrove, to acquire goods to feed the refugees.

Neil sighed and had to think of the irony of that fact. The humans and most of the other races wanted nothing to do with the elves, and now, once the danger to them was exposed, they would to turn to the one race they always wanted to avoid. Maybe this was the one singular event that could finally bring the races together. He hated to admit it, but it just might be. Tasha and himself had tried various events, the most recent being the now cancelled 'United Games'. All had had some measure of success, but there was no one single event that could bring everyone together in trust. Now, a witch that had been on the verge of launching an attack a year and a half ago was back, and this time Neil was pretty sure she would follow through on any threat of conquering Avalon. Tasha gripped his hand tightly and he looked over at her. She didn't look very well.

"Are you okay?"

Tasha used her free hand to lean on the wall and breath deeply. She nodded and closed her eyes, swallowing hard.

"I'm fine, just a bit nauseous, but it'll pass."

"It will? This has happened before?"

Tasha smiled at him reassuringly. "Yes, but it always goes away. Just nerves, really, it is nothing."

Neil frowned. "If it keeps happening, please tell me. It might be more than just nerves. I know Helana's magic has its influence on everyone. It might be affecting you a bit more than usual considering her hate for you and what she's become."

"I'll keep that in mind. Now, I think we should get our gear ready and talk to our soldiers," she urged.

"Uh, sure, don't try and change the subject on me here," he laughed. "If you keep getting sick, tell me, okay?"

Tasha frowned at him this time and finally gave in. "Fine, I'll tell you. Happy? Now can we get some work done?"

"Sure, but only if you promise," teased Neil.

"Oh my, I promise to tell you, now, can we go?"

"Yes, we may," he laughed as she gave him a smack on the shoulder. "Hey, easy now!"

"Then be nice," she laughed. The two kidded around as they wandered inside Cambridge to collect gear and to begin prepping their own forces for the ride ahead.

Xanthus found Malcolm reading through the book of magic in the elf library. The wizard had moved the book into the library after Zach and Riane had been transported back to the old world. He felt it would be safer to be out of sight of any curious eyes that may wander through the council chamber during this trying time. Malcolm wanted it locked away for safe keeping and there was no better place than in the elf library.

"How is your reading coming along old friend?"

Malcolm looked up and shrugged. "Quite well, I believe. I think I might have found a simple spell that should help protect the king and queen, but I'm just reading further, in case I find something a little better."

"Always the perfectionist Malcolm. You never could stop competing with yourself."

"A fault of mine I'm afraid, even back when Schredrick was trying to decide who would succeed him, I was always trying to outdo my competitor by that little extra I could muster. That always made him mad."

"Who? Schredrick?"

"No no, he always encouraged that. My competitor hated me, always did. Never knew why he was like that. He was somewhat jealous of my abilities because he wasn't quite as efficient at spell casting, but I think Schredrick overlooked him in the end because he never tried to overcome that. He kept trying to make me mess up instead of working at it more himself." Malcolm sat back, and chuckled. "Funny, that seems so long ago now."

Xanthus shook his head. "It has been some time has it not, perhaps you are thinking of your own student, Shar, and of what she's capable."

"Perhaps. I have no worries about Shar. She is far more gifted than I ever was, or ever could be. She is endowed with an enormous amount of skill. To what extent I am unsure, but the unicorn stallion knows, and he only alluded to her skills at the Dark dragon confrontation."

"Is she capable of being your possible successor, just as you were all those years ago?"

"That could very well be. I have thought about a successor on and off for some time. I had at one point thought Helana could be such, but, well, she has decided on other roads to travel down. I have no desire to rush any decision, I am happy as guardian but if and when the time comes I would have to seriously look at Shar. She seems the only logical choice to continue as guardian. I am curious to see how she evolves with her abilities."

"How is her training going?"

"Extremely well! I have every confidence in her and I am quite sure she may have to use her skills at some point before her return here. I have urged her to keep her attempts at magic to a minimum unless absolutely necessary. As long as Helana does not think she has an adversary to face before her arrival here, the better our chances are to catch her off balance."

"Sound advice. I understand we have to keep our plan a secret, but I do wish we could have used your transporting skills to alert the other elves of what's happening. Sometimes I may get spoiled by you," Xanthus snickered.

"You think so?" Malcolm laughed, "I know you do!" Both men shared a good laugh, which proved to be a good prescription for the heavy cloud that had settled on all since Helana's arrival. It made them feel good about themselves even if it was for only a short time.

Xanthus left the room after their jovial outburst to see to other matters and Malcolm returned to his ideas on the protection magic he could use for the king and queen. A few more pages turned in the book of magic and he finally decided on what was best. It would provide minimal protection but it would be enough to give him at least some peace of mind. With that out of the way, his thoughts wandered to Zach and Riane and how they might be faring. He was quite confident the two had crossed over successfully. Helana had not been able to catch their magical casting of the astral gate in time.

Malcolm ran his fingers over the cover of the book of magic book and sighed. Now, the bigger question was, how and when would they succeed. He winced slightly as he felt Helana's strength grow and continue to drain his own energy source-the lands themselves. He had never felt such a drawing of magic, even when she had been able to throw Avalon into chaos before. That had been but a trickle to what he was feeling now. Malcolm did not like it and began to really fear about what his former student was doing to the balance of magic. If she had created chaos before, this time it might be total annihilation!

Chapter Nine

Helana stood on the land outside her castle, Livinia, just beyond the drawbridge and looked on as the trolls began to approach from the west. The wraith she had sent to urge them on had succeeded in hastening their arrival. Phase one of her force was now complete, the second was coming and the third and final additions would follow shortly thereafter. Helana waited patiently as the trolls were being herded on. When they had arrived she stopped them and walked over to Gartog and smiled at the troll.

"Nice to see you and your kind at my doorstep Gartog, I extend my thanks to you for moving as quickly as you have."

Gartog still could not help but stare at her and tried to grasp what this 'thing' was in front of him. It was one thing to see her briefly before, but now, up close and personal and having a good look it was something completely different. She even looked somewhat altered than when she had appeared before them just a while ago. The troll bowed.

"True queen, we to help, what need?"

"That will show itself in due course, be patient. As promised I have food for you and your kind," she pointed to a pile of carcasses of assorted animals. "Feel free to help yourselves. Eat well, we have a long journey and it starts this night."

"This night? We tired, need rest."

"Rest? You have some time now to rest, and eat. I suggest you take advantage of it." With that Helana turned and left the trolls to desecrate the carcasses she had left for them as food. It was time to act on her next phase of the force she was creating.

Helana walked over to a spot on the barren ground in front of her castle and knelt down to grab a handful of the dead soil. She let it fall through her fingers while reciting words of a specific incantation meant to bring about the rise of the dead.

"*Ex vestri cinis cineris vos vadum anhelo, ex vestri cinis cineris vos vadum orior oriri ortus, vos vadum ago, vos vadum pareo, ut ego narro illi lacuna is ero sic, sic mote is exsisto*". Helana blinked, paused and then repeated the spell with another handful of soil. "*From your ashes you shall breathe, from your ashes you shall rise, shall live, and you shall obey, as I speak these words it will be, so mote it be.*"

Around her the dirt began to stir and swirl. Helana stood and watched as the magic took hold. As the soil fell away, bones of men began to form and rise and solidified as they once were when alive. The skeletons rose from the ground and stood up, then skin began to cover each body slowly, inch by inch and then the tattered clothing began to mend itself and the men's features took shape. In what was a matter of minutes, Helana stood before all of the fallen men from the assault a year and a half ago! They stood there, alive, taking in their surroundings. They saw Helana smiling at them.

She walked over to one of the men, a fallen general, and

ran her fingers over his cheek. "General, welcome back to the living."

"Helana? Is that you? And how did this, this, happen?"

"It is I, with the demon, as one. A price for freeing me from my prison, and yes, you live. As long as I live, so shall you."

"My queen," he bowed and the rest of the now living dead did the same.

"Our time to even the score with the elves, and the rest of this world, has come," she hissed angrily.

The general looked at her with a grin. "I look forward to it."

"Good, now I will call on the last of those we need to complete our arsenal."

"And who would that be?"

"Who are they? They are those who dwell in the abyss my general, those of which you and the rest will command as we march on the races of Avalon." Helana moved back over the bridge and into her courtyard once more. Her risen army followed and stood off against the walls of the castle to witness what their queen was about to attempt.

Helana positioned herself near the center of the courtyard and stared at the ground in front of her. She concentrated on the spell whirling through her mind, trying to focus on the words. The demon within her conflicted with her human side but she fought it to get the correct incantation in the language she wanted to speak.

"Creatures of night, dark and foul, your servitude I do seek, wreak your havoc on this land by my demand, on this night you shall rise from the dark and into the light, so mote it be!"

Blue light shot from her hands to strike the ground and it was absorbed without stirring a single grain of sand. A moment later the ground began to shake and a crack started to form where the magic had struck and began to spread outward like a spider web. The land began to fall away, and a burst of fire exploded skyward sending flame into the clouds and sent a deafening roll of thunder out over the lands. A hole started to take shape growing ever larger by the second. Howls, screams and sounds of scraping claws over rock echoed up as the chasm expanded. When it was done, Helana walked to its edge and stared down.

Xanthus and Malcolm were standing on the balcony outside the elf council chamber when the thunder echoed in from the south. The wizard and elf king stared at the southern skies and noticed a slight red tinge to the cloud cover in the distance. Malcolm shook his head and closed his eyes in sadness. His former student had crossed a line that no one should even attempt. Her magic abilities were venturing into forbidden territory. With such anger fueled even more by the demon part of her, there was likely no boundary out of reach now.

"She has let the demons loose, has she not?" Xanthus questioned. He knew the answer but wanted his friend to confirm it.

"Yes she has, and I fear what lay in the darkness, of things she has freed."

"What do we know of the demons?"

"Very little I am afraid. Schredrick had discovered them some time ago, but their abilities are rather limited unless called on. The one, Valgor, has been able to escape every so often, helped by the ones who like to dabble in dark magic. He has tried to meddle in the affairs of this land when given the chance. Until Helana and her ambition came along, even that wasn't significant."

"Why so angry? Where is this coming from? I do not

understand it. She has done more damage in her short time amongst us than all of those before, including the Dark Dragon," Xanthus sighed.

"The Dragon did its damage, which we were able recover from, but this," Malcolm looked to the south. "I do not understand her either. Is it the demon manipulating her? Or is it something else? I do not have an answer. I do know this evil knows no bounds and may now destroy us all, and even threatens our old world. No one is safe. I have never been more afraid than I am now."

Xanthus put his hand on Malcolm's shoulder. "We will prevail. We will not let this witch destroy all that we have built."

"We need Zach and Riane to succeed, without that, this is a war we could lose!"

Helana breathed in the foul, putrid air freed from the darkness. "Come forth, it is your time," she snarled.

Creatures of every shape began to crawl out of the opening she had created, some stood, some crawled, while others erupted in flight and screeched in jubilation at their new found freedom. The witch could not help but smile at the sight. She was quite confident that there was nothing, or anyone who could stop her now completed army. Theirs would be a force to sweep through the races and take control of the throne she had so long wanted as her own. However, Helana would not stop there, she wanted more. Helana had grandeur thoughts of crossing back to the old world and throwing chaos into a world where magic had been long forgotten. The possibilities of what she could do there was too good to evade. Once the throne of Avalon was hers, she would go after the next prize, ruling over those who would be easily subdued thanks to their lack of understanding of magic. Just the thought of watching all those who had spurned magic be subdued by the very same was exhilarating.

The demons massed throughout the castle and Helana pointed to the gate.

"Gather outside, the time to wait is over!"

The dark beasts, her servants, marched obediently to the grounds outside the castle and waited for her orders. There stood the risen dead, demons, and trolls, all devoted to her and the quest ahead. Helana walked over the bridge, and surveyed her army. It was massive, even she was overwhelmed at what was now hers to control. Now it was time to get organized.

"General Vadeez, break your men into pairs and divide the demons accordingly, make as many divisions as you wish, and get the trolls sorted out in front to lead the march. They will be our first line. Try to use them to hide the demons until it is their turn to strike. Get them ready as soon as you can, we move east to the gnomes once you are set."

"My queen, I will make it quick, and have them all in line shortly. We will march before dawn, you have my word."

"I believe you general. I have very little doubt you will." Helana nodded and returned to the castle. She would leave her generals to get all in order. There were a few others she had to call on. A few other errands had to be taken care of.

Helana whispered as she walked and came to a stop where the chasm began. Several large winged creatures emerged from the depths, crawling out of the darkness. One by one they clambered out to stand, reaching nearly three times Helana's height. These wraiths were considerably larger than the others and took a position nearby waiting for their orders. This species of wraith were not gifted with changeling abilities but it didn't really matter. They were lethal to anyone or anything who dared confront them so there was no need to hide who they were.

"You have one quest, I am opening a door to Tir Nan Og, and you are to go in and find me the fairy queen, bring her to me. Feel free to take whatever demons you wish with you. Eradicate the faerie home, leave it in ruins. Do what you want with the sidhe, show them no mercy! I really don't care what you do."

"Yesssssssssss, masssssssssssster, we will obey."

"You will, or else contend with my wrath, and believe even you don't want to test me." Her threat was more of a statement confirming her strength to keep them aware of their place. "Bring her to me by tomorrow night at the gates of the gnome's castle!"

The wraith needed no further instruction. They bowed respectively and turned to look down into the void that had been her prison, their home. Each of the wraiths let out a screech that resonated down into the hole and all around the castle walls. Moments later hordes of goblins, boggarts, and other demon creatures appeared that walked, slithered or jumped. The wraith turned back to Helana and waited for the demon queen to open the door to the faerie realm.

"Find me the queen, bring her to me, alive, Do you understand?" They nodded. "Good. Now, all of you, here is a special gift from me to you." Helana waved her hand and the horde now brandished iron knives, swords or mallets. Iron was the one weakness of the faerie. They could not fight against it, even with all of their magical abilities. Not even the queen of the faerie could resist iron.

Helana shouted out the incantation to open a breach into Tir Nan Og. "*Open the gate to faerie I demand, split it wide so that all may go to conquer and divide! This I command, so it shall be!*" Her final words were spat out with venom and the magic took form. A mist formed before her and the magic began to weave itself into it.

In Tir Nan Og, Leasha felt the threatening magic immediately. She countered with her own magic to strengthen the realm's defenses but the intruding incantation was overwhelming in its power. Her defenses would not stand for long against it.

Helana smiled at the challenge and raised her voice again. "***Open the gate to Faerie I demand! Split it wide so that all may go to conquer and divide! This I command, with all the power of dark at my hand, so it shall be!***" Her hands thrust forward and a blue stream cascaded from her fingers at the wall of mist in front of her now. It tore at the mist, trying to find a crack, any crevice in which to get a foothold. It didn't have to seek for long. A small fissure opened and the magic struck at it, forcing its way in. The fissure became a gap, and soon an opening began to ever so slowly expand.

Leasha felt the evil explode into Tir Nan Og in a wave that swept through the realm. Faerie of every size and shape stopped what they were doing and looked towards the far horizon, fully aware that something felt terribly wrong. A hush came over Tir Nan Og as all faerie listened to the air around them. There was no wind, no sound. Then it began. Sounds of those who had penetrated their realm began to echo in from the distance and the wind started to blow with a foul aroma. The faerie turned and fled at any speed they could. All were in direct line to the castle where their queen, Leasha, lived. She would know what to do.

Leasha leaned on the balcony railing and wretched. The darkness that had entered her home had sent an overwhelming feeling of nausea over her. This was an evil she had never encountered, ever. She sensed the demons, they were in her realm. How they had gotten in she had no idea but whatever it was that had breached Tir Nan Og its malevolency was evident in the air itself.

Leasha looked out over the gardens and saw her children in flight, they were already nearing the castle and they would be looking for answers. These demons would not be negotiated with, they were here for a reason, and that was likely for her. There could be no other logical reason for their entry into her world, her home. She waited for her children and the inevitable questions.

Helana watched the demons, led by the wraith rush into the land of faerie. She stepped back from the portal, the faerie magic burned against her skin and she wanted nothing to do with it. Humans were not allowed in to any fairy realm unless taken or invited by the faerie. Despite being merged with the demon the magic still burned against her human side. Thus, that was her need for the wraith and the other minions. They would do her bidding and would bring her the queen she wanted. The queen she intended to make an example of to the rest of the races to demonstrate that her power could reach anywhere. The portal closed after the last demon entered and the mist faded away with a blast of wind. That task was taken care of. Helana turned and returned to attend to the preparations to begin their march on to the gnomes at Eldridge.

Leasha did her best to calm her brethren down but it did very little to ease the tension from the approaching storm. The wind was gaining strength and the stench of the demons was reaching an intolerable level. Each fairy looked to the queen for what they should be doing next, only Leasha was as confused as they were.

"Is there something to do that will stop them from coming any further?" asked Alisha.

"I am afraid not, they are here to wreck havoc, why they have come I am not sure," replied Leasha.

Howls echoed from the distance and then a number of screams followed. That gave the faerie the answer to why they had come. Leasha went wide eyed with fear, not for herself, but for all her children. The demons had come to hunt them down.

"All of you!" she shouted to the gathering. "Flee as quickly as you can to Avalon! Get yourself and the rest out of here as quickly as you can!"

"But where would we go?" asked Eden.

"Go to Malcolm, he will know what to do."

"My queen, you are coming too are you not?" inquired Alisha.

Leasha shook her head. "Not right away, I will stay behind to give you time to escape. I will come after you have all gotten away."

"Then we will stay with you," said Eden defiantly. "We will stay to fight these things."

More screams and more fairies flew up to the gathering shouting as they arrived, absolute fear evident in their panic.

"They have iron! They are killing everyone and destroying everything in their path!"

Leasha faced her kind with renewed determination. "I command all of you to leave immediately! Alisha, Eden, you will guide them to Malcolm, tell him what is happening. I will join you as soon as I am able. Now, all of you, you must flee Tir Nan Og before it is too late!"

Alisha and Eden, albeit reluctantly, bowed in obedience

to their queen. Both took charge and cast the spells to open portals back to Avalon. Two swirling mists formed and a doorway opened amidst the mist. Each pointed to the portals and beckoned the faerie to enter. It didn't take much encouragement to get them moving. The fairies took the lead quickly and looked more like streams of light as they escaped into the portals.

Leasha nodded in satisfaction and went into her chambers to grab her staff. She was going to need it shortly. Her goal was simple, to allow enough time for her children to escape from these demons. She would fight them if necessary and perhaps even teach them a thing or two about faerie. Her father would not stand by and watch while their home is destroyed and neither would she.

The wraith pointed their underlings in various directions to hunt, to seek, to destroy the faerie. The goblins, hobgoblins, boggarts and other demons wasted no time ravaging everything in their path. Those faerie unfortunate enough to get caught felt the wrath of their weapons and were annihilated by the iron blades. Other demon torched the gardens and tore trees and plants from the ground as nothing was left untouched while they marched onward to the castle and their objective of capturing the fairy queen. The wraiths led the horde, and were first to the outer gardens just on the rim of the castle. They paused as they detected the queen. It did take long to locate her since she made no effort to hide from them. She stood on the balcony, staff in hand, waiting for them. This confused them momentarily. However when they noticed the faerie fleeing into what appeared to be several swirling mists they assumed she was there to defend the escape of her kind.

"Queen! Sssssssurrender your realm and your kind to usssssss," taunted one wraith.

"You cannot defeat usssssss," snarled another.

Leasha sent a stream of faerie magic from her staff into the throng of demons who had encroached on the inner gardens. The demon unfortunate enough to get caught by the magic vanished in a flash of fire and the Fairy Queen stood tall, holding her ground. They had their answer to their demand.

"Your choice ssssssidhe," hissed a wraith.

The wraith spread out and moved in on the castle. They crept to the faerie queen from different angles and did their best to avoid the faerie magic sent at them randomly by the queen in an effort to dissuade them. The cluster of other demons bolted for those faerie attempting to escape to try and stop them. The fewer faerie that made it out, the less chance they had to warn others of what was happening.

Leasha took notice of the other threat and now had to try and give protection to her children on top of keeping the wraith at bay. She aimed her staff at the horde and let loose several volleys of faerie fire that torched a number of the goblins as they neared the fairy escape gateways. It gave the others a reason to stop their advance, if only for a few moments, as they waited for their masters to make their move on the queen.

Leasha turned to fend off one wraith with another discharge of her magic. The fire impacted with it full front and sent the creature reeling backwards but to her surprise, it did not die like the other demons! What monster was this that could withstand faerie magic? Was there enough strength in her magic to destroy it at all? She whirled around to propel another at her foe and again the creature was forced back but not destroyed. The masses waiting to cut off the other faerie escaping darted in once more to stop them and Leasha quickly turned, hurling fire as she did. Once more the pack fell back away from her magic. Two more wraiths moved in on the fairy queen and Leasha sent both flailing with streams of fire. Once recovered the two began to advance again. Leasha breathed hard and felt her strength begin to ebb.

Alisha and Eden watched the attack on their queen feeling absolutely helpless. To divert their attention they instead focused on the other dark beasts attempting to stop their escape. Both fairies tried to come up with a way to slow the encroachment and allow their queen to key in on the wraith.

"We can tap into the wild magic, conjure up some storm or wind to stop them," suggested Alisha.

"We cannot, we don't have enough knowledge of it! We risk losing ourselves to it," warned Eden.

"We must try! We won't be able to get out if we don't!"

"Fine, what do we do?" asked Eden.

"We must focus on what we want, and let our will create what we need," said Alisha. "We should be able to do it together."

"What do we want?"

"A very strong wind I think would work best."

Eden shook her head and shrugged. "Wind it is."

The two sprites joined hands and murmured the words they had been taught over time.

"*What we want is what we wish, our desire to raise the ire of what is wild, to blow strong against all that is wrong, rise wind, rise as we command! So mote it be*!"

The two sprites looked at one another not knowing what to expect, but at the same time hopeful that something would happen. Their faerie magic, while virtually powerless outside their realm, had the possibility of conjuring up a reaction in their own home. The result always depended on those casting and their 'devotion' to the incantation.

Leasha struck one of the wraiths with the end of her

staff, driving it back. She felt the spell the fairies were casting and felt a sense of pride for her kind to take the chance to stay and fight by casting magic that may or may not work against a foe that was capable of killing them. Another wraith lunged and Leasha drove her staff directly into its abdomen. It became lodged and the queen looked directly into the wraith's eyes and spoke words she had never spoken.

"Veneficus of faerie ego dico in thee, per totus vox vos usus, attero is creatura per totus vestry zest, permissum non is ago, permissum non is anhelo haud magis, sic is ero." Leasha twisted the staff as it glowed with the faerie magic and stared at the monster before her. Its eyes glared in utter hatred as it reached up and grabbed the queen by the shoulders. Before it could do anything she repeated the phrase as the magic began to spread into and over the creature.

"Magic of faerie I call on thee! With all the power you possess destroy this creature with all your zest! Let not it live, let not it breathe no more, so it will be!"

The wraith's disfigured face began to distort and it screeched in agony as the faerie magic ripped it apart and shattered it into dust. Just then, one wraith then came up behind the queen and took a swipe at her with its claws. The force sent the queen hurling through the air and crashing into the hedge near the escape gateways. Alisha and Eden hurried over to help her as Leasha slowly propped herself up with her staff. She waved the two pixies off and stood on her own, too proud to let the demons think her weak. Battered, and cut, the queen still stood tall.

"Get out of here you two, follow the others out, and get to Malcolm. Now go!" she urged.

A pack of imps charged abruptly and one threw its weapon towards the queen. Alisha, seeing the impending threat moved to block the attack and put herself between the knife, and Leasha.

"My queen!" she shouted and took the full brunt of the blade in her chest. Alisha collapsed to the ground and Eden screamed in shock!

"Alisha! No no no!" She picked up her fallen friend and watched as the life left her. Alisha smiled one last time and then turned to dust in Eden's arms.

The wind that the two sprites had called on only moments earlier had begun to rise and compounded in strength by each passing second. The charging demons were now finding it hard to move forward and soon found themselves being pushed backwards. The wind had begun to grow out of control as it tore at everything. Leasha touched Eden on the shoulder and pointed to the gateway.

"She is gone Eden, you must go to save yourself, I will follow when I am able!"

"You promise?"

"I promise, now go."

Eden nodded. She took one last look at her now destroyed home, turned and flew into the gateway out of Tir Nan Og with the last few faerie. Leasha turned to face the wraith once more, which now moved to surround her. The wind had little effect on them and appeared to be nothing more than an irritation. Leasha stood her ground and did her best to keep them at bay with her magic. The wind blew her hair every which way and her injuries had stained her torn clothing. She would not surrender to these heathens.

One wraith got close enough to rip its claws into her back and the fairy queen fell to her knees, holding herself up with the staff. Leasha tried to stand while sending out another burst of magic from her staff, but the wind took the magic in every direction and it faded harmlessly into the surroundings. Another wraith grabbed her by the neck and threw her down to the ground. It opened its jaws to tear into the queen but one other wraith came between it and Leasha.

"She mussssst live," it hissed.

"NO, kill her," retorted the other.

"She musssst live!" repeated the first. To emphasize its point the wraith drove its one clawed hand through the others neck, killing it instantly. It crumpled to the ground and the remaining wraith stood there, gloating.

The one wraith reached down and dragged the fairy queen to her feet and then clamped a collar of iron around her neck. Leasha gagged at the touch of the iron. It burned against her skin and she gave the wraith a definitive look of contempt. Then the creature took her staff and snapped it into pieces. Her magic was spent.

"With usssssss you will come," the wraith hissed.

"For what purpose?" She asked angrily. "Why not kill me now?"

"That is for the masssster to do." It gave the faerie queen a nasty grin and attached a chain to the collar on her neck. "Now, call off thissss wind."

Leasha lowered her head in defeat, and fell to her knees, weakened from the fight. She murmured a few words and the wind subsided. As it diminished the other demons circled the queen, anxious to have a close look at someone they would very rarely ever see.

The one wraith pointed to the castle. "Rip each ssssstone out, leave nothing sssstanding!"

The goblins, imps and everything else screeched in glee and tore off to the castle. Leasha could do nothing but watch as her home fell, stone by stone, into rubble. She looked up at the wraith.

"How can you? This was your home once, before you fell into the dark."

The wraith pulled in close to the queen and snarled, teeth dripping with saliva, the disfigured face that had once been faerie only inches from her own. "The more reassssson to desssssstroy it. Watch queen of faerie, watch."

It held her head up with the leash, and would not let her look away as the castle slowly toppled into nothing more than a heap of stone. Rock by rock, piece by piece, it was slowly obliterated. Leasha tried to look away at times but the wraith would grab her hair and pull her face forward once more. There was no escaping it. The demonkind relished every moment of the destruction. One wall would collapse and the monsters would dance around the fallen rubble in celebration and then would move onto the next object of their wrath. Some of the demons ripped stones out and threw them into the flowers or at a nearby tree. Even a few would throw the rubble at other demons in jest. The stones would ricochet off or knock them down and a few would laugh at the others pain. One section of the castle tumbled to the ground in a rumble of stone and dust and the horde moved onto the next level. Piece by piece it crumbled and Leasha was forced to watch it all.

After what felt like several lifetimes had passed, the last stone was torn from the foundation and tossed aside as any other stone that had stood in the way of finishing the task at hand. It was over, the castle was gone. There was nothing but debris of what had been once the proud center of Tir Nan Og. Leasha looked around and saw nothing of what it had been. Gardens were burnt, or in the process of burning. Trees had been uprooted, and all that had been alive was now dead or dying. Her home was gone.

"There will be repercussions for what you have done here," Leasha stated angrily.

The wraith grabbed her arm with his free clawed hand,

tearing into her body as it did, and lifted her high. It laughed at her and pointed to the surroundings.

"Isssssss that sssssso queen of a dead land? There issssss no one to sssssstop usssssss."

Leasha, tears streaming down her face, and blood escaping her wounds, said nothing to dispute the statement. It seemed that the creature of darkness might very well be correct in making the bold comment. The wraith lowered the queen and ordered the demons to finish destroying what may have been left untouched. It turned to her once more.

"Ssssssoon the masssster will take care of you."

Leasha stared up at it. "I look forward to meeting it."

"You will wissssssssh to be elssssssewhere." The wraith let out another wail of laughter and pulled the queen by the chain so she could see the rest of the annihilation of the faerie homeland. It did not want her to miss out on all the festivities. She would meet her fate soon enough, but there was nothing said about torturing the faerie as it wished in the meantime.

Leasha, battered, bruised and beaten could not fight back anymore, her spirit was broken, and her power contained. The proud queen stumbled along, doing her best to keep up with the wraith as it dragged her on. She could only hope that her children had found Malcolm and Xanthus on Avalon. It was now her one and only chance of survival.

Chapter Ten

Birds chirped as they flew from branch to branch and the occasional fish would leap from the water to capture the one bug foolish enough to get too close to the water. The lake surface was calm, and the leaves on the trees barely twitched due to the lack of any wind.

That all changed abruptly as a breeze formed out of nowhere causing the water to ripple and then waves took shape as the wind increased. Leaves shook in the sudden squall and the water crashed against the rocky shore. A distortion in the air just above the shoreline formed and took on the shape of a whirlwind of cloud. A tunnel of sorts formed within the cloud and two figures appeared. Mere outlines at first, they became clearer as they neared the opening of the gateway.

Zach and Riane then emerged from the vortex, and tumbled onto a shoreline of loose shale. They turned just in time to see the vortex implode unto itself and vanish in a blast of wind and thunder. All that remained behind was the two of them, on a lakeshore, in the middle of someplace. The wind that had been prevalent seconds earlier had vanished as quickly as it had come up.

Zach groaned and slowly stood up. He helped Riane stand and both took in their new surroundings. Zach stared at the lake, and then he looked up towards the trees and then back to the lake. He had been here before!

"You've got to be fuck'n kidding!" he muttered.

"Excuse me?" wondered Riane.

"Uh, sorry, we've, um, I've been here once already. This is where we had to come to cross over to your world the first time! Son of a …."

"Where do we go now?"

Zach threw his gym bag over his shoulder and pointed to the trees. "We go this way."

Zach led with Riane right behind him. They entered the forest and followed the path that wound its way amidst the trees. It was all coming back to Zach from that first excursion a year and a half ago. Tony's bad coffee, his disbelief in there being anything other than a lot of fog and Neil's persistent hope that they were about to go somewhere he could only imagine by playing that game of his, what was it called again? Oh yeah, dungeons and dragons. What were the odds of actually ending up where this had all started in the first place? 'Apparently pretty good' he thought to himself and managed a grin.

The birds that had vacated the area with the sudden alteration in weather had returned to their usual song and even the squirrels were getting in on the fun this time around. Riane listened to it all, in awe of being on the old world and yet there was nothing out of the ordinary that made her feel like she had left her home behind. She did her best to keep up to Zach who was moving rather quickly down the path to some unknown destination that he only knew about.

Zach broke free of the trees first and stopped to take in his surroundings. He took in a deep breath and let it out slow, letting the freshness of the day bring him around to where he was now. A glance upward to a sky filled with just a few clouds and one sun brought him to the realization that he really was home. He turned to see Riane emerge and the woman who had insisted on coming with him, no longer looking like the elf he had first met, smiled back at him.

"Why are we stopping? Are we there?" she wondered.

"We aren't anywhere yet," he chuckled. "But we are back on my world, or the old world, as you keep calling it back on Avalon."

"Is it? I cannot really see much of a change."

"Really now," he smiled. He moved to stand beside her and pointed up to the sky. "Have a look up yonder there little lady."

Riane gazed upward to where he was pointing and saw in the sky, the one sun, and she realized she really was on the old world. She looked back at Zach and had an even larger grin on.

"We are here! But yet, it does not feel or look much different than from where we came."

"Oh trust me, that'll change soon enough," Zach assured her. The distinct aroma of a camp fire alerted his senses and he looked towards the campground. "The bigger challenge at the moment is to figure out how the hell we're going to get back to town."

"There is a town near?"

"More like a big city, but we have to get a ride because there is no way we can walk that far."

"A horse?"

Zach laughed and shook his head. "No, not a horse. We need a car, or truck, or anything that has wheels. Here we do things a little differently."

"I see. So where do we find a car?" she asked curiously. Riane looked around the area but could see nothing but tables of a sort and lots of forest. "Why are there so many tables?"

"We call them picnic tables, they're here for anyone who'd like to take break and have something to eat."

"Okay," she nodded. "I do not see a car? Or a, truck? As you call it?

"No there isn't either of them around. The least Malcolm could have done was have a car waiting," he quipped. "Come on let's see who's in the campground."

"Campground?"

Zach scratched his chin and realized he would be asked a lot of questions about just about everything. Did he ask that many questions in his first journey over to the magical world of Avalon? He wasn't sure, but he imagined he probably did.

"It is a place where people here go to camp, to sleep outdoors."

Riane nodded. The answer seemed to satisfy her. He stared at her for a second longer and she noticed.

"Yes?"

"Um, just trying to get used to seeing you look like a person and not an elf, it's going to take some time to adjust to it."

Riane moved in beside him and put her arm around him. "I am still the same person, even if I do look, human." She gave him a kiss and he smiled back at her.

"I'm sure you are, but Malcolm did say you might develop some of our, uh, habits, once you've been human for a period of time. So I'll have to keep an eye on you," he winked. "I can't have you become addicted to junk food, or TV."

"What are those?"

"Oh you'll see. Come on let's see if we can bum a ride

from somebody in this campground. I am in no mood to walk over 60 miles."

"Is that far?"

"Oh yeah."

The duo walked through the path into the campground and saw a group of teen-agers packing up their gear to leave. They were in luck! Zach jogged up to the company of teens and nodded as he said 'hello'. The kids looked at him curiously and then saw the woman come up beside him. One of the guys really took notice of Riane with a large grin and nodded back, to her, not him.

"Hey beautiful, ya lost?"

"Uh, hey," waved Zach. "We're together."

"Oh, sorry dude."

"Yeah, sure. Is there a chance the four of you are heading into Seattle?" he asked

"Maybe, who wants to know?" asked one of the other guys.

"I am, seriously, our ride forgot to come and get us, probably got the days mixed up when he was supposed to pick us up and we need a lift back into town," explained Zach. The two guys didn't seem too receptive to the idea but the girls were.

"Oh come on Steve, we can make room for them." The one girl winked at Zach and Zach winked back.

Riane saw the interaction and felt a little flush and then caught herself. She frowned at herself, unsure of what had just happened. Zach looked at her and leaned in close to whisper.

"I think the girl's are going to make a case for us to tag along."

"Why is that, because she showed an interest in you?" she snapped quietly. Zach looked at her, rather surprised at her reaction.

"What did you say?"

"Um, nothing, sorry, not sure where that came from." Riane took a few deep breaths and Zach couldn't help but chuckle.

"You're jealous! See, Malcolm said you'd feel some human feelings at times, very cool."

"No it is not, it makes me uncomfortable."

"Don't worry, it'll pass soon enough."

The conference between the four teens finally came to a conclusion and one couple approached. The girl who had winked at Zach spoke up first.

"Yeah, we can take you back into Seattle but the guys want you to cover some gas money, if that's cool by you?"

"No problem I can do that. I didn't catch your name?" Zach asked as he shook her hand.

"It's Christina," she said as she smiled at Zach. Steve spoke up at that point.

"We're together," he snorted to make his point. Zach couldn't help but grin.

"Hey, lucky you. Well the two of us are pretty much ready whenever you are, need any help with anything?" offered Zach.

"Nah, tha's okay dude, we're good. Just haul your stuff over to the back and toss'er in. We should be headin out in a few," replied Steve. He and Christina went back to packing up their own belongings while Zach and Riane wandered to the back of the van and tossed in what they had.

It wasn't long before Zach and Riane were making themselves comfortable in the back seat of the van amidst gear as the company left the campground making their way out to the main highway and en route to Seattle. The teens chatted up the duo about their weekend and wondered where they had been camping.

"We were all over the place, never saw ya anywhere," said Taylor.

"We were off the regular path, hiking around the lake. Chances are you wouldn't have seen us," replied Zach with the first thing that came to his mind.

"Cool, hey, did you feel that weird storm that came through just a while ago? It was like so calm and then like 'bam'," Taylor emphasized with his hands, "this wind comes up and almost blew our tent away! That was totally weird."

"Yeah, wasn't it though? We got caught in it too when we were getting close to picnic grounds back there," said Zach.

"So, where are we dropping ya?" asked Steve.

"Um, I'll guide you once we get there." Zach looked at Riane for a second realizing he had no idea where to go! He leaned and whispered in her ear. "I'll look up a hotel I know of and get its address. We can stay there for the time being."

Riane nodded and then saw a big semi truck and its trailer race by as they came to a stop sign at the end of the grid road from the campground. She went wide eyed and ducked behind the seat. Taylor chuckled and looked at the truck that had just gone by.

"Yeah, they scare me too. He's gone now. You can sit up babe," chuckled Taylor.

"Hey," piped Rachel. She gave him a light smack on the shoulder and he laughed.

"What I do?"

"Dude, never compliment another woman in the presence of your girlfriend, trust me on that one. Been there, done that," snickered Zach.

"Listen to him," she pointed. "He knows what he's talking about."

"Sorry babe," he looked over at Steve and just shrugged. "Women."

Zach laughed quietly and Riane had sat back up to take in the scenery that had already begun to change. The traffic on the highway kept her fascinated and she was looking every which way to see as much as she could while they drove.

"She sure likes lookin around," Taylor quipped.

"She's not from around this neck of the woods, it's all kinda new to her," Zach replied.

"So where are you from then?" Rachel asked.

"I am from Cambridge castle," replied Riane.

"Where?" checked Taylor.

"Uh, she's from England originally." Zach corrected her. Riane looked at him and then looked back to the group and nodded.

"Yes."

"Oh cool, I was wonderin about that accent, very nice," Taylor smiled.

"Are you really looking to get your ass kicked?" Rachel asked with a smack to his shoulder.

"What?"

Zach laughed lightly and shook his head. He decided to change the subject to save the kid from any further gaffes that could get him into the doghouse with his girlfriend.

"Do you have a city map by chance?

"No idea dude, this isn't my ride," shrugged Steve. He stepped on the gas and moved to pass a slower moving truck. Riane grabbed Zach's arm and he thought she might just rip it off.

"Easy girl," he whispered. "Relax, he's just passing."

"I do not like this. What did you call it?" she asked while clasping his arm even tighter.

"A van," he took her hand into his own. "You have your

seatbelt on, so you're kind of protected, to a point. So just sit back, and enjoy the ride, we'll be in Seattle in no time."

"I have a map of the city," piped up Rachel. She smiled at Zach as she handed over a map to him. He nodded his thanks and opened up the map to find the hotel he wanted.

As soon as they had passed the truck and had gotten back to a slower speed Riane finally relaxed and went back to her sightseeing. Zach let out a sigh and began to look through the city index. It didn't take him too long to find which street he needed.

"The Warwick Hotel is on Lenora, 401 Lenora."

"Oh I know where that is. It's near the art museum. Ever been there?" Rachel asked.

"Yeah actually, once," Zach said.

Rachel turned around in her seat to get a better look. "Really? I didn't take you as an art person."

"Is that so?" chuckled Zach. "Well, your right. I only went there because the woman I was dating at the time worked there."

"Very cool. So why did you two break up?"

Zach was getting just a little annoyed at her persistent questions. "Well, she was into art, and I wasn't. That's pretty much it."

Riane was oblivious to the conversation. She was too far absorbed in the changing countryside. The traffic was becoming more congested and there were a lot more structures coming into view. It was all fascinating to her. This was the old world, and she was really here experiencing what had been her ancestor's home. It wasn't quite what she had expected, but regardless, she was definitely living a dream!

"We're coming into town. Where are we going again?" asked Taylor.

"The Warwick hotel, 401 Lenora," repeated Zach.

"I'll point the way," offered Rachel. She turned around and began to guide Steve to the best of her ability.

"You aren't from Seattle?" wondered Taylor.

"Not now, I used to be. We're just in town to visit, get a few things. The usual tourist thing," replied Zach.

"So what did you do when you lived here?" inquired Christina.

Zach grinned and scratched his cheek. "I used to be a cop here." He felt the van instantly slow down and couldn't help but grin. "Easy guy, I'm not a cop anymore."

"Gee dude, ya freaked me there for a second!" laughed Steve.

"I was actually a detective, so behave," Zach leaned in closer, "Because I could be watching you." Rachel looked over her shoulder and he winked at her. She, Christina and he started to laugh at the joke. The guys eventually caught on to the tease and started to laugh with them, albeit rather nervously.

The drive into Seattle was for the most part, uneventful. Riane was glued to watching the passing sights and Zach had begun to dig into his back pack to find the money Neil had given him, and the ever important credit card that he would undoubtedly need. He found the card amidst the clutter of the other paperwork he had, and noticed it had his name on it, and not Neil's. That was weird. He shrugged and assumed Malcolm had done his usual hocus pocus. It had better work!

Their arrival at the Warwick Hotel came sooner than he had anticipated. He recognized the place instantly. He had spent a number of nights in the bar in the hotel and from what he remembered it was a pretty nice establishment. It was a good a place as any to call home for the time being. It was centered near the places they would likely have to investigate or have access to what they needed, so it would serve nicely. There wasn't anything that wasn't nearby to accommodate their needs.

The gang pulled up to the front of the hotel and Steve jumped out to open up the back of the van. Zach and Riane stepped out into more noise than Riane had ever heard in her entire life, and that was a long time! At first she covered her ears but slowly she realized her hearing was adapting to the noise rather effectively and she was able to remove her hands after only a few moments. She shrugged, and thought it must be the human side of her again helping in this situation. Maybe being human wasn't so bad after all!

Zach grabbed the rest of their gear and handed a pack to Riane who tossed it over her shoulder and wandered over to stare at a few of the sights before her. Zach chuckled as he watched her. He found his wallet and the money Neil had given him and handed over a few bills to Steve.

"Will that cover it?"

Steve nodded, "Oh yeah, plenty dude. Enjoy your stay in town, maybe we'll catch up to ya later!"

"You never know," he nodded. Christina jumped out of the van and stuffed some paper into his hand as Steve wandered back to the driver's side.

"Here is my cell number, and Rachel's. If you guys want to hit the town tonight, give us a call and we'll join you." She smiled and went back to her side of the van and waved as she climbed back in. The gang beeped the horn as they drove off and Zach waved. He turned to see Riane staring up at the sky and could only imagine what she thought of the Seattle skyline. He tucked the phone number into his jeans and grabbed his pack.

"Come on you tourist," he grinned. "Let's get a room and make ourselves at home."

"You live here?" she asked.

Zach laughed. "This is much like your inns back in Fairgrove, only a little more fancier."

"Cool."

"What'd you say?" Zach asked.

"Is that not what you say? They seemed to say it a lot."

Zach snickered. "Yes they did, well, shall we?" He offered his hand. Riane smiled and took hold of it.

"Yes, we shall."

To Zach's relief, a room was available and better yet, a suite and even better still, the credit card worked! They got the key to the room and rode on up in the elevator in which Zach had to keep Riane from asking questions about it, at least until they were off of it. To his surprise she had forgotten about the elevator as soon as they had stepped out and into the hallway. She was touching this picture and that picture, running her fingers over the walls, smelling the flowers in the vase. There was nothing the elf did not investigate. When Zach opened the door to the suite she walked in and gasped at the room. He smiled and threw his bag off to the side and stretched.

"Home sweet home, for now anyways, make yourself comfortable gorgeous," he urged. Riane's smile was so huge that Zach thought it might become a permanent fixture on her face and he couldn't help but chuckle at the sight.

"What is it that you find so amusing?" she asked.

"Oh just your reaction is to everything around here, I can imagine it's a bit of a, um, shock!"

"Think of when you were new on my home; were you not just as surprised? Especially when we elves made an appearance?"

Zach nodded and sat down on the edge of the bed. "You got me there. Here, sit. Let me show you something we call TV. If you think what you see out the window is eye catching, wait until you get a load of this."

In the small tea shop, the waitress finished wiping up the tables and carried the remaining dishes over to the sink. She washed up what there was and finished up a few odds and ends to close the doors for another day. Her teacher and her boss wandered into the lounge from the back room and sat down at one of the tables. He placed a laptop computer down on the table and motioned for his student to join him. She tossed her towel onto the kitchen counter and ambled over to sit across from him.

"What is the computer for?" she wondered.

"I need you to create a website for us."

"For what purpose?" She opened up the laptop and turned it on. "Since when do you care for any sort of technology?" she teased.

He shrugged and pulled out a pipe. "I think perhaps we should," he paused for a moment, thinking. "We need to advertise more, it might bring in a few extra customers."

"Really now? And why can you not do this yourself?"

He lit his pipe carefully, and inhaled. Ever so casually he exhaled, the smoke slowly filtering up to the rafters of the lounge. "Magic and technology do not mix well. The results are usually, well, shall we say, incoherent. I will add of it as it were once you are done, just enough to accomplish what I need done."

"Well, it won't take long to do up a site. Something basic I can have up and running by morning."

"I need it by tonight. Tomorrow morning will be too late."

She looked up at him. "Too late?" Now she was curious. "Why would it be too late sir?"

"Simple really, those who may need to find us won't be able to unless our site is there for them to find."

The young lady sat back in her chair and crossed her arms. "You know that answer isn't going to satisfy me."

He laughed and took another whiff of his pipe. "Very well, if you insist, you recall me mentioning visitors coming soon?"

"Yes, I do," she nodded.

"They will need to find us first, and if we do not have a site for them to seek out, they will likely never locate us."

She sighed. It was another vague answer from her mentor. "You do not believe in a straight answer do you?"

He merely shrugged as he smiled at her. "No, and soon in time, you will be doing the same."

The lady turned her attention to the computer and logged on to a particular program and then looked up at her teacher. "So what do we call this site?"

He reached into his shirt pocket and withdrew a small piece of paper. "Use the names on here. Incorporate them into it somehow, be creative."

"That is quite extensive," she commented after glancing at the list. "This is going to take some doing."

"I have the utmost faith you will succeed," he smiled at her.

"As you wish sir." The young lady sat up and went to work on creating the website her teacher would hopefully approve.

Zach sorted out his letters and assorted gear to prepare himself for the task ahead. He had decided his first plan of attack was to hit Neil's former law office and talk to his partner. After that, it would be off to his old detachment to make use of some resources, that is, if his former boss would allow him.

He glanced back at Riane who was busy changing channels on the Television. She was completely absorbed by it all. What he found surprising was her ability to adapt to everything so quickly. It only took her a few moments to figure out how to use the TV remote. He thought that might have taken a little longer but she was 'channel surfing' in no time.

There, strewn over the desk, was the letter to Matt Riordan, Neil's partner at the law firm, his old cell phone which he'd have to get reactivated and the cash Neil had given him. Rachel had been nice enough to let him keep the city map, which might come in handy at some point yet. Zach tapped his fingers on the desk and looked at the phone. He picked it up and dialed the front desk of the hotel.

"Yeah, hi, can you connect me to the law office of Baxter and Riordan? I can't find the number for them. Thanks." He sat there, waiting and in a few moments he heard it ringing on the other end.

A voice answered. "Hello, law office of Riordan and Baxter, how may I direct your call?"

"I'd like to speak to Matt Riordan please," replied Zach. He found it odd that the name of the law office was reversed. It appears Matt was taking a liberty of being first on the bill since Neil was absent.

"I'm afraid he's in court the rest of the day, I can set up an appointment for tomorrow morning if you wish?"

"Uh, sure, what the hell."

"How is 11am?"

"That'll be fine."

"And who shall I say is calling?"

"Zach Thomas. Tell him it's an old friend of Neil's. That should keep him in the office until I get there."

"Yes sir, I will pass that along. Have a nice day."

"You too, thanks, bye." Zach hung up the phone and sighed. Well, the lawyer would have to wait. May as well pay a visit to his old detachment and do some research in the meantime. Now, what to do with Riane? He looked back at her and saw her intently watching the Television. There was the million dollar question.

"Hey you, anything interesting on there?" he asked with a smile.

"Everything!" she replied in earnest. "There is so much to see!"

"Believe me, after a while you'll be like the rest of us sayin there's nothing on."

"Are we going to start out soon?" she wondered as she paused to look at another program on the tube.

"Well I need to go to where I used to work and use some of their resources, but I can do that by myself. What we need to figure out is what you can do in the meantime."

"I can go to the Seattle public library on 4th avenue and do some of my own research on the man we are supposed to find. That may be of use for you in your own quest."

He looked at her in shock. "Uh, and you know about this library how?"

"I saw an ad on this," she pointed to the television. "I can find it on the map you have and go there. I will meet you back here later this afternoon."

Zach sat back in his chair dumbfounded. "Are you sure you haven't been here before?"

"No, I have not." She grinned. "But I am a quick learner."

"I gathered that."

"Then we have a plan, as you say?"

"Yes we do. I'll drop you off at the library, and I'll go on from there. The sooner we can take care of this, the sooner we can get back."

They collected what they needed and set out promptly. They took a cab over to the library and Riane was quickly out the door and running up the steps to the building before Zach could wave to her. He laughed and shook his head.

She was really getting into this world! Maybe when this was all over and everything was taken care of, they should come back and spend some real visiting time to check out the sites without having to be rushing around. He nodded to himself as he watched her wave at the door before she went inside the library. Hopefully she wouldn't draw too much attention to herself.

"Where to?" asked the cabbie. Zach gave him the address and sat back as they drove off. He was pretty sure it was going to be a little odd being in his old place of employment and would undoubtedly turn a few heads when he walked in there.

He looked up from the desk he was sitting at and yawned. What was he really doing here? A glance around the office confirmed what he had been thinking earlier, he didn't miss the place a whole lot. Amazing! A year and a half away from the paperwork, the yelling, and the pressure had made him realize that he wasn't all that happy in his last line of work after all! His attitude had made a huge turnaround during the time he had been away. A year and a half ago his life had been spinning in circles, like a tire on a slick surface. It seemed to be in a continuous spiral downward and it was only a matter of time before he would have crashed flat on his face. His girlfriend had left him, he was up to neck in debt and a bottle of vodka had become his best friend. Now, he was sober, with the exception of his excursions with Axel and Ruskin but that couldn't be helped. He chuckled at the thought. He was out of debt and just as inconceivable, in love with a woman, or an elf, a race he never would have thought existed before that fateful day a year and a half ago. A strange man had shown up and made him and the other two, in his deep calm voice, 'an offer you will find very hard to refuse.'

The series of events that followed shortly thereafter had changed him and given a whole new outlook on life. Now, after all that had happened, he was sitting at his old desk where he had spent eight years as a detective. He wished he was back with the others to help them but he had been sent back to Seattle to try and find somebody. That was what he intended to do. If this so called legendary wizard did exist someplace, then he would find him. It was in his nature to succeed. He hated leaving anything unresolved, and worse, he hated to fail.

His former captain walked over to him and interrupted his train of thought. "Zach, got a second?"

"Uh, yeah, sure." Zach wandered into his captain's office and took the seat across in front of the desk.

The captain looked a little confused and the first question he blurted out confirmed his observation.

"Where the hell have you been for the last year and a half? Not a word, no letters, no calls, and not even an email from you. Then, 'poof', you show up out of the blue and ask to use or resources to help you find somebody. Who is so damn important that you need to crawl out of the woodwork to find? As far as I'm concerned you ain't a detective no more for this force, am I right?"

"You're right, I'm not. I gave up on that part of my life not long after I left here. It's just that, well, let's just say this person is very important to a friend of mine."

"You have a friend? And I'm supposed to accept that? You know Zach, you were on the edge before but I think you've gone and jumped off into the deep end of the pool. Where you been hidin yourself?"

The captain was a down to earth person who needed every possible angle covered before accepting an answer so Zach wasn't even going to try and explain where he had been. If he did, the captain would likely lock him away to be observed by the proper physicians.

"I've been," Zach paused, thinking his answer through carefully, "doing a lot of traveling."

"Traveling? Where about?"

"Here and there, no place special." Zach tried to change the subject and steer their conversation away from where he had been for the last 18 months. "So, can I use the computers and our files, or not? I promise not to make a mess of anything."

"This person is that important huh?"

Zach nodded and smiled. "Yes, he is."

"Well, at least I know it's a 'he'," cracked the captain. "You never were one to explain things clearly. Yeah, sure, go ahead." He shrugged and stood. "Use what you need to use. Before you leave this time, at least have the decency to say good-bye huh?"

"Ahhhh, did you miss me captain?" teased Zach.

The captain brushed him off as he blushed. "Do what you need to do and don't screw anything up or I'll have your ass in a sling, got it?"

"Yes sir."

"Good, now get the hell out of my office."

Zach didn't say another word as he walked out of the room and back towards his old desk. He couldn't help but grin. Now maybe he can get some work done. His thoughts turned to Riane and he hoped she was having more luck over at the library with her research. He sat down at his desk and clicked his computer on to surf the internet. He brought up a search engine and paused with his fingers sitting on the keyboard. Where would one start to look? What name or phrase would you use? Where in the world do you even begin looking for some mythical wizard by the name of 'Merlin'?

Chapter Eleven

In the forest near Aberdeen, and elsewhere on Avalon, sprites appeared in flashes of light. There had been no set path in their escape from Tir Nan Og, hence there was no way to determine where they would finally emerge. It was inevitable they would be scattered throughout the land. The biggest priority was to survive and to that end, they had succeeded.

Eden and several other fairies emerged into the forest nearest to the gnomes. At first the faerie hovered amidst the branches, unsure of what to do next. Eden settled down on the ground at the base of a tree and wept openly. Her closest friend was gone and her home was destroyed. It was all too much to absorb in such a short time. A few of the faerie nestled in close to provide comfort. Others floated around the forest trying to determine where they were.

"Every tree looks alike, who is to say we are near the dwarves, elves or even the human folk," sighed one fairy.

"How are we to know which way to go?" asked another.

Eden looked up, tears rolling down her petite cheeks. Her eyes scanned the forest and then she glanced to her right. Something felt familiar. A light breeze stirred in the forest and brushed over her body. Someone she knew was near, the wind told her so.

Shar watched the gnomes impatiently. They were taking too long in moving out of Aberdeen. The process of getting the populace organized had taken an extremely long time. It was only now that they were finally moving to the lower chambers to evacuate through the tunnels that worked their way northward through the mountains, opening somewhere out into the forest a safe distance away. Shar stood on the terrace of Aberdeen, letting the breeze of the early evening flow over her face. It was the wind that brought her attention to the sudden thrust of fairy magic into Avalon. She felt the magic tingle on her cheeks and listened to the wind speak of their arrival. There was something wrong, out of place but she could not determine what it was.

Eden stood and flew into the shrubbery abruptly. The other faerie followed as the wind guided them on. Eden emerged from the trees and paused, the castle walls had caught her eye. She instantly recognized them.

"We are at the gnome's castle!" she blurted out.

"I feel other faerie magic, maybe there are more here!" said one.

Eden shook her head. "No, just one, and she can help us!"

They returned to their natural form and once more became mere speckles of light racing up the castle walls to find the one who could help them. A friend they would desperately be glad to see.

Adeena found Shar just as she noticed the oncoming

faerie. She looked at her fairy friend and pointed downward.

"It appears we have company."

Adeena nodded as she peered down. "Yes I know I felt faerie magic nearby. Who are they?"

"We will find out momentarily."

Eden and her entourage reached the top of the wall and Adeena recognized her immediately. Eden stepped down onto the stone and materialized. Each hugged the other and Adeena felt the sorrow within her.

"What is wrong? Why are you here? What, has happened?" she asked.

Eden started to cry immediately and Shar knelt down to console her.

"It is fine Eden, no harm will come to you here," assured the mage.

"At least not yet," added Adeena.

"Our home is gone," Eden started. Another wave of tears steamed down her cheeks and she continued. "Demons, destroyed everything, killed many of us." Eden was now sobbing uncontrollably. Adeena put her arms around her friend and held her close. The fairy kept on with her story amidst the tears. "They came with iron weapons, so many gone now, Alisha," she paused, "Alisha is gone too."

With that news Adeena began to cry and held Eden as close as she could get her. Shar stood and gasped. What had happened? The land of faerie destroyed? How was that even possible?

Eden looked up at Shar. "They have our queen, she is their captive, I think, but she may be dead now too. There is no place for us to go, so we left. She told us to leave, to find Malcolm. That maybe he could help us. Do you think he is able?"

Shar looked down at the faerie and then to the rest now standing there, "He and the elves will offer you sanctuary, and that is a promise. You cannot stay here, it is not safe either. You must travel to the elves where he is and tell him what has happened. I cannot do much for you here and I have to see to the safety of the gnomes. If your home has fallen, then they will be coming here next. Go to the elves, find any others of your brethren that may be lost and take them with you. If your queen is alive he will know what to do to determine that. Are you all able to continue on?"

"We are, and we will tell Malcolm everything," nodded Eden. She brushed her cheeks to wipe away the tears. A new look of determination was taking their place. "Are you coming as well Adeena?"

Adeena shook her head. "I must help Shar, but you, Jindra and the others will be okay. Stay out of sight and do not stop until you reach the elves, okay?"

"I promise," she nodded.

"I will see you, all of you, very soon," assured Adeena.

Jindra walked over and gave Adeena a warm hug. "I will take care of Eden," she whispered. "We will find the others."

"Thank you," smiled Adeena. She looked at the rest. "Fly safe and quick, but watch out for everything out there. This is not our home, so we must be extra careful."

"We will watch," nodded Eden. "Be safe yourself. Come, let us go!"

Eden and Jindra took the lead and the rest followed right behind. Soon the tiny speckles of light vanished into the confines of the forest. Adeena watched sadly and then slumped over the railing of the terrace.

"My home is gone, I have nothing anymore."

Shar put her arm around Adeena. "Not at all my friend,

you have me and you will always have a home here on Avalon."

Adeena put on a small smile. "Thank you Shar."

"You are most welcome." They watched the forest for a time and then the mage motioned towards the stairs. "Well, how about we get those gnomes to pick up the pace a bit?"

"Yeah, like that will ever happen." Each had a small chuckle at that and went on to try the impossible, the chore of speeding up a rather urgent evacuation.

Vasilis and a handful of elves had completed a run into Fairgrove, collecting supplies to store at Cambridge. The community had been rather defensive at first, but once the elf captain had begun to throw the coins around the attitude had taken an about face. Suddenly all the vendors were lining up to hand over whatever it was they wanted. As much as most of the races mistrusted the elves, when it came to make money off of them that prejudice quickly disappeared. It did not take long for the expedition to gather up what they required and were traveling back to Cambridge with more than the horses could carry. The group had purchased a couple of wagons to help carry the stockpile of goods. It would be easier on all of them and the horses wouldn't have to be burdened with the load.

"Do you think Markham and North Meadow will provide enough for their own people?" asked one elf.

"We can hope, it will make our task considerably easier," replied Vasilis.

The entourage rounded a bend in the trail and came across a scene that made all stop and the horses neigh uncontrollably. Before them a band of men, a rather gruff looking bunch, and standing before them was a wraith. It took notice of the elves immediately and let out a screech that sent a chill through the entire forest.

Vasillis belted out orders as he drew his sword. "We need to get the wagons down the trail!"

"We will keep them busy long enough to accomplish the task!" said one elf. He and two other elf guards pulled out their weapons and moved in next to their captain.

"The rest of you get the supplies back to the river! Now go!" shouted Vasillis. He and the three soldiers charged in on the wraith and the men. The men, not expecting an attack, were not really prepared to face the much better trained elves. They scattered in every direction, leaving the wraith alone.

The three elves positioned themselves between the wraith and the wagons, keeping it from stopping their escape. The company guiding them stampeded by, leaving their compatriots to fend for themselves. One elf moved in on the wraith and it turned its head to face this would be attacker. It swung its tail around and caught the elf completely by surprise. The creature had moved so fast the elf did not see the attack coming. The impact of the tail sent the elf flying off his horse and into the brush.

"Foolisssssh elvesssssss," it hissed.

Vasillis backed his horse off, but the other elf drew his bow and quickly shot an arrow into the arm of the wraith. It snarled and yanked the arrow out as if it was nothing more than a piece of dirt stuck to its scaly skin. The menacing creature stood its full height, nearly a full fifteen feet, and bore down on the elf that had dared to wound it. The elf had no chance to get away. The wraith crashed into the elf and horse, snapping the horse's neck instantly. The elf jumped from his ride and managed to get his sword up to deflect what would have been a fatal blow to his head. The blade cut into the claws of the creature and it took a step back as it screeched in anger.

At this point the first elf who had taken a fall stumbled

out of the brush to renew his attack. He drew another arrow and let it fly. He had three more arrows into the wraith before it could react. The wraith fell to one knee and the one elf closest ran in to use his sword. The creature reached up abruptly and grabbed the elf's sword and snapped it from his hands. The elf realized too late the thing was only pretending to be hurt. He was dead a moment later as the wraith cut him in half with its claws. It refocused its attack on the remaining two elves and stood tall once more.

Vasillis leapt from his horse and sent it running into the woods. If he were to have any hope he would have to do this on foot. He withdrew his other blade and made a run at the creature. The wraith closed in on the one elf still determined to fire off as many arrows as he could, but they were having no effect on it. The elf moved back in an attempt to give himself some room for escape but the wraith was quick and on him in seconds. It let out a roar as it drove its clawed hand into the elf, killing him.

Vasillis ran in from behind and threw his one blade at the creature. It stuck into the back of one leg and the wraith turned to see his newest attacker running at it with sword raised and yelling at the top of his lungs. The wraith let out a roar of its own that echoed throughout the forest and lifted its claws, ready to tear into this last elf who had dared to attack it.

Helana stood on her terrace and watched the march of her army northeast to the valley of the gnome's homeland and Eldridge castle. They would arrive within the day and begin their merciless destruction of it. She would leave nothing standing, and would spare no one. It was only the beginning of her conquest of this land of Avalon.

Her army was complete. The trolls were fed and marching as ordered and prodded along by her risen army from the ashes of the sand. The demons moved along orderly, commanded by more wraiths she had called up from the depths of her prison. The machines to tear at the walls of the castles that would stand in their way were pulled by the overgrown ogres she had drawn out of the hills to the south of her castle. As one they made a formidable foe.

The ground shook as this army of evil marched on, its soul intent to destroy all those who stood in its way. Helana sighed and breathed in all the fetid, foul air that escaped from the recesses of the dimension she had been confined in for far too long. A small piercing pain shot through her body to remind her once more of the price she paid to escape the dark. What she had been was virtually gone, and this new creature she had become was far more satisfying in a wicked way that she could not believe she had not thought of it sooner. All of her weaknesses were gone, replaced by a power she could have never imagined. There were no longer any boundaries to what she could do, to what she could achieve. Malcolm, the elves and those on the old world would soon discover such abilities soon enough.

Chapter Twelve

Tony watched the dwarves move in an orderly fashion, with the women and the young being ushered along by their male brethren. Mia had gone out into the forest to have a look around and to see if there were any unseen enemies that might catch on to the fact the dwarf castle was being evacuated. The less who knew of what was going on, the better it was for them. Tony had wanted to go along but Mia had assured him that she would be all right and that she could accomplish more whereas having a second body would double the chance of detection. One body would be much easier to hide within the forest. He had reluctantly agreed and had gone about helping Axel and Ruskin get the dwarves moving into the tunnels out of Aberdeen. It had taken a lot of convincing but now that they were moving, the process was very efficient. With the dwarves ambling along without argument anymore it was time to finish some other projects that had been started but needed to get completed.

"Hey boy, don't just stand there. C'mon an'give us a hand settin up a few gifts fer th'witch," encouraged Ruskin.

"Gifts? Such as?"

"Just a little somethin ta greet th'witch when she gets here," promised Axel.

Tony grinned. "But of course, it would be rude not to say 'hello' when she arrives."

"Oh yeah, an'we'll be sayin hello th'best way we dwarves can, with a bloody ax an' everythin else we can throw at'er!" said Ruskin with a chuckle.

The trio ventured out onto the catwalk of Aberdeen and wandered over to one group of dwarves setting up a weapon that was commonly used in medieval times, a trebuchet. It was a small catapult capable of hurling smaller boulders or whatever 'thing' you wanted to put into a sling of sorts and the machine would swing the sling up and over, send the rock, or other item down and out towards the target. Of course when its done firing, you hope it actually came close to hitting whatever it was you were aiming for.

"I don't know if those will do much damage to her army," commented Tony. He scratched his cheek and looked them over.

"Not meant ta, more ta annoy her than anythin, an'if it keeps her dodging a few an 'on her toes, then th'better we are fer getting away before she knows we're gone," said Axel with a shrug.

"Well let's hope it works then. So, where do we get started?" asked Tony.

"That one there, c'mon then," urged Ruskin leading the way over to the nearest Trebuchet.

They spent some time assembling some of the weaponry and the two dwarves showed Tony some of the other 'greeting cards' they would be using for the oncoming army. Within the walls, hidden from view was another common medieval weapon, a very large crossbow weapon of a sort, known as ballista's, and were only able to be seen if you were up close to the outside walls. There were holes dotted throughout the face of the stone walls through which the spears would fire through. It was another line of defense the dwarves commissioned to defend off any intruders.

"I wonder how big this army is that's comin this way," commented Tony. He dropped an average sized rock, to be used in the trebuchet, next to the one they had just completed.

"All ready. One up on ya there boy," bragged Axel. "Th'council sent out a scoutin party a day ago ta have a look see."

"Oh, cool, that'll help give us some idea then," replied Tony. "I'm kinda curious to see what all the fuss is about."

"We should know in a couple days, maybe sooner, dependin on how fast th'boys ride back," added Ruskin.

On a hill looking to the southwest, a bit of distance from the gnome settlement of Eldridge, four dwarves and two gnomes sat on their rides, staring into the distance. The group had arrived a few hours earlier, and was scouting out the so called army that was rumored to be moving on the settlements. Thus far they had seen no evidence of such an assault. The four dwarves had stopped in on Eldridge to let the gnomes know what they were doing and two of the gnomes had tagged along to get their own confirmation of things.

The evening was quite cool, overcast and the threat of rain hovered over the quiet of the forest. The company sat, waited, for anything to show itself but to no avail. They did take notice of how quiet the forest was though. No birds called, the leaves barely rustled in the virtual non-existent wind. The air felt colder than usual.

"She's gonna be a cold night I think," muttered one dwarf, Ricker by name.

"Aye, she may be," conceded a gnome with the name of Amery.

"How long we plan ta stay an'watch?" asked another dwarf who went by the calling of Thane.

"Until we know there ain't anything comin our way," said the first dwarf Ricker.

"That could be awhile Ricker," Bram chuckled. "Might we start a fire an'warm th'bones a bit?"

"No, nothin ta alert anyone, or anythin to us bein here," Ricker warned. "Pull yer cloak on better an' save yer energy by less talkin."

"Ya know he ain't gonna be able ta keep quiet that long," Thane joked.

"Shaddup," Bram grumbled.

"Lads, take a look, out there. Is that part of th' plains movin or are my eyes playin tricks on me?" asked the second gnome, Oren.

Thane laughed lightly. "In this cold, I be bettin on th'cold freezing yer eyeballs!"

"Nay, he be speakin th'truth. Look, the ground, it be movin," nodded Ricker. He pointed to the southwest. "Look close, there is movement down there, an' it movin along at a good clip I might add."

Iver, the fourth dwarf in the group nodded in agreement. "I see it, an'yer right, there was nothin there a moment ago, now it be all over th'place. My word, look at that will ya, th'plain be alive."

"Bloody hell, I'm afraid of what we've been told is true! Tis th'army of darkness an' it be movin our way," muttered Amery.

"They be at th'gnomes by dawn, if not sooner," said Bram. "Yeh best tell yer kind ta move out a wee bit faster."

"Oh that won't be hard ta do after seein that," motioned Oren.

"By th'word of the mage Shar, she was telling th'truth. There is no end ta them," said Thane with a wave of his hand. "I don't want ta see any more, I don't like this. If they see us, we're done fer."

"Agreed, let's move on. We stop at Eldridge ta warn'em, an' on ta Aberdeen we ride. There won't be much time," stated Ricker pulling on the reins of his horse. "C'mon, before I get sick of seein anymore of 'em."

"Smell that?" asked Iver. "There's a stench, an' it's getting worse."

"Aye," grunted Ricker. The wind was beginning to pick up speed and the leaves on the trees were now rustling with more intensity, and the foul odor Iver spoke of was getting worse as the wind strengthened.

"Look lads, in th'sky! Somethin's flyin over them," pointed Thane. A number of winged creatures were crisscrossing ahead of the advancing army and they did not look friendly!

Bram stared at the mass of the army and shook his head. It was enormous! The threat approaching was spread out almost as far as the eye could see. If this was what they were going to be up against the odds did not favor them or any of the races in the battle about to be fought. The speed at which such a force could move was astounding and that was even more frightening. They would storm through each kingdom in no time before any of the races could mount any sort of assault or defense.

"Move, into th'woods," instructed Ricker with a sense of urgency. "Now, before we're seen!"

"Make it quick lads, they're a flyin in quick, they'll be on us shortly!" encouraged Amery. He kicked his horse to hasten their retreat into the woods as the flying monstrosities grew with each passing second.

"Make fer th' cave behind them elms, th'one we passed comin up!" barked Ricker.

"Aye! Good idea!" concurred Iver.

The group raced deeper into the forest, hoping they could reach cover before the flying 'things' would find them. Ricker led them through the brush until he found the elm trees he had spoke of. Hidden nicely behind was a cave that they had discovered quite by accident when Thane was looking for a secluded place to 'relieve' himself. It would provide the necessary cover until the creatures moved on or flew back to report on anything they had seen. Once inside the cave they dismounted and herded the horses deeper into the cave to keep them quiet. One of the gnomes and one of the dwarves stayed with them while the rest returned to the mouth to watch and determine when it was safe to move on again.

First one shadow flew over, and then a second. The third paused in its flight and lowered itself into the forest to have a closer look at its surroundings. It came low enough that the group got its first glimpse at the thing.

"Bloody hell," muttered Ricker quietly.

The creature had several features of which included a body of a lion with a tail that was spiked similar to that of a porcupine, clawed legs and a head that vaguely looked human in a much distorted way. It was ugly to the core and the men knew it was something they had better keep from meeting. It hovered in the trees as if waiting for something, its wings moving back and forth the only sound they could hear. Suddenly out of the woods a herd of deer appeared, spooked apparently, and the creature reacted immediately. Its tail flicked and a number of spikes flew from it and into the deer. The animals fell where they were and then the other two creatures appeared next to the third. At once all three landed and tore into the deer in a feeding frenzy such as the dwarves and gnomes had never seen in their entire lifetime.

The company did not move a muscle or say a word as they stared in horror at the sight before them. Every so often one of the creatures would look up as if to make sure nothing was watching and then would return to devouring the deer it held in its claws. When the feeding was over, all three lifted back into the air and moved back towards the army from which they had come. After a short time Ricker decided it was time to move.

"I don't want to be around when they return! Get th'horses, we're leavin, an' we ride hard, no stops!" he spoke firmly. None of the company disagreed. In moments they were riding at full gallop towards Eldridge and Aberdeen to warn of what was coming.

Shar watched the dwarves ride off towards Aberdeen and knew they had to get Eldridge emptied before the army of Helana's arrived. The scouting company's report was disturbing. The creatures they spoke of reminded her of old stories that Malcolm would talk of when she was a child with Tasha. He would tell scary stories to keep them from venturing too far off into the woods or away from adult supervision. These things he often talked about she couldn't put a name to, but she would have to do a little research of her own and see if there was a name for them. That was all for a later time, at present they had to get the gnomes out of Eldridge for time was getting short.

"Adeena, how are they coming along in the lower tunnels?" she asked as the fairy flew into view on the rampart.

"They are moving along, as fast as they move you know," sighed Adeena. She sat down on the railing of the catwalk and crossed her arms in frustration. "If it were me in charge I'd be pushing them out the door."

"I am sure you would," Shar teased.

Adeena wrinkled her nose. "What is that smell? Ugh."

"The smell just started a while ago. Its preceding what is coming from the south, from the army. The scouting party spoke of it when they told us what they saw."

"I don't like it, smells like something is rotting."

"I know. Come on little one, let us go down once more and encourage the gnomes to move a little faster. I hope the report from their scouts has the desired effect!" motioned Shar.

"Well good luck with that, unless they've got a reason to move a little quicker I doubt they are in any rush," scoffed Adeena.

"Then I suggest you start pushing," winked Shar.

Mia was on her way back to the confines of Aberdeen. She worked her way through brush, stepping around the occasional tree stump that had at one time been a much larger tree. The remnants of that tree usually lay nearby, the result of a storm wreaking its havoc on the forest. Her search of the area had seen nothing out of the ordinary with the lone exception that the wildlife was few and far between. She had seen several flocks of birds flying northward and had seen only a single deer, and it too was moving quickly north. If the animals were fleeing then something had to be coming and it was spooking them enough to cause the flight. That was cause for concern.

Ahead of her a branch snapped and the sound of brush being moved through caused Mia to stop in her tracks. Quickly and quietly she stepped behind the nearest large spruce and hid amidst the branches to avoid an unnecessary confrontation with whatever was approaching. It was was making no effort to hide itself. When the branches of the brush parted Mia almost gasped out loud but caught it in time. The wraith might have heard her otherwise.

She had never been that close to one before and Mia wished she had not come across it now. The creature stood over nine feet tall and its clawed hands ripped several branches of the tree right off and tossed them aside. It sniffed the air through nostrils protruding from its extended nose, its teeth, row upon row of razor sharp knives were grinding as it smelled the surroundings. Mia was wondering what it was looking for and realized it was looking for her. It had caught her scent and was hunting. Now she began to panic, how was she going to get away from this thing? What was it doing this far from its kind?

The wraith extended its wings momentarily and then drew them in close, its long scaly legs with clawed toes took several steps forward and then it turned to look straight at her. The black and yellow eyes narrowed and focused. Mia knew it had found her and without even waiting to see if it came after she bolted for the nearest thick underbrush. It would be her only means of avoiding those claws and immediate death.

She was in and running through brush as quick as her legs could move and Mia could hear the wraith in pursuit. She ran in the general direction of Aberdeen but it was going to take some doing if she stayed within cover. The wraith let out a howl and Mia pushed herself harder! It sounded as though it was closing in and for the first time felt genuine fear for her life. She heard branches breaking so near it could have been on top of her and she would not have known. Mia tripped and as she fell a large branch flew over top. It would have knocked her down had she still been standing! Mia changed direction and did her best to confuse the creature and buy herself some more time.

Another shriek from the creature sent a chill through her body and as she broke free of the trees realized there was no place left to hide. She sprinted for the castle as fast as she was able, pushing her body to its limits and beyond. Mia risked a quick glance back and saw the monster tear out of the brush and see her. It started in pursuit! Mia withdrew a couple daggers and let them fly in full stride in an attempt to slow it down. One dagger lodged itself in an arm and the other found the chest. All the wraith did was pluck them off as though they were twigs that had fallen on it.

It was the sight of several spears flying through the air that made her gasp in shock and pause, not sure whether to go on or stay put. She took another look at the wraith and as it dodged those spears and still continued its pursuit her mind was made up in quick order. Mia ran on towards Aberdeen and almost ran over Axel and Ruskin in the process.

"Watch it will ya!" shouted Axel.

"Axel! Ruskin?" she gasped.

"Aye, an' whole lot o' others," Ruskin pointed. "Let'em go boys! Let that thing know we don't like it visitin us!"

Another volley of spears flew through the air and Mia turned to watch the wraith maneuver around several but took a few others in the legs and one of its arms. It howled and stopped its drive forward for the moment. A whole mob of dwarves moved past Mia armed with more spears and axe's than she could count. Tony ran up and she hugged him instantly.

"I am so glad to see all of you," she managed between breaths.

"Thought we better come looking after one of the guards on watch saw the wraith," he said with a sigh. "Boy am I glad we did."

"What took you so long?" she replied, trying to make light of the situation she had been in.

"Yer not welcome in these parts!" Axel shouted. "Ya go back ta yer witch an' you tell'er we'll be waitin!"

"Send th'thing home men!" bellowed another of the dwarves, Brenn.

The wraith screeched at the dwarves, as though daring them to try and they obliged hardily. Spear upon spear, and a few arrows were sent at the creature and though it tried to avoid most, there was just too many to overcome. It gave up and opted to leave while it still could. The wings expanded and the dark creature lifted into the sky, much to the dismay of the dwarves who were looking forward to finishing off the thing. It vanished into the clouds and the company decided it was time to return to Aberdeen.

"Ah there lass, yer all right now," assured Axel.

"I had it right where I wanted it," expressed Mia with a light laugh between tears. "I thought I might not actually get away this time."

"Hell no, I ain't going to let that happen, and next time, I'm going with you," said Tony firmly.

Mia nodded. "I will not argue about that anymore, I promise."

"Back to the castle men, we have work to do yet!" ordered Brenn.

"Never seen any of them that looked like that one before," muttered Ruskin.

"Ah, who knows what th'hell they look like most often? They be always changing how they look," added Axel.

"Come on then, I think a keg is in order after this," chortled Ruskin as he rubbed his stomach.

"Aye brother, I think yer right, huntin always gets me thirsty!" agreed Axel with a grin.

Chapter Thirteen

The elf guard on the catwalk of Cambridge saw the rider approaching from the south, and alerted the other guards to notify the king and the wizard Malcolm. All were present when the bridge was lowered and in rode a slumped and battered Vasilis. He nearly fell off his horse as it came to a stop near the stables. A few of the elf guard helped him down and propped him to help stand. He was covered in blood, his shirt was torn and there were deep gashes on his legs. His face was bruised and his breathing was rough. Still, the elf captain managed to smile upon seeing the king.

"The supplies, did they arrive?" Vasilis asked.

"Yes they did captain, some time ago, safe. I believe because of you and your men. Where are the others?" asked Xanthus.

Vasilis shook his head is despair. "They did not make it, I barely got away myself. It caught us by surprise."

Xanthus waved his hand at Vasilis. "Enough talk for now," he motioned to the guards. "Get him to the healers; he must be attended to immediately."

"I am all right sir, I can walk on my own," assured Vasilis.

"Don't be the hero now captain, you are home, let us get you healed. We have a great deal of work to do and we will need your help. Having you to assist is more beneficial than having you hobble around, wouldn't you say?" the king smiled and Vasilis nodded.

"Yes sir."

Malcolm watched the injured elf go with the assistance of a couple elf guards and shook his head sadly. "We are already suffering at the hands of the witch."

"She is showing her arrogance in venturing this far north with her minions, an arrogance that could be of benefit to us. It may cause her to make a mistake or two," commented Xanthus.

"Let us hope so," agreed Malcolm. "Have we heard of any news from the other elf colonies to the north? I heard one of the messengers returned late last night."

"Yes, the one messenger that went to the woodland elves. He reported as having delivered our letter, they were to send us a reply within a day or so."

"That is rather vague," sighed Malcolm. "I don't like how that sounds."

"You worry too much my friend," assured Xanthus. "My brother leads the woodland elves, I have the utmost faith he will stand by us."

"I have not seen or talked for that matter to Ledal in some time, I have to admit I have lagged in my visits to the others in the past few years."

"We all get busy in our own lives; even I haven't talked to Ledal in years. That is something I have to fix after we deal with all of this. With my wife gone, perhaps it will do me good to go visit a few of my other brethren," sighed Xanthus.

"My king!" shouted one of the watchmen in the towers. "Another rider approaches!"

"Perhaps another messenger has returned!" smiled Xanthus.

"With good news I hope!" added Malcolm. Both men strolled back to the main gate as the elf guard stood waiting to welcome this new rider into Cambridge.

Vasilis was walking by an open window when he saw the rider entering the gates of Cambridge Castle, and he paused to watch. The two guards accompanying him took notice of the newcomer as well.

"Another messenger returns," commented one.

"Messenger?" asked Vasilis.

"Were you not at the council meeting? Oh yes, you were already gone by then," said the other.

"Gry, your observing abilities never cease to amaze me," cracked Vasilis. "It is a wonder why you never advance past the rank of guard."

"No need for insults Captain," replied Gry.

"What messenger?" Vasilis inquired again, this time with more emphasis on the word 'messenger'.

"They were sent to the other colonies, no idea why, that is between the other captains sir. You best ask them for more information."

"I will Gry, thank you for the update. I can make it to the healers on my own, you two can go about your business," urged Vasilis.

The two guards moved on down the hall and Vasilis returned to watching the messenger dismount in the courtyard. Xanthus and Malcolm were welcoming him back and appeared to be in discussion with the elf. Vasilis scrutinized the scene for a few more minutes and then moved on. He would have to talk with the other captains at the first convenient moment, apparently there was more going on than he knew about. With that thought Vasilis nodded to himself and winced as he pulled the bandage on his arm tighter.

The messenger was allowed to attend to his horse after reporting his news and both Xanthus and Malcolm were relieved to see the letter he had brought back with him. The elves from the ice fields were sending their best archers and swordsmen by nightfall of this day. The remainder of their army would be arriving at Cambridge within the week. Both elf king and wizard could not have received better news. Both were hoping any further letters from the remaining messengers would bear the same good news.

They had their answer over the course of the day as each returning courier relayed the same. All were to provide their best soldiers and most would be arriving by that evening or by morning of the next day. Thus far the strategy of striking first was coming along quite nicely. Even Jacinto had sent word that he and his men would be waiting for them on the forest edge near Markham until they arrived. They were more than willing to march on Helana with the advance army and help in any way or offer up any strategy that might help.

"So far we are on schedule to depart by tomorrow afternoon, provided all have arrived by morning as promised," said Kieran.

"Perfect, my honor guard is prepped and ready as well," added Neil. "Both Tasha and I have our horses ready."

"I still think you risk too much my lord," said Taith. His sentiments were agreed on by everyone else in the room.

"Don't worry about us, we'll be fine. Malcolm will have our lucky charms ready before we leave," added Neil with a chuckle.

"Charm?" questioned Kieran.

"Talisman," corrected Tasha. "We will have our own

protection, more so than the rest of you. So do not extend yourself on our behalf, be aware of your own safety and we will all get through this just fine."

On the rampart of Cambridge Castle the elf watch kept vigil on all that was happening outside the walls. Over the course of the last couple days tents had been constructed for the forthcoming combatants and in short order, refugees from the gnomes, dwarves and wherever else that may come to the elves for aid. Activity for the most part was limited to the occasional elf guard who wandered through the camp to make sure all was well. Thus the oncoming sight of a great many colorful speckled lights drew the attention of the elf watch.

"Captain Kieran!" shouted one guard up towards the general direction of the council chamber.

The captain showed himself on the balcony. "Yes, what is it?"

"There are a large number of, um, lights, approaching the castle!"

"Lights? Can you try and be more specific?" asked the Captain, a little confused at the remark.

"I wish I could sir, but it's just a bunch of lights, moving fast," shrugged the watchman.

Malcolm wandered out at that point. "Did you say 'lights' my good man?"

"Yes sir."

"Faerie," he said quietly. "That does not bode well."

"Faerie?" asked Kieran. "Here? What for?"

"We need to find out," pointed Malcolm. "I will be right down!"

The Faerie 'lights' came to a stop on the outside of the castle. The guards lost count after trying for a time and just shook their heads in disbelief. So many were moving around that it made it almost impossible to get a proper number. The Faerie transformed into their full form and all stood, along the moat circling the castle. There were hundreds upon hundreds and the elf guards were amazed at the sight. Most had never seen that many fairies in one spot and chances are they wouldn't again so they made sure to take in the vision this particular time.

Malcolm appeared through the castle gate and wandered onto the bridge that crossed over the moat. He paused to take in the sight, and feared the worst. One fairy he recognized at the front of the pack, Eden and motioned for her to come forward. She and another fairy, Jindra, came over at his request. Each faerie stopped in front of the wizard and Malcolm took notice of their disheveled look.

"Eden, what has happened to bring all of you here?" He asked.

"Oh Malcolm, where do I even begin," the fairy sighed, her voice sounded tired.

"Take your time," assured Malcolm.

"Our home is gone, destroyed by demons," started Jindra.

"What?" asked Malcolm incredulously.

Eden continued on, "It is all gone; they came, killing us, ripping everything apart. We all fled here, we've been able to find most of our faerie kind, but some may still be out there, lost."

"Our queen sent us to you, saying you would know what to do," added Jindra.

"And what of Leasha? Is she here as well?" he wondered, but knowing that was not likely true.

Eden shook her head. "No, she stayed behind to fight and give us the chance to get away. I am scared she might not be alive," tears welled up in Eden's eyes and Malcolm patted softly on the shoulder.

"There there little one, I will go and find your queen. What is of other importance is that we find the rest of your kind and bring them here."

"I would like to take some of the others and do just that sir, it won't take too long. We have covered a lot of the land as we made our way here and can finish off our search within a couple days," stated Jindra.

Malcolm smiled at the fairy. "Yes you may. I don't think we have had the chance to be formally introduced. I am Malcolm," he offered his hand.

Jindra took his hand and bowed before him. "I am Jindra. It is nice to meet you sir."

"And I you," reiterated Malcolm nodding.

"When will you go and find our queen?" asked Eden.

"This evening, once I have prepared a few talismans that will allow me to crossover. It should not take long and you have my word Eden, I will find her."

"Thank you sir, what of the rest of us?" she wondered.

"Take refuge in any of the tents you see scattered around. Rest and we will provide you some food and drink a little later. I will have the elves prepare something just for the faerie."

"Thank you sir, we will. I will depart this evening with those who wish to accompany me in the search for the rest of the surviving faerie," said Jindra.

"Make yourselves at home," shouted Malcolm to the entire faerie tribe. "You are welcome to stay as long as you have need to." Malcolm pointed to the tents. "Pick any you wish to use, and I will check in on you shortly."

"We appreciate it Malcolm," bowed Eden. "Follow us everyone!" shouted Eden. She and Jindra led the faerie off to several tents off to the far side, away from the rest so they could have their privacy.

Malcolm walked quickly back in to the courtyard and Xanthus was just as quick to approach him.

"The Queen, she is missing?" he asked.

"Yes my lord, and Tir Nan Og is destroyed. Helana sent an army of demons in and according to the faerie nothing was left standing. I need to crossover and see if I can find Leasha. She might still be alive. The chances are slim, but I need to take the risk and see for myself what has been done," replied Malcolm.

"Then I am coming with you. You cannot go in alone. I will not allow it."

"I am not sure what we will find," warned Malcolm.

"True, but you risk more by going alone. I am going with you," emphasized the king.

"Very well, I need to gather a few things and then we'll be ready to go."

A tower on Cambridge rang its warning bell and both looked skyward to see what was going on. Guards were pointing to the sky and in the distance there were a number of flying creatures of a sort approaching the castle.

"What are they?" shouted Xanthus.

"I cannot see from this distance! They are closing in fast though!" replied the watchtower guard.

"More visitors or intruders?" wondered Malcolm aloud.

Kieran and Taith emerged from the castle in full run. Each took command of a regiment of armed elves and guided them to the catwalk of Cambridge. Neil and Tasha appeared in the courtyard and jogged up to Xanthus and Malcolm anxious to ask what was going on.

"What's all the fuss?" asked Neil.

"There," pointed Malcolm. "We have someone, or something moving in from the northeast."

An arrow appeared from the sky and slammed into the

ground in the courtyard. A flag was attached to the arrow and Xanthus recognized it immediately. It was from the woodland elves. He knew his brother's signature anywhere. Every elf colony had their own flag so that they could alert the other elves to their arrival and to avoid any other race from impersonating them. It would avoid any unnecessary bloodshed or any intruder from gaining entry into their home.

"Stand down Captains! The Woodland Elves arrive from the sky!" bellowed Xanthus.

"Yes sir! All elves lower your weapons!" Kieran barked.

"The first of the reinforcements have arrived," Xanthus smiled.

"A good sign indeed," Malcolm winked.

The elves on the catwalk lowered their weapons and all waited for the Woodland elves to land. The flyers broke off into two groups, the larger of the two maneuvered to settle on the land outside the castle whilst the smaller group guided their ride to the center of the courtyard of Cambridge. The animals they rode were unrecognizable at first, but Neil soon gasped as he realized what they were!

"Gryphons? That is what they are?" he checked with a look at Tasha.

"You know your beasts I see," she acknowledged with a nod.

"Only from fairy tales I have read, but wow, never thought I'd see the day I'd actually see one them!" he exclaimed. He watched the creatures land one by one as they obeyed their rider's requests to lower them down. The Gryphon had the body of a lion and the head of an eagle with white wings to match the feathers on their head. The legs had the muscle tone of a lion but where paws would have been, there were instead talons. They were a formidable sight to see and without question one creature you would not want to cross. The talons would tear any combatant to shreds.

"Malcolm, they're magnificent," Neil commented.

"I will have one of the elves allow you to touch one. Interested?" he smiled.

"What do you think?" Neil joked.

Xanthus started forward arms open to greet one particular female elf that had dismounted. "Brielle! Welcome!"

"Brielle!" Tasha waved to her, obviously acknowledging a prior acquaintance.

"Who's she?" Neil asked.

"Hello father! It is good to be home again!" Brielle shouted with a wave.

"Riane has a sister?" Neil looked at Tasha.

"Yes, she does. My aren't you on your game today," Tasha laughed.

"Okay you, the sarcasm isn't really necessary," cracked Neil.

"But you make it so easy," she teased.

Brielle ran up to her father and both gave the other a huge embrace. The other elves that had landed in the courtyard all wandered over and waited their turn to greet Xanthus- albeit in a different more formal way.

"It is good to see you again," Xanthus said.

"You as well, you know you could come to visit every so often," she teased. "Uncle Ledal said to remind you of that," she laughed lightly.

"I'm sure he did," Xanthus laughed.

"There is someone you need to meet, again. When was the last time you saw your niece?" Brielle asked.

"Oh my, it has been ages."

"Captain!" beckoned Brielle. A woman stepped away from the group of woodland elves and strode over to face Xanthus.

"Captain?" checked Xanthus.

"Meet the newest captain of the woodland elf guardians, your niece, Captain Elise," introduced Brielle with a grin.

"Uncle," Elise bowed politely to her uncle with the respect one would give those in rank higher than their own.

"No need to be so formal! Congratulations on your new position captain!" nodded Xanthus. He walked up and gave Elise a big hug equal to the one he had endowed upon Brielle.

"Thank you sir. My father sends his greetings, he and the rest of our forces will be here in a few days once they have finished organizing themselves and securing our home," Elise said.

"My thanks for coming on such short notice, but we have little time to waste in this matter," said Xanthus.

"We needed to take the Gryphon out for a ride anyway," Elise jested. "We are ready to go whenever you and your forces are prepared."

"Tomorrow afternoon is the plan, once the others have arrived we will set out," Xanthus explained.

"Our bows are ready, and our swords are at your command Uncle, we will do everything we can to assist," assured Elise.

"I know you will. My home is your home Elise, you and your guard may rest in the tents we have set up outside the walls. Feel free to choose those you wish and we will send word once we have prepared the evening meal." Xanthus gave her another hug and had a smile as large as he could muster.

"Come then cousin, I need to introduce you to a friend of mine," motioned Brielle leading the way over to Tasha.

Neil watched the interaction and took notice of how the Woodland elves were dressed a little differently than their brethren here at Cambridge. Their clothing consisted of darker colors blended in brown and green, no doubt to mesh with their surroundings of their forest home. A few of the Woodland elves had darker hair, again, a stark contrast to the more blonde oriented elves of Cambridge. He observed Brielle with darker hair too, while Elise was more of a blonde. A bit odd considering that Riane was as blonde as you could be he would have thought her sister would have been the same.

"Hi Tasha!" exclaimed Brielle as she ran up. The two hugged and were giddy with laughter upon seeing one another again.

"I hear you are Queen now, your majesty," bowed Brielle. She stood back up laughing. "And this must be your king?" she looked at Neil.

"Just call me Neil," he replied shaking her hand.

"So formal," Brielle teased. "Very well, Neil."

"He is just a little uneasy with the whole king concept," mocked Tasha. "I'm working on him though."

"Well congratulations, on your new title, and your marriage. My apologies for not getting here for the event but I was off on my own little adventure to the east. Remind me to tell you about it later. Allow me to introduce my cousin, Elise, captain of the Woodland Elf guardians. Elise, this is Tasha, Queen of Avalon," she giggled somewhat and then pointed at Neil. "And her king, Neil. Just call him Neil," she smiled.

"It is a pleasure to meet you both," bowed Elise.

"There is no reason for any formalities between us Elise; we are both just Tasha and Neil. It is nice to finally meet the cousin I have heard so much about!" grinned Tasha.

"Do not believe all that she may have said about me, Brielle does tend to exaggerate somewhat," kidded Elise. Brielle gave her a shove and both laughed.

"It is nice to have you both here, we're going to need all the help we can get," Neil said.

"Brielle, Elise, welcome to Cambridge," added Malcolm as he wandered over.

"Malcolm nice to see you again," smiled Brielle giving the wizard a huge embrace that almost knocked the wind out of him.

"Sir, it is an honor to meet you," nodded Elise.

"We will talk more later, but may I ask first if you could have one of your riders introduce Neil here to the Gryphon, he has never seen one before and I believe he would like to pet one of them."

"Oh that I can take of myself. Would you like to do that now?" Brielle asked.

Malcolm interjected, "I have some urgent matters to attend to, and I need to speak with you two for a moment," he nodded to Tasha and Neil. "Then you can show him the Gryphon."

"Agreed. Well cousin, let us send the others off to find a bed and get some rest. We can take care of the Gryphon ourselves."

Elise nodded. "As you wish cousin."

Malcolm took Neil and Tasha aside. "I have to leave for a short time, and Xanthus is coming with me."

"Does this have to do with the fairies?" Tasha asked.

"Observant my dear," Malcolm said with a smile. "We should not be gone for long, but I am relying on you two to watch over things until I return."

"We'll do our best. Do we wait until you get back before we head out tomorrow afternoon?" checked Neil.

Malcolm shook his head. "No, delay is not a good idea. Proceed as you have planned, and we will return here as soon as we are able. I have your talismans ready and in my room. You will find them on my desk. Wear them around your necks, do not, and I mean, do not take them off at any time," instructed the wizard.

"We won't," assured Tasha.

"Good. I will talk to you both once I return. Safe journey as you march to meet Helana."

"And you as well my friend, I hope you're able to help out the fairies," Neil said.

"As do I," Malcolm sighed. "Now, go pet your fairy tale," teased Malcolm.

Neil laughed and nodded. "Okay, take care."

Malcolm walked off and Xanthus joined him. Together the two vanished inside the castle. Neil and Tasha walked over to visit with the Gryphon and as he patted the creature on the side its neck, he still could not believe he was touching a living legend. The Gryphon looked over at Brielle and Elise as if to ask 'how long do I have to stand here' and both elves snickered.

Wizard and Elf King held their respective staffs and as Malcolm finished casting the incantation to allow their entry into the land of faerie, mist formed and slowly an opening took shape. What waited on the other side of the mist was unknown but both were ready for the worst. A foul odor escaped from the opening warning them that the demons were still present somewhere within and the men feared they may be too late to do anything but they had to try. When the magic had fully taken hold, both men stepped into the doorway and vanished into the mist. As they disappeared the magic faded and the mist dissipated, taken away by a light breeze that drifted through the council chamber. The odor lingered momentarily and then it too, dissipated.

Chapter Fourteen

Zach yawned and tipped back his drink, finishing it in one swallow. It had been some time since he had had an old fashioned vodka. After elf brandy, dwarf ale and whatever else he had consumed the last while, this ordinary drink was quite refreshing. He picked up a leftover piece of pizza and took a bite, savoring the taste of it as he chewed. Zach had ordered in after picking up Riane at the library. She had printed off paper after paper of information and they had decided to make it an evening in to go over the material. So he treated her to a good old fashioned pizza, but to her, it was quite the new experience. A pizza and a half later and a couple of average beer and she had passed out on the bed with papers strewn all over the place. He chuckled as he looked over at her, snoring loudly with paper in hand. Zach sighed, stood up and wandered over to take the paper out of her hand. Riane didn't even move as he took the paper and pulled the blanket over her. He strolled back to his chair and laptop and poured another drink, and threw in some orange juice for mix.

"How the hell am I supposed to find this guy," he mumbled. The information Riane had dug up was useful in its own way but it gave him no clear angle on how to pursue a mythical wizard. After reading of King Arthur, the Knights of the Round Table, and countless other historical stories his mind was full, yet it felt empty. He scratched his chin and decided to wander down to the bar and clear his head. Zach scribbled a note as to his whereabouts for Riane in case she woke. He threw some water on his face, changed his shirt, combed his hair and grabbed his room key on the way out.

In the bar, he found a seat and ordered a rye and cola, a change from all the vodka he had drunk so far. After a few sips he turned around and listened to the sounds of the establishment. It felt like he hadn't been in a bar in ages. True, the taverns back on Avalon were similar, yet they were not anything like here. A familiar voice made him look about in shock.

"Hi Zach, out on the town?" Rachal asked.

"Hi there, didn't think I'd see you again, and Christina," as the other lady came into view from around the corner. "No boyfriends?"

"They went off to some football game, so we thought we would venture out on our too," Rachal smiled.

"Enjoying your visit so far?" Christina wondered as she took a seat next to Rachal.

"Well, been busy for the most part," he replied. "Can I get you ladies a drink?"

"Sure, two brandy," Christina smiled.

The bartender nodded and brought up two glasses to fill. Zach threw a few dollar bills on the bar and lifted his own drink up.

"And another rye."

"Coming right up sir." The bartender went about pouring the ladies drinks and then moved on to mix his. Zach watched him pour the brandy and noticed how similar it looked to the elf brandy back on Avalon. He shrugged it off and went back to visiting.

"So why come here, to this bar?" he asked.

"Well," Rachal looked over at Christina and then back at him. "We were hoping to run in to you and your girlfriend. We thought you two could use a night out and we could be your hostesses, as it were. Is she here with you now?"

"No," snickered Zach. "All the excitement of the trip, and a few drinks has worn her right out. She's up in the room sleeping."

"What's keeping you so busy?" Christina wondered. She took her brandy and sipped from the glass.

"Oh we're trying to find an old," he thought for a second. "An old friend of a friend."

"Any luck?" Rachal checked.

"Like trying to find a needle in a haystack, as the old saying goes."

"What does he or she do?" Christina asked.

Zach didn't mind the questions, but was surprised they were so interested in his goings on. "Well 'he'," he emphasized the word 'he', "dabbles in, um, historical stuff, from way way back."

"Historical," Rachal said out loud as she appeared to be thinking about it. "Does he work for a museum? University?"

"Neither, as far as I know," he replied with a shake of his head.

"Wouldn't hurt to ask at a museum, they might know him in some way, you never know. Or visit the university, the faculty might be able to set you down the right path," added Christina.

Zach looked at them curiously. "You two sure are different."

Both ladies laughed lightly. Rachal tipped her glass back, finished off her brandy and placed it back on the bar.

"Being different is one way to stand out from the rest," she gave him a quick smile and licked her lips.

"True," he laughed lightly.

"Well I'm going to guess you are too tired to venture out with us this evening?" Christina asked politely. She finished off her brandy and returned it to the bartender, waving off his offer to refill.

"Sorry ladies, perhaps we'll cross paths again and we'll take you up on your offer."

"You promise?" Rachal smiled at him.

"Yes, I promise," he chuckled.

"Then have a good night Zach, good luck finding your old friend of a friend," Christina said. She adjusted her dress after standing up and Rachal gave Zach a little wave.

"Take care."

"You ladies as well, have fun," he said as he lifted his glass to them. The two stunning brunettes slowly made their way out of the bar, and every man in the room took notice as they passed by. When they vanished outside Zach couldn't help but snicker at all the men shaking their heads and sighing after enjoying their stroll out.

He finished off his drink and decided it was time to return to the room and catch some sleep himself. The ladies did make a good point though during their conversation. Perhaps someone from a museum or university might have an idea on how to locate a person of historical significance. As he rode the elevator up to the room he decided it might not be a bad idea to visit an old acquaintance at the museum. The only bad side to that thought was the acquaintance was an old girlfriend, and she might not be too happy to see him.

Zach and Riane entered the museum of Natural History and Culture the next morning, just as it was opening for the day, and ambled over to the customer service desk. Zach wanted to stop in to the museum first before their appointment at Neil's old law office. The young lady sitting at the desk looked up and greeted them both with a warm smile.

"Can I help you?" she offered.

"Yes, is a Michelle Bruce still on staff here by chance?" Zach asked.

"Let me check for you." The lady went about entering something into her computer and looked back up after just a few moments. "Yes she is Michelle is downstairs at the moment. Apparently you caught her just in time!"

"Oh," Zach started. "Why is that?"

"According to this, she has transferred to another museum. Today is her last day."

"Wow, what are the odds of that," Zach said with a smile. "Thank you," he looked at her name tag. "Thanks Jasmine."

"Your welcome. The elevator to the downstairs level is just around the corner."

"Okay, great," Zach waved. The two of them found the doors easy enough and were gliding down to the lower level seconds later.

"She is an ex girlfriend you say?" Riane asked again.

"Um, yes, so I have no idea how this might go."

"Why is that? Did you two not get along?"

"Well we did, but it didn't end very well."

"How so?"

Zach stuttered and stammered trying to find the right words but in the end just gave up. "I didn't call her back after she had left me a few messages, I just kinda forgot to. After a bit I thought she would just forget about me, so I never did bother trying to call her again. It was back in a time I was really gambling a lot."

"That was not very nice," Riane said with a frown.

"I know, I know, I didn't mean to forget about calling her. It just sorta happened."

"Men," Riane huffed.

Zach looked at her, and smiled. "Say what?"

"You men are all alike." Riane realized after saying it that was quite unlike herself to say that. "I have no idea why I just said that."

Zach laughed lightly and gave her a kiss on the cheek. "It's the human thing to say."

"Human, like the pizza and beer last night?"

"Now that was very human thing, a tradition amongst us folk," he said with a chuckle.

"I will stick with my brandy from now on," she rubbed her temples. "My head still hurts."

"It'll pass," he assured her. "Now let's hope Michelle is in a good mood today."

They stepped off the elevator and worked their way down a hallway towards an office door that was ajar. A couple young men carrying boxes emerged and went by them. The work clothes they had on made them out to be movers so Zach thought it was safe to assume that it was Michelle's office. At the door he peered around it and saw the lady sitting at the desk. She was gathering up papers and filing them into folders. It had been some time since Zach had seen Michelle but it was her all right, and he had to admit, she looked as good now as she did back when he had dated her. The blonde hair with dark tips was a bit of a different look for her, but it suited the straight long hair that came down to her shoulders. Michelle was dressed a little more casual than usual, likely because of the fact she was moving. Her black shirt hung on her loosely, but there was no denying she had curves and was quite the attractive lady. Zach wondered if she would remember him.

"Excuse me," he coughed upon entering the room.

"I'm busy right now, go and talk to one of the other staff, I'm sure they can help you," Michelle replied without looking up from her work.

"Michelle," Zach said her name. Then she recognized his voice and looked up. He waved and added "Hi."

Michelle stared at him, her eyes fixated on him. She took a quick glance at Riane and then fixated back on him. "Zach?"

"Yeah, it's me."

Michelle stood up and walked around the desk. "What the hell do you want?"

"Um," he took a couple steps back, and she stopped her advance. "I need some help with something, and I thought you might help."

"Really, me? You want me to help you?" Her voice started to quiver, the anger evident in her tone.

"Michelle, I know I can't apologize enough for what I did back when, but believe me when I say, I am sorry for how I handled, us," Zach explained, trying to amend a broken bridge that might just be impossible to do, but he had to try.

"Is that so, you know, all you had to do was call, that's it! How hard is it to return one of my messages? Huh? One little call! You just didn't have to guts to tell me we were finished!" she snapped angrily.

"I know, I wasn't in a good place back then, you know the trouble I kept getting in to. I just got, well, scared."

"Scared? Of what? Me?"

"No, scared of everything, work, my gambling, maybe even us, but things are different now and I really am sorry for what I did, or I guess, didn't do." Zach was doing his best to set the record straight with Michelle, and he hoped, from what he remembered of her character, that she might be a little open to the idea of accepting his apology.

Michelle sighed and sat on the edge of her desk for a moment. She crossed her arms and looked over at Riane. "I'm guessing you're the girlfriend?"

Riane nodded. "Yes, the girlfriend."

"Is he being honest here?" she asked.

"I believe he is trying," smiled Riane. "He can mix up his words at times, but I do believe he is truly trying to say he is sorry."

"You hurt me Zach, and it took me a while to get you out of my system. But geez, here you are again, after a couple years, trying to apologize. It must be important if you've made the effort to come see me," Michelle said. She stood there, arms crossed, thinking things over. "Fine, apology accepted. I guess."

Zach sighed and walked over to shake her hand. "Friends?" he asked hopefully.

Michelle started to reach over and then she swung her hand up to slap him but he caught her hand just in time, but she was quicker with the other hand. Her fist slammed into his jaw and he fell back from the blow. He leaned against the wall, rubbing his cheek.

"You did deserve that," Riane smiled.

"I like her," Michelle commented with her own grin. "I like her a lot. How did you ever end up with him?"

"Not sure," Riane teased.

"Now I feel better," Michelle said. She went to sit down at her desk and looked over at Zach who was still rubbing his cheek.

"You've got quite the left hook," he complimented.

"Thanks, I've been going to the gym regularly. Now,

what in the world brings you back to me?" Michelle was curious now, her anger vented.

"I recall you were quite the historical guru, I need some info on a person from long ago," he started.

"Oh really, do tell?" she beckoned. "This should be interesting."

"What do you know of an old wizard by the name of Merlin?" he asked.

"Merlin? Are you referring to the same Merlin who was King Arthur's teacher, mentor, and so on?" Michelle checked. Her curiosity was peaked now and she sat back to hear him out.

"I guess so. I am trying to find," Zach had to stop and think for a moment on how to tackle this issue. "I am trying to find someone who studies him, old English history, sort of specializes in it." It was a roundabout answer but it sounded a lot more realistic than him saying 'I'm looking for Merlin himself.'

"Well, well. Are you what, a private detective now?" Michelle asked.

"For the most part, I left the force about a year and a half ago."

"Really, now there's something I thought I'd never hear. I figured you to be a lifer for sure. Well, if there is someone out there who specializes as you say in Merlin, chances are you won't find him here, but over in England."

"England? Why there?"

Michelle looked up at him and shook her head. "Zach, Zach, Zach, Merlin is a figure of old, and I mean real old English mythology. So if I'm studying some legendary wizard, I would do it there, not here. Think about it."

"I guess your right," Zach agreed. "Makes sense when you put it that way."

"You did say you were a detective right?" Michelle teased.

"Funny," retorted Zach. "So I'll ask you again, what do you know about Merlin?"

"To begin with, Merlin is really just a person that may or may not have existed. There are so many stories passed down over time that for all we know he might have been a guy who made up a good batch of ale one day and went from being a 'wizard' at brew making to a man who can turn lead into gold. There is no actual documentation on him, what there is, is so vague that it leaves the storytellers a lot of leeway in making him out to be more than what he ever really was."

Zach sat down on one of the chairs and Riane followed suit. He looked at Michelle and shrugged.

"That's it?"

"Of course not, I'm a guru on old stuff, isn't that how you put it?"

"More or less." Zach put on a small smile and Michelle just frowned in return.

"I've studied King Arthur history, folklore, for years. It's such an unknown part of a so called history that has next to nothing in print. The romance of the period drew me in at first but the more I delved into the more it pulled me in. There are so many different versions of what may have, may have not happened. Merlin for the most part is a piece of that King Arthur legend, he's another part of history over there in England that has very little documentation of so once more people tend to take liberty with what information they do have. Now if you want something really obscure, try studying up on Norse mythology."

"Yes, I have done some reading on Arthur and Merlin but the Norse stuff, no clue what you're talking about. The Arthurian period, see, I did read a book or two," Zach chuckled. "It seems one writer says this, another says that, how do you know which way to turn?" he asked.

Michelle laughed lightly. "You don't, that's just it. I can go on for hours on all of the myth's, stories and what have you but you'd still end up scratching your head like you always did and pouring yourself another drink."

"I did that?"

"Every day," she snickered. "Does he still like to drink?" Michelle looked over at Riane.

"Very much," she confirmed with a nod of her head.

"Shocking," she giggled. "Your accent, is it English?"

"Yes," nodded Riane. "I am from north England."

"Very cool. Anyways, Merlin for the most part, was King Arthur's teacher, and friend. Merlin guided him while he was growing up and while Arthur was king. At some point, Merlin was either vanquished, or imprisoned by a student of his, Nimue, or in some texts she can also be the 'lady of the lake'. There's more I can tell you on that, but let's just stick with Merlin for now. He had apparently fallen in love with her and taught her everything he knew, and she in turn used it against him. He has never been seen since. While she went on to either kill her self at some point, or disappeared into the lake from whence she came. Either way, she died from most accounts. As for Merlin, some stories say he died in his prison created by Nimue, or he might still be in there. That all depends on who's telling the story at the time." Michelle took a sip of her drink and looked over at her two guests, who were listening intently.

"Is that the Coles notes version?" Zach joked.

"Pretty much," she grinned. "I knew the long version might bore you."

"So if I were to go to England and find this, um, historian guy, where would I start?"

"My guess would be The Museum of London, as good a

place as any to start. They actually have a medieval London exhibit, so that might be useful. Do you have an email address? I can forward some information to you if you'd like."

"Sure, that would help a lot. The same as it was before." He pulled out a pen and started writing on a piece of paper.

"Save your bad hand writing, I remember it, hard not to, number one cop zach, am I right?"

"Uh, yeah," he chuckled.

Michelle glanced over at Riane. "Is he that predictable with you too?"

"That all depends on the day," Riane replied with a wink.

"If I think of anything else I can toss in there, I will," Michelle added.

"Thanks, I appreciate it Michelle." Zach stood up and shook her hand again. She squeezed it hard and he grimaced. "I owe you one."

"I'll remember that," she said with a sly grin. "Now I have to get back to packing, I'm moving on to my new job next week so I have to get out of here by tomorrow."

"Good luck with your new job then. I'm sure you'll do great."

"Yes, thank you for your help and I wish you well on your new adventure," Riane smiled.

"Watch over him, he tends to get into trouble," Michelle grinned.

"I always do," Riane replied. They shook hands and she with Zach turned to leave.

Michelle watched them leave and then sat down back at her desk. She let out a deep sigh and then went on to her computer. Before she would do anything else she would get that information sent off or she might just forget about it with everything else she had to do that day. She looked down the hall for a moment, and a small smile adorned her face. It was nice to have some closure with Zach, though she had to admit, there was still some emotion there. Well, since they had now had finally closed the book on their relationship maybe in time that would disappear as well. Michelle pondered that for a moment and then went back to collecting the information he needed. Her new job overseas would surely help by keeping her busy at first and then what emotion there was would likely dissipate. Only time would tell.

The elevator door opened and Zach and Riane stepped out of yet another and into Neil's old law office. Riane and Zach wandered over to the receptionist and he introduced himself.

"Hi there, I'm Zach Thomas, I have a meeting with Matt Riordan."

"Yes, he's in his office down the hall, second door to the right. I'll let him know you are on the way," she smiled back. The lady picked up her phone as Zach motioned to Riane and the two of them were strolling down towards the lawyer's office just as the receptionist hung up the phone.

Zach paused in front of Riordan's door and knocked. A muffled 'come in' was said and both he and Riane entered. A disheveled heavier set man was seated behind a desk covered in papers and a box of donuts was open on an adjacent table. The man sipped down some coffee, the distinct aroma giving it away, and sat back as they entered.

"Hey there, grab a seat. I'm Matt Riordan, and you are, um, old friends of Neil's?"

"Yes we are," Zach replied.

"And how is he doing these days? Is he planning on

coming back to legal land sometime soon?" Riordan asked more as a plea as opposed to a question.

Zach grinned and shook his head. "Sorry, I don't think so."

"Crap, I was hoping otherwise."

Zach let out a chuckle and made himself comfortable in his chair. "I think this letter from him will pretty much explain that for you." He pulled out the envelope and handed it across the desk to Matt.

"A letter? Oh geez, that's never a good sign." Matt grumbled a few more colorful words and tore into the letter. He read it through, let out a few more snorts and then tossed the letter down on his desk. "He's leaving me the law firm. He made mention of some other forms he's supposed to provide to make that happen?"

"I don't have anything like that with me, but I'm sure those will come along in the not too distant future. He's a little busy at the moment," Zach replied.

"I'm sure he is," sighed Matt. "Well, he goes on to mention you may need a few things," Matt picked up the letter again and looked for something in particular. "Oh yeah, money, or whatever else I can provide you. For what?"

"We have a few things we need to take care of and Neil suggested you could help us if we needed it. Money, not so much. However, we have to travel overseas to England so if there is any way you can speed up the passport process, that would help a lot," Zach explained.

"You don't have passports?" the pudgy lawyer wondered out loud. "Who the hell doesn't have a passport these days? You can't do sweet tweet without one it seems."

"Well we would be two of those people," Zach quipped.

"Yes, indeed. Is there any way you can help us?" Riane

asked. She put on a smile and blinked to give her eyes a sad look to them.

Matt caved in completely with her mild flirtation. It was rare that any woman would so much as notice him let alone flirt. "Oh who am I to deny a pretty lady such as you a chance to do some traveling. Lucky for you, and you as well," he nodded to Zach. "That I have a friend who owes me big time. I saved his ass on a lot of alimony to his ex wife. So I think I might just be able to have those taken care of, with any luck, in the next couple of days."

"Neil wasn't kidding! You are good," Zach passed the compliment on. A bit of a lie but since Riane had been so good at flirting it was the least he could do.

Matt was barely even conscious of the remark and paid little attention to Zach. He wore a big grin on his face and smiled at Riane as he picked up the phone to make the call. A few words shared between him and his former client and within a few minutes he hung up the phone. He gave Riane another wink and she smiled back at him.

"Good news, he can speed up the process and have it ready the day after tomorrow. All I need to do is get a picture of both of you that he can use for the passports and presto it's done."

"Thank you very much sir, I really appreciate the effort you have put forth on our behalf," Riane added.

Zach looked at her, and he almost wanted to laugh out loud but restrained himself. She was really getting into this flirting thing!

"Glad to do my part to help. After all, you are a friend of Neil's. You be sure to tell him I'll keep his office ready, in case he ever changes his mind and wants to come back to the legal system."

Zach stood up and moved to stand between Riane and his gaze. "I will be sure to tell him that. Thanks for the help

Matt." Zach held out his hand and Matt reciprocated. They shook and Matt went about fumbling through his desk to find a camera he could use.

"I have that stupid camera in here someplace, ah, there it is," he muttered. Matt held up a digital camera of sorts and motioned for the two of them to go stand against the wall. "Smile pretty now, you are on Matt TV," he joked. "Well, camera, not really the TV."

"No, really?" Zach cracked. He couldn't help himself, the guy made it too easy.

"Oh be nice Zach, Matt is going to help us out even though he doesn't really have to. Where should I stand? Over here?" Rianed asked.

"That'll be perfect. Smile!" He urged.

Riane put on a picture perfect smile and struck a pose as though she was modeling. Zach shook his head in disbelief and had to really contain his desire to break out laughing. He took his turn, eventually. Matt had to take a few extra pictures of Riane just to make sure he got the 'right' one. With Zach, it was one quick shot and they were done.

"Okay, I'll get these over to my man over at the passport office and get it done for ya. Is there anything else you need?" Matt checked.

"Not off the top of my head, but if I come up with something I'll give you a call. Appreciate you seeing us, I'll be sure to pass a hello on to Neil from you," Zach said.

"You do that, and tell that son of a bitch I hope he's happy," Matt snickered. "I'm sure he is though. Ain't quite the same around here without him but I guess I'll have to make do. You two stop in the day after tomorrow and I'll have your passports ready."

"Thank you Matt," Riane said with a quick wink. He blushed and motioned for them to move on out. Zach took

Riane by the arm and the two of them left Matt Riordan behind to take care of business.

In the elevator Zach smiled as he faced Riane. She looked at him and shrugged her shoulders.

"What?"

"If you were flirting any harder, the guy might just ask you to marry him," he quipped.

"Whatever do you mean?" she replied with a small grin.

"You're really using this being human thing to your advantage aren't you?"

"Well, I can't help myself, it just, happens," she giggled. "I can't stop it."

Zach chortled and put his arm around her. "Well your charm worked wonders on old Matt in there. Just try and control it a little bit."

"No promises," she teased and gave him a kiss on the cheek. "Where to now? Shopping?"

Zach groaned. "Oh please don't tell me you've taken an interest in shopping?"

"I would like to try it, we have some time on our hands, so why not?"

"Ugh, because I hate shopping. But since we do have a little spare time, I'll go along with it this time. But in the future, don't get your hopes up," he sighed as he smiled at her.

"As you wish, where to first?"

"Not a clue, let's just walk and see where we end up."

"Okay, sounds good." Riane gave him a hug and together they exited the elevator to get started on their shopping 'spree'. Zach grimaced at the thought of it but decided it might not be so bad since he had Neil's credit card. Going shopping on somebody else's dollar was always a good thing.

Later that evening, after shopping all afternoon and spending money like it was going out of style, then enjoying a fine meal in the hotel restaurant the duo retired to their room for the night. Riane had lain down on the bed to watch some TV but Zach heard her snoring after a couple of minutes. He laughed quietly to himself. The poor girl was actually all shopped out. Never in his lifetime would he expect any woman to be tired of shopping! He poured himself a drink and logged on to the internet to do a little more surfing. Zach paused on the keyboard, wondering what he should type into the search engine. He thought back to earlier in the day when they had met with Michelle and for fun, typed in the words Merlin of England. A number of different sites popped up on the results page, but one of them caught his eye. He scrolled down and clicked on it.

A web page for a tea house in England came up and he read what was on the home page for the establishment. 'Merlin's Tea House – Friend of King Arthur & A Friend of You – Famous Tea's from the Island of Avalon'. Zach thought that was rather odd and read a little more. 'Tea's of every flavor and every taste, No matter where you may travel from around the world; this is where you can find the answer to the question, where do I go to find the best tea! Come on in, and you will find the answer to your question.' Zach sat back and took down a good swallow of his drink. That was the weirdest slogan he'd ever seen. 'Awful wordy' he thought to himself. He explored the site further and after he had gone through it page by page, word by word he exited and lay down next to Riane. For some strange reason, he had a strong desire to have a cup of tea.

Chapter Fifteen

Neil adjusted the straps on the saddle resting on his horse and turned around as Tasha came up behind him. She gave him a quick hug and ran over to her own horse to do the same with her gear. The last of the advance forces had arrived earlier this morning from the woodland elves as promised by Brielle. The Iceland elves had shown up late the previous evening and the others over the course of the night. There were a good many of the different races of the elves gathered in the courtyard and for Neil it was a sight. Each race had their distinct features whether it is clothing, hair color or style, or even manner of speech.

One race stood out just a tad more so, the Dark Elves, a race who rarely ventured outside their realm, had even replied to the call from Xanthus. They were a small group of approximately 50 but they were here and for Tasha that was enough. Brielle had welcomed them on behalf of her father and their leader, Riss, had been very courteous in response. The Dark elves resided in caverns Northwest in the mountains bordering the ice fields. They are the only elfin race that did not make their home above ground. It was the one common thread between them and the dwarves, but other than that, the dwarves who did not trust the elves in general, were even less trusting of the Dark Elves due to their seclusion. The Dark elf appearance was quite stunning, with pure white hair and darker skin that had the look of a good summer tan in comparison to their rather pale brethren. Their clothing consisted of dark brown shirts and pants with black cloaks which made the term 'Dark Elf' rather genuine.

The entire company was almost ready to depart as scheduled.

"Jacinto is going to be a little overwhelmed with all the elves riding with us," said Tasha with a chuckle.

"I'm sure he'll get used to it pretty quickly and once the fighting begins he won't even notice," snickered Neil.

"Is there anyone not ready to ride as yet?" she asked.

"I think everyone is pretty much set. I'll go take a quick roll call so we can get this thing going," said Neil. "Kieran!" he shouted.

"Yes my lord?"

"Gather all the captains so we can go over things quickly before we depart," Neil said as he walked up.

"Yes sir," he bowed. Kieran jogged off shouting orders as he did. Neil with Tasha joining him now that her horse was secure strode over to the center of the courtyard and waited for the rest of the Captains to join them. It did not take long for Kieran to round up everyone and in quick order they stood before them. Neil could not express how it felt to see all these men and women before him but it gave him some reassurance that maybe they could win this war against Helana.

"Everyone," he paused, "Thank you again for coming on such short notice, and committing your forces to what we are about to attempt. We won't be able to stop Helana, but I am sure we can give her some serious thought about all of us giving up without a fight. We will rendezvous with a force of men led by a friend of ours near the forest bordering Markham, from there we will ride as fast as we can and try to get to the dwarves before Helana does. Failing that, Thatcher here has said the falls west of Aberdeen will be our best place to inflict some damage on Helana's forces."

"Aye, both dwarf and gnome that be th'place to meet if we were to abandon our homes," Thatcher nodded.

"I remember the falls. It is a perfect place to launch a surprise attack," Brielle said.

"At this point we must assume the gnomes have left Eldridge because the witch has to be on the verge of her assault on that castle," Kieran stated.

"If so then the gnomes will be on the march. They and the dwarves might need some assistance just to put some distance between themselves and whatever the witch has for an army," Riss commented.

"Might it be best to let Aberdeen abandon itself and concentrate on launching our attack at the falls? We might spread ourselves too thin to accomplish anything at the falls if we try to defend Aberdeen as well," Elise suggested.

"The dwarves and gnomes might need some help, as Riss said to escape. Is there enough time to get them clear before Helana shows up?" Neil questioned the group.

"There might be as long as the dwarves have begun their evacuation. If they are being true to their nature, that is being stubborn and staying to fight, then we could be in some serious trouble before we even begin," Darg, the captain from the grey elves, stated.

"My friend is there, along with Axel and Ruskin, I have the utmost confidence he'll get them mobilized. If he can't, then the latter two sure will," Tasha chuckled.

"Ah yes, knowing them, I can vouch for that," Brielle snickered.

"Then we focus on setting up at the falls, and get the gnomes and dwarves to safety. We'll play it by ear once we get to the falls, agreed?" Neil checked.

"Agreed," everyone said in unison.

"Then let's ride, Jacinto might be getting a little antsy by now, we don't want to keep him waiting," Tasha urged.

"Let us move then," Brielle nodded. "Captains, safe journey!"

The group broke apart and each went to their separate companies. Neil and Tasha climbed on to their horses and with a wave set off out of the courtyard with his royal guard riding behind. As they rode, one by one, the companies fell into line behind. Brielle, Elise and the woodland elves flew in overhead as the woodland elves rode the gryphon. Those that watched were impressed but none knew what waited ahead, and for those that rode as well as those who watched were likely better off not knowing. On occasion it was better to not understand or have knowledge of what waited, and in this case, being ignorant of it all was a blessing in disguise.

At Aberdeen, Mia walked briskly along the catwalk with Tony. The dwarf's evacuation had finally progressed to a point where half of the population had left the castle and early that morning the first of the evacuee gnomes had passed by on their trek northward. It gave them some relief knowing that Shar had succeeded in getting Eldridge evacuated. So far though, there had been no sign of Shar or Adeena.

"I hope they aren't still there. From what I've heard from the dwarf scouting party, I would not want to be anywhere near Eldridge when that army arrives," Mia said.

"Yeah, that place hasn't got a chance. Hell, I don't even think what Axel and the others have set up here has any hope of putting a dent in that pack of thugs," Tony added.

"Demons and who knows what she might have conjured up? Did Axel say how much longer before the rest of the dwarves will be out of here?" she asked curiously.

"Hopefully by tomorrow, all that will be left will be a few to operate the contraptions they set up but that ain't my idea of fun."

"That is foolish suicide," she mumbled.

"I'm still tryin to get Axe and Ruskin to just leave it all. They can deal with Helana's army on our terms instead of hers."

"I wonder what Malcolm has planned?" she wondered.

"If Neil and Zach have any say in the matter, they'll have something goin on," he smiled at her.

"Look!" pointed Mia. Down below they could see more gnomes parading along, carrying packs and supplies. A few carts were being pulled by horses that had carried some of the smaller gnomes and others were hauling various odds and ends.

"Let's go and get our own rides ready, just in case," Tony warned.

"A very good idea, that odor is getting worse by the minute," Mia said.

"Since this morning I think it's beginning to stick to my clothes," Tony cracked. "It is really starting to get bad."

"Precedes what may be coming," Mia whispered.

Jacinto was waiting as promised near the forest edge on the outskirts of Markham, and he was equally impressed with the contingent that Neil and Tasha had brought along. His forces took their place in the throng and the large man who had become good friends of Neil and Tasha, and dependable in times of need, settled in beside the duo.

"I like this idea of meeting the witch before she can

make any inroads towards our homes- gives us a fightin chance," he grinned.

"I have no idea of what she has prepared for an army Jacinto, but we'll definitely give her something to think about," Neil assured his husky friend.

"My sword has been quiet as of late. It will be nice to swing it again, on something other than trees!"

"Rest assured my friend, you will have ample opportunity to swing that blade," Tasha added.

"I recommend we do not stop for the night and that will put us at the falls by morning," Kieran said.

"What of the dwarves?" asked Vasilis who had joined the company on the ride after his visit to the healers. He had trotted into the mix to catch up on what was going on

"We cannot stage a worthwhile defense if we push ourselves to get there, the falls is our best hope of stopping Helana, albeit for a short time only," Keiran replied. "I am impressed with your stamina Vasilis, I would have thought you might have stayed back to recoup a little more."

Vasilis shook his head and chuckled. "No thanks, I can rest after this is over with."

"We are glad you could make it," Tasha acknowledged.

"Anything to assist as best I can, your highness," Vasilis nodded.

"Then let us move on fellow riders. We have a witch to stop!" Jacinto bellowed as he lifted his sword. His men let out a shout in unison and the rest of the elf contingent joined in on the ruckus.

"On to the falls then, lead on Thatcher," Neil beckoned.

"It would be my honor sir," the gnome replied. He gave his horse a quick kick and the advance force moved on at full gallop.

Malcolm and Xanthus wandered through the ruins of what had been Tir Nan Og. Fire was everywhere; it had consumed and was still enveloping trees or plants that it had missed with a vengeance. There was nothing left alive and both were shocked and stunned at the appearance of the fairy realm. Several damaged iron weapons were strewn about, abandoned by the demon that had carried it. Malcolm winced at the thought of how many faerie had been killed and Xanthus paused to shake his head in disgust.

"This is unfathomable! I cannot believe she would destroy such a peaceful world," Malcolm scoffed. "She has gone beyond even what I thought possible."

"We must not forget my friend, she is sharing her mind with the demon, one fallen from faerie. There will be a strong desire to wreak havoc on those it once befriended."

"I do not know if this realm can ever be restored, it is too far gone," Malcolm said.

"We will have to revisit here when we have taken care of her and the demons, then we will see if it is possible for the fairy to return home."

"The castle I believe was over this way," Malcolm pointed.

The walk through the ravaged land was painful and slow as they avoided the fires with caution. As they crested a hill that would have given them a glorious view of the fairy castle where Leasha lived they were instead shown a sight that made both gag in horror. Rock was strewn everywhere, and smoke and fire filtered through what was left of the foundation of the castle. The once tall towers were gone, the walls torn apart, and the gate was in shambles, with pieces of stone and lumber cast over the landscape. Malcolm fell to his knees and gasped at the mess. Xanthus shed tears as he could not control his emotions with what had happened.

"The queen, my word, what of the queen," Xanthus murmured.

"She must still be alive, she must be. Helana would not invade this realm without a purpose, Leasha must still be alive," Malcolm stated with confidence.

"If she is, she cannot be for long. We must find her quickly," Xanthus said.

Malcolm looked around the stricken landscape and took notice of several new eruptions of smoke in the distance. The demons were still languishing in Tir Nan Og, making sure their job was thorough.

"That way my lord. They are working their way towards the mists."

"Where will they exit do you think?" Xanthus did not wait for Malcolm to reply before determining the answer on his own. "The gnomes, they plan to appear outside Eldridge."

"That is Helana's plan, to use the faerie queen as an example to the rest of us. To kill the faerie queen will show off her power. I will not allow that to happen," Malcolm said in anger.

"It will take both of us to free Leasha. It must be quick or we will fail and then she will make an example of all three of us," Xanthus pointed out.

"Yes, indeed. Hurry my lord; we must catch up to the demon before they exit Tir Nan Og."

Malcolm and Xanthus picked up the pace in pursuit of the demons within the fairy realm. The blazes in the distance were still erupting with regularity which gave hope of catching them before their exit. The two avoided the newly started fires as best they could, but on occasion they had to make a detour to avoid a rather large inferno still enveloping a grove of trees. On once such occasion a cry for 'help' barely audible above the roar of the fire made the two pause to make sure they had heard it. A repeat cry echoed amidst the ruins and the two began an immediate search to seek it out.

Both nearly stumbled across a stray demon that had fallen behind to toy with a couple faerie it had cornered against a smoldering tree stump. They managed to hide in behind some fallen debris before they were seen.

"Gotsssss u little globsssss of light," it sneered while waving its blade of iron.

"Let us go!" one fairy screamed while holding its brethren close.

"No little ones, ordersssss are to kill you all!" It let out a laugh and waved the blade threateningly, enjoying each moment of its torture of the two faerie.

Malcolm looked around the area to make sure this demon was by itself and then leaned in close to Xanthus. "I will take care of this! Stay hidden until I have dealt with this thing."

"Are you sure? It might alert the others?"

"I am confident it will do nothing of the sort," Malcolm promised. As he finished the sentence he morphed into the shape of a demon creature that even made Xanthus take a step back.

"I see what you mean," Xanthus grinned.

Malcolm in his new demon form stepped out from behind their cover and strolled up to the demon still torturing the two faerie. The demon did not see him until he was almost upon him and was a little startled at the sight.

"What you want? These two are mine!" it snapped in anger. The thought of losing its prey did not sit well with it.

"Have them all you want, I will find my own," Malcolm snapped back.

"None left, just these two, ssssss they are mine!" it repeated.

"Then kill them already and let us get back with the rest," Malcolm urged as he stepped in closer to the monster. The two faerie cowered closer to the tree stump as death appeared imminent.

"I will do when I ready!" the demon growled. It turned its focus back on the two faerie, turning its back to Malcolm as it did.

The wizard stepped in closer and touched the demon with his staff. The demon gurgled out a few words as it suddenly whirled around but in seconds it had turned to stone and then crumbled to ash. The two faerie stared at this other demon and slowly Malcolm morphed back into his usual appearance and smiled at the two.

"It is safe now, you are no longer in any danger," he assured them.

"Who," stammered one, "what?"

"I am Malcolm," he said. The two faerie recognized him upon hearing the name.

"Thank you sir," bowed one.

"Are you two the last still here?" he asked.

"Yes sir. We did not reach the castle in time to escape with the rest. There were others behind but they have been hunted down. We are all that are left here."

"Have you seen your queen by chance?" Malcolm wondered.

"Yes, she is being dragged by one of the demon, a very large one. They are moving that way," pointed one of the fairies.

"Thank you both, now, go through this door," Malcolm pointed. He spoke a few words and small opening of swirling mists congregated next to them. "It will take you to the elves to be with the rest of your kind. I will go and find your queen."

"We will take our leave then sir. Good luck; she is not in good shape."

"I will take care of her. Now go before any more demons decide to come looking for their missing friend."

The two faerie flew into the small opening and it closed immediately afterward. Malcolm stood tall and motioned for Xanthus to come out from his hiding spot.

"Very well done sir. I hope you can make us both look like that when we find the rest of them," Xanthus smiled. He wandered down to the wizard and Malcolm nodded in the direction they had to go.

"The queen is alive, but in bad condition. I think, from what the fairies have told me, she is being held by one of the wraith. It is the only demon large enough to capture her. We must hurry on. It will not be long before they reach the mists."

"At least we know she is still alive! That is some good news amidst all this destruction," Xanthus sighed. "I hope you have an idea of how we can get close enough to her. The wraith will not be as easy to fool as that demon."

"I am counting on the wraith focusing all its attention on other things. Come on my friend," Malcolm beckoned.

It was only a short time later when they discovered the entire demon horde. They were all at the edge of the mists, waiting for something to happen. Their wait wasn't too long before the mists started to break apart and an opening began to take shape. Malcolm and Xanthus watched from a safe distance behind a number of overturned boulders that at one time were part of a much larger faerie garden.

"The magic used to break into this realm has to be immense," Xanthus whispered.

"Her strength is escalating," Malcolm replied. "When

they begin to exit, we will transform and mix in with them. Stay close because we won't have much time to accomplish our escape."

"Understood," Xanthus nodded.

A couple of the large wraith emerged from the pack; one was dragging along the queen who by now could barely stand. She was being pulled along with a chain attached to a collar around her neck and the lady was scarred with cuts and bruises, her hair covered in dirt and soot from the ashes, and her clothing was torn. Leasha would fall but be yanked back up by an unsympathetic wraith.

"Out of my way,ssssssss," it hissed.

Xanthus and Malcolm both wanted to cry for Leasha and all that she was going through, but at the moment they had to wait for their chance to free her and worked hard at staying focused on the task at hand. The wraiths were the first to step into the opening and the remainder of the demons followed close behind.

"Now we go," Malcolm urged. As the two stepped out from behind cover, their bodies transformed into a couple fellow demons and the two took their place amongst the rest. The smell of the creatures was quite overpowering and Malcolm almost heaved but held it in and did his best to ignore the odor. Bit by bit the cluster of creatures, demon and otherwise, stepped into the breach that would take them out of a now decimated Tir Nan Og and back to Avalon.

Chapter Sixteen

Shar stood in one of the towers and watched as Helana's army took position outside of Eldridge. She could not fathom how many there were. They were everywhere you looked and who knew how many lay within the cover of the forest. The ground vibrated as they had approached and the stench of rot was almost unbearable. It was as described by the scouting party earlier, except this was now up close and personal. Shar wished she was elsewhere. She and Adeena had stayed behind to make sure every gnome had made their way out of Eldridge and at this point, besides themselves, there were only a select few remaining. As she stared at the army before the walls Shar was glad the evacuation was virtually complete. The army had situated itself and had done nothing since settling in, which was a bit unnerving!

"What are you waiting for?" she whispered.

One of the few gnomes still in Eldridge wandered in to the room and spoke quietly to the mage. "My lady, we have set a few of th' assault traps as a precaution to help hide our escape. Is there anythin you need?" he asked.

"No, just be ready to go once I figure out what they're up to," Shar replied. She looked back at the gnome and smiled reassuringly. "I would get the others down to the tunnels, just in case they move quickly."

"Aye m'lady, I will see to it personally," he nodded and left the room. Adeena was next to show herself and the sprite moved to stand next to Shar. She frowned at the sight below and rubbed her nose in disgust.

"My they smell, ugh, what are we waiting for?" she asked impatiently.

"I need to know what we're up against, shhhh," Shar hushed her.

"Smelly, rotting and really ugly trolls," Adeena cracked. "I really don't like those flying things," she pointed to the tree tops where several of the creatures were hovering.

"Yes, I have no idea what they are but we best stay out of sight," Shar replied quietly.

Below, the trolls, demons and the risen soldiers milled around impatiently. Helana's orders upon departure were to wait upon arriving and not to begin their assault. They would wait until told otherwise.

"Why do we have to wait is what I'd like to know," grumbled one commander.

"We do as we're told, or would you rather be dust again?" another snapped.

"No, but standing around here is not accomplishing anything either," he retorted.

"She has a plan, and we must do as she asks."

A breeze erupted abruptly and the trees began to sway in its grasp. The army looked around curiously, wondering what was causing the sudden gusts when a mist began to form near the castle walls. The General in charge of the entire horde stepped forward and smiled. The wraiths were returning from the faerie realm. Soon Helana would arrive as well and then this would be the first kingdom to fall under her wrath and therefore would begin her domination of Avalon.

The mist thickened and then began to split as the door to the fairie realm began to open. The first wraith bearing the faerie queen in tow with her chain leash stepped out of the whirling mists and pulled the queen in next to it.

Shar watched as the mists began to form and then part and gasped as the wraith had emerged, dragging Leasha with it. The fairy queen did not look well and could barely stand. The wraith would tug on the leash and drag her to a standing position every time she began to fall to her knees. So this was what they were waiting for but Shar felt there was more to it than just bringing Leasha out of Tir Nan Og. That would serve no real purpose. The rest of the demons and other wraith stepped out of the doorway and moved off to the side awaiting their next orders. Shar could not believe the number of demons emerging from the vortex, and the wraith that guided them were different than she had seen before.

The wraith stepped towards the man it recognized, the general given command by Helana, and held the faerie queen up to show off his prize.

"We have the queen asssssssss requesssssssted by her," it hissed. "Issssss sssssshe near?"

The General looked at the fairy and then back at the wraith. "She will be here momentarily. Be patient. A job well done! She will be very pleased with the result. What of the other sidhe?"

"Dead, or esssssscaped, land gone, dessssstroyed asssssss ssssshe sssssaid to do."

"Good," the general nodded. "Keep her near; don't let her die just yet!

Adeena shook her head. "This is not good Shar, we have to do something!"

"We cannot do anything right now. We have to wait," Shar replied.

"If we wait my queen will die!"

Shar faced Adeena and put her hands on her friend's shoulders. "I know you're worried about her, but right now, we cannot do anything. I will not let her die if I can help it."

"You swear," Adeena asked imploringly.

"If necessary I will do what I can to help her," Shar assured her.

A blast of thunder, followed by flashes of lightening interrupted their conversation and both returned to the window to see what was going on. The rabble of Helana's army had begun to move back closer to the forest just as the lightening struck the ground just outside the walls of Eldridge. Where the lightening struck, a funnel of cloud had begun to form, almost taking on the shape of a tornado tail that would reach down from the sky just before touching down. Out of the cloud stepped Helana, and the demons all screeched in delight upon seeing her. She raised her hands to silence them and turned to her general in command.

"Is the assault ready to begin?" she asked.

"As soon as you give the word my queen," he bowed.

"You will have it as soon as I deal with one other small issue," she smiled wickedly. Helana glanced over at the wraith holding the fairy by the chain and strode over to the Queen of a dead land and knelt down in front of Leasha.

"Faerie queen, nice to see you, again," Helana hissed.

Leasha forced herself to look at the witch even as the pain of the iron and beatings pulsated through her body. "I do not know you."

"We met once, when I was a mere student of Malcolm's years ago. You ignored me for the most part. This time you can't because I will not let you *sidhe*."

"Sidhe," the queen whispered, "a name only the demon use," Leasha scoffed. The wraith gave a quick pull of the chain and the queen winced in agony.

"Perhaps, but then they were once fairie, *tamen es haud magis*," Helana retorted.

Leasha looked at her, fear showing for the first time. A language she had not heard in centuries, the language of the old fairy and of the ancient elves. A language abandoned as the races had evolved over time. It was a language only the demons had maintained because darkness does not evolve, but festers in its own world.

"But are no more," Leasha whispered the words back.

"Yes, are no more," Helana nodded.

"You are still somewhat human witch, or you would have come into my home on your own to do your minions work, but why use a language we have left alone? Or is the human in you dead after all?"

"No, I am still human, but the power of the demon is in me now and together we will be unstoppable. Which brings us to you, I am going to kill you and show all the races the capability of my power and you are the perfect example to demonstrate such."

Leasha slumped low again, only to be brought back up to a standing position by another yank of the chain by the wraith. "Then do it and get this over with."

"Patience queen of a dead realm, first, I need to get their attention." Helana smiled and turned to face the walls of Eldridge castle. "***Gnomes! I know you are in there, I want you to watch what I am about to do to the so revered Queen of Faerie! Do you hear me Gnomes? The Queen of faerie shall die this day and you will be the witness to it! Those who hear my words elsewhere, you will bow down to me, or you will die like she is about to!***" She bellowed, her voice echoing over the walls and beyond. The echo of her words floating over the land, until the dwarves heard the echo at Aberdeen. Then the citizens of Fairgrove heard the words, and then the advance army stopped in its tracks to hear what the witch had said. The elves at Cambridge soon heard the threat as did all who camped outside its walls. Helana's threat reverberated over all of Avalon, and there was not one individual who did not stop to listen.

"The queen," whispered Tasha as she pulled back on the reins of her horse. She and the entire advance forces came to a stop to hear the words of the witch as they floated over them on the wind.

"Is it possible?" Neil asked.

"Anything is possible now; I hope Malcolm is near, he might be able to do something."

"Maybe Shar is still nearby?" Neil said with a shrug, his comment merely a thought of vain hope.

"She is no match for Helana," Tasha shook her head. "This cannot be."

They listened for more and the wind soon brought the words the group did not want to hear.

Shar held back her desire to spring into action because Malcolm had warned her to not expose herself or her abilities unless absolutely necessary. Her mind raced with options, but all she kept returning to was that she had to do something to save Leasha. Adeena was in tears as she looked up to her for an answer, an offer of help but she had nothing for her friend. Each returned to the window as Helana spoke again.

"My power is growing as each new day passes and soon not even your guardian Malcolm will be able to stop me! Bear witness to the end of faerie and the beginning of my reign as your queen!"

Helana did not notice two of the demons edging their way closer to the wraith that held Leasha. She was so self absorbed with her announcement that the two demon were able to get right next to the wraith. Even the wraith failed to notice the rather two brazen demons getting close. Helana turned her attention back to Leasha but still did not pay attention to the two demons situated behind the fairy queen.

"Now that I have everyone's attention, I think my lady that you have outlived your usefulness. Soon enough I will find the rest of your kind and do away with them or convert them over to my new order. All of you will soon be extinct."

Leasha fixated her gaze on Helana. "My realm is but one of a few witch, you cannot kill us all."

"Oh yes I will, once I cross over to the old world I will do the same there as I have done here. You and your sidhe will be gone, forever," Helana replied. The venom in her voice made Leasha cry in despair as she realized the demon witch would do exactly as she promised. The tears slipped down along her cheeks to her chin and then falling silently to the ground. She had no hope left, her spirit was broken and all of her resistance was vanquished. Leasha used what energy she had left to try and stand and face her death as proud as she could.

The demons began to howl anxiously, their patience was gone after a long march and all were eager to start tearing into the gnome castle. Helana moved to stand before her army and she admired their desire, their hatred and how eager they were to satisfy her orders. She reveled in it for a time basking in the power of it all and then she turned around to face Leasha.

"Now we begin my reign as queen of all the land," Helana said. She took notice then of the two demons who had circled in behind Leasha and both had their arms around her. It was odd to see the demons doing such a thing and she had to stop and think about their actions.

"What are you two doing?" She snapped angrily.

The two demons changed shape then and before her stood Malcolm and Xanthus, the two men she hated most. Malcolm smiled and winked at her and spoke a phrase she recognized all too well. In a flash he, Xanthus and the fairy queen vanished from sight as the amulets flared to life and transported them away in a blinding array of lights and wind. Her prisoner was now gone, the wraith stood there holding an empty leash and looked at Helana abruptly, immediately fearing the wrath of the demon witch.

Helana was too dumbfounded at first, and wondered how the two men had managed to find her, let alone the fairy queen. Then her anger boiled over and she let loose a volley of magical waves that scorched the immediate surrounding area, destroying anything and everything, including the wraith and demons that had strayed too near. She faced the walls of Eldridge then and began to chant an incantation.

Shar felt something extremely dangerous in the magic being formed and she grabbed Adeena by the arm. "We must go, now!"

The mage and sprite ran as fast as they could, all the while Helana's magic grew, and Shar could feel its power. They had to be as far away as possible or they would not live to see the next day. Down the halls they bolted, reaching the stairs that would take them down to the tunnels and out of Eldridge. Adeena changed into her true fairy self and flew on ahead, with Shar running as quickly as she could behind her.

Helana's words grew in strength, their sound reverberating over the walls of Eldridge. The stone began to shake and the dark army stood back, shrinking back into the forest for protection from what the witch was about to do.

Shar reached the bottom of the stairs, gasping for air and pointed to the remaining gnomes. "Ride! Ride now!"

There was such urgency in her words that the gnomes did not wait to ask her why, they merely obeyed and were off at full gallop down the tunnel ahead. Shar leapt on her horse in one fluid motion and gave it a swift kick. Adeena, still in her sprite form, flew alongside her friends as together they fled, racing on ahead of the ever growing incantation of Helana. The magic was reaching its zenith as the walls of the tunnel were beginning to crack, and dust began to fall. They were almost out of time. On they galloped, pushing their horses as hard as they dared in the confined space before their very means of escape would turn into their final resting place.

Helana unleashed all her fury then! She screamed with such fervor that her entire army cowered in fear. The scream resonated over all of Avalon as the magic was let loose. It slammed into the walls of Eldridge in a giant wave and the walls disintegrated at its touch. Wall upon wall, building upon building collapsed and turned to dust as the magic expanded inward on the gnome kingdom. The wave continued on, leaving nothing standing. The land surrounding the castle shook from the force, and many of the demonkind were unable to stand from the vibration. The magic reached the lower chambers and the walls buckled and imploded. The escape tunnels began to cave in and those fleeing could hear the noise grow louder as they raced on to reach the end of the route.

The gnomes reached the opening first and did not hesitate in getting clear of the collapsing tunnel. They emerged and kept on riding hard as they did so down the trail the previous evacuees had taken. Shar turned to look back and saw the stone walls falling, closing in, and catching up to her. She gave her horse another kick and held on for life as the magic neared. Adeena flew out of the escape tunnel first and paused to make sure her friend would get clear. Shar and her horse jumped free of the tunnels as the last of the magic took hold and pulled the tunnel down into a solid wall of rock. The mage only took a last glance back of what had been the kingdom of Eldridge. The magic that had been used was incredible! How would she be able to put up any sort of defense against it? Shar did not dwell on the thought but shoved it aside for the time and nodded to Adeena to keep moving. With any luck they would reach the dwarves and Aberdeen in less than a day. The dark army would not be far behind, and this time would be even more frenetic for destruction after having been denied the chance to wreak havoc on Eldridge.

Helana was breathing hard, and fell to her knees, drained from the magic she had just used. She looked skyward and spoke a warning to the one man she knew would be listening. The words she spoke resonated over Avalon to reach her former teacher.

"***You escaped this time Malcolm! Next time you will not be so lucky! You hear me wizard! Next time I will win the war of magic's!***"

Malcolm stood in the courtyard of Cambridge and listened to the threat. A threat she would very well follow through on. He turned his attention back to Leasha as he and Xanthus held the fairy queen to keep her from falling over. A number of elves raced up to help and he nodded to them.

"Get her to the healers immediately! She is not well!" he instructed. The elves nodded in acknowledgement and together they carried the now sleeping fairy away to take care of her.

Xanthus faced his friend. "Very well played sir."

"Thank you. It was both of us who pulled off the impossible," Malcolm winked. "I am going to prepare myself to join the forces on the march to the falls."

"Do you think that is wise? Helana may be looking for you now and your presence could risk the very element of surprise we have against her."

Malcolm paused in thought. The elf king made a valid point. "Perhaps, I can do more here in preparation for her arrival. Shar will be joining them shortly and she can use her abilities to help." Malcolm sighed and leaned on his staff. "One small victory but now I leave the king and queen alone, on their own, again."

"I understand my friend," Xanthus patted his friend on the back. "They have more of a chance to succeed without our presence. We have saved the queen of faerie, and that my friend, is a small victory we needed."

"Indeed."

Tasha looked at Neil and a grin adorned her face. "Malcolm did it! The queen must be safe."

"I think you might be right, but, that means she's going to get even madder as she keeps coming," Neil replied.

"If I were to take a safe guess, we might not see Malcolm join us, for that very reason my dear. Let's hope we find Tony, Shar and Adeena with the rest at the falls."

"Yeah, I sure hope so." Neil looked back at the company and waved them on to continue their march. With a kick to his horse all were riding at a gallop once more with the hopes of reaching the falls that much sooner.

Helana was breathing hard, and fell forward, her arms outstretched to hold herself up. The magic had left her weakened, but the end result had been achieved. Eldridge, the gnome kingdom was nothing but rubble. Dust still filtered skyward and the occasional rock would tumble from its perch as the debris shifted. There was nothing remaining of what had been a castle. The demon army had watched in disbelief as it happened and the general in command risked venturing near the witch.

"My queen, are you all right?"

"I will be fine in time. Get them on to Aberdeen. This time you can start your attack without my word. Go, and let them destroy everything and everyone that gets in their way."

"But, with your magic, you can just do to them, what you just did here," the general commented.

Helana looked up at the general and shook her head. "No, it takes too much of my power and leaves me weak. I want all my strength when I face them again, I want them groveling for mercy as I rip them apart. Let the army have their fun. Let them do as they wish. I must return to rest, and replenish my magic. I will see you again in a few days."

"As you command my queen," he bowed.

Helana spoke a phrase and slowly vanished in a whirl of wind and blue light. The general turned to face the army and pointed to the north. "Onward to Aberdeen! It is time to kill some dwarves!"

The horde let out a screech of excitement and began moving quickly on to the north, each general taking charge of their division and organizing them for a quicker march, determined to breach the walls of Aberdeen within a day.

Chapter Seventeen

Zach stepped out the doors of Heathrow airport and took in a breath of air. It was a tad more humid but the aroma of flowers and fresh cut grass greeted him along with the smell of a bakery and freshly baked bread. That was weird but this was after all, someplace new to him. He looked around, taking in the sights and sounds, and chuckled. Matt Riordan had come through on his promise to arrange their passports and two days after collecting them make travel arrangements. Here they were standing on a sidewalk outside one of the largest airports in the world waiting for a taxi in London, England.

After relaxing in Bar 5 with a couple drinks after arriving, Riane had been enthralled with the optic displays, both of them were ready to get to their hotel and begin the improbable quest of finding someone who supposedly existed, but according to any sort of recorded history, likely did not. Riane was watching the jets fly in and out and much like back in Seattle. She was completely excited about yet another new location to visit. Zach glanced around and took in another breath of air. There was something about this place that felt different than back home in Seattle. He couldn't put a finger on it but he just shrugged it off as a tourist thing and motioned for a taxi. They climbed in.

"Welcome to London! Where you two comin from?" the cab driver asked in his very noticeable English accent.

"Overseas, but the lady was originally from here," Zach replied.

The cab driver looked back at Riane and gave her a big grin, "Well then, welcome home would be in order."

Riane nodded and smiled back. "Thank you sir."

"Where you two off to?"

"The Park Plaza Riverbank London, on, um," Zach fumbled for the information he had gathered online prior to their departure.

"Oh yes, know it well, on 18 Albert Embankment. Nice choice for th'stay, very nice hotel."

"Good to know," Zach acknowledged.

"Then let us get you two over an' settled in, and I hope you enjoy th'stay."

Zach chuckled at the driver and his very obvious efforts to get himself a sizeable tip upon arriving at the hotel. Since it wasn't his money he was spending, he would be more than happy to oblige him. In moments they were off to their hotel, and their next temporary home until their quest was complete.

They checked in to their room after almost an hour of driving and made themselves at home as best they could. Zach opened up his laptop he had acquired back in Seattle and fired it up so he could begin his search for places and their locations. Of course there were a few things Riane wanted to see as well, including Big Ben which was only a short walk away and Buckingham Palace. Both attractions were on their agenda for the day, so the trip wasn't just a complete business venture. After all, Zach had never been here either and he was just as curious as she was to see such legendary landmarks. After some sight seeing they would begin the business of trying to find the man for whom they were looking. The belief that a legend was actually alive and well in the present day seemed a bit of a stretch to Zach, but Riane had the utmost confidence they would indeed locate the man of myth and legends.

"I want to take a quick shower. Can you make us some tea?" Riane asked as she started for the bathroom.

"Sure, I guess so. I have an urge to try some as well," he joked.

"Really? I don't see you as a tea drinker my dear," she teased. "After watching you drink a couple cups of that coffee stuff each day since arriving on this world, seeing you with a cup of tea would be very, odd," Riane commented with a grin.

"Tea on its way, go shower," he pointed to the door. "I'll show you who's odd," he murmured. Zach went about making some tea as Riane took her shower and changed. They both drank up their tea and embarked on their sightseeing tour before visiting The Museum of London, which would be both a tour and work combined into one.

With map in one hand, and directions to each location in the other, both strode out into the streets of London to take in a few of the sights, sounds and smells. The jaunt over to Big Ben which adorned the north end of Palace of Westminster wasn't that long of a walk, and they admired the majestic view of the Thames River on their way over as they crossed the Westminster Bridge to get a different view of things. After posing for several pictures and stopping for a bite to eat, they meandered over to Buckingham Palace to take in the changing of the guard. They managed to get there in time to see it begin.

"Excellent timing," Riane said with a smile. "There is so much to see, and do, but we won't have time to see it all will we?" She looked at him hopefully, but she knew full well it was wishful thinking.

"Sadly no, but once we get everything taken care back on Avalon, we'll come back. How does that sound? We can take some time and travel around back here, we'll go all over the place, sort of a real vacation," Zach suggested.

"Really? That would be very nice, and then I say we promise to do just that."

"I promise," Zach nodded.

"And I as well," Riane reiterated the promise. She leaned in and gave him a kiss and then they returned their attention back to the changing of the guard and all that went with it.

Zach watched the ceremony and all the while glimpsed around at the whole area, taking in this, noticing that, and each time his gaze returned to the castle itself. There was something about it that caught his attention each and every time. He took a few pictures of it, but still couldn't put his finger on why he was so fascinated by it. Zach chuckled to himself, 'boy am I getting caught up in all this sightseeing stuff' he thought. It was a nice refreshing change from all that was happening back on the world of Avalon, and he wondered why he hadn't done more traveling before? There was so much to see, so many places to explore! That could apply back on Avalon as well. The land was vast and he had barely even ventured outside the areas he already knew! He nodded to himself after making a promise to not only Riane but to himself to see, experience and to live more.

Together they watched the ceremony come to a finish and made plans to take a tour of the castle a little later after grabbing a bite to eat first. The remainder of the day was spent relaxing, and taking in their new surroundings. For Riane it was a chance to see where the elves had come from long long ago and for Zach it was just a nice change of pace.

The tour of Buckingham was fun, and both made sure to take in all of the tour, at times falling behind and being ushered back up to the group to keep from getting into trouble. Once they were back outside they paused to sit down and determine their next course of action.

"That was fun, I can't believe the queen still lives there," Riane said as she put her arm around him.

"Ah well, everything seems to be a tourist attraction these days," Zach joked. "It's a little different than Cambridge back home huh?'

She nodded. "A bit, but still very interesting. How did you like it?"

"Felt like home," Zach cracked. "Wanted to put my feet up on a couch and watch TV." He laughed lightly and gave her a kiss. "I say we hit the museum before it gets too late, and then maybe we hit one of those tea houses or something, so we can say we did it."

"Aren't we the adventurous one?" Riane teased. "Getting a bit of a taste for th'tea are we?"

"Maybe just a little," Zach laughed with her as they surveyed the map of London to get the location of the museum. Once they knew their route they were off again! This time their journey would take them to LondonWall at the junction of Aldersgate Street, and into the Museum of London. Where they would go from there, well, they had absolutely no idea.

The tour of the museum was interesting and it took a few queries to locate someone who might know a thing or two about medieval history. Finally one man, a young student who was actually interning on his free days, brought them to a small office near the medieval showcase and showed some genuine interest in their questions.

"How old are you?" Zach asked curiously.

"22 sir, but I'm wise beyond my years," the student joked. "At least that's what my professor says."

"I'm sure he does," Zach sighed. "So, Kerry, is it?"

"Yes."

"Kerry, what do you know about Merlin? Anything at all?"

"Well, he's a mythical wizard, who may, or may not have existed at one point in history. No one really knows there isn't any documented proof of his existence, just stories that are passed on from generation to generation. There are a few passages here and there about a 'wizard' of sorts, if you will but nothing of any significance. Was there anything in particular you were looking for?" Kerry asked. Zach scratched his cheek after hearing a rerun of what Michelle had already told him and shrugged at the student's question.

"Where we might find him," Zach chuckled and Kerry laughed with him.

"Good one sir," Kerry winked.

"Yeah, I know. Are there any, um, places, where if you or I were a wizard, we'd like to go and hang out?"

"Like a magic shop?" Kerry shrugged, unsure of how to answer that.

"Well sure, but are there like, gatherings or meetings of sorts, someplace? There are druids still in existence these days, at least that's what I've been reading about. They must meet every once in a while to talk, or drink coffee."

"Tea," corrected Riane with a small chuckle.

"Right, tea," Zach said. "Anyplace for stuff like that?"

"Wish I could help you on that, but I don't really know much about those who practice druidism, my major is more on the historical side of things."

Zach sighed; they had reached yet another impasse on trying to find any sort of location to start their search for

Merlin. The student was eager to help but lacked any real knowledge of what they needed.

"So where are these magic shops?" Riane asked curiously.

"I can write a few down for you, my cousin likes to pretend she's knows something about magic. She's been to a few. Just give me a moment," Kerry said as he went about trying to find a pen and paper.

Zach leaned in close to whisper in Riane's ear. "Magic shops?"

"We have to begin somewhere, may as well start there," Riane replied.

"I guess your right, as good a place as any I suppose."

Kerry handed over a piece of paper with a few names and addresses and Riane thanked him for the help.

"Wish I could be more helpful, but the person replacing the retiring Mr. Wren won't be here till next week," Kerry apologized.

"That's okay Kerry, you've been a big help," Zach smiled at the student. "We won't keep you any longer, but thanks again."

"Anytime, enjoy th'stay here, I do hope it is a good one." Kerry accompanied them back to the gallery and bid his farewell as he ran off to take care of other errands. Zach and Riane were left to ponder where they would go next.

"Well, that was a complete waste of time," Zach muttered. "We're no further ahead than we were back in Seattle."

"Quite true, but we do have a few magic shops to check out," Riane smiled. "It is something."

"Well, let's hope we can find something there. So, up for some late afternoon tea?"

Riane nodded. "My, yes I am. Where shall we go?"

"I found some tea shop online before we came over here,

it caught my eye. It is supposed to offer up all kinds of teas from Avalon believe it or not."

"Where is it?" Riane asked.

"In some park, Raven something or other, I think." Zach opened up the map of London once again and found the park he was looking for. "Yes, its Ravenscourt park, not all that far from here."

The cab ride over to the park wasn't too long and they were breathing in the fresh scent of the trees the moment they stepped out onto the walkway. After paying the cab fare the two of them moved into the park and followed the signs that led them to a tea house, an actual old house that had been transformed into a tea shop. Zach stood and stared at the place for a moment, and gazed at the sign above the front door.

"Merlin's tea shop," he murmured.

"Now what are the odds that a tea shop would be named after Merlin?" Riane wondered aloud. "The very man we're looking for."

"Oh about a million to one, come on, I'm curious to see what kind of tea this place has," Zach urged.

Zach grabbed the door knob and turned it. Upon entering a bell attached just above the door jingled as it swung open. A young lady working behind the counter looked up and smiled at them. An elderly couple was just finishing paying for their order and the woman waved good-bye to them as the two ambled out of the tea shop. Zach looked around the establishment and took notice of the various paintings adorning the walls. He slowly walked around looking at them while Riane walked up to order herself some tea.

He came to a stop in front of one painting and looked at it curiously. A knight holding a sword was the centerpiece of it all, with a castle in the background. The young lady behind the counter wandered out to see if he wanted anything to drink. An older gentleman leaned over the railing from the upstairs loft and took notice of the new visitors.

"Excuse me; your lady friend suggested I ask you if there were something you wanted. She was not too sure of what tea you would like."

Zach turned to look at her and then pointed to the picture. "Who is this supposed to be?"

"That is King Arthur; the castle in the background was Camelot, home of the Knights of the Round Table. Do you know anything about them?" she wondered.

"A little, I've been doing a lot of research lately so I might know some, but not a whole lot. Um, I'll just have some tea from Avalon that you were advertising on your website," Zach replied.

The young lady looked a little surprised at the comment he had just made.

"What?" Zach asked.

"You are the first person to mention the website, I find that rather, curious," she said with a shrug.

"The first? You must not get many surfers to your website then," he cracked.

"We've only had it up for a couple days thus far; I wasn't really expecting to get feedback so soon. As for the tea from Avalon, we have many to choose from."

"Surprise me then," he smiled. "Is the owner of this establishment around by chance?"

"Yes, he is. I'll see if he's available," she replied. The lady returned to the counter, glancing upstairs as she did. The elder man nodded back down to her and he vanished from view. The waitress made up both orders of tea and brought them out to their table.

"Are you in town for a visit?" she asked while placing the tea on the table.

"We stand out that much do we?" Zach laughed lightly.

"Just a little," the woman teased.

"Yes, we are in for a visit, and it has been quite the experience so far," Riane said.

"What brings you our way?" the waitress asked.

"Oh we're here to see a few of the sights, see if we can find someone, you know, the usual," Zach quipped.

"Really now, well then, good luck and enjoy your tea," she bowed.

Zach thanked her and as he did heard footsteps on the stairs that led up to the loft. Riane sipped her tea and paid little attention to the man walking down. Zach however did. The elder man was rather distinguished in appearance. He had short cut grey hair, his beard short as well, and his mustache well trimmed. He wore a simple pair of brown dress pants with a white sweater and grey vest over top of it. Zach had no idea how old the man was but he looked to be in rather good shape regardless. The man approached their table and Zach stood up to greet him.

"You must be the owner of the place?" Zach asked.

"I am indeed, and, what do you think?" the gentleman returned the question.

"Quite nice, very down home," Zach replied.

"I am glad you like it." The man glanced at Riane, and squinted for a moment. "My my, this lovely lady is a sight for the eyes."

Riane blushed and stood up, nodding to him as she did. "Thank you sir."

"So what brings you to our side of the world Mr. Thomas?" the man asked.

"Vacation, sight seeing," Zach replied. He failed to notice the man using his name in the question.

"Is that so, well, the tea is to your liking I hope?"

"Yes, I'm starting to get used to it. My lady friend here has me almost converted from coffee," Zach laughed lightly. "You promote it as being from Avalon, but, is there such a place or is that just part of your marketing strategy?"

"What do you think?" A question returned instead of an answer and Zach was getting a little curious about the man.

Zach shrugged. "What do I think? I think you do a good job of marketing, since Avalon really doesn't exist."

"Is that so? Well don't tell anyone around here, after all, legend has it that Arthur over there in that picture you were admiring is buried there," the man winked.

Zach was really curious now. "Do you know much about Arthur?"

The man motioned for Zach and Riane to sit down and he joined them, pulling up a chair and sitting across from them. "I know a good deal about the man, and other things. You mentioned to my manager that you were looking for someone. Anyone in particular?"

The young lady, the manager, brought over a cup of tea for her boss and he accepted with a smile. She returned to the counter and went about cleaning up. The elder man took a sip and nodded his approval of the choice of tea. He repeated the question.

"You were looking for someone?"

"Um, just someone who might be a specialist in medieval histories," Zach answered.

"Really now? Well, I'm quite good in that area; why not try me with a question or two?"

That sounded like a challenge to Zach and he couldn't resist. "Okay then, did Arthur really have a group of knights?"

"Yes, he did. Quite the group to I might add, always getting into trouble. Next question?"

Rather vague, but Zach continued on. "Where do you get your tea from?"

"Avalon, as we promote in our marketing strategy, as you put it. Another question?"

"What is Avalon?"

"A small island off the coast well protected from everyone. Next question?"

"Where is Avalon?"

"I already told you, next question."

"That wasn't really an answer," Zach said.

The young manager couldn't help but get her own comment in. "Tell me about it, I get that all the time."

"Falon, let the man finish his queries, he is after all a visitor here," the man said and encouraged Zach to continue. "Next question?" Zach thought carefully for a moment on what he wanted to ask him next and an idea hit him.

"Do you know what an elf is?" Zach grinned at what he thought was a trick question.

The man smiled. "You really want me to answer that?"

"Yes, I do."

The gentleman turned to face Riane. "You are quite the attractive woman my lady, but what of your true nature?"

Riane looked confused. "I do not know what you mean?"

"I think you do," he winked. The man passed his hand over Riane's face and as he did her human face morphed back into the elf she really was. Zach's jaw dropped and the young manager of the tea house smiled at the sight.

"My word, a true elf," she whispered.

Zach stood up abruptly and stared at the man. The owner of the tea house swept his hand back over Riane's features and she returned to the human form that Malcolm had given her. The man stood and turned back to Zach.

"You say you were looking for someone, well Mr. Thomas, it appears you've found who you've been looking for."

Zach could not contemplate what the man had just said and stood there, disbelief, shock, and a string of many other emotions racing through his body. Zach looked at Riane, then the young lady who the man had called Falon, and then finally his gaze returned to the man himself. It hit him then, the man knew his name.

"How do you know who I am?"

"Your signature on your traveler's cheques," the man cracked with a grin.

"Oh," Zach murmured.

"You were expecting some other answer?"

"Actually yeah, I was waiting for you to say magic or something like that," Zach said.

"Well I might have used a little bit," he winked, "I did use magic on your lady friend."

"Good point, so how did you know she was an elf?"

"That my friend caught me a little off guard, but," the man chuckled. "A good spell, but nothing too hard to see through, for myself that is, once I realized what was going on."

Zach looked around the room, it was empty, and they were the only people in the place. He scratched his chin, rubbed his neck and let out a sigh. This tea shop had been named after the man himself, but that was too coincidental, or was it? The man had used magic easy enough to unmask Riane! Could it be that easy? A tea shop run by the very master wizard he had been sent to find. At this point it couldn't hurt to ask, they really had nothing to lose

"So, are you," he paused before saying the name he thought he would never actually say to a living person, "Merlin?"

Chapter Eighteen

Shar and Adeena arrived at Aberdeen after a hard ride from their narrow escape at Eldridge. Their horses were exhausted, and so were they. The dwarf home jutted out through the mists shrouding the mountainside and to the duo it was a very welcome sight. The gnomes who had fled with them were already riding at full gallop to the gate and both mage and fairy had opted to take their time and let their horses have a chance to rest. Their stay here would be short. The dark army would not be too far behind and after the experience they just had, neither wanted to be around when they arrived.

"I wonder how many are still left?" Shar wondered out loud.

"Oh, knowing Axel and Ruskin, they're probably all still here waiting to put up a fight," Adeena scoffed.

"Now Adeena, I'm sure they tried to use common sense on their fellow dwarves," Shar smiled.

"Only if ale was involved," Adeena quipped.

At the gate, a lone dwarf greeted them. The dwarf wasn't his usual argumentative self and that only told Shar that even the dwarves were on edge over this entire matter. The gate opened enough to let them pass through and the small company entered into a rather quiet courtyard. On a normal visit there would be dwarves all over milling about but today there were only a scattered few. To their surprise, Axel and Ruskin appeared from a doorway and greeted the group.

"Well well, if it isn't th'lady Shar an'er tiny trouble maker," Axel grunted.

"Boys, it is good to see you again, but at the same time, why are you here?" Shar asked. Adeena merely frowned at the two and managed to refrain from returning her own remark.

"We came ta make sure we get th'place ready fer th'witch, an' to get th'rest of us outta here," Ruskin said. "Th'scout party we sent out came back with some rather ugly news, so we were able ta get th'council on our side to evacuate."

Another familiar voice joined the comment from Ruskin. "Which wasn't an easy task as they didn't believe they were in any danger," Tony added as he and Mia both entered the courtyard.

"Hello you two!" Shar smiled. She dismounted and gave both of them a hug as they came up.

"We were wondering when you two would show, we've been watching gnomes go by in groups the last day or so, all heading north," Mia said.

"I stayed back to get a look at the army of Helana's, risky, I know, and to make sure the last of the gnomes got out," Shar replied.

"And what of this army? The scouting party gave us a pretty good description, but what do you think?" Tony asked.

Shar sighed and shook her head. "They are many, and her power is beyond anything I have could have thought possible."

"Our home, tis gone, nothing is left but rubble," one

gnome said as he wiped dirt off his face. He and the other gnomes had climbed down off their riders and were stretching their legs. The ride had been hard and dusty the whole way from Eldridge and they were all in need of a bath.

"Gone?" Mia wondered, "How is that even possible?"

"Helana unleashed some sort of magic, I've never felt anything so dark, and it flattened everything. There's probably nothing but a big hole left in the hills where the castle once was. The dwarves need to get out of here, they cannot stay. They will not survive," Shar warned.

"They are mostly gone, only a few of us left ta make sure they get away," Axel assured her.

"You aren't going to do something stupid like try and fight?" Adeena remarked with a sigh.

"An' what if we were?" Ruskin challenged her. The fairy moved to stand in front of the dwarf and crossed her arms in defiance.

"Cause I'll have to kick you good and hard to make you think otherwise," she responded sternly.

"Oh is that so," Ruskin snickered. "Ya hear that Axe? She's gonna kick me!"

"That might be a tad entertainin, give it a go will ya sprite, see if ya catch'im," Axel taunted.

"You kids can play later, right now, I think we better listen to Shar and get the rest of the dwarves out of here," Tony urged. He looked at Shar. "If what you say is true, then what chance do we really have against her?"

"There is always a price to invoke such a magnitude of magic. She will have weakened herself and will need time to rest. That is what will likely keep Aberdeen intact, but the army will do enough damage and there is no way we can keep them at bay for any length of time. Even with your defenses Axel," Shar glanced over the dwarf. He merely shrugged and agreed.

"We never thought ta be able ta do so, but we'd like ta hurt'em at least a wee bit," he grinned.

"Aye, give'em a taste of dwarf spirit," Ruskin added.

"You can save that for another time as we should get going, and soon," Shar emphasized. "I don't know how far they are behind, but they can't be far, the air is already carrying their stench."

"An here I thought it was you all th'time," Axel said, aiming the joke at Ruskin.

"Me? I thought it was you!" he retorted.

"Oh gee, we'll be here forever at their speed," Adeena muttered. She ambled over to pet Shar's horse and the mage merely chuckled at the remark.

"We're pretty much ready to go now, we just have to get the rest of the dwarves to move out," Tony said as they walked towards the steps leading up to the rampart.

The remaining dwarves congregated in the courtyard as Axel and Ruskin sent word to get them all there. There were only about a handful left, and they were not in any hurry to leave.

"We're stayin Axel, there ain't nothin yer gonna say ta change our minds," Bram said.

"Stayin here is askin fer a death sentence, yer ain't gonna stop them things," Axel replied, his statement was more of a plea. He did not want to see any of his brethren fall victim to an assault they could not win.

"If we don't stay an' hold'em off as long as we can, then those who've left won't be getting far. Yer fergettin boys, a lot of them are families with young'ens, an'they won't be movin fast," added Iver.

"We don't have families, that's why we've stayed behind and ain't no one gonna miss us," another dwarf, Duncan cracked. He was trying to make fun of a sad situation and for the most part, it was working.

"Ya don't have ta do this," Ruskin urged.

"Aye, we do lad," Bram smiled. "You go on, ya leave Aberdeen ta us."

A shout from the rampart got everyone's attention. "There's something flyin in! Can't make it out!"

"To yer weapons men!" Iver shouted. The group scattered and Shar quickly grabbed her horse by the reins and guided her ride into the cover of the nearest building. Tony, Mia and Adeena followed right behind. Axel and Ruskin had disappeared from view in search of their own battle gear.

A creature came into view of the courtyard, and landed right in the middle of it, letting out a loud screech as it did. The thing took stock of its surroundings and soon found itself surrounded by a group of dwarves armed with axes and spears.

"What th'hell is that?" Iver muttered as he took aim with crossbow.

"No bloody idea, but shoot it anyways!" Bram shouted.

Iver let the arrow fly and the arrow struck the creature in one of its legs. It squealed and reached down, jaw open and yanked the arrow out with its teeth. The remainder of the dwarves attacked with spears, and other weapon of choice. The creature backed off a little to give itself some room but the dwarves would not let it. Soon arrows were sticking out from all over its body and the creature lifted its wings to fly off but the dwarves would have none of that. Axel and Ruskin appeared rope in hand and with the help a few others tossed it over several times and pulled the creature down to the ground. The dwarves attacked with a fury that even shocked Tony and the rest. The thing was dead not long thereafter as several spears jutted out from around the creature's neck.

"Now that's dwarf spirit," Axel snorted with a chuckle. "Ain't that right men!"

A shout echoed from everyone and they basked in the glory of their small, but important victory. They would not go down without a fight, this was their home and not one of them was going to stand by and let these demons take what was theirs.

"What is it?" Iver asked, again.

"Does it matter, it's dead," Bram joked.

"Yer right," Iver nodded, grinning.

Shar wandered over and took a good look at the fallen creature. It was extremely grotesque facially, but the body was of muscle and the claws were sharp enough to shred anyone who came near enough. It had badly miscalculated its attack, but if there were others they were not likely to do the same.

"Manticore," Shar whispered. Her memory of Malcolm's old stories suddenly surfaced. She looked up as Axel and a few other dwarves ambled over to her. "You got lucky. That tail, with those spikes like a porcupine, you would all be dead with one flick of it."

"Yer not serious?" Ruskin asked.

"I am, next time if there's another, and chances are there will be, all it will take is one thrust and a hundred spikes go flying into all of you. Think about what you are doing, you cannot stay," Shar repeated the warning.

"Lass, whether another shows or not, we ain't leavin, but you best be goin. If this one is here, th'rest will be here shortly. Ya need ta get away while ya can," Bram said.

"Is this what you really want?" Tony asked.

"Aye lad, tis our choice," Iver nodded.

"Then we go, mount up, we best be movin," Axel motioned towards the stable.

Ruskin embraced his fellow brethren one by one,

knowing full well he would never see any of them again. "Yer all fools ya know."

"We know," Bram snickered. "Now go my friend."

Those leaving gathered quickly in the courtyard, the remaining gnomes, Shar, Adeena Tony and Mia along with Axel and Ruskin and a few other dwarves prepared to move on. The stench preceding the army of Helana was beginning to strengthen on the wind warning of their approach.

"Good luck sir," Axel nodded to Bram.

"You as well, we'll give ya th'time ya need ta get on," Bram winked.

The gates were opened and the company rode out at full gallop, veering northward to the trail that would lead to the 'Falls'. Once there the next part of their journey would be decided upon. The group did not know of the approaching advance forces led by Neil and Tasha, so they were bound to be in for a pleasant surprise as opposed to one of demon origin. With the wind at their backs, the company merged with the forest as they galloped further down the trail, the trees disguising their escape.

Bram whistled for his fellow dwarves to take their positions and to wait. The gate was closed and secured, followed by the closure of a second gate designed specifically for an attack such as the one forthcoming. It would give the forces inside a bit of an advantage to reorganize if need be. A third and final gate was then closed, the final defense before a breach into the courtyard and into the confines of Aberdeen. Each dwarf took their position on the rampart or in the towers, weapons, ready for the assault.

The wind picked up and the foul aroma floated up over the walls of Aberdeen and Bram had to cover his face at first because of his desire to wretch. The ground began to shake and the castle shook. The dwarves shouted out words of support to one another while waiting for their foe to make an appearance. Bram saw several more of the flying manticores but these chose to stay up above, perhaps waiting for the actual attack before committing their own assault.

Then the army appeared, bursting through the trees in an enormous mass led by trolls bearing several giant ramming logs with ogres, pulling catapults right behind. Bram could not make out what the rest of the creatures were but there were many, more than he ever could have imagined. It had looked massive from a distance when he and the scouting party had seen them the first time, but now it was overwhelming.

Iver came over and patted him on the back. "It has been an honor servin with ya sir."

Bram nodded with a grin. "Aye, an'with you as well Iver. Let's take as many of th'ugly bastards as we can with us."

"Aye, agreed."

The filth of Helana's army howled in anticipation and the general in charge pointed to the gate of Aberdeen. The trolls bore down and the first shock of the ramming log was felt throughout. Two more groups joined in and soon the first gate was beginning to crack under the assault.

Bram gave the order then. "Fire at will! Let them know we mean business!"

The dwarves let loose their own volley of firepower, spears and rocks rained down on the army below but all that appeared to do was enrage the mass even more. Soon the first gate of Aberdeen shattered and the first wave of demons were through. The trolls continued on to the next gate and began to ram it as well. The dwarves let loose everything they had at their disposal, taking down a slew of the creatures but still more poured out of the woods. Bram paused to watch, wondering if there was any end to them.

"Retreat to the second defense line! Move, move move!" he shouted as he pointed. The manticore flying above flew in to the courtyard at that point beginning their attack. A group of dwarves moved to fend them off but were dead in moments when the creatures hurled the spikes from their tails. The spikes pierced the armor of the dwarves and the group of five dwarves fell to their deaths instantly. Bram swore and grabbed his axe. They were getting through too fast. They had to slow the attack down.

"To the inner walls everyone! We make our last stand there!" Bram bellowed. The dwarves were running to take up their new positions just as Bram heard the second gate collapse from the battering ram. It would not be long before the third gate would be breached. The dwarves in the towers managed to kill off two more of the manticore with a flurry of strikes from their larger form of crossbow, the ballista. The remaining three creatures flew back up to regroup and Bram knew their next attack would be the final blow.

Bram, Iver and the remaining dwarves took up a spot on the rampart running alongside the mountain wall and prepared for the inevitable invasion about to enter Aberdeen. They watched as the third gate began to buckle and shatter.

Bram listened to the sound of the wailing demons and other things brought into this world and anxiously took aim with his ballista. "Stand ready, here they come!"

The final gate exploded into the courtyard as the troll's slammed their ram into the last of its resistance. Monsters of every shape, and size overflowed into the dwarf home of Aberdeen determined to destroy it all, just as they had in Tir Nan Og. Those left to defend it stood ready, prepared to fight for their home until they had spent their last breath. Bram took aim and fired.

Chapter Nineteen

Neil looked up at the falls and admired the sight before him. Tasha stood next to him and held his hand tightly. Here is where they would make a stand against whatever Helana had congregated as her army. They had arrived late that night above the falls and had waited until dawn to venture below and determine how they would set up their line of defense. He and Tasha surveyed their surroundings and could see why this would make a good location for a surprise attack. Any army moving in here would be facing an assault from above and below. It was without a doubt the best location to spring their forces on an unsuspecting foe.

"My lord, good morning," Thatcher smiled as he strolled up.

"Neil, we're too good friends for such formal stuff," Neil urged.

Thatcher chuckled. "As you wish, Neil. Impressive sight isn't it?"

"Yes, it is," he replied.

"Biggest valley in these parts, have ta go further east ta see more of'em," Thatcher commented.

"Maybe one day I'll have to do just that as it wouldn't

hurt to do some traveling after all this is over," Neil sighed. He looked at Tasha. "What do you think?"

"I like the idea, there's a lot of Avalon I have yet to see," she smiled back.

"Brielle, Elise and the others are ready ta talk of where we be settin up," Thatcher informed. He pulled out his pipe and dropped in some fresh tobacco to light up. A moment later he was puffing out little clouds of smoke that lingered in the damp morning air.

"Let's not keep them waiting," Tasha motioned for Thatcher to lead the way.

All of the captains, with Tasha, Neil and Thatcher and Jacinto gathered under a very tall grove of trees near the falls themselves. Greetings of 'good morning' were offered around and it was time then to get down to their strategy. Kieran took charge and had a rough map drawn out to use. He rolled it out on the ground and everyone stood around and paid attention to what the elf captain had to say.

"The army will come through the valley, and follow the river up to the falls, they have to cross here in order to get by. If they go any further to the north, they'll have to deal with a lot more mountain and forest. Here, this is where they can cross and go on to Cambridge with the least amount of delay. We need them to congregate near here, and attack the largest part of the force to inflict the most damage. If they get past and over the river, they will start to spread out again and make our work near to impossible," Kieran explained. The captains nodded and agreed.

"It will be best for our attack with the gryphon here, if they get across as you say, then trying to strike at them once they enter the trees again is as good as finished," Brielle added. She knelt and tapped the map at the river. "Here, when they are most vulnerable is the best option to drive them back."

"I do not think we will be able to drive them back, but merely delay the inevitable," Riss said. "Our numbers are not that great, and we have no idea what we are expecting."

"Aye, yer right sir, but we can still make a wee bit of a difference, even if it be a small one," Thatcher said with a wink. He took a puff of his pipe and exhaled several tiny clouds of smoke. "My people will be near shortly, we may add a few more to th'ranks if we're lucky."

"We have scouts out already looking for them," Kieran assured the gnome. "We'll make sure they and the dwarves are guided out quickly to keep them safe."

"Any word at all from either Aberdeen or Eldridge?" Darg asked.

Neil shook his head. "Nothing as yet."

"Why not send out a few others to investigate some of the surrounding area, just in case this army of Helana's is able to find away around us?" Vasilis suggested.

"A good idea as we can't be caught off guard. We can send out four scouts to see what lies behind the falls, and to the south," Brielle pointed.

"I'll go south," Vasilis volunteered. "I've been through those woods enough to know where to look."

"Good, Alai, Rythen, Pendus, you three go search out the land behind the falls. Be back in a few hours, and we'll plan accordingly," Kieran said.

The four elves departed and the strategy session continued. Elise took her turn and pointed to the top of the falls.

"From up there we will wait with the gryphon, and I'm assuming the archers as well?"

"Yes, we'll line the entire upper ridge and send a thunderstorm down, they will wish they had never left their hell," Teague smiled. He was the captain of the elf archers of Cambridge and was never shy on bragging about his brethren's abilities.

"Well you better make every arrow count as we can't afford too many misses," Riss challenged.

"You don't worry about my archers. We will find our marks," Teague assured the Dark elf captain.

"Captains," interrupted Brielle. "We are here as one force! Whatever differences we may have are to be put aside. We are all elf here," she emphasized.

"Aye captain," Teague nodded. Riss nodded his acknowledgement as well.

The group noticed a rider approaching from the east; it was one of the earlier scouts they had sent out and was now returning and judging at her rate of gallop she had news of importance. The elf scout reined in her horse as she neared the river and slowed to cross. The company had erected a temporary crossing bridge to go back and forth. The depth of the river was just a bit too much for a regular crossing. So to make things a little easier the bridge was made and could just as easily be dismantled when required. She trotted up to the group and dismounted.

"The gnomes have started to pass through the valley," she informed them.

"Thank you Lilach. Anything else out there that caught your attention?" Brielle asked.

The scout shook her head. "Nothing out of the ordinary, the gnomes started passing through earlier this morning. I would imagine the dwarves will not be far behind," Lilach said.

"True. Are the gnomes moving along well enough?" Brielle wondered.

"Yes, for the most part. Some of the carts seem to be a bit of a challenge, they really overloaded them with a lot of things!"

"It's not easy to leave home, and your personal belongings. It must have been hard," Neil sighed.

"I know what that's like, all too well," Tasha nodded. "I've had to do it twice now."

Neil winked at her as she squeezed his hand. He looked over at Jacinto.

"Jacinto sir, are your men ready to give the gnomes a hand?" he asked.

"Oh, they're ready, itchin to do something for a time. It ain't a fight, but it'll do for now," Jacinto said.

"Steer them up towards the eastern forests. The township of North Meadow should be out of the path of Helana's army for the time being," Tasha said.

"Good thing too. We'll make sure the gnomes an'dwarves find their way. You be sure to save some of them things for us to kill," Jacinto winked, a huge grin on his face.

"I think we can arrange that," Thatcher chuckled.

"I will hold you to that little man," Jacinto pointed at the gnome. "I will have my men go back down the trail and assist any of the stragglers. If the witch is comin, she won't be far behind'em."

Kieran pointed to the map. "She may, but she may use a more direct route straight here," he motioned. "Both gnomes and dwarf are coming through the mountain pass. That may give us a little more time to move them on."

"Either way," shrugged Jacinto. He was more interested in getting into a fight than being a guide to homeless gnomes and dwarves but he understood the necessity in keeping them safe.

"We will see you soon," Tasha nodded. Jacinto waved and ran off to gather his forces to move on to the job at hand.

"Enough talk everyone, we need to set ourselves in," Brielle said. The rest nodded in agreement. "Then let us get down to it. Elise, have your group take a sweep of the surrounding area, see if there is something or anything out there we need to know about."

"Aye, on our way," Elise replied. She was the next to disappear and the rest followed after her.

"Any word from the other two scouts we sent out?" Neil asked.

"Not as yet sir, they should be back shortly," Kieran replied.

The remainder of the morning was spent preparing their defense of the falls and the arrival of an uknown type of army.

Deep in the forests, shrouded from any curious eyes, a single figure waited amidst the trees. The individual was standing right amongst a thick growth of willow and no one would have seen him had they ridden by or even strolled by on an afternoon of sightseeing. The cloak blended in with the color of brush and the person did not move, not even to turn his head and take a glance of the surroundings. It waited, silently, motionless and had been for some time. Birds flew up and perched on nearby branches and then moved on when they found nothing of interest. A couple deer ambled by and did not notice the person standing in the trees. They ate some grass and moved on to find something more appealing. Still the person did not move.

A rider approached eventually, and the one waiting still did not stir. The rider dismounted and moved near the brush.

"I bring news," he said.

The figure in the willows finally moved and stepped out from cover.

"This better be worth my time to travel out here," she

murmured. Helana removed the top of her cloak and let herself be seen by the rider.

"It is my queen." He bowed down to her and then stood once more.

"So what is so important you needed to see me?" she asked.

"The king and queen plan to ambush your forces at the falls west of Aberdeen. They have amassed a sizeable force capable of inflicting some damage."

"Is that so? Well then, this was worth my time. How large is the army?"

The rider shook his head. "I am not sure of the exact number, but it is sizeable. A number of the other elf tribes have joined with Xanthus in this effort. The humans have supplied a very large number of their own fighters for this as well. It can delay your march on Cambridge significantly."

"Then my friend, they will be the ones surprised in this ambush, with one of our own. Keep me informed on anything else you may hear, summon me at your discretion," Helana said.

"Yes, my queen, I am here to serve," the rider bowed again.

"And your reward will be equal to your support. Now go, and be wary of what you do," she warned. "I cannot risk my best spy at the hands of the elves."

"Yes my queen."

The rider returned to his mount and was galloping off back to the assembled forces of elf and human. Helana watched him go and smiled. Her strength was near restoring itself and soon she would be able to witness the massacre at the falls, her massacre of a feeble attempt to stop her. She vanished in a swirl of mist, leaving the forest empty where she had once been.

The last of the elf scouts returned from their exploration of the outlying area and Kieran approached him. The elf climbed down from his ride and nodded to the captain as he approached.

"Cael, you are extremely late on returning. You were out since early this morning; even the second group of scouts has come back. Why are you the last?"

"I went a little further than I perhaps needed to sir; I felt it necessary considering the circumstances."

"Just how far did you go?" Kieran asked.

"I ventured further to the southeast, almost too close for comfort towards Aberdeen. The smell is atrocious the further I went," Cael explained.

"There was no need to go that far. Since you did, anything of note we need to know about?"

"There are things flying the sky, not sure what they are, but they are very thorough in their pattern over the trees. I hid several times in the heavier thickets so they would not see me. They will give our gryphons a good fight."

Kieran looked at the elf and nodded slowly. "All right then, go and check in with Taith for your next assignment. How long do you think we have before that army is on the move?"

Cael shrugged. "They must already be. Those creatures in the sky were moving this way slowly. I thought it best not to risk going any further."

"Good choice. Now go and check in with your captain," Kieran pointed.

"Aye sir."

Neil had watched the conversation take place and strolled over to visit with the elf captain as the other returned to his detachment. Kieran nodded at him as he approached and let out a deep sigh.

"You look troubled captain?" Neil asked.

"He was out too long. I don't know whether to take that as a good thing, or not."

"You think something is wrong?"

"I am not sure, but I will keep an eye on him sir. He might be telling the truth, but," Kieran looked back across the river, "one can never be too sure on who is or is not on our side."

"Very true. Are you up for an ale, or brandy? That might help ease our nerves a bit," Neil suggested.

"That it might! How is the lady Tasha this evening? She looked a little sick earlier in the afternoon?" Kieran wondered.

"Better, or so she says. She's not really forthcoming on stuff like that," Neil joked. "She could be as sick as anything and she'd still say she was fine."

"She is a stubborn one," Kieran chuckled.

On the trail leading to the falls, a group of riders galloped on as the evening sky grew darker. As the final rays of daylight faded into twilight the group came across a few stragglers from the dwarf kingdom of Aberdeen and slowed to make sure they were all right.

"Hey there, is everything going okay?" Tony asked as he reined in his horse.

"Goin fine, a wee bit slowly at times, but we're managing," the dwarf replied.

"Any chance you can move things a long faster? The nightmare we left behind won't be too far off," Mia wondered.

"Are ya gonna carry us now?" the dwarf chuckled. "We can try lass, but th'carts are a bit sluggish on this darn trail, if ya can call it that," he grumbled.

A booming voice echoed through the dark in reply to the dwarf comment. "Then if we have to carry you, we will!"

Jacinto appeared with a few more of his men and he was a pleasant sight to see!

"Jacinto! Hey, good timing," Tony remarked with a grin.

"As always," Jacinto teased. "What's the word on Aberdeen?"

Shar shook her head. "Not good, I doubt there is much left by now."

"And Eldridge?" he further queried.

"Rubble, a big pile of dust," Adeena replied.

"Ya don't say, well, that's sad to hear. Heading up to the falls are ya?" he asked.

"Yes, quickest route to Cambridge, or so says Axel," pointed Tony.

"Is he back there? Couldn't see the little guy. Are ya hidin somewhere?" Jacinto joked.

"Shut up ya big oaf, ya tryin ta be funny?" Axel retorted.

"He's too big to be funny; all his brains are in his arse!" Ruskin added with a chuckle.

"Would you like to be fodder for my horse, ya little twerp?" Jacinto scoffed.

"Don't we have to be somewhere?" Adeena whined, her patience running a little thin with the banter.

"Quiet sprite, we'll get there at some point," Axel said.

"You'll find some other friends there at the falls, they've managed to put together quite the army to give the witch a good headache," Jacinto informed. "They're getting set to ambush what be comin," he nodded back at the way they had come.

"Really? Is Malcolm with them?" Shar wondered.

"No my lady, he stayed back at Cambridge last I heard, but he may have shown up by now," Jacinto shrugged. "He was tending to other things."

"It'll be good to see Neil and Zach," Tony said. "Are they staying out of trouble?"

"Zach ain't there either my boy, he's off somewhere else at Malcolm's request, so says Neil. He and the queen are there though, getting it all set up," Jacinto rambled on.

"Well thanks for the update sir, appreciate it," Tony smiled as he saluted the larger man.

"Glad to boy. Ya best get movin, we'll get these dwarves all caught up to the rest. We'll be back sometime tomorrow, hopefully in time to lend a hand if need be before ya have all the fun."

"I ain't savin any for ya, after th'hell we've been through to get th'hell outta their way I'm plannin on evening out th'score," Axel snorted as he tapped the axe handle strapped to his back.

"See you back at the falls then sir, have fun," Tony winked.

"I'll try to control myself," Jacinto replied sarcastically. "See you all soon."

He rode on with his men to aid the fleeing dwarves as best they could and keep them on the correct path away from the oncoming danger. The wind came up abruptly for a moment and the stench they had all smelled back at Aberdeen was beginning to strengthen. Helana's army had to be on the move if the aroma preceding them was already riding the currents of the wind.

"Come on everybody, let's get to the falls. I have a feeling we aren't going to have to wait too long for her army to get there," Tony said. He gave his horse a kick and the group was moving back down the path and on to the falls to meet up with the rest of the assembled forces.

General Vadeez shouted orders to the trolls to keep them moving along and urged his men to keep at them until they were back on track to make up for lost time. They had spent far too long ransacking the dwarf castle. Some of the ogres and trolls had found some hidden food caches and had gorged themselves to the point of almost being sick. It had caused the already sluggish beasts to move even slower. The demon contingent had already taken the lead and was well ahead of the remaining forces.

Those few dwarves that had stayed behind to fight were disposed of easy enough and the demons, trolls and everything other creature had disassembled Aberdeen with such vigor that Vadeez was curious as to what they had done in the realm of faerie. If they could inflict such damage to a structure built into a mountain in such a short time frame, what had they done with a free standing structure? It was amazing to watch such destruction. The only remaining thing left of Aberdeen to even suggest there had been a castle was the outline of it left in the mountain wall. If the dwarves ever wanted to rebuild, that is if any survived after all of this, it would take forever to rebuild the structure. Two kingdoms down, and the resistance had been next to nothing. Both dwarf and gnome had opted to flee instead of face them. Considering what this army had been able to do thus far, it was probably the best and only option for them. Vadeez reveled in the power of this army and could not wait to face off against the elves and whoever else got in their way. He returned his attention to the task at hand and failed to notice a mist form behind him.

"Move on, come on then, keep it going, you can all rest later you ugly slugs, now move!" He barked.

"Problems general?" Helana's familiar voice caught the man off guard.

"My queen, I did not see you," he bowed to her. "The trolls and ogres had a little too much fun at the expense of the dwarf's food storages and they ate rather too well."

"Stupid animals," she snorted. "I have a new plan of action for you general, I need you to split the forces and reroute the second wave to the west and bring them directly north along the river up to the falls."

"My queen, is that wise? It will weaken us considerably and leave us vulnerable to any attack."

"Not really general, we far outnumber the elves and humans. I have information that says there is an ambush waiting for us at the falls. By splitting up the group and sending them west and then north, we will be able to catch them off guard. They will be focusing their attack on the first wave coming in through the valley. They will not be expecting us to come up the river."

"Is this information correct my queen?"

"I have my source and he is quite reliable. Not to worry general, we will be able to catch this so called army off balance by moving up the river."

The general nodded. "As you wish, I will tend to the arrangements immediately."

"Excellent, I will meet you all there within a day as my strength has nearly been replenished."

"Then we will give this army of theirs a surprise they will not be happy to see," the general smiled wickedly.

"I expect we will," Helana added with her own evil sneer.

Chapter Twenty

Zach stared at the man sitting in front of him. This man was casually sipping his tea as if it was the best tea he had ever enjoyed. This man was a complete legend, and in theory, supposed to have been long gone or in some circles, never to have even existed! Yet, here he was, a man or master wizard, according to Malcolm, that he had been sent over to find alive and well and running a tea shop no less. Zach sat up and he made himself a little more comfortable in his chair, still staring at the man. How was this even possible? When Malcolm had asked him to find this so called master wizard he thought it was a long shot at best, but he did as he was asked because it was necessary for the good of his new home on a new world that was at risk of being destroyed. He was beginning to realize that almost anything was possible, especially considering all that he had seen and done in the last year and a half. Now here he was again, with another unbelievable and mythical person staring back at him.

"Zach?" Riane said, poking him as she said his name.

"Huh?" Zach blinked and looked over at the woman.

"Are you okay?" she asked curiously.

"Um, yeah, I'm fine. I'm, just trying to get a handle on," he moved his hands around in a circular motion. "This."

"Meaning me?" Merlin gave him a quick little smile.

"Yeah, you," Zach nodded.

"More tea?" Falon checked. She had wandered over to gauge Zach's reaction when he had asked her teacher who he was and she expected exactly what she was witnessing now. It was quite amusing but to help him ease into the reality of it she thought it best to see if he needed a refill.

"Um, no, thanks, I'm good right now."

"Okay, thought I'd ask. Sir, should I close up for the night?" Falon pointed to the door.

"Yes, I think it best we have some private time with our guests. We have much to talk about, wouldn't you say Mr. Thomas?" Merlin winked.

"Yes, apparently we do," Zach replied. He leaned over and put his arms on the table. "So, you're really, Merlin?"

"I am the man, I am he, I am the one, and only," Merlin joked.

Zach shook his head in disbelief. The guy was a comedian! "Prove it."

Merlin took his turn to sit up. He put his cup of tea down on the table and scratched his chin. "Prove it you say, what would be worthy of proof in your eyes Mr. Thomas? I have already unmasked your lady friend here, what more do you need to see?"

"I don't know, do something I wouldn't expect, surprise me," Zach said.

"Careful what you ask for," Falon warned with a wave of her hand.

"Shush Falon," Merlin said with a smile. "He asked, and I shall oblige. Very well Mr. Thomas, let me see what is it I can do to make you believe. I can go on and on about history, what I have seen, been a part of, still a part of for that matter or why you are here. Which by the way, you carry a letter for me, actually two, the one I wrote long long ago, and another from a fellow wizard. So let's see, what is it I can do to possibly convince you, oh, I could make every picture dance around the room," Merlin flicked his finger and each painting left the wall and proceeded to float around the tea shop. "Or I could change you into a mouse, but no, that would be rather rude, so maybe I can just change your color instead." Merlin moved his right hand and Zach turned a dark shade of blue.

Zach lifted up his hands and stared at the vivid blue they now were. Riane giggled at him, pointing to his blue face and now pure white hair.

"You look a lot like the elves from the ice fields on Avalon," she said, trying to contain her laughter.

Merlin flicked his hand and Zach returned to his natural color again. The wizard looked over at Riane. "And how are the blue elves these days?"

"They are doing quite well," Riane replied courteously.

"Very good to hear," Merlin nodded.

"Okay, you made your point," Zach sighed. "I'll go with it, your Merlin." Zach sat back in his chair and crossed his arms.

"If Neil could see me now, he'd love this," he added.

"A friend?" Merlin asked.

"Yes, he's big into the history stuff, loves the king Arthur," he pointed to a still floating painting, "Knights and all that. He plays some sort of dungeon and dragon game too."

"Interesting game that one, a little far fetched at times," Merlin chuckled.

"So how is it you are here, like, now?" Zach asked, his curiosity getting the best of him.

"We can get into all that another time. You have a letter

for me. Let me see what it has to say," Merlin beckoned for him to hand it over.

"Oh right." Zach reached into his jacket and withdrew two envelopes. He handed over Malcolm's letter first and then held up the rather faded envelope and Merlin recognized it immediately.

"My my, I thought I would never see this again," he murmured. Merlin took it and held it for a moment. "That was so long ago, so very long ago. A different time, but then, today is a much different time in comparison to when I wrote this. So many years gone by, most just fade into one another. Once in a while, a year stands out, but those are few and far between. I am impressed the letter has held up so well. However," Merlin sat back. "If you are here, and with the letter, then all is not well on the new world. I entrust this letter from my fellow wizard will explain it all?"

"Yes, it will. Probably a lot better than I ever could," Zach said.

"Sir, I am very sorry to interrupt, but I have to say, it is an honor to meet you," Riane smiled and held out her hand to shake his. Merlin obliged and smiled in return.

"It is an honor for me as well my lady to meet someone from the new world, I honestly thought that I never would, but as the years have gone by, I realized that one day I might. More so because of varying circumstances that would bring that about, but I have learned a lot myself over the years. There are things you cannot change; no matter what it is you do to try."

"What do you mean?" Zach asked.

Merlin pointed to his tea cup and Falon wandered over to refill the cup with some fresh tea. "I will explain more on that a little later as well Mr. Thomas, not to worry. Allow me to read your letter and then we can enjoy the rest of our evening."

"Knock yourself out," Zach agreed. He stood up with his own tea cup and let Falon refill his cup too. "Thanks, Falon, is it?"

"Yes sir, it is nice to meet you Mr. Thomas."

"Just call me Zach, no need for the formal stuff."

"As you wish, Zach. My lady, a refill for you as well?"

"Yes, thank you," Riane nodded. Falon emptied out the last of her tea into Riane's cup and returned to the kitchen to brew up a fresh pot of hot water.

Zach sipped his tea and nodded towards Falon. "She knows who you are?"

"Oh my yes. What good is an apprentice if they do not know who is teaching them?" Merlin grinned. "Her reaction was not as good as yours though."

Zach frowned and put his tea cup down. "Quite the joker aren't you?"

"When you have been around as long as I have, you tend to learn to laugh at more things, you may not otherwise."

"I see."

"Now if you will, allow me to finish reading and we'll talk some more," Merlin said.

Riane took Zach's hand and stood. "Come, let us look at the paintings some more, and let the man read his letter in peace."

"Oh all right," Zach sighed. He got up out of his chair and followed Riane from picture to picture, which had resettled back in their proper spots on the wall, and noticed how much detail had gone into each picture. Zach who was never much into art at all, even though he had dated someone who was in a roundabout way interested in it, he found these rather 'catching'.

He stopped once again at the picture of Arthur and his knights of the round table. Zach grinned at the thought of Neil missing out on all this, the meeting, the artwork, and who knows what else that may lay ahead. Riane put her arm around his waist and leaned on his shoulder.

"They look so serious, as though they have a lot on their minds," she observed.

"Probably did at the time. So," he looked at her, "having fun yet?'

Riane chuckled. "Very much, I am glad I came along."

"Yeah, I'm glad you did too," he smiled at her.

They wandered through the tea house, looking it all over to allow Merlin the time he needed to read through the letter Malcolm had sent. Falon was keeping herself busy cleaning up the shop and readying it for the next day of business. Neither Zach nor Riane had any idea how long it was until they heard Merlin stand up from the table and stretch with a 'grunt' and a mumble of 'getting stiff'. The legendary wizard motioned for them to rejoin him and they obliged.

Zach pointed to the letter now resting on the table. "Did Malcolm explain it easy enough?"

"Yes, he was quite thorough; tell me, how is he doing? Or how was he doing before you left?"

"He was looking tired, almost like I used to feel after pulling an all nighter when I was still on the force," Zach replied.

"I see. So, what he says is all true, the demon merging with the woman, and the rest of it," Merlin checked.

"As far as I know, yes, I don't know what he put in there but if he has it in writing, then it is true. He's not one to beat around the bush with anything," Zach said.

"Beat around the bush, slang, such terms I have grown used to hearing and seeing over the years. Well, if what your guardian says is true then, we must move quickly. He will be quite weakened by this time and will not be able to sustain the magic of the amulets for much longer," Merlin explained.

"So what are we going to do? Go back now?" Zach questioned curiously.

"Back? Oh, not yet my friend. We have to collect a few things, one being a, a talisman of sorts to help against the demon witch," Merlin replied.

"Talisman?" Riane asked.

"Yes, a weapon that will help us defeat her," Merlin said, the answer not really satisfying Zach.

"You'll have to explain a little more on that one. What weapon?" he pushed.

Merlin tipped his tea cup back and finished what was left. He placed the cup down and sat up. "We need to collect an old, artifact, shall we say. One that is capable of stopping this evil. It has been used centuries ago, and is hidden away in a place to which we must now travel."

"And just where is that?" Zach wondered.

"That you will see in time, but now, it is time to gather a few things and depart. Get your belongings from your hotel, and be back here in an hour. We must be on our way as soon as we are able," Merlin instructed. He stood up and nodded to Falon. "Put a sign on the door Falon saying we will be gone for a time, a vacation perhaps. That should satisfy the customers."

"Yes sir," Falon nodded. "Am I to accompany you?" she asked hopefully.

"Indeed Fallon, you are. As I said a few days ago, you will be able to have some fun with your new talents," he promised. "Quickly now, go and get your things from the hotel. Don't waste any time."

"I guess we're going then," Zach shrugged.

"I will make sure we make it here in the hour," Riane assured Merlin as she poked Zach.

"Aren't you glad you have an elf to keep you on track," Merlin joked.

"Sometimes yes, sometimes no," Zach replied with a chuckle. "See you both soon."

An hour later the four gathered in the tea house once again, bags in tow and Merlin dressed in a cloak of sorts, carrying a walking stick that Zach assumed was his own version of a 'staff' that Malcolm was always toting around. Falon had on her own cloak and was dressed similarly as Merlin for an outdoor excursion. Riane and Zach felt a little underdressed and she pointed to her jacket.

"Will this be enough?" Riane wondered.

"My yes, I am merely comfortable in my old cloak, had it for a long time you know. Hard to part with it," Merlin replied.

"I hope you washed it once in a while," Zach said mocking the statement.

Merlin looked at him. "And this would be where you are trying to be the funny man? Am I correct?"

Zach shrugged. "I guess."

"Then you and I will get along nicely," Merlin chuckled. "Let us go, our cab has arrived," he pointed to the vehicle just pulling up to the front of the shop.

"Where are we going?" Zach asked. To this point Merlin had said nothing of where it was they had to go and it was starting to really annoy him that he had no clue where they were going.

"At a small harbor on the coast, there is a boat waiting for us there. It is a couple hours drive so I had some tea and coffee made up for the journey," Merlin replied. "Falon makes really good coffee," he winked at his apprentice.

"Thank you sir, I have to admit, I do," Falon chuckled.

"There should be enough caffeine for your requirements Mr. Thomas."

"Zach, just call me Zach."

"Zach," she nodded. "The coffee is a bit dark, but you will find it smooth enough and strong enough to keep you awake." The group of four left the building and moved on to the waiting cab.

"Great, I'd hate to miss out on anything," he remarked. "This whole trip has been quite the whirlwind as of late," he said shouldering his tote bag.

"Rest assured Mr. Thomas, where we are going will be enough to keep you awake," Merlin commented as he closed the door behind them and locked it.

"Oh really, and just where the hell are we going in this boat of yours at nine o'clock in the evening?" he asked.

Merlin stuffed his keys into his cloak and motioned to the cab. "Go on, get in."

"You're not going to tell me are you?" Zach sighed.

Merlin lifted up his tote bag of sorts. "Oh sorry lad, we are going somewhere I haven't been in a long time, a very long time. Everything we require is there. We are traveling to the island of Avalon."

Chapter Twenty One

Malcolm sat down on the edge of his bed, exhausted and worn from the day. His magic was draining at an alarming rate. Every time he awoke his body ached and it was that much harder to call on his magic when he required it. Soon enough, the amulets would be useless to him or to anyone else because the magic needed to bring them to life would be unavailable. He let out a deep breath and tossed his cloak aside. Such a long day but it was still a successful day in regards to organizing their preparations for Helana's arrival. He knew the army they had sent out to delay her would only be able to do so much and Malcolm kept his hopes up that the casualties wouldn't be high. He admired Neil and Tasha's desire to inflict some pain back on Helana but it was a risky venture at best.

He had just returned from checking in on the Faerie queen, Leasha and her progress in recovering from her wounds. The elf was doing well but was still a long way from being her usual self. The scars were taking longer due to the fact they were inflicted by the demons and iron, both of which act like a poison on the body of a faerie. They had managed to just get her away in time before the damage would have been fatal. The remaining faerie had sent out their own search parties to find others who had escaped the destruction of Tir Nan Og but had been scattered throughout the land. A few were returning already with some of their kind with them so their searches were fruitful and a chance for them to be reunited in a better place. Albeit that was a short term solution for the faerie but a more stable situation than their now destroyed home.

A knock at the door brought him out of his thoughts. "Yes, the door is open."

Xanthus appeared from around the corner and smiled at his old friend. "Are you well?"

"As good as I can be at the present time," Malcolm nodded.

"The magic is being drained faster isn't it?" the elf asked.

The wizard sighed and that was answer enough for the elf king.

"You should have rested a time longer at the keep, it might have helped you now," Xanthus said as he moved into the room.

"Perhaps, but not likely, it may have only delayed the inevitable," Malcolm said. The wizard stood and wandered over to the small table on the far wall. He poured himself a cup of tea and lifted the teapot for Xanthus to see if he wanted any.

"Yes, a cup will be nice to conclude this hectic day," Xanthus nodded. He joined his friend at the table and waited as Malcolm filled his cup. Together the two took their tea and themselves out onto the balcony adjacent to the wizard's room.

"A question for you," Malcolm turned to look at the elf. "What do you think of Shar?"

"Shar? Well, that depends on why you ask the question?"

Xanthus chuckled. “Usually when you start a conversation about somebody like that, you have a point to make.”

Malcolm laughed, welcoming it after the long day. “Can’t fool you at all.”

“No, not in the least,” Xanthus quipped. “In response to the question, I think Shar is a very gifted mage, perhaps your best pupil ever over the years. Very adept at all types of magic it appears.”

“True, more so than I could have imagined, and the unicorn stallion saw it in her as well.”

“I recall you saying that, so what do you think that means?” Xanthus was curious to see where the conversation was steering.

“I believe Shar is even better at the gift than I, it is only a matter of time where she might be teaching me a thing or two.” Malcolm leaned against the railing of the balcony and sipped his tea. “I am thinking of handing more responsibilities on to her, letting her take charge in circumstances instead of me.”

“You are thinking she is your successor?” Xanthus asked.

“I do, everything is pointing to her. Ever since she used the amulets something has awakened in her and her abilities are expanding faster than mine ever did. She is someone special, someone who comes along ever so rarely. I believe she is the next guardian of Avalon.”

Xanthus took a sip of his tea and looked at his friend. “A bold statement! You thought Helana could have been a successor once, although, this time, I believe you may be right. I have seen her gifts expanding as you have and I have never, nor so I believe had my father, seen anyone as able as she during his lifetime. He had seen many gifted in magic but he never talked of any being exceptional. Except one, the very man Mister Thomas is currently seeking.”

"That, old friend is a more bold statement than mine," Malcolm smiled.

"Tis true though, talent of that caliber is very rare, and I believe we have one of those with Shar," Xanthus said.

Helana stood amidst the tall trees and listened carefully. She did not have to wait long before the sound she was waiting for emerged through the thick brush. Footsteps, that began quietly but grew exceedingly louder as they neared. Trees began to bend and shake as whatever manufactured the footsteps came ever so closer to her. Patiently she hid from sight keeping her eyes open for her target. Her patience paid off as the creatures came through the brush and into view.

She stared up at the giants, enormous creatures that lived far in the eastern regions of Avalon. In her search for slaves in her first attempt to conquer Avalon she had visited with a fellow she had met in the woods in this vicinity and he had suggested she recruit the giants. Of course she thought it unnecessary at that time, but now, they would come in very handy on the march to Cambridge and the elves. So she had returned to the east and sought them out.

Helana looked the group of five giants over and selected three that would serve her well enough. The giants were a larger version of a troll in her mind, big muscular simpletons that vaguely looked like a man, with dark grey skin and big teeth that could use a dentist's care and dark matted hair that needed a good brushing. A bath couldn't hurt either! Their odor was rather repugnant and they were covered in dirt. They did not pose a threat to anyone unless threatened themselves. She moved out into the open and cast a spell that put all five into a trance before they could act. The magic flew from her hands and the blue light settled on them, immediately putting the giants powerless and subject to her commands.

"You two," she motioned, "leave, go back to where you came from." Two of the giants turned and stumbled back into the trees, leaving the three she wanted behind. "We have somewhere to go my pets, stand ready."

Helana spoke several different words of another incantation and all three were caught up in the whirlwind of magic. She vanished with the three giants leaving the forest empty with a few dented brushes and broken trees to remind anyone they were there in the first place.

General Vadeez prodded the trolls along with more shouting and threats and to some extent it had been working. The creatures were finally burning off their excess intake of food at their conquest of Aberdeen, and were able to move a bit quicker. It still was not enough speed for him though. He wanted to be ready when this so called ambush would take place. A strong wind abruptly appearing made the general stop in his tracks and wait to see what awaited him this time.

Helana appeared and with her the three largest creatures he had ever seen. They were as tall as the trees and with two steps would overtake them all. He looked up, his eyes locked on the behemoths.

"General, I have a gift for you."

"What are they?"

"Simply put, giants, from far in the outlying Eastern lands. They will come with you and be at the front of your lines when you attack the resistance. These things will inflict more damage than a troll ever could."

"I am impressed! How were you able to find these, giants?" he asked.

"Friends elsewhere guided me to them, which are what's

not so important right now. What is important is getting to the falls to launch our own ambush," Helana said.

"I will use them well," Vadeez nodded.

"Good, I will rejoin you and the others at the falls. My powers have been nearly restored, in case I do not, be sure to finish them off. Leave no one alive," Helana instructed the fury quite evident in her voice.

"There will not be one left standing," General Vadeez assured her.

Chapter Twenty Two

Tony dismounted his horse and shook Neil's hand enthusiastically. It was good to see a familiar face amidst all the new faces he had seen the last few days. Tasha was just as relieved to see Shar and Adeena return from their trek to the gnomes alive and well, albeit not under the best of circumstances. The entire group of captains, along with Neil and Tasha had an impromptu meeting to hear what Tony, Shar and Adeena as well as Axel and Ruskin had to say about the journey back and what they had seen. Each took turns to describe the destruction of Eldridge, and the further inevitable defeat of Aberdeen. It was at times very hard for both dwarves to talk about leaving their friends behind to fend for themselves, but all of the information they provided would be essential in helping their impeding fight here at the falls. Everyone was stunned and taken aback at Shar's description of Eldridge's destruction and the power that Helana had in her ever growing abilities.

"There is one advantage though. If she expenses such magic, she needs time to recover and let the magic strengthen. How long that may take, I do not know, but it is something we can use to our advantage, if the timing is right," Shar explained.

"Then she must be near full strength again?" Brielle wondered.

"Perhaps, but then, maybe not. If she is unable to help her army here at the falls, the advantage lies with us," Shar said. "There is no way to find that out though, until it actually happens."

"Let's assume she will be able, that way we won't be taking their forces lightly. Even if she isn't there, they are still a surmountable army to contend with," Neil said.

"Aye, they are. There are so many different things in that army, I 'ave no idea where ta even begin ta describe'em," Axel muttered.

"We have to be prepared for anything. Demons have no rules they follow, they want only one thing, to destroy or kill," Riss commented.

"We set our forces in place tonight, and are ready for anything after that. They are already on the move according to our scouts and could be here as early as dawn," Kieran added.

"Then the time for any more discussion is over. We owe our gratitude to Tony, Shar and the rest for their safe arrival and information," Neil nodded with a smile. "As of now we are on watch for Helana and her army, I don't know what else to say except we have to do our best to slow them down. We have to give Cambridge enough time to set up their final line of defense."

"And to give our other friend Zach time to do what he needs to accomplish back on his home," Tasha added.

"Which is?" Darg asked.

"He has his own job to fulfill at Malcolm's request; it has to do with our situation here and if he's successful will go a long way to stopping Helana," Neil said. He didn't really want to get into any more detail because the less said the better.

"Not much to go on," Riss grunted.

"For it to work, the less said the better! We will all find out in time. Now, is there anything else we need to bring up?" Neil checked. He wanted to make sure all the bases were covered before they embarked to their specific areas.

"I think we have it covered," Brielle nodded. "Let us all dig in, and to all, a good fight. Do not let the demons get past, hold your line for as long as you can."

Kieran pointed to Elise. "If for whatever reason your line is breached, call on Elise and her forces. They and the gryphon's can help you retreat back to the river up above the falls. That is our only escape back to Cambridge, Teague, your archers must protect that retreat at any cost. If you fail then it will cost us all our lives."

"We will not break Captain, you have my word," Teague said reassuringly.

"Then that is it, safe keeping to all," Kieran motioned to all around the room.

"Aye, let's take some of them demons an' make'em pay fer what they done to our homes," Axel added. Ruskin grunted his agreement and Thatcher nodded as well.

"We will, not to worry my friend," Neil said with a nod. "Good luck everyone."

With that the group disbanded, breaking off to their separate divisions in preparation for the arrival of the dark army. There was a nervous tension throughout the encampment. More so because of the unknown and what their enemy was capable of. Exactly what their defense would be able to do would be determined once the fight started. One thing was certain though, they all knew they had to hold them off for as long as possible. The last line of defense against Helana had to be at full strength when she would inevitably arrive at Cambridge or their entire effort to stop her would be futile. Here at the falls, would be their determining factor at success or not. Zach's efforts on the old world depended on their success as well. If they broke down far too soon Zach could very well return to an already conquered world. The next day would establish a lot on how this war unfolded.

Up above the falls, Elise and her forces fed the gryphon and wandered around making sure all was ready for a quick departure if needed. She walked over to the edge of the ridge and stared out into the night. The dark clouds looked as though they were actually getting thicker and the dampness in the air was oppressive, adding to the already nervous tension throughout camp. Elise had to admit her lack of experience in the field was her greatest fear, but as her cousin Brielle always reminded her, 'everyone responds to situations differently, and each has their own gifts that will come forward when the time is required'. This was going to be a great test under pressure against a foe of which they knew very little. Elise watched the clouds, and glanced occasionally to the campfires below. Only a few were permitted so they could keep their numbers hidden from any foe and to minimize their location. There were no fires allowed on the ridge. That was to keep them completely concealed and the gryphon weren't really fond of fire all that much, so there was an extra reason to keep the campfires away.

Teague and his archers were entrenched along the entire ridge and were not in view at all. Each archer was amidst brush for better cover and unless you stepped on them, one would never know they were even there. Elise sighed and returned to her gryphon. She drew her cloak in tight to keep the cool of night at bay and petted the creature calmly and it snorted its satisfaction of her touch. This night would be a restless one for both her and the gryphon.

Kieran walked along the front lines with Taith, making sure the first line at the river was prepared and ready. This is where the initial attack would occur and it would go a long way in keeping the demons at bay. Their use of the river was immeasurable in its importance. The 'things' as Taith called them would have to get through the water before they could do any sort of offensive, so the river would be used against them and in doing so, hopefully the elves first line of defense would decimate a great many of the dark foe.

"They are ready as can be," Taith said. He nodded to a group and they walked on. "They have enough spears to inflict serious pain, and after that, they move to arrows. It will work," he smiled.

"Keep their shields up at all times! We have no idea what these creatures will hurl at us, they need to protect themselves always," Kieran reminded. He was confident of what they had for weaponry, but it was the unknown of the dark army's response that had him concerned.

"I will make sure they do. My only concern will be the demons using their own dead to get over the river. It isn't flowing as fast as it could be," Taith remarked.

"Aye, that could be a problem. Use lighted arrows if the bodies' mount, if they are burning perhaps that will give those second thoughts on using them as a bridge."

"Very well, it might not work very well but if it is able to slow them even a little I will be happy," Taith acknowledged with a nod. The two elves paused at a bend in the river and looked out across the field on the other side of the river. The army had to cross it, using the forest to the south would be too burdensome and give their army a too big of an advantage. They would have to cross the field to get to them.

"I don't like being down here for too long, we can be easy targets if this starts to go bad," Kieran said.

"You worry too much my friend, our back way is clear and Teague will make sure it stays that way. Come, let's keep going down the line, more walking and less talking will keep your mind busy," Taith chuckled.

Back near the second and third lines of defense, Tony and Neil strolled through the groups to plan and ease their minds of what lay ahead. Mia, Tasha and Shar had gone off somewhere else and they had no idea where Axel and Ruskin had wandered. It was quite apparent that they and Thatcher were upset at losing their home to the demons. Chances are they were off drinking a good portion of ale to ease the pain.

"Zach is back home?" Tony asked.

"Yeah, he's off with Riane somewhere to find the so called master wizard Malcolm keeps talking about."

"A master wizard, really, and who would that be?"

"Merlin," Neil said. Tony stopped in his tracks.

"What?"

"You heard me! Don't make me repeat it, because who knows who might be listening," Neil whispered as he held his finger to his lips.

"Well he's got his work cut out for him then," Tony remarked with a chuckle. "I don't envy him."

"Time will tell. So we have to wait for him to get back, hopefully, with him in tow," Neil said. He slapped Tony across the back, "Never a dull moment huh?"

Tony laughed. "Never! How is Malcolm holding up?"

"Not sure, we haven't had any contact with him for a couple of days now. All I do know is he had to go into the faerie realm to find the queen. Apparently the demons got in there and destroyed it. This whole thing is becoming quite the mess," Neil replied with a sigh. "Never in a million years would I think all this could happen. Not even in my wildest dreams!"

"Such is life in a world of magic; let's just hope we can get through this particular mess."

"No kidding."

Axel and Ruskin had finished off a few flasks of ale and Thatcher had lent a hand as best he could, but could not come anywhere close to keeping up with the two dwarves. After a time he gave up trying, opting to drink at his own pace. It would pay off in the long run with less of a headache come morning.

"Yer a might slow there Thatch, ya wanna another swig?" Ruskin offered, waving the flask in front of the gnome.

"No thanks, I've had enough for th'moment! You go on, drink what ya wish," Thatcher waved him off.

"Sad 'bout Eldridge?" Axel wondered, as he let out a burp.

Thatcher chuckled at the burp, and nodded. "Aye, it is hard ta believe it ain't there no more. I won't grasp it til I see it for myself, but if Shar says it to be true, she is to be believed!"

"She's not one to mix words that one! Hey, have ya noticed her hair goin more blonde?" Ruskin asked. He handed the flask over to Axel and sat back against the log on which they were resting.

"Tis th'magic, her gift is getting stronger," Thatcher replied.

"Is that so? My, she'll be givin ol'Malcolm a run fer his money now won't she," Axel chortled. He took a deep swig of ale and wiped his beard afterwards.

Thatcher laughed along with the two dwarves and took his turn with the flask on this go around. They finished it off with a few more passes and opted to sit back and give the drinking a break. The trio had a small fire going and was warned to keep it to a minimum for safety so a log was added to the embers as it neared ash to keep it from building but not too late that it wouldn't burn at all. It provided enough warmth to keep the chill at bay and the dampness just at the edge of their site. The ground was soggy so no matter what spot they tried to sit on, so they always ended up back on the log to keep dry.

"I hate th'dampness, why'd we get stuck near th'river?" Ruskin grumbled.

"Cause ya asked ta be near th'front of th'action," Axel snorted.

"Aye, yer right. What was I thinkin," he muttered. "Can ya toss another stick on th'fire there Thatch? Me toes are gettin cold," Ruskin snickered.

"Are ya sure? We can't be makin it too high now," Thatcher said as he tossed a small stick on the coals.

"If it were any smaller, th'bugs would be freezin," Ruskin cracked.

"Aye, if they aren't already," Axel added.

"Quit yer gripin' lad. Morning will be here soon enough, an'you'll be too busy to worry about th'cold," Thatcher said.

"Yer right, go on then, throw another wee stick on'er," Axel joked. "So I can find th'next flask."

Shar gazed at the sky and the ever darkening clouds. The breeze had only just begun to carry the aroma of rot and that meant the dark army was on its way. She watched the clouds change shape, and wondered if the stars or moons would ever be able to show themselves again. Tasha poked her, bringing her out of her trance.

"Ouch, not so hard," Shar smiled.

"Just checking to see if you were with us," Tasha teased.

"I am here so stop poking me. It's not nice," Shar kidded.

"How are you feeling my lady, I noticed earlier you looked somewhat, ill?" Mia wondered. Her observation skills were too strong and the queen knew better than to lie to a tracker.

"I am better now, thanks for asking. Must be the weather, or all this tension," Tasha put on a smile for her two friends.

Mia looked at her and merely nodded opting to leave it at that. Shar however, was more curious.

"How sick have you been?" she asked.

"Just some nausea here and there. Not a big deal, really!" Tasha answered with a shrug, "just nervous about all this."

"Really?" Shar commented. She took Tasha by the hand and spoke a few words. Tasha pulled her hand away, but Shar arced her eyebrow at the queen.

"You know you can't lie very well," she winked. "Does he know?"

Tasha sighed. "No, he doesn't. If he did do you think he would let me come out here?"

"Of course he wouldn't and I have the urge to send you home as well," Shar said. "This is risky, for both of you

"What is going on?" Mia asked, not sure what the two were talking about.

Shar looked over at Mia and gave the tracker a smile. "Think for a second Mia, why would Neil not want her out here due to her health?"

"No idea. Because she would get hurt?" she merely shrugged.

"Yes, true, but no, that isn't why. Think, she's not feeling well, and she's risking two lives, not just one."

Mia shook her head, at a loss, and she was getting more confused as the conversation continued.

"We will be fine, Malcolm has these talismans for us to wear," she held up her necklace. "We are perfectly fine."

"Regardless, don't take any foolish risks," Shar warned her with a wave of her finger.

"I think both her and Neil are capable of fending for themselves," Mia piped in.

"Yes they can, but still, no foolish risks, and I think you should tell him," Shar urged.

"Tell who, what?" Mia glanced from one woman to the next. "Can either of you tell me what is going on?"

Shar smiled, "The queen is expecting."

A figure that had been shadowing the three ladies heard the comment and was a bit surprised at the remark. This would be information worth reporting back to his queen. She would be quite anxious to hear this kind of news. He slid back into the shadows and away from the three ladies, leaving them to continue their conversation. He had what he needed, and at his first opportunity would alert his queen about his new information and what he had just heard. Just what she would do about it was unknown, but she would definitely want to know about it all and especially this little tidbit.

Chapter Twenty Three

Zach leaned on the railing of the boat and tried to steady himself. 'Why in the world did it have to rock so much' he thought to himself. The boat they had taken from the harbor wasn't exactly a small boat by any stretch but it still rode each little wave as though it was something a surfer would enjoy and not a passenger on a boat. Riane and Falon were settled inside the lower cabin area while Merlin himself steered the boat. He couldn't see a thing in the dark and he was amazed that the legendary wizard could have any idea as to where he was going. But then, he of all people should know where this so called island of Avalon would be.

The ocean calmed as the ride continued and the boat's incessant rocking eased somewhat allowing Zach to relax, enough so that he could actually enjoy the trip. He turned around and Merlin was standing there, catching him completely off guard and he nearly jumped in the air from the surprise.

"Geez! Don't do that! Hey," Zach glanced up at the steering apparatus of the boat and then back at Merlin. "Who's driving this thing?"

"The boat is on course, and will guide us to where we need to go. Not to worry young man. It knows the way," Merlin assured him with a pat on the shoulder. "Care to have a seat inside, and join me for a drink?"

"Sure, beats standing out here all night," Zach replied with a motion to the cabin. The two men found a seat around the small table just inside. They could see the two ladies sitting in the lower cabin around the other table playing cards. Falon was teaching Riane how to play various different games.

"She's been quite quick at learning the games. Falon is having a tough time trying to win," Merlin acknowledged with a smile. "Has she always been such a quick study?"

"Oh yeah, but here I thought she'd be a little more timid, but Malcolm's spell on her to look human has made her even more hungry to learn everything. It's bizarre, but then I've seen a lot of weird stuff in the last year and a half."

Merlin pulled a bottle of whiskey from the cabinet next to the table and grabbed two glasses to go with it. He poured two shots into each glass and handed one glass to Zach who accepted it with a nod.

"To all that is weird," Zach joked as he lifted his glass.

"I can toast to that," Merlin laughed lightly. They each took a sip and put their glasses back down on the table.

"So tell me, has anything you seen in the last year and a half as you say, been a bit more extraordinary than any other?" Merlin wondered curiously.

"Hard to say. I've seen a lot of stuff, a lot and every time I think I've seen it all something else shows up, case in point, you," Zach pointed at the wizard.

"Fun isn't it?" Merlin winked.

"Sure it is," Zach chuckled as he sipped his whiskey.

"I've been around a long time Mister Thomas, and there are things I still see today that surprise me. Mind you, we live in weird times! Just look at some of the TV shows out there, egad, such junk," Merlin shook his head. "It seems no one seems to care about the actual story anymore, sad really."

"And just how is it you can still be, alive, I guess. I don't know how else to put it, but how are you able to be here, now, talking to me?" Zach wondered. The need to know was eating away at him.

"Long story," Merlin sighed. He tipped his glass back, tasted the whiskey and then swallowed. "Are you sure you want to hear all the boring details?"

"Well, you can skip out the boring stuff," Zach chuckled.

Merlin smiled and sat back. "Very well, a question for you first. The elf, do you love her?"

Zach was a little caught off guard by the question but he glanced down to Riane and then looked once more back at Merlin. "Yeah, I do."

"She loves you that much is certain. She would do anything for you, and perhaps one day she might do more than you could ever think possible, but love is strange that way. It can make a man, or women do things they might not otherwise do."

"You loved someone, at some point?" Zach was curious to see if that's where he was going with this conversation.

"I did, she was an extraordinary woman, and quite cunning at the same time. You see love can cloud one's judgment. It happened with me a long time ago. Like young Falon there, I was looking for an apprentice to teach and she was quite eager to learn. I was young, so to speak," Merlin chuckled. "Naïve perhaps. After all I had never fallen in love, and I think at first I just thought of her as a student but that grew into more until I was truly in love with the woman. She knew this and used it to gain more knowledge than I should have let her know. A student must be patient, to be able to control their gift, if they are able, before they take that next step. Too much knowledge can corrupt, and that is what it did with her."

"Malcolm had an apprentice like that, too. She's the one who's the problem back on the other world," Zach said.

"I am guessing he had feelings for her as well. At one point, we are all guilty of it at some time or other. Until we learn from that mistake, it is bound to happen to all of us who take on an apprentice, especially if she is a woman. You see Mister Thomas; one can only be alone for a time before that loneliness can be too much to bear. When someone arrives who is interested in what you have to teach, then we are all too eager to show them the intricacies of magic. You are two of the same, gifted whereas most others are not. My love for her was turned against me at one point, and she imprisoned me within a cave, trapped by magic. I was unable to prevent the death of my dear friend Arthur, at the hands of his own bastard son Mordred," Merlin further explained.

"I recall reading about that at some point when I was doing all this research and trying to find you," Zach said. "Oh, sorry to interrupt, go on."

Merlin winked and tipped his glass back, finishing off what he had. "More?"

"Fill'er up, this could be a long night," Zach grinned as he held up his glass. Merlin refilled their glasses and settled back to continue his story.

"Where was I, Oh yes, I was stuck in this cave, which at first I didn't care for, but after some time I got used to it and settled into my fate and merely relaxed, for lack of a better word to use. After all, I wasn't going anywhere." Merlin chuckled and scratched his chin.

"So did this woman ever love you?" Zach asked.

"I thought not, but after a long time relaxing in my cave, which I decorated quite nicely by the way," he smiled. "She appeared one day. She had aged and was near her death, and overwrought by guilt for what she had done to me. She confessed to me she had aided another woman, Mordred's mother, in concealing who she was in order to sleep with Arthur, thus conceiving Mordred. Her doing so had brought about the death of Arthur and for that she could not live with herself and the guilt any longer. As she lay dying she professed to love me, which nearly broke my heart right there. She then requested I seal her within the cave where she had imprisoned me, as her final resting place. Her final gift, if you want to call it that, was something I did not expect. In time she had amassed so much knowledge in magic, so she transferred that to me and with that knowledge she included her life spirit, life force, whatever it is you wish to call it, and in doing so, gave me a much extended life."

Zach stared at him and then took a swig of his whiskey and put the glass down. "So how long are you supposed to live for now?"

Merlin sighed and shrugged. "I am not even sure. I am aging yes, but a much slower rate and according to Mother Nature; my time will end when my successor becomes ready and one who shall lead comes forth."

"Mother nature?" Zach looked at him with a stupid look. "Yeah right."

"Actually yes, maybe one day I'll introduce you, if she's up for the visit. Anyways, I digress," Merlin said. "So I left the cave, and sealed her within after she passed as she had requested. I found after a number of years that my aging wasn't really progressing and again had to get used to all of that. I saw many things going on around the world, magic was being forgotten or eradicated in some places, and all that needed magic to survive was dying. I went in search of a place where I could find a haven for all those of magic and in time found one. Hence, the world from whence you came. The island we are going to still has some magical races there, guarding what needs to be guarded. The majority crossed over to the new world and at the time, I had hoped would prosper eventually weeding out what was evil." Merlin was about to go on but Zach interrupted.

"The woman you, loved, what was her name?"

"Ah," Merlin sighed as he remembered days long past. "Nimue. No doubt you came across her name in your studies, some storytellers have her as someone else, and another lady as someone else, all of which I find very amusing. But Nimue was and always will be the one and only woman I have ever loved. I have had other apprentices over time, but she and one other were the most gifted. The other being part faerie and someone you will meet upon our arrival at Avalon. Young Falon is quite gifted too, but time will determine if she is truly gifted."

"Okay, you find this other world; send the magic folk over, hoping to prosper and weed out evil?" Zach wondered about the last part. It seemed a bit odd.

"Yes, it was my dream that on a world where magic could thrive, that they would be able to do away all that is evil. Sadly, over time I found this to be unrealistic. I did hope that someone such as yourself would never come seeking my assistance, but I have grown to realize that evil cannot be stopped."

"Oh, why is that?"

Merlin took his time in answering that question, as he looked for the right explanation that would best describe what he meant.

"Mister Thomas," he began.

"Just drop the mister stuff, call me Zach."

"Zach then it is. Zach, I have seen many things over the

years, good and bad alike. I have come to realize that there are things we cannot control. Evil is such a thing. I thought long ago that it could be vanquished, but I have since come to realize that it can only be contained. It is an entity unto itself, and uses us as its tool to achieve whatever it is it wants. Evil cannot exist without good, and good cannot exist without evil. The two balance each other. At times one may supersede the other, but in the end it must remain in balance in order for existence. However, with evil, it will do what it can to destroy that balance, because it feeds off of it, like a starving animal that cannot get enough, so is evil. It feeds and feeds, and if it is allowed to overfeed itself, then havoc ensues and complete destruction will follow. It does not care if there is anything left behind, for that is what it wants. The war between good and evil has been going on for all time, and will continue to do so. What has happened on the other world is new, and there are no longer any boundaries, evil has found a way to achieve what it has always wanted. Utter chaos and destruction."

"That doesn't sound very good," Zach said.

"No, it isn't."

"So what exactly are we going to get on the island? You said something about a talisman?"

Merlin sipped his drink. "You shall see. Let's talk about other things, something a little less, depressing," he snickered.

"Hey, since you knew Arthur, his knights, what about today's royal family? They drop by for tea once in a while?" he teased.

"I said less depressing," Merlin cracked. Zach laughed at the remark because it wasn't the answer he was expecting and he almost spit his drink all over the man.

"I am kidding of course," Merlin added. "They are nice people for the most part, some stand out more than others.

Diana, she was a rare exception, I do miss her dearly. She was an extremely unique individual who had a heart as big as the world. Very sad, but her boys have her heart and will continue to do good as she had. Anything else you care to know?"

"Well if Neil were here he'd likely have pages upon pages of stuff to ask you, but at the moment, I'm kinda drawin a blank. Any idea how much longer until we get to the island?" Zach asked.

"It is not that far, within the hour, but we cannot go ashore until dawn. So if you have nothing to ask of me right now I think I will go and get some sleep, and before you say it, yes, I do sleep. I'm not that abnormal you know," Merlin said.

Zach laughed again, and lifted his glass to the man. "Cheers."

He watched the wizard venture down the steps into the cabin and something Merlin had said earlier had just triggered another question or two but he would get around to it later. They weren't that important.

Merlin passed Riane and Fallon in the lower cabin, saying goodnight as he did, and disappeared behind one of the bedroom doors on the boat. The ladies returned to their card game, with Falon taking her turn to deal. Falon passed the cards between the two of them and settled back in her seat to look her own hand over. Riane did likewise and let out a sigh. Fallon glanced up at her, and squinted, trying to read the other's eyes for a sign of what she may or may not have in her hand. Much to her chagrin, the elf was just not an easy read. Just when Falon thought she might have Riane figured out, she would go about doing some sort of different reaction. Falon was getting a little frustrated at how hard of a time she was having against a supposed rookie at cards.

"And you've never played these card games before?" Falon checked, for what felt like the hundredth time. She was too flustered to accept it.

"I have played mostly poker, but these, are new to me," Riane smiled as she lifted up her cards.

"Really," Falon squinted while studying Riane's facial features.

Riane merely nodded, "Yep."

Zach's voice echoed down the steps. "Don't let her fool you Falon, she learns quickly. She had Axel and Ruskin coughing up money after just two hands of poker."

"Friends?" Fallon asked.

"Yes, dwarves, you'll get the chance to meet them when we go back," Riane answered without looking up from her cards.

"Dwarves? Well that'll be interesting," Falon said.

"More than you'll ever imagine," Zach cracked from up on the deck. "Hey, any ice down there?"

"Nope, we're all out," Falon replied.

"I will take two cards," Riane held up two fingers to make her point.

Zach stood up and stretched, he may as well catch a few minutes of shut eye as well before they got to Avalon Island. Who knows when he might get another chance to get some sleep? He ambled by the ladies, saying 'good night' as he did. Neither really acknowledged him since they were so entranced by their game of cards, and Falon's determination to beat Riane. Zach took a glance at Riane and she winked at him. He thought for a brief moment that the elf was merely toying with the wizard's apprentice and when she winked at him, he knew she was up to something. A few 'choice' words by Falon when the particular hand of cards was finished answered that thought easy enough. Zach closed the door and fell down on the bed, and was snoring moments later.

A knock on his door brought him out of his brief slumber and Zach sat up groggily. He didn't know what was worse, a lack of sleep, or waking after not enough sleep. Each made him feel miserable. The knocking persisted and he rubbed his eyes to get the cobwebs out of them.

"I'm awake, what?"

"We have arrived Zach, feel free to join us up on deck when you are ready," Merlin's voice filtered through the door.

"Yeah, okay," Zach mumbled.

It took about ten minutes before he finally walked up the steps to join the other three on the deck of the ship. All Zach could see all around the boat was fog, and more fog. The boat wasn't moving at all, that much he could tell but as for seeing anything else, completely impossible with all the fog.

"The sun does shine here once in a while doesn't it?" Zach joked.

Merlin turned around to look at him. "Depends on which way the wind is blowing."

"The wind?" Zach looked around at the fog. "There isn't any."

"Very observant," Merlin remarked with a chuckle. "Has he always been that keen in sight?" He asked Riane.

"Always," she answered with a light laugh.

"That's enough from both of you, so, are we there yet?" Zach chuckled as he asked the stupid question.

"We are waiting for daybreak, which will be any minute now," Merlin said.

"And you know this even with all this friggin fog," Zach yawned.

"Yes, I do," Merlin simply replied. Zach left it at that, and leaned on the railing, waiting, along with the rest of them for whatever was supposed to happen next.

Nothing moved in the fog, not even the slightest sound escaped it. They stood; waiting until Merlin finally moved to the front of the boat and lifted his 'staff' into the fog. A light breeze started up and the fog lifted enough to reveal a shoreline that the boat had come to rest on. One would have never seen it until the fog dissipated, revealing how thick the fog really was.

"Well I'll be," Zach murmured.

Merlin turned to face them all. "Now do as I say and you will follow me, one by one onto the shoreline. Once we are on land do not go anywhere, just wait there. I will have to get permission to go any further. Understand?"

All three nodded and he led them up to the edge of the boat where he proceeded to speak a few words and then he used his staff to touch the side of the boat. A white light glowed around the staff and a series of steps began to lower until they touched down on the sand of the shoreline. Merlin stepped down first and he motioned for them to follow. One by one they took their turn and once they were on shore they found a spot just away from the steps and stayed in place as instructed.

Merlin took a few steps forward and lifted his staff. "I have come on a matter of vital importance and seek your counsel. Do I have your blessing to come forth onto Avalon!"

All was quiet as the fog remained thick, obscuring the rest of the shore and whatever lay beyond. Then the fog began to stir and a form began to take shape. The silhouette of someone began to coalesce in the mist and all three watched as the process continued until the distinct outline of an individual could be made out. As the contours solidified it became apparent that the person was a woman. The lady materialized at last and floated down through the mist to walk on the sand and approach Merlin. Her hair flowed in the fog as though it was still a part of it, much like the mist that trailed behind her as she advanced. The dark hair was long and though there was no wind appeared as though it was being blown back into the fog. The mist never left her, at times shrouding the woman as though it protected her from any threat. She stopped several steps away from the wizard and looked him over.

"It has been a long time Merlin, good to see you well after all these years," she said with a sly smile.

Merlin nodded and stood up straight as he faced her. "Hello Morgana."

Chapter Twenty Four

Helana stood at the edge of the forest before the suns broke the horizon, and watched the clouds flow by overhead. They would hide any such sunrise this day, and as she whispered an incantation, there would be a whole lot less to see, anywhere. The clouds thickened and lowered onto the treetops, ever so slowly edging to the ground. The grey mist took hold of the land, and would not let go. It spread from the forest over the open plain, creeping along as it took hold of each blade of grass, each stone and every crevice. It was so thick nothing, absolutely nothing was visible. Helana watched the fog spread and then turned to another of her generals.

"Wait until the fog has advanced to the river, and then slowly move our forces out into it. Keep them straight, and keep them quiet, the mist will hide most of the noise from their advancement. If all goes well you should be right on top of them before they have any time to react. General Vadeez will be approaching from the south, and will catch them wide open without any defense."

"Understood my queen," the general bowed.

"I will return shortly, I have another errand to attend

to. Remember, keep them quiet as you march forward," she repeated.

"It will be done."

Brielle watched what should have been an open field but the fog hid it completely. She had watched the fog advance as the morning dawned and it brought more of the damp night chill with it. The elf did not like this particular fog, it did not feel right, and it obscured their entire view of anything or anyone that might approach them. There would be no way of knowing if their enemy was anywhere near. She could not even hear if there was anyone out there. This whole situation did not sit well with her.

"How are we going to know if there is anything out there? We can't see anything," she grumbled.

"No army can hide, even with this fog, we'll know if there's anything out there," Axel assured her.

"Are you able to feel the ground moving?" she teased.

"Are ya referrin' to my height by chance?" Axel snorted.

"No, not in the least," Brielle smiled.

"Th'sprite is enough ta put up with, don't ya start in now there girl, don't care if yer dad be th'king of elves or not," Axel chuckled.

"Relax, I will behave, promise," Brielle winked.

Elise stood on the edge of the falls and stared into nothing but grey cloud and mist. The moisture in the air stuck to her skin and she wiped the dew from her cheeks. This was not good, there was no visual on anything. She could not even see the archer that was a mere few feet from her. This cloud gave away no secret as to what may lay within. They were all blind to its grasp.

"Teague!" she shouted.

A voice, but no face, replied back through the fog. "Yes Captain?"

"Can you tell if there is anything out there?"

"None at all, can't see a thing in this mess, how about you?" he replied.

"Try and use your hearing, focus on that instead of sight. That might help somewhat," Elise suggested.

"Hear that one and all? Use your hearing, listen to the fog, and see if it has any surprises out there for us!" Teague shouted to all the archers.

Elise concentrated and listened as best she could, still there was nothing. It had to be after dawn at this point she assumed, and if there was an army out there, they were being awful quiet. She had a very uneasy feeling and Elise bit her lip nervously. Their well planned defense strategy was absolutely useless against this aberration of weather.

The figure waited in the woods, anxious to pass the latest news to his queen. He did not have to wait long; she appeared after a short time in a flash of wind and mist. Helana beckoned him over to her and he slipped out from behind the trees to face her. The man bowed and she motioned for him to stand up.

"No need for that every time we meet, so, what news do you have for me this time?" she asked, her curiosity peaking since it had only been a short time since his previous visit.

"I bear news about the queen herself, among other things, but the news about the lady Tasha I thought you might find of particular interested."

"Do tell," Helana shifted her stance, now she was really curious.

"The lady Tasha is expecting," he smiled.

Helana sneered, "Is that so. Well, the little play queen is with child is she? How much do you wish to serve me?"

"I am but to serve my queen," he replied.

"What other news?"

The spy continued. "I overheard talk of one going over to the old world, to find someone who can aid them against you, it is quite hush and no one is talking of it but I believe they mentioned another wizard of sorts."

Helana looked at the man, "Is that so. Interesting, I do not know of anyone who can do much." She paused in thought for a moment, and her demon side spoke. "A vinco veneficus, legend has is."

"I do not understand?" the man inquired about the last comment.

Helana shook her head. "There is a legend of one wizard, just a story, it is nothing more."

"I see. That is all I have for now, but I will keep watch."

"Then, my faithful spy; here is your next quest. You find the queen, and you kill them both, her and her unborn child, do so and you will be at my side when we conquer this world. Are you up to the task?" She wondered.

"It will not be easy, but I am up for the challenge," he answered confidently.

"Then the task is yours, and yours alone," Helana smiled.

"I am honored."

"Succeed and you will have an army at your command when we cross over to the old world, succeed and this new monarchy will fall," Helana said. She drew her cloak in tight and whispered the words she needed and in a flash of wind and mist, vanished.

The man turned and returned to his waiting ride. He climbed on and steered the animal back to resistance forces waiting at the falls.

"I will succeed my queen; it will be an absolute pleasure."

The ranks waiting along the river grew ever more nervous as the fog failed to negate at all. No sound or very little carried any distance and if there was an army out there in the fog, they could very well be standing on top of them and they would not know. Axel and Ruskin shifted continuously while waiting and were beginning to lose their patience with all of it. They were not the only ones, the entire force was restless, and unable to see or hear was extremely uneasy.

Shar did not like the fog from the beginning, but as Malcolm had warned, to use her magic now would give her and her abilities away to Helana. At this point however, she felt it necessary to take the risk. The danger was greater to more than just her if she did not do anything. There were too many lives at risk. She could sense magic was involved with this fog and it could conceal a great many things.

Axel stood up and stretched to listen, he thought for a moment he had heard something, albeit vague.

"Th' water, there's somethin splashin in th'water."

"Are ya sure, I can't hear a thing," Thatcher turned his head to try and put his ear to the river.

"Brielle, Kieran, I am going to do something about this fog, have everyone stand ready, just in case," Shar said.

"We'll be ready," Kieran assured her. He ran off, stopping at every group to have them prepared for whatever may happen.

"Are you sure you can do something about this?" Brielle checked.

"Yes, not to worry, we'll be able to see something, if anything momentarily. Be ready," she replied without taking her gaze away from the fog in front of their forces.

"Aye," Brielle nodded. She moved to take her place with the rest, and lifted her bow.

Shar pulled her cloak in tight and thought of the words she needed to use. Carefully she began to speak and moved her left hand out with an open palm held up as though she were stopping traffic.

"*Go no further, with these words you will vanish, with this wind I send you will give way, expose the land as it was before, this I ask, so it shall be, so mote it be,*" she murmured. A light breeze began and immediately the fog began to thin and lift. Shar let the magic do its work and soon the river began to appear.

Elise saw the mist begin to thin and with it her hearing improved, there was a noise in the air that sounded like 'flapping' and it became more predominant as the fog lifted. She turned and ran back to her gryphon, shouting commands as she bolted.

"Teague! Aim at the sky! Get them shooting!"

The Captain of the archers heard the noise as well and was already running along the ridge line.

"You heard her! Fire at will! I don't care at what, just shoot and hope you hit something!" he barked.

Elise heard the arrows as the archers let loose the first volley skyward. There was something out there and now the enemy was virtually on top of them.

"To your ride! Get into the air and be sharp, go!" Elise commanded as she reached her gryphon. The other riders did as ordered and mounted their own animal. The entire group was airborne in moments and flying into a still shrouded sky.

Elise dug her heels into the side of the gryphon and she felt the animal resist at first but it slowly gave in as she began to guide its course. She could see the group go into formation and hold their position above the archers, and away from their current line of fire. They held steady, waiting for the fog to dissipate further and ascertain the situation.

As the river came into view, Axel and Ruskin went wide eyed at what they saw. They weren't the only ones. The entire resistance force was overwhelmed at the sight that beheld them as the fog lifted. Not one arrow was fired as all stared, at the hell that had been let loose from the depths of darkness.

Demons of all sizes, monsters of every shape, and trolls were sloshing through the river with the smaller of the filth standing on the troll's shoulders. The masses were almost half way across the river already and would not take long before they reached the near shore of the resistance forces. Though the river was deep but the lack of any significant current was allowing the trolls to stay above the water with ease. The demons and other minions were so thick that there was no way to avoid hitting any of them with whatever weapon of choice.

Brielle was the first to break out of her trance and was shouting as she pulled her bow back to fire. "Shoot! Fire at will! Make'em count!"

"Look at'em all," Axel muttered as he rubbed his beard. "How th'hell are we supposed ta fight that!"

"Just do what ya can! An' save some fer me!" Ruskin shouted as he let his axe fly. It whisked through the air and the blade slammed into the skull of the nearest troll. It jerked back in response and sank below the water. The dwarf picked up his secondary axe and stood ready for the onslaught.

The front line let loose with all the stock in their cache and at first saw very little effect due to the size of the dark army. A few would fall into the water but there were dozens more to replace those and their encroachment on the resistance closed. As the dead mounted the surge across the river began to slow but the gap still narrowed between the demons and the first line of the defenses.

"Light your arrows! Get them on fire!" Kieran ordered. He watched as the first line began to light their arrows but the time to do so was too long. The elf captain turned to Shar but she already had the incantation under way. At this point there was no hiding her magical abilities and if they did not do something soon they would be overrun.

"*Fire burn, Fire strike, hit your target as they aim, so mote it be*!" Shar whispered. The arrow tips of the elf archers sparked to life and the arrows were let loose into the throng of demons.

Helana reappeared at the end of the far side of the field in whirl of wind and blue light as she rejoined her army just as the attack had begun. She was somewhat disappointed her cover fog was gone and immediately sensed the use of magic. The question she had, was from whom? It was not Malcolm's doing, this was a different form of magic. The elves perhaps? She detected it again as the burning arrows were flying through the air. No, this magic was beyond the elves capabilities. A new foe to contend with and she smiled at the thought.

"Very well, let us see who is the better," Helana hissed. She lifted her hands and countered the burning arrows.

Shar watched as the fire on the arrows extinguished as they hit their targets. At first she was taken aback, but then felt the magic. As quickly as they extinguished Shar had them relit and the fire took hold of the host. Shar assumed it was the work of Helana, and that could be dire for the resistance. If Helana interfered in their defense of the falls, it would give the demon army a heavy advantage. Yet she knew the witch could not risk using too much of her magic for it would drain her and she would need time to rest to regain her strength.

Helana nodded in appreciation towards the magic invoked to relight the fires. This person knew her magic well. She would wait a while to test this mage further. Her remaining forces would arrive shortly and would undoubtedly cause more havoc on those defending the falls. The witch stood there, waiting and watching the battle unfold.

Elise saw the first manticore break through the fog near the middle of their formation. It flung its tail around and its spikes flew into the two nearest riders and the gryphon. Both tumbled from the sky in a heap, instantly dead from the poison darts. Elise and another rider had their crossbows aimed and fired just as quick but too late for the fallen. The riders changed directions to avoid the oncoming attack of the deadly creatures. A few more of the manticore appeared and Elise began to think of alternate ways to fend them off. An idea came to her, speed, it was the only answer to the slower creatures. She signaled the other riders with her arms. The riders communicated that way to change strategies or signal others. Each signal had different arm motions and together they would react.

Brielle and Kieran were shouting orders to keep firing as the enemy pushed their way through the water to reach the near shore. Arrows were fired en masse but no matter how many of the demons fell the force still advanced through the water. Due to their lack of advance notice of the attack the front line was about to be overrun. The initial plan of defense was now thrown to the wayside.

"Move back to the second line! Move! Move! Move!"

Kieran bellowed as loud as he could to get his message out above the carnage.

Axel, Ruskin and Thatcher didn't want to argue the order, they were more than eager to move back and away from the dark army now almost to their shore line. The dwarves who rarely backed down from any fight knew they were at an extreme disadvantage. The three hustled back with the elves to reposition themselves with those waiting at the second line.

Neil shook his head and Tony nodded with him. This well thought out plan was somehow coming unraveled really quickly. The first line took their spots next to the second defense group and the archers took aim once more.

"We need to slow them down Kieran, they're advancing too fast! At this rate we'll be retreating well ahead of our timeline!" Neil shouted.

"I know sir! We'll hold them here, we will hold them!" Kieran hollered back, the tone of determination quite evident. He took his place next to his fellow elves, shouting orders while he pointed at the advancing army.

Up above Elise and her riders got their gryphon to fly as fast as they were capable and together the unit soared in and around the manticore, confusing the monsters and keeping the poison darts off their intended targets. As they raced by they would fire their crossbows, sometimes hitting, sometimes missing but it kept the manticore off balance. Neither side was winning the fight in the sky but neither was losing the war at this point. Elise knew they had to break the manticore defenses and get the advantage back so they could lend a hand to struggle below on the land. Once more she signaled her flyers to a change in strategy and as one they responded, refocusing the attack on the manticore.

Arrows flew from the resistance forces at will, hitting everything that crossed from water onto land. There was no way to miss. The demons fell and were stampeded over by other minions who in turn collapsed dead as the elves fired relentlessly. The dark army began to slow, impeded by the dead that were piling up.

Neil smiled; at last, they were making some progress. He pulled another arrow and let it go, and reached back for another. His supply was getting low, and if his was, no doubt the others were dwindling. He paused, and put his bow down. He ran along the line until he reached Shar.

"Shar, we need your magic, the arrows are nearly gone, can you replace them?" he asked.

"It is too soon, I risk using too much magic and expending my strength. Helana is here somewhere, you may need me to assist in other ways," she replied.

Neil let out a breath, and nodded. She was thinking ahead. "You're right. Are you sure she's here?"

Shar nodded. "Yes, she's tested me once already with the fire I brought out. I can't have her knowing how much ability I have."

"Move back to the third line, if she is here we might need you up on the ridgeline. Take Tasha with you," he urged.

"Wise," Shar smiled. She ran off to fetch Tasha from her position. The queen would not agree with the retreat, she was enjoying the fight too much. To have to pull back would make her considerably frustrated but Neil needed her safe. He returned to his bow, grabbing it as he ran by to Kieran.

"We have to go to the next phase! We'll run out of arrows pretty quickly!"

Kieran nodded and shouted out orders. "Advance line! To your feet!"

A long column of elves stood up and lifted their concaved long blades, similar to that of a sickle. They were the advancement unit of defense who would move in towards the demons and cut them down, allowing the second fortification to regroup and re-establish the line. Each elf stood next to the other and the troupe advanced towards the demons with Taith taking command of the offensive. Axel and Ruskin lifted their axes and joined the melee with zeal.

Tasha was not too pleased with Shar when the mage grabbed her by the arm suddenly and began to pull her back away from the barrage.

"Wait Shar! What are you doing?"

Shar took a firm tone with her friend. "I am taking you with me to the third line, if this goes bad quickly we need to keep you safe!"

"What about Neil? Tony? The rest?" Tasha asked angrily.

"They will be coming shortly, but first we need to get you back. Don't argue with me, there is more than just you at risk. Remember?" Shar shot back.

Tasha had no response to that, and reluctantly followed Shar back to the third and final line of defense before the foray would have to go into full retreat. The two ladies took shelter amidst the brush that the forces were using as cover on the third line. Vasillis was in command of the third fortification and directed the two ladies to the back end of the defenses to allow for the ease of their retreat.

"If you need anything, just ask my lady," Vasillis bowed. He moved off to check on the forces, leaving Tasha and Shar by themselves.

"I don't like leaving anything, this fight is just as much mine as it is the elves," Tasha said angrily.

"Yes, it is. However, Helana is here, I don't know where

but she is somewhere. We need to keep you safe and Neil as well. I promised Malcolm I would keep watch of you both, don't make it any harder please," Shar smiled. Tasha managed a light laugh, and Shar laughed with her.

"Very well, I don't want to be more of a pain than I need to be," Tasha teased her friend. "Are you sure Helana is around?"

"Yes, I believe she is watching this fight unfold. I don't know what, or if, she will do anything."

"That will depend on how well we are doing against her army," Tasha sighed. "She won't allow us to get a step up on her."

"Therein lays the fear," Shar nodded.

Elise and her gryphon captains keyed in on one manticore at a time, letting loose with a volley of arrows from every rider as they flew in! It was a slow process because they had to keep their speed up to avoid any retaliation from the toxic darts of the manticore's tail. The end result was what they hoped, the sight of a dying creature hurtling towards the ground. After a few of them were dispatched the elf sky riders began to feel the tide turn in their favor. The confidence was evident as they keyed in on another manticore and the creature retreated back towards the forest. A few of the elf riders began to pursue but Elise pulled them back with her arm signals. They could not afford to risk splitting the group.

It was their chance now to lend a hand to the ground forces and Elise motioned for the group to swing downward, and do what they could to help.

"Down! Make your shots count!" She shouted while waving them down.

Taith and the advance troupe marched into the demons

with blades swinging, cutting the creatures with every ounce of energy they had. The blades sliced through scales, fur, skin and bone. The demons and dark creatures fell to the wayside as the elves pushed the dark army back to the edge of the river. The determination of the elves was making a difference despite the numbers favoring the minions of Helana.

Taith cut down one demon and as it bled profusely he finished it off with a broad swing that beheaded it. A man of twisted shape and deformity stepped in front of Taith and drove his blade into the stomach of the thing. It had no effect. The man merely grinned and grabbed the handle, ripping it from his hands.

"Not today demon," Taith shouted as he quickly withdrew his sword and brought it around across the creature's upper torso. It left a huge gash, but still the man stood there with a grin.

The elf was dumbfounded at the ability of the thing to survive his attack, but it only drove the elf to push harder and several swings later the 'man' lay in three pieces on the ground, incapacitated but still alive.

Taith was worn out by the attack and saw that the other elves were having the same difficulty finishing off the other men resembling demons. There was something different about these spawn. The dark army, now led by trolls pushing their way through began to push the elf troupe back.

"No ya don't ya dark thing!" Axel shouted as he drove his axe into the neck of one scaled and hairy creature. It gagged and fell to the ground in a heap. The dwarf yanked his axe free and focused on the next creature moving towards him.

Ruskin was just as active with his own blade as he cut down an imp, slicing it cleanly in half. The smaller demonic creature fell to the wayside and Ruskin was targeting his next fight.

"Why don't ya take on something yer own size!" Axel cracked.

"Shaddup, keep yer own count, an' don't ya mind what I'm doin!" his brother retorted.

Elise and her elf riders flew by then just as the advancement troupe began to slow and let loose with their volley of arrows, and the gryphons used their clawed feet to grab several trolls and toss them back into the river. A cheer broke through the ranks of the elves and with a renewed determination began to push back against the demons.

Elise and the riders flew near the south tree line in an arc to turn and go for another fly by over the attack, but as they neared the forest, two spears flashed out from the trees and struck down two of the gryphon, their riders tossed off as they lurched. Both rider and gryphon hit the ground dead. Elise pulled her gryphon up hard and looked back to see where and who had launched this new attack.

The trees were pushed aside and Elise almost lost her grip on her gryphon at the sight she saw. Three enormous creatures, things she had only heard of in stories, giants, stomped into view leading another horde of demons and monsters onto the fields just south of the resistance troops. There was nothing standing in their way but open space.

Chapter Twenty Five

Merlin stood on the shoreline of Avalon, and waited for the lady Morgana to allow their further travel on the island. The mystic woman, former student of his and protector of this hallowed isle was surveying the situation and stood staring at the rest of his party with curiosity. The wizard leaned on his staff and shifted his stance while he waited for her to speak. She took notice of his impatience and grinned at the man.

"What is the matter old friend? Is your passage that important?"

"It is Morgana, there is very little time to waste on this issue," he replied.

"Is that so? My name is Morgan Le Fay, Merlin, I would think that after all these centuries you would get it right."

"Morgan Le Fay," Merlin cracked a smile. "I have not used that name since you were but a small girl, learning how to say your first incantation. I doubt your sisters call you by that name Morgana, speaking of the ladies, where are they hiding?"

"They are busy elsewhere. I am the keeper of this isle and it is I you need to be concerned with. You show your face and you expect me to just let you wander through? You bring three," she began and then paused for a moment as her gaze shifted back to the other three. "One is different. She is protected by magic."

Morgana floated over towards Zach, Riane and Falon, the mist staying with her as she approached. She faced Riane and looked at the woman closely. Riane bowed her head in acknowledgement of the lady suspended before her. Morgana smiled at her and looked back at Merlin.

"An elf? Hiding as a human. Yet she is not from here, from where then?"

"Observant as ever Morgana! Think for a moment, and you may come to the answer on your own," Merlin challenged her.

"Oh Merlin you waste my time, there are no elves on the mainland, or elsewhere on this world save here, on Avalon." Morgana stopped in midsentence and looked back at Riane. "You are from the new world. Amazing!" Morgana stared at her. "Then the magic, the races, are thriving on the new world?"

Riane nodded. "Yes my lady, we are."

"Amazing, truly amazing." Morgana drifted back to Merlin and gave the old wizard a small hug. "You are always welcome Merlin. You may pass. Why is it you need to enter our fair realm once again?"

"The new world faces a great threat that may cross over to this world; I am here to collect what I need to stop it."

"Ah yes, you are here to retrieve it once more. It has not been touched since the death of Mordred. Are you sure it is required?" Morgana asked.

"It is," he said with a nod.

"Then we will have to gather the others in order to release it. This will take time," Morgana said.

"I understand, but we have no choice."

Morgana sighed. "Very well then. I will retrieve the council immediately. The fairy king will not be happy being disturbed during the spring season, but I will make him understand. You know the way?"

"Yes I know where I am going," Merlin chuckled. "I do still have my memory after all these years."

Morgana smiled. "I had to be sure," she smiled. "I will meet you all up there." At that Morgana disappeared into the mist, leaving the four of them standing on the shoreline. Merlin motioned for the rest to join him and together they began to walk up the path leading up a hill.

The trail meandered through tall grass and sand and slowly the terrain changed into shorter grass and the ground more solid, gradually evolving to a firm dirt path lined with short brush. It was a steep climb and the fog kept most of the island hidden from view and Zach was beginning to run out of patience, and breath.

"How much climbing do we have to do?" He grumbled.

"The exercise will do you good," Riane teased.

"Didn't ask for your opinion," Zach snorted back.

"We are almost there Mister Thomas, Zach, put aside everything you've known and let your mind be at ease," Merlin shouted back at him.

"Enough of the mumbo jumbo. Where are we going anyways?" he asked.

"There," Merlin replied as he stopped at the top of the hill. The other three came in alongside him and looked down into a valley shrouded in fog. But amidst the fog, tall spruce trees jutted out and the tall towers of what appeared to be a castle of sorts.

"What, is that?" Zach murmured.

"That my boy is Camelot, as it was all those years ago.

Come on then, we have little time to waste." Merlin strode on and was quickly vanishing into the mist.

"Camelot?" Zach said. He looked at Riane and Falon. "Camelot?"

"Yes Zach, if he says it is Camelot, you can take him at his word," Falon assured him.

"But, how?"

"Sometimes if you want an answer, you just have to ask, I'm sure he'll tell you," Riane smiled. She and Falon began to jog down the trail leaving Zach to stand there by himself for a time. He stared at the towers piercing the fog and scratched his head in disbelief. This was almost like a dream and if he closed his eyes he might just wake up from it all. To make sure he blinked several times, and the towers of Camelot were still there. He had read a lot on the so called castle in his research on Merlin, but to actually see it was unbelievable! This was no dream, it was real. He took in a deep breath and started down the path after the rest.

Zach emerged from the forest to stand before the walls of the legendary castle Camelot. He gawked up at it, taking in every stone as his gaze strayed up to the catwalk, where a number of guards stood on watch. He couldn't make out whether they were human, elf or other. Merlin, Riane and Falon stood waiting in the arch of the front gate of the castle. Zach took his time sauntering over, his eyes never leaving the castle. He was completely in awe of the spectacle.

"Enjoying the view Mister Thomas? I think I've actually aged while waiting for you," Merlin said with a wide grin. The wizard was enjoying having a little fun at Zach's expense.

"Very funny," Zach retorted. "Who's on watch upstairs?" He pointed.

"The elves. It is their duty to protect the castle, the

island, all its inhabitants," Merlin answered as he motioned to the elves on the catwalk.

"There are elves?" Riane wondered. To see elves from this world would be something to tell her father about back home.

"Yes, there are. One contingent remained behind to fulfill the task assigned to them by their former king," Merlin said.

"May I meet them?"

"You shall," Merlin assented.

"So, why are we here? What weapon are we supposed to get?" Zach asked curiously. He couldn't wait any longer to see why they had traveled all this way.

"You have a need to know everything, don't you Zach?" Merlin sighed.

"Yeah, I do. The detective in me I guess," he shrugged with a chuckle.

"Then I will keep you no longer, follow me and we shall see what we are here to collect," Merlin motioned for him and the others to follow.

The four walked into the courtyard of Camelot castle and once inside the three stared in awe at the magnificence of it all. All three felt like they were entering a part of history, a mythical past that no one had been able to witness before at least no one in this day and age anyway. They took it in, absorbing each new sight that came into view. Merlin and company were greeted by an elf that leapt down from one of the upper catwalks and bowed in greeting. He stood in front of a door that led into what would be the main hall of Camelot and held his sword front and center.

"Greetings! We have consent from the lady Morgana to enter the halls of Camelot," Merlin stated.

"I know sir, she informed us of your arrival not long before you appeared. I am to welcome you and to be your guide," the elf bowed again. He stood tall. "It is an honor to meet you Merlin. My father told me about you over the years, I am sure he would be happy to see you again."

"Is he still around?" Merlin asked politely.

"He is sir, he will be back later after his patrol of the island."

Riane stepped forward and offered her hand. "It is an honor to meet a fellow elf from the old world."

"You are an elf?" the guard questioned her. There was no indication that she was such, due to Malcolm's spell.

"She is transformed to fit into her surroundings; she is an elf true enough, from the new world."

"Really?" The elf smiled on hearing that and shook Riane's hand enthusiastically. "The honor is mine my lady; again, my father has told me many stories of how our fellow elves migrated to this other new world."

"Perhaps one day you will have the chance to visit," Riane smiled.

"I hope so my lady."

"I hate to break up our hellos, but my good elf, can you guide us to the lower chambers?" Merlin asked.

"Yes sir, follow me," he bowed. The elf opened the door and led the way into the main hall. Merlin had to pause upon seeing the room. It had been a very long time since he had set foot in the hallowed halls of what had once been his home. He took in a deep breath and exhaled slowly. The memories, good and bad flooded back and the wizard wiped a tear that slid down his cheek.

"Are you okay sir?" Falon checked as she moved to stand beside her mentor.

"I am," Merlin acknowledged. "Every time I am in here the memories come back, of a time when things were very different."

"Need a tissue?" Zach cracked. Merlin laughed lightly and shook his head at the man.

"You must be the life of a party Mister Thomas, but my thanks, you help an old man to remember that life is just as much about today as it is about the past. Come then, let's retrieve what we need and restore the balance of magic," Merlin said with nod of appreciation.

"This way sir," the elf guard pointed. Once more he took the lead and the rest followed.

He led them down a couple halls, pausing on occasion to allow the group to take in the different sights. At a stairwell that led down the elf guard motioned for Merlin to take the lead and the wizard obliged. Falon, Riane, and Zach trailed behind and did their best to keep up. It wasn't long before they reached the end of their descent and found Merlin waiting for them.

The room was relatively dark, with one torch lit on the nearest wall, undoubtedly lit by someone prior to their arrival. It was an empty room with the exception for one area near its center, where an object sat, hidden by the darkness. Near the back of the room was another much larger door, that had a symbol of sorts painted on it and was secured with an enormous beam saddled across it. It would take several men, or elves to lift it off before gaining entry. There was a reason it was that way and Merlin noticed the trio looking at the door.

"That is a tomb my friends. A final resting place for an old friend and no one without my permission is granted access. The dead deserve to rest in peace," Merlin informed them.

"Who?" Zach asked as politely as he could.

"That is where Arthur rests, and forever shall do so, away from those who may want to disturb it, protected by the guardian's magic of Avalon. Only on permission from me may they enter and then they will change the incantation to allow it. He deserves nothing less, a man who brought this land together, a leader that has had no equal in the years since," Merlin further explained.

Zach remembered something from their boat trip and walked up to Merlin. "You had mentioned on our ride over here, something about one who is supposed to come and lead. There are stories I had read saying that Arthur will rise again and is king, is that what you were referring to?"

Merlin chuckled. "No Zach, Arthur is very much passed on. Those are stories created by those who have too much free time on their hands, and perhaps a strong desire that such a thing could be true. No, the one I was alluding to was Arthur's heir, a descendant of his."

"A descendant?" Falon asked with a gasp. She could not comprehend such a statement could be true. "But how?"

"Why could it not be my young student? After all, the lady Guinevere had fallen in love with Lancelot, Arthur was distraught, would it not be feasible that he found comfort with another woman? I admit, I found it hard to apprehend when mother nature told me of this, heir, but she was adamant this person existed, somewhere, someplace on this world. She could not however, tell me who it was or where this person would be. If you think I am vague at times, you should try having a conversation with Mother Nature." Merlin let out a deep sigh and looked back to the door that led to Arthur's resting chamber.

"In all my studies, there has never been any mention of a descendant. There has always been the tale of Arthur himself returning," Falon continued.

"Those of us in a small circle have taken steps to hide all references in any writings that may have mentioned such a thing. It has not been easy, but we have kept that fact, a secret. You are the first three to know of it," Merlin said.

"I thought you were joking about Mother Nature! She really exists?" Zach asked.

Merlin nodded. "Yes, she does. Though you may not recognize her as anything you may understand. She is, rather unique."

"So why are we down here?" Zach wondered.

"What we need is down here, hidden away, secure from any curious onlookers. It rests with Arthur, as it should since he was the last one to wield it. There, in the center of the room," Merlin pointed. "*Ignite, suggero nos per lux lucis, pulsus tergum umbra per vestri vires, sic mote is exsisto.*"

The torches situated alongside the outer wall ignited and the room lit up as bright as though the sun was shining through a large number of windows. The room was bare with the exception of a large stone object in the center of the room as Merlin had mentioned. The stone was misshapen, with no particular form to it. It looked as though someone had merely picked up a big rock in a field somewhere and had dropped it in the chamber. In the stone was another object, and as they walked closer to it, the hilt of a blade was clear while the blade itself was imbedded into the stone.

"So, we hit the witch with the rock?" Zach jested with a shrug.

"Please Zach, stop joking around," Riane urged.

"Sorry," he apologized.

"That is all right, no Mister Thomas, we don't use the rock. It might just give her a slight head-ache," Merlin quipped. "No, what we need is the sword itself."

"Why the sword?" Zach asked.

"It is more than a mere sword! It was forged by magic with the elves, a few others, and I included all having a hand in its creation. It was made for one purpose, to kill evil. This blade and no other can do what we need on the new world.

It is the only weapon with the power to kill the witch and the demon, to restore balance to the magic."

"Wait a second; is this the same sword from the stories, the sword in the stone tales? Arthur drew it from the stone and was named king because of that, is this that same sword?" Zach quizzed.

"The very same," Merlin acknowledged. He wandered over and touched the hilt with his fingers. "The sword, of course, is Excalibur."

"My word," Falon gasped. All of her childhood was being lived out in one day, all of the mysteries were unfolding before her and she felt like she was living a dream.

"May I touch it?" Falon requested.

"Feel free, it won't bite," Merlin teased. "Give it a go on pulling it free, if you wish, though you will find it impossible."

"Maybe we'll get lucky," Falon replied confidently.

"It will be fun to try," Riane added.

"I will be back shortly, I have to retrieve my book of magic, and wait for the arrival of the rest of the council. Only together will we be able to free the sword from the stone. Then we can prepare for our journey back to your world my lady," Merlin bowed to Riane. The wizard turned and wandered over to Arthur's tomb and touched the door. More memories flooded back, of a time when he was teaching a young Arthur about what was good, and what was wrong. He closed his eyes as the memories overflowed and he felt a tear trickle down the side of his cheek. It had been so long ago but felt like it was only yesterday.

Over at the stone, Riane reached out and grabbed the hilt of Excalibur with both hands and gave the sword a good pull. It didn't budge and the elf giggled at her effort. She stood aside and Falon did the same. As Riane the effort fell short of dislodging the sword. The two ladies laughed and began to tease Zach.

"Whatsamatter? Big strong man like you scared to be shown up by a couple ladies?" Falon goaded him.

"You two have shown that thing ain't movin, so why should I break my back trying?" he replied with a chuckle.

"Oh give it a shot Zach, show us how bloody strong you are," Riane needled him.

"Everyone here on Avalon has tried sir, you may as well try yourself," the elf guard said.

"Oh really, everyone?" Zach checked.

"Yes," the elf guard assured him.

Zach sighed and shrugged. "Oh what the hell." He walked over to the stone and looked at the sword for a moment. He looked closely and saw some words engraved on it.

"Take mihi sursum," he whispered.

Merlin vaguely heard Zach say the words. "What did you say?"

"Just reading off what's on the blade here."

"What words?" Riane asked. "I didn't see any words."

Zach merely shrugged, "Guess you didn't look close enough. "Well, here goes nothing," he cracked.

Zach put both hands on the hilt of Excalibur, and was somewhat surprised that the handle felt warm to the touch. He took in a deep breath and gave the sword a good strong pull.

Merlin turned from facing Arthur's tomb to see Zach put his hands on the handle and brace himself to yank. The wizard watched as he began to pull.

Zach fully expected to feel resistance but instead the sword withdrew as he heaved and the distinct sound of metal scraping on stone echoed throughout the room. He nearly lost his balance as Excalibur uprooted itself from the stone and Zach repositioned himself, and then stood there in disbelief, with Excalibur in hand, free of its stone casing.

Merlin stared in awe, at the sight he had just witnessed. He sat down on the steps to Arthur's tomb and scratched his chin in shock. The sword, Excalibur, could only be freed from the stone by magic, or, by the one person Mother Nature said existed. That person could be no one other than Arthur's descendant. Those were the conditions imposed on Excalibur, and so it was, and had been for centuries.

Zach stared at the sword in his hands, and looked over at Merlin for some sort of explanation. The wizard merely stared back, perhaps as shocked as he was at the turn of events. Zach looked at the others in the room; both Falon and Riane were gawking at him and the other elf was kneeling and bowing towards him.

"Mister Thomas, you have just made my job a whole lot easier," Merlin murmured.

Chapter Twenty Six

Malcolm sat on the edge of the bed, and watched as Leasha finally began to stir after a long rest. The queen of faerie slowly opened her eyes, looking around the room at first, taking in her surroundings and then she saw the mage at the far end of her bed. She smiled weakly and tried to sit up but Malcolm held up his hand to encourage her to think otherwise.

"You are still quite weak my lady, lay back, go easy. It will take time to restore your strength after what you have been through," he said calmly.

"Thank you, for saving me Malcolm. I truly thought my life was at an end," the queen said while trying to hold back tears.

"You are welcome, but you don't give yourself enough credit. You are quite the stubborn prisoner," he chuckled, trying to lift her spirits up.

Leasha managed a light laugh. "I must have a little of my father in me."

"I imagine you do," Malcolm agreed.

"Have you seen my children?" she asked.

"Yes, they are here. Eden and Jindra have been gathering

the strays and guiding them back here to Cambridge. They are safe."

"But no home to return to," Leasha whispered. A few tears slipped through her defenses and slid down her cheeks.

"We will repair your home after this is all over with, and one day they will be able to return. In the interim, Xanthus has welcomed all of faerie to stay here. This will be home, for now," Malcolm said. He smiled and took Leasha's hand in his own.

"Thank you again, for everything. I will thank Xanthus for his warm hospitality when I am able. This is a horrible dream that never ends," she murmured.

"True, it does feel that way. Well, perhaps we may all end this nightmare soon enough. Just to keep you updated, since you've arrived we've had a lot of our reinforcements show and we've begun to prepare for Helana's eventual arrival here. We will be able to give her a welcome she won't soon forget," Malcolm commented with a reassuring smile.

"The evil she commands has no conscience! They will be a challenge."

"Yes, I know. Her full strength is not yet at hand, though that may change as each day passes. Her ambition might cause her to get careless. If that happens, we have a chance to end this."

"Perhaps with yours and Xanthus's help, we can restore even a small piece of Tir Nan Og so that we can return even if for short periods to maintain our magic."

"We might be able to do it, but until this fight is over, we will have to wait. I am unsure whether our combined abilities can suffice."

"If my strength is there, the three of us, maybe even your student, can do it."

Malcolm nodded, her idea had merit. "Yes, there is that

possibility. For now, let us concentrate on you getting better, we are going to need as many as possible to carry a sword," he winked.

"It has been some time but I will lift one if it is necessary," she smiled back.

Malcolm chuckled. "I will have a special sword made just for you."

"Good, be sure to save a wraith for me," she smiled back.

"I am sure we can arrange that."

Out in the fields surrounding Cambridge castle Xanthus was touring through the assorted tents, housing their new visitors, reinforcements to battle Helena. He was accompanied by a few of the new Generals that led these new arrivals. Their discussions centered on different strategies they might use and of course they chatted about news back in their own kingdoms.

"Any word on your brother's arrival?' the General of the ice elves asked.

"Ledal should be here by morning, his lead scout arrived last night so his party should be following," Xanthus replied.

"It has been some time since I have seen Ledal, it will be good to see him again," the General of the desert elves said with a chuckle. "I think we were causing trouble for your father the last time we were together."

"My father was not impressed with your antics," Xanthus agreed with a small grin.

"Oh we were not that bad," Escalan commented, trying to hold back his laughter.

"Kemal wanted to run you out to stay with my father," Captain Melaken joked. "He thought staying in the ice fields would cool you off."

"Well, I am glad he never followed through! Staying in the ice is not my idea of an enjoyable holiday," Escalan scoffed.

"You should visit, you'd never know we lived in the ice," Melaken winked.

"You come out to the desert first, not warm at all," Escalan retorted.

"Gentlemen, we all had our fun in our youth and what we did, well, is done," Xanthus snickered lightly. "Time now to foçus on what we need to do together, it will be like old times, though a different target to expend our energy on."

"Agreed old friend, the witch is an abomination," Melaken stated.

"When Ledal arrives we must break open some brandy, and visit a tad. It will be good to have us all together again," Escalan added.

"I will extend the invitation to Peresca. We cannot exclude our other ally," Xanthus said.

"As you wish. It will be interesting visiting with the Dark Elf, I hear she's quite the fighter," Melaken said, his comment had a tone of admiration.

"Indeed, her reputation precedes her, I'll send one of my men over to her camp with the invite," Escalan offered.

"By all means do so, in the meantime, let us talk some more strategy," Xanthus pointed to the fields on the way to the Norcross River. The group of three men strolled into what would be the final battle ground against Helana and her army.

Eden and Jindra and a large number of bright flecks of light whisked across the open plains as they approached the Norcross River, dipping in and out of scattered bushes, and letting the wind currents brush against them. The two had gathered the last of the lost faerie and were returning to their new home of Cambridge Castle. Their kinds had survived the attack in Tir Nan Og, but were far fewer in numbers now. It would take some time before they could repopulate but that was the least of their concerns. Living in a land other than faerie was going to take some getting used to. The two had traveled all over in the near forests, mountains and lakes. There might still be a few stray faerie out there, but in time, they would be drawn to their own.

The two leading the group paused by a small grove of trees and motioned for the entire gathering to pause and catch their breath. They had been going at full flight for some time, Eden and Jindra were the most tired and on the verge of collapse. They had pushed themselves so they could find their brethren but it was beginning to show.

"My wings ache, I do not know how much more I can do," Jindra sighed. She sat down on a small stump and let out a deep sigh.

"We will be back to the elves soon, we can all sleep then," Eden said. The faerie moved beside her friend and patted her on the back. "Thank you for everything, Alisha would be smiling at you now."

"Miss her?"

Eden nodded, and wiped a few tears from her cheeks. "Yes, very much. I have not had much time to think, since we fled. She did not deserve to die."

"Very true, none of our kind deserved what those things did to us and our home. I hope they get what they deserve!" Jindra said bitterness evident in her tone.

"Yes. I have never wanted to bring anything bad on anyone, but these demons should be punished for what they have done," Eden said.

Another few faerie joined them. "Yes they should," one agreed.

"How will we survive outside of our home? Won't it affect us?" one wanted to know.

"I am as lost as you," Eden smiled. "Malcolm will know. He knows best."

"I hope so, as nice as the elves are, it isn't home," one other faerie added.

"Is it much longer?" one other asked.

"No, we will be there soon. Are we ready to continue?" Jindra asked.

The group nodded in majority. They were ready to move on. Eden and Jindra took the lead once more and all returned to their faerie form and were flying off towards Cambridge. It was as close to home as they could get.

Malcolm had adjourned to the elf library after his visit with Leasha. The faerie queen had fallen back asleep and the wizard decided to revisit some old magic texts. Somewhere in the pages of the ancient book was a spell that must be able to stop Helana and what she had become. In case Zach and Riane failed to find the one person who could restore the balance of magic, he needed to find an alternative.

Two candles flickered, casting shadows on the walls around him as he read. The late afternoon sunlight was not quite enough to allow him to read the faded words on the pages. He would read one page, and then turn over to a new one and begin again. After a time Malcolm rubbed his eyes to get the tiredness out. All the words were beginning to blur into one another. Still there was no incantation to do what he required to fight Helana. It was time for another fresh cup of tea to help rejuvenate the mind. He waved his hand and his cup refilled with more tea, the steam rising from the warm liquid.

"Wherever will I find an answer to your power Helana," Malcolm murmured to himself. He sipped his tea and sat back in his chair. After a few minutes of relaxing, and letting his thoughts wander Malcolm placed his tea cup down and returned to his reading.

One spell's words became another and after a time he felt like he would find nothing amidst every known casting. Then one caught his eye.

Malcolm sat up, took another sip of tea and looked closer at the page and read the words aloud. "*If there is need to overcome an incantation where magic has joined together, one can overcome such a joining by taking the life of the two. Both lives can end by only one means, a weapon built to kill evil, thus freeing the other life it holds. Then the other life can be taken, but remember, there is always an exchange for such magic, there must be give and take in order for the spell to work.*"

Malcolm looked up from the book and glanced at the candles still flickering. The spell was saying that in order to end the joining, both lives must end. One by a weapon, a tool of which there was no prior knowledge. A weapon built to kill evil? Where would he even begin to look for such a thing? The other by taking the life but there had to be an exchange, a life for a life.

The wizard sighed. "***There is a price for every spell of this magnitude***." He remembered saying those words back when they had revived Tony. The Dark Dragon was reborn with his return but this time, in order to take a life, one must give a life as well.

"There is no other way," he whispered. Malcolm knew what had to be done if the time came, and he would tell no one, even Xanthus, his oldest and dearest friend.

Chapter Twenty Seven

Helana watched as the second wave of her army appeared from the south, emerging from the forest. Satisfied this battle was well in hand she vanished in a whirl of wind and light to attend to another matter. She resurfaced at another location some distance away where several large wraiths were waiting. The creatures had been instructed by her to return to this grove of trees and wait for her; she had a special quest for them.

She smiled on seeing them; they had obeyed and were where they had to be. Helana was going to test her magic's strength, and these wraiths were going to be a part of it. She had to know if her ability had reached a level that would overcome the amulets and any enhancement from the elves. With her minions occupied for the time being it was as good a time as any to push her magic and see where it could take her.

"Good, you are all here. I am going to open a portal and I want you five to go through it. Once you have crossed, you have my permission to do what you wish," Helana said.

"Where isssssssssss thissssssss portal to take usssssssssssssss?" one wraith questioned.

"Somewhere that your powers will give you free reign," Helana replied.

"Isssssssss thisssssssss sssssssso, then we go asssssss you assssssk," another wraith hissed as it nodded its head in agreement.

"The portal will open you near someone I need you to find, the magic will guide you," Helana instructed. "Do not let this person escape alive."

The entire wraith bowed in agreement. The creatures moved back as she motioned for some space to cast the magic required. Helana took in a deep breath of the forest air and let it out slow. She held her arms out and began to draw in power from the surrounding land.

Malcolm felt the draining of magic immediately and rushed out to stand on the terrace outside his room. He stared to the east, and felt every fibre of his being having its magic drained. He listened to the wind and it whispered in his ears, warning him of what was happening. The wizard grasped the railing and held on tightly as he felt the magic being created start to form. He turned abruptly and went in search of Xanthus, if what he thought had happened, the two of them would have to act quickly to repair the damage.

Helana drew her hands together and began the words to open the portal. *"All this power, I call on you, do as I command and open the bridge between our world and the other! Take my charges and guide them to the one they need to find! Open the door and let them through! Do as I say and make it so!"*

A ball of blue magic formed within her hands and she thrust her arms skyward, letting loose the magic as she did. It expanded as it reached the clouds and exploded in a flash of light! A vortex began to form and the clouds began to rotate inwards. The portal she sought began to take shape.

Malcolm fell to his knees as the magic cast by Helana exploded and he held on to his staff for support. He caught his breath and waited until his strength returned. Once he was able to stand again he was up and moving quickly to find Xanthus. There was no time to waste. He knew this magic, Helana had opened the door to the old world on her own, something unheard of, and they had to close that doorway before she sent something through.

Helana faced the wraith and pointed to the portal. "Go, find the one and make sure he doesn't return alive. Do not bother coming back unless you succeed."

"Asssssssss you command," one wraith bowed. All five spread their wings and rose off the ground, flying with the wind into the vortex. One by one they vanished into the twisting mists, and into the pathway through to the old world.

Neil watched the magic burst across the sky and his attention was focused on what was happening far to the east. A shout brought his train of thought back to the task at hand. How could they contend with a new enemy force approaching from the south? Another segment of Helana's army had appeared with three giants leading the pack and was closing quickly on their ranks. The giants were a new twist on the attack, and he had no idea from where they had come. The bigger challenge was how to defend against this new threat.

"We need to bring some of the archers down to defend the south!" Brielle shouted.

"Bring some of the ground team over to do it, have them focus their arrows on the giants!" Kieran ordered.

"We need more! We need the archers from the ridge!" Brielle added.

"There is no time, and they are busy fighting off the manticore!" Kieran shouted back. "Take the ground team. It is all we can do, we risk spreading the rest of the ranks too thin!"

"We won't be able to hold them long," Neil said with a nod towards the southern enemy.

"I know. We need to start moving back to the third line, and then up the ridgeline," Kieran agreed.

"I'll get the ground archers over to fend the south, we'll hold the line as long as we can!" Tony said. "Just make sure our path back is clear."

"It will be," Kieran assured him.

"Do what you can Tony!" Neil smiled. "See if you can take out one of those big thugs!"

"Room service for a week if I do," Tony winked. He was off and running to gather the ground archers and move them to form a line to face the south.

Shar watched the magic take form and could vaguely make out the vortex that was taking shape. She felt the magic being drawn from the land and did not like how it felt. Tasha had joined her and together they witnessed the event.

"What is Helana up to now?" Tasha wondered aloud.

"Not sure, but it almost looks like the portal spell. She might be opening a doorway, a path elsewhere," Shar observed.

"To where?"

Shar shook her head. "That I do not know. I do know

she is using a lot of power to do this; she's taking the risk on weakening herself. That might work to our advantage."

"What if she's testing herself, to see how much power she does have?" Tasha countered.

"That could be, if it is then she's getting extremely confident in her abilities," Shar said.

"As I am confident in yours," Tasha complimented.

"Thanks," Shar smiled.

Vasilis approached the two. "Ladies, we need to move you up to the ridge. There's another group of Helana's army moving in from the south now."

"The south?" Shar asked.

"Where did they come from?" Tasha wondered.

"We are not sure, but they are moving quickly. We've been ordered to move back just in case. They're going to move back the other lines soon."

"Thanks Vasilis," Tasha nodded.

"Yes my lady," he bowed and ran off to tend to the rest of his forces.

"I'm going to Neil," Tasha said.

"No, not a good idea," Shar objected.

"Then you'll have to come with me," Tasha flashed a small smile and ran off. Shar cursed under her breath and ran after her; she wouldn't be able to live with herself if something were to happen to her friend.

Malcolm found Xanthus in the council chamber, and the elf king knew full well why the wizard was seeking him out. The elf king already had the book of magic opened to the required page to counter what Helana had concocted.

"She is beginning to test herself," Xanthus sighed.

"Yes, she is. Are you ready?" Malcolm motioned towards the book.

"I am. Let's not wait, who knows what damage she has done already, and the risk to those on the old world."

Malcolm stood before the book and Xanthus moved to stand next to him. Both wizard and elf began to speak the words to engage the spell and close the portal Helana had opened. As the incantation took shape the amulets in the staff flared to life and with the final phrase spoken the magic burst forth shooting into the sky from the amulets. It sought out the portal and all those on the ground saw the beam of light streaking through the sky. It did not take long before it found the abomination of Helana's and it struck at the dark magic, shredding it as it did.

Helana watched angrily, but resigned herself to watch the magic get erased by her nemesis. The wraith had gone through, and that was what she intended. She would not lose any more strength to fight back against the amulets; it was a fight she would save for another day.

The amulets magic streaked in and out of the vortex, pulling the dark spell apart until the clouds closed and the wind ceased. The counter spell faded away with a few final bursts of light and the clouds were as they were before Helana's magic. She stared at the sky for a time and then looked away to the west. The Wraith was on their way to the old world, quest in hand, and her duty now lay with her army. There might be a need for her on the frontline. Though she doubted it, but it was better to be safe. She could not let this small band of resistance stop her advancement. They were a mere minor roadblock in her path to Malcolm and the elves.

Malcolm closed the book and both he and Xanthus had moved to stand outside and gaze at the sky. Their spell had worked, that much they did know. Just what Helana had accomplished was still a mystery but both were sure that in time that would make itself known.

"Ledal arrived earlier when you were hiding out in the library, he brought half his force with him. The rest will arrive tomorrow," Xanthus informed Malcolm.

"Very good, have you had the opportunity to visit with your brother?"

"Not as yet, we have scheduled a strategy meeting later on with all the leaders. It should be a lot of, well, fun," Xanthus grinned.

Malcolm chuckled. "Having all of you together again should be interesting, and what of Peresca? Inviting her as well?"

"Oh yes, the invitation has been extended. I am sure she will be there. We are after all joined together for this common cause."

"Well if I can, I will join you all later. Go easy on the brandy!" Malcolm urged.

"No promises, especially with Escalan," Xanthus said, holding back his laughter as best he could.

Malcolm sighed. "It is good to laugh despite what we are going through. Say hello to Ledal for me, I will catch up as soon as I am able."

"We will save you some brandy," Xanthus assured him.

Chapter Twenty Eight

Zach sat on the steps over near Arthur's chamber, holding the sword Excalibur in his hand, with it draped over his legs. He was as confused now as he was when the sword abruptly slid free of its stone casing. How was this even possible? Zach looked down at the weapon, and looked at the inscription on one side, 'Take Mihi sursum' in its original latin or 'take me up' in English, and then he flipped the sword over and read the other inscription in its original latin 'Iacio Mihi Absentis' or 'cast me away' translated in English. Just then he noticed some smaller writing, in Latin he assumed, etched into the hilt itself. He leaned in close to get a better look.

"'Tamen est bonus', For all that is good", Zach whispered, surprised at his ability to understand the Latin. He looked up and scratched his chin. "What the hell does that mean?"

"What does what mean?" Merlin asked as he approached.

"The other inscription here, 'for all that is good', its here on the handle," Zach pointed.

"My word," Merlin smiled. He moved to sit next to

Zach. "Only the man that is resting in there," he motioned with a nod, "has ever seen those words. You are only the second to ever see them. What it means is that it is meant for good, to be wielded for good. Does that help you understand a little better?"

"I guess," Zach shrugged. "But why is the sword warm to the touch?"

"The magic within has awakened, brought to life by your touch, that is how the sword is released from the stone. A condition we placed on Excalibur when we put it in the stone, much the same way as it was when Arthur removed the sword all those years ago."

"Why me though?" Zach asked with a sigh. "I am the last person in world who should be a so called leader of people."

Merlin chuckled. "You sound like Arthur; he said the very same thing when he first held Excalibur. Contrary to what you may think Zach, your leadership will show itself when the time calls for it."

"This is all way beyond me," Zach muttered.

"I can see why you may say that," Merlin grinned. He patted Zach on the back. "But we can talk more on the subject a little later, for now, we must prepare for the arrival of a few guests. With Excalibur being pulled from the stone, it will signal those who encased it. They will be anxious to meet you."

"Why? Oh, never mind," Zach snickered. "I forgot I'm Arthur's heir." He stood up holding the sword and looked over at Riane and Falon. "Well ladies, your thoughts?"

"What can I say, I am honored to meet you," bowed Falon.

"Likewise my king," Riane smiled and bowed as Fallon did.

"Stop that," Zach said. "I got lucky, nothing more."

"It is more than luck Zach, we know that now," Riane said. She came over and gave him a hug.

On the far side near the entrance, a mist formed and once more the form of Morgana took shape. She stepped down into the room, the mist following her as she strode over towards Merlin.

"I sensed Excalibur's magic. What has happened?" She asked quickly and then saw the empty stone, "Who?"

"Morgana, apparently we will not have any need for the council to free the sword. Its true owner has found it," Merlin answered. He motioned towards Zach and he stepped forward, holding the sword.

"How is this possible? I sensed nothing when all of you arrived here," Morgana stated, looking as stunned as the rest.

"You? What about me?" Merlin laughed lightly. "I believe now that there is no way we would have known Morgana, only the sword would have that ability."

Morgana nodded. "You are right old friend, the others, they will be here soon then." She turned to face the elf who had been their guide. "You need to alert your General. He will need to know, and send word to have a special meal prepared! Be sure to include something for the Faerie, otherwise the king might be somewhat appalled, he is after all a selective eater."

"Yes my lady, I will tend to it immediately," the elf bowed and left the room.

"King?" Zach looked at Merlin.

"Yes, the king of the Faerie, he is one of the council, among a few others. I would think they should be here momentarily," Merlin said as he looked around the room.

"I thought the land of faerie, well, whatever it's called, was back on the other world?" Zach wondered.

"That is only one realm of many. A few have disappeared

but there are still a few left on this world. They do not leave their realm very often as there is no need."

"The Faerie king, The Elf General, the Lady of the Lake whom is part faerie herself, myself, my fellow sisters and Merlin make up the council. We are the only ones who can free the sword, that is, until you arrived," she bowed, "heir of Arthur."

"Oh man, will you stop that bowing stuff!" Zach groaned.

Riane laughed and gave him another hug and then a kiss. "Look at it from their side of things. Someone long lost has finally found his way back."

"I'm here because I was sent here. All of this other stuff is just a fluke!" Zach chuckled.

"Maybe, but perhaps your destiny brought you here," she winked.

"I'm getting a head-ache," Zach mumbled.

Another formation of mist began against the far wall and the company turned to face this new arrival to the chamber. Merlin and Morgana moved to the front and awaited their new guest so they could greet appropriately. This mist took on the form of a thick fog and settled against a section of the wall and remained there, fixated. A man stepped out of the mist, his robes, in various dark colors from blue, to grey to black intermingled flowed behind him. The Faerie king had arrived and he paused for a moment to gather his bearings and upon seeing Merlin and Morgana he smiled.

"Ah old friends, it is good to see you again! It has been a long long time!" His open outstretched arms welcomed Morgana first, and then Merlin. He stepped back then to look around the room. "My my, it is has been some time since I set foot in here, which brings me to why I'm here, of course. The magic of Excalibur beckoned me and my curiosity got the best of me I have to say. So tell me, what is going on?"

"The true heir has claimed what is his, something I admit I did not see coming," Merlin smiled back to the king of Faerie.

"Really? Amazing, I never thought it would happen! It has been such a long time. Where is this heir?"

Merlin turned and motioned for Zach to come over. Zach strolled over nervously and nodded to the king. This new guest was as tall as him, but had short dark brown hair and looked no older than someone of thirty years, with bright blue eyes. A man of average build but his robes hid him quite well. The dark blue, grey, black colors almost merged with the mist much like Morgana's body did.

"Nice to meet you sir," Zach bowed.

"It is I who should be bowing to you, I have dreamt of this day for many years. Albeit time really doesn't affect me," the king chuckled. "But I'm sure you know that already. Or do you?"

"I have a vague idea how it works with the faerie, kind," Zach replied.

"Oh bother, where are my manners? Allow me to introduce myself; I am Oberon, King of Faerie." He shook Zach's hand and Zach recognized the name.

"I'm Zach, Zach Thomas. Oberon? I've heard that name before."

"Really? I can't imagine where," Oberon said with a slight shrug.

Zach snapped his fingers. "It was in high school! I read some Shakespeare book, well, I had to read it for class, can't recall which one but you were in it."

Oberon rolled his eyes. "Ah yes, I remember the Shakespeare lad, made a mistake talking to that one. He was always writing things down, never understood that.

Wasn't much of a talker, asked a lot of questions though. A story for another time perhaps, but enough about him, what of the others?" He looked at Merlin and Morgana.

"They will all be here shortly my lord; will your wife be joining us?" Morgana asked.

"No I'm afraid not, Titania is busy in the gardens these days. She sends her greetings though."

"May I introduce as well lady Riane, an elf from the new world, and my young apprentice Fallon," Merlin introduced.

"An elf?" Oberon looked at her closely. "Ah yes, the magic hides her, a very good spell for these times. The new world! Excellent! Have you any word from my daughter? She watches over Tir Nan Og, her home."

Riane shook her head. "Sorry my lord I have not seen the queen for a time, I did not know she was your daughter!"

"My yes, the youngest of my children, and the most adventurous one as well! When old Merlin here mentioned to me about sending one of the faerie realms over to this new world to assure our continued existence she was the one who asked to go. It was hard to let her go, but in the end she won out," Oberon sighed.

At that moment the elf guard returned and bowed on seeing Oberon. The faerie king waved him off and beckoned him to stand. The elf captain faced Merlin and Morgana, bowing to them as well.

"The other council members are on their way master Merlin. The Lady of the Lake just arrived."

"Thank you captain. Show them down will you."

"Yes sir," he replied and was off again to do as he was told.

"Keep your sisters restrained Morgana," Merlin teased. "They tend to get overzealous when company arrives."

"They will behave, or they will have to answer to me," Morgana assured him with a smile.

"Very good, everyone let us move and stand by the stone. That will give us plenty of room for introductions," Merlin instructed. He pointed where he wanted each person and they all took their place accordingly.

The elf captain was back in short order and behind him trailed the remaining members of the council. One by one they entered the chamber, an elf, a number of ladies enveloped in mist similar to Morgana, they were her sisters and another woman draped in a dark cloak that clung to her appearing as though it was soaked and the woman's blonde hair was slicked back as though she had just gotten out of a shower. She of course was the Lady of the Lake. The company spread out and the chamber was quite full, with everyone staring at everyone else.

"Welcome all; you are here for one reason. Believe me when I say you were going to end up here regardless because of something happening on the new world and would have been called to assist in the release of Excalibur. However, due to an unforeseen circumstance, we are all here to meet one who has finally found his way here, I do not know how, but he is here and freed Excalibur with his own hands. We all know that in order for that to happen it must be an heir of Arthur, and after all this time his heir is among us!"

"Merlin my dear friend, this is a momentous occasion! Long have I waited to put my eyes on this person, to know one does exist," The Lady of the Lake spoke.

"Who is it?" asked one of Morgana's sisters.

"Everyone let me introduce you to some new visitors to Avalon. The first in many centuries, first my young apprentice Falon, the lady Riane, an elf from the new world, and last but not least, Zach Thomas," Merlin moved to stand next to him, "Arthur's heir."

The group all turned their gaze to Zach and he felt a little uncomfortable with all the attention focused on him. He adjusted his stance a few times to find a comfort zone, but no matter which foot he switched to, he remained uneasy. He held the sword Excalibur in his hands front and center and lifted it to satisfy their curiosity.

"Welcome home Zach," the Lady of the Lake said as she smiled at him. "Let me tell you a little history," still smiling she began to explain, "Long ago we made the sword to combat evil, and Arthur was the one man who was able to carry the blade to serve its purpose. There have been others before him, but each time they used Excalibur for their own agenda's, so a select few of us placed conditions on the sword and encased it in stone. In order for it to be freed the one who could wield it must be pure of heart. Many tried, but failed. Arthur was the first and the only one since to free the blade and use it as it was meant to be. After his death we returned it to the stone with the same conditions, and with one extra, it had to be a descendant of Arthur. There was no way to determine if there was one, but Merlin," the Lady glanced over at him, "said there had to be because Mother Nature told him there was. None of us have ever had the call from her, only he has. So, we put our faith in him and therefore the added condition on Excalibur's release. Now, our faith has been rewarded, and you have proved Nature, and Merlin correct."

Zach looked down at the sword and sighed. "Are you sure it isn't a mistake?"

"My boy, Excalibur knows its keeper, and you, are the one," Oberon winked.

"Just my luck," sighed Zach. Riane smiled and Falon couldn't help but chuckle at his remark.

"I must shake the hand of a distant cousin," one of Morgana's sister cackled.

"Say what?" Zach asked incredulously as the woman shook his hand enthusiastically. "You are kidding right?"

Morgana snickered, "No, we are related to Arthur so though we are distant relatives, we are related."

"Well the surprises just don't stop do they?" Zach mumbled.

Merlin laughed and put his hand on Zach's shoulder. "Come; let's go have something to eat before we begin our trek back to the mainland."

The group never had the chance to go anywhere before a shock wave reverberated through the chamber. All were confused and wondering what was going on. Merlin was quick to act; he beckoned everyone aside and made his way to the doorway.

"Stay here everyone; I will determine what is going on! Please wait here," he urged. The wizard was running up the stairs, and Zach, Riane and Falon were right behind him with the Elf General and his captain trailing.

Outside there were elves scattered throughout the courtyard running with bows drawn, following others that were making their way up the steps to the top of the rampart. The Elf General that had been in the chamber shouted at those on the catwalk.

"What is going on Captain?"

"General, the clouds grew abruptly dark and then a shock wave exploded from the sky!" replied the elf captain.

"That would explain what we felt below," Merlin said.

"What's going on Merlin?" Zach asked as he stared up at the sky. The dark clouds were beginning to move in a circular motion and it looked familiar to what he had seen several times before.

"Magic is at work here, but not of our doing," he answered, staring at the same formation that Zach and the rest were locked on.

"All elves to the catwalk! Defensive positions everyone!" The General shouted.

"General, do you have an extra crossbow handy?" Riane asked. "I might be of assistance."

"Captain, get the lady a bow, see you up on top," The General nodded and was off to join the rest of his elf contingent. The elves were all taking position while the General barked orders. Archers loaded their bows and a number of other elf defenders loaded the larger version of a crossbow, the ballista and took aim at the sky. If anything was coming through the clouds, they would be prepared for it.

"The magic was not used from this world," Merlin said as he stared at the sky. He was concentrating on the forming vortex, trying to determine the source of the magic.

"That shock wave why did that happen?" Zach asked.

Falon was as entranced as Merlin in trying to find a source for this anomaly. She looked around the castle, and then back to the sky and then back to the castle surroundings once more. She looked at Merlin and Zach, there was a realization in her eyes.

"The magic protecting Avalon! I don't detect it anymore sir, do you?"

It was Morgana that answered her. "No, it has been broken." She had emerged from the chamber and had joined them in the courtyard. "I felt the alteration almost immediately; I am after all, this isle's guardian."

"The shock wave," Zach said.

"Yes, it would seem that would be why," Merlin agreed.

"Merlin, we need to re-establish the protection spell for Avalon, we are going to need the rest of the council," Morgana pointed back to the door that led to the chamber below.

"Bring them up, and hurry Morgana. I will deal with the vortex," Merlin nodded. "Be sure they protect themselves."

"I will remind them," Morgana said. She floated back to the entrance to the lower hall and vanished inside.

"Sir!" Falon shouted. She was pointing to the sky and Merlin returned his gaze to the twisting clouds.

The first wraith appeared, bursting out of the vortex with wings spread wide to control itself and gauge where it was. It was quickly followed by four more; all five screeched their unearthly sound and took stock of where they had to go. The horde caught sight of Camelot, screeched several more times, communicating with one another to confirm that this was their destination. The five began their descent and bore down on the castle. It became apparent they were there for a reason, and their target had now been selected.

Chapter Twenty Nine

Captain Elise guided her force of gryphons in quick circles over the advancing army that had breached the river from the east and kept her fellow air group firing at will to do anything and everything possible to slow the dark minion's of Helana. The new threat approaching from the south had cost her four of her best fighters and she had commanded them back closer to the falls to ascertain their best order of defense with the least loss. The regiment had decided on the nearest threat, so they could give their own forces time to retreat because with the latest change the resistance would soon have no alternative but to fall back to the ridge. The air threat from the Manticore was gone for the time being, the vile creatures had vanished from view but she knew they could return at any time. She had a few of her riders stay back to keep watch, just in case.

Elise signaled her team with a new arm signal and the group broke into three smaller groups to give the attackers a less easy target to aim for. With another signal she called in one of the guard gryphon's to take her place. She withdrew and guided her ride to a safe distance back near the third line of defense and had the gryphon land. Elise jumped off and with a series of hand gesture's commanded her gryphon to wait. It drew in its wings in understanding the command of its master. The Captain went in search of someone she could talk to and update them on the situation she had seen from above. The first person she came across was Riss, another of the elf captains.

"Riss! Are Neil and Keiran aware of the army coming up from the south?" she shouted above the ruckus.

"Yes Elise, they are trying to get the troops back to the ridge!" Riss replied.

"They need to work faster, the south army will be on them shortly!"

"They are doing the best they can! There are just too many to hold off! I've lost a quarter of my regiment alone!"

Elise shook her head. "I am sorry Riss, I will get my riders to push harder on the front line and give you more time to withdraw. If you see Neil and Tasha, or anyone else, get them back to the ridge, now, not later."

"Aye, I shall. Good luck sky rider," Riss bowed and ran off to relay the message.

Elise was running back to her gryphon and patted the creature on the side of the head as she came up. "Easy my friend, we have some more flying to do."

She was then back up in the sky directing her squad with more hand signals to refocus the attack and give their ground forces some more time to re-establish their retreat.

Tony pointed to the elf archers he had commandeered and was shouting as loud as he could to get them set up. The south army was advancing quickly and there was nothing to keep them from overtaking their own forces if they didn't at least slow them down.

"As soon as you are set, shout out!" He bellowed.

One by one the elves shouted out their readiness and

lifted their bow in correspondence with their signaling. As the row all came ready bows were drawn and Tony barked out the command to 'fire'. A slew of arrows rained through the air striking the nearest enemy attackers from the south, sending them tumbling. Those that trailed behind were next to feel the second wave of arrows as the archers reloaded and fired in unison with Tony's orders. The archers were prompt and accurate, and were determined to do what they could to hold the line of defense a little longer.

Neil watched the giant's moving in closer with the southern army and wondered how they were ever going to stop these behemoths. There was nothing in their arsenal that could slow them down, let alone kill them. He returned his focus to getting the second line back and reforming so they could get their fall back plan in motion.

"Thatcher! Have you seen Axe and Ruskin?" Neil asked on seeing the gnome.

"Not in a bit sir, been a bit busy myself," Thatcher chuckled as he lifted his bloodied axe.

Neil laughed and pointed, "If you see them, get them back to the third line! We need to start backing out!"

"Aye sir! Shall do! I'll be sure ta tell'em!" Thatcher disappeared as he scurried off to find the two dwarves.

Neil turned to go in another direction and came face to face with Tasha and Shar. He was not impressed on seeing Tasha so close to the action.

"I thought I asked you to stay back?" Neil frowned.

"I tried Neil, but she wouldn't listen," Shar said as she drew her cloak in close.

"You need to move back! We're starting to pull everyone to the third line, and starting back up the ridge," Neil informed them both. "We've got more company and we're going to get overrun."

"Then I can help you organize the retreat!" Tasha pointed to the forces still waging war against the demons.

"I'll stick with her," Shar assured Neil.

He groaned and threw his arms up in defeat. "Very well, get the left flank moving back first. Keiran is up somewhere near the front of it all keeping them focused on pushing them back to the river."

"I'll grab Brielle over there to help as well," Tasha nodded and was gone with Shar right behind her.

"So much for this going according to plan," Neil muttered to himself as he jogged off to see if Tony needed any help.

Tony and his archers were firing volley upon volley into the forthcoming demons. They were not having much of an effect on the giants. The three monsters kept rumbling on, carrying torn tree trunks as a weapon, and were swinging them back and forth ready to make use of them. The throng of demons and trolls were herding themselves around the giants once the arrows began to fly and it was becoming increasingly difficult to take out the demons.

Neil ran up next to Tony. "How goes it?"

"Not good! We're not gonna hold out much longer," Tony informed while shaking his head.

"I don't like how this is starting to take shape," Neil said, he shook his head as well.

"We're losing this," Tony mumbled.

On the hillside, to the east, Jacinto and his men had returned from assuring the refugee's safe retreat towards Cambridge and were watching the spectacle below in the valley. The large man took note of the distance between themselves and the demons and moved along the line of riders to confer with his top men.

"Riley, Keller, Mister Baker," Jacinto shouted as he nudged his horse along.

"Yes sir," Riley replied urging his horse forward a few steps.

"How long ya figure to ride down on that mess down there?"

"Oh I don't think it'd take long. We'd give the bastards a good scare I think," Riley chuckled.

"Anxious to get in on it sir? A bit tired of ridin," Keller added.

"Baker, your thoughts on it?" Jacinto asked.

"I'm with the two lugs here. Need to give my sword some action, as it's getting a bit rusty," Terry said, getting his own thoughts in on the decision.

"Agreed," Jacinto said with a large grin. He moved his horse front and center to face his men. "All right then, ride to the right side of the dark army, the side closest to the valley ridge, we can push'em back onto themselves and allow room for us to get through over the river an'back up the ridge with the rest. They ain't gonna last much longer, looks like they're takin a beatin down there. Keep yer heads up and give them ugly things a headache they won't soon forget. On my word, ride hard, and take a few of them with ya on the go by, ready?"

The entire regiment roared their enthusiasm and the sound of clanking swords on shields echoed through the entire line. They were more than anxious to get in on all of the fighting in the valley and lend a hand to give the other forces a lift in morale.

"That other army there comin from the woods is gonna be a bit of challenge sir," Baker pointed. "What of them?"

Jacinto just shook his head. "Nothing we can do. There ain't enough men to hold them off, we need ta focus on pushin the others onto themselves and get the others up the ridge, that's our job. We don't do that, this is going to be nasty for us, got'er men?"

Another roar broke through the ranks to acknowledge him and Jacinto nodded, he was proud of his men and their willingness to risk their lives. He lifted his sword high and bellowed as loud as he could the command to 'charge' and the men of the North villages stampeded on down into the valley.

Taith was exhausted from the fighting. His sword was nicked and bloodied and every muscle in is body ached beyond their ability to take any more but he still pushed himself and his men did the same. When he caught sight of Jacinto and his men rushing across the field to their aide, the elf captain felt a huge wave of exhaustion leave his body, to be replaced by a renewed enthusiasm.

Helana watched as this new unforeseen attack from the eastern hills approached her forces on the plains. She did not like what she was seeing and would give her opposition a slight advantage, albeit a small one. Her forces moving in quickly from the south would overrun the elf forces, but if this new hurdle succeeded in their attack, it would give the elves the time to retreat. That was something she did not want. Her magic was drained from opening the vortex so she had to wait and see what would develop. To use her magic again so soon would drain her even further. She would wait until it was absolutely necessary.

Tasha, with Shar right behind was running around shouting orders to begin their withdrawal back towards the ridge and the third and final line of defense. The new threat from the south was closing quickly and they had to get back to a safe distance. They came across Kieran doing the same.

"The left flank has begun to move back, Elise and her riders are covering them from the sky!" Kieran barked. He was looking exhausted and his face was covered in dirt.

"Perfect, start the front lines as soon as you can," Tasha said.

"Aye, they'll be next," he nodded. "We'll be doing the retreat in phases; Elise needs time to move into position."

"Don't wait too long captain. We'll see you back at the tree line," Tasha motioned with her sword.

Keiran ran off to begin the retreat of the front lines and the two turned and moved off to collect Neil, Tony and the archers holding on the right flank facing the southern threat. The other segment of Helana's army was almost upon them and the three giants leading the mass were on the verge of overtaking the archers.

"Release!" Tony hollered. Another wave of arrows soared through the sky, taking a slew of demons with them. The arrows were nearly gone and the dent they had made on the invaders was minimal. The giants, carrying the tree trunks they had torn from the earth, were being waved around like enormous clubs and the earth was vibrating more and more as they approached.

"Tony! We've done all we could, time to move them back!" Neil ordered.

"A little longer, we've still got a few arrows," Tony replied.

"No more. It's time to go!" Neil repeated his order.

"All right, will do," Tony nodded. "That's it everyone, let go one more and get back to the third line, it's time to get the hell outta here!"

Neil saw Tasha and Shar running up and he decided it was time to see if the mage would use a little of her magic to give them a chance.

He faced Shar as she approached and she had an idea of

what he was about to ask. "I know Malcolm said you weren't supposed to use magic unless necessary but right now we could use a little of it to slow them down."

Shar looked at the approaching onslaught, and then back to Neil. "I have an idea, but once I use magic Helana might retaliate, we need to get the retreat in full force."

"I understand," Neil nodded. He looked at Tasha. "It's time we got out of here, and this time don't argue with me."

"I won't. Come on Tony! We've got a bit of a run to get to the ridge!" Tasha beckoned.

"Don't wait for me! I'll be right behind you guys!" Tony smiled. He ordered the archers to retreat and one by one they obeyed and soon their entire group was fleeing back to the third line and the waiting forest that would cover their flight. Only Shar was left standing there, alone, to face the entire mob.

Malcolm's apprentice stood tall, and threw her cloak hood back to get a good view of the army approaching. She focused on the giants and keyed in on the tree trunks they carried. An idea formed and Shar began to whisper the words she needed.

Helana felt the magic immediately and whirled to look at the war raging on the plains. Where was it coming from? And from who? Infuriated she turned back to the trees and strode into another waiting group of minions, her last surprise for the elves. More Manticore sat patiently, hidden from view.

"Rise into the sky my pets, do as you wish to them, let none survive," she snarled.

The Manticore rose up and emerged from the trees in one large mass on a flight path directly to the ridgeline and the waiting elf archers above. Helana enjoyed the view of them flying towards the falls; they would be the final thrust that would put this little miserable effort to hinder her conquest of Avalon into its death throng.

Shar remained focused and brought her magic to its zenith! She cast her arms outward and motioned her hands in a round about motion and the tree trunks flew from the giants hands. The behemoths stopped in their tracks, confused as to what was happening to them. The tree's whirled around and each giant was hit by what had been their weapon of choice. All three collapsed to the ground from the force of the attack. Their tumble reverberated right up to Shar. She thrust her arms forward again and sent another wave of magic into the ground in front of the dark minions. The earth exploded skyward, debris hurtling into the demons, sending them scurrying backwards, but only a little. Then the ground caved in and a large ravine formed in front of the advancing force and a good quantity fell into the ravine, excluding the giants, who were lucky enough to avoid the fall. Shar instead sent the giant tree trunks hurtling back onto the giants to hinder them further. She let out a deep breath and took in her result. It would do for the time being. Satisfied, Shar turned and began to run back to the rest of the retreating forces.

Helana sensed the magic end and stared at the abrupt result of it all. The southern army was stopped in its tracks but she knew it would only be a temporary setback. The Manticore would make up for that. Instead she thought of other ways to halt the retreat of the elves and their allies. One idea did come to the surface, but she would wait until the time was right.

Teague wiped his brow and then he saw the new threat

coming across the sky. He stared and tried to grasp the situation. How were they going to defend against this attack? He ran down the line checking their arrow situation.

"How many left in the arsenal?" he shouted.

"Only a few here!" shouted one archer.

"Just a handful captain!" Answered another.

"We can't hold another attack sir," one elf puffed as he ran up. The manticore had been seen by the archers and all looked to their captain for an answer. The elf captain glanced over all his archers and then gazed back at the approaching manticore.

"We don't have a choice men, stay behind cover and make sure each arrow makes its mark on those heathens! We have to give our forces a chance to get back up the ridge!"

"Aye sir!" the company shouted in unison.

Each archer took position and waited for the inevitable attack. Teague moved along the line encouraging his archers and then looked for Elise and the riders. He lit an arrow and let it fly, hoping it would catch the elf captain's eye and alert her to the returning enemy.

Elise caught the flight of the lit arrow out of the corner of her eye and guided her gryphon around, and as she did, the elf saw the approaching demon storm in the sky. She pulled back on the reigns of her gryphon and assessed the attack. There was no way they could defend this mass. The archers on the ridge would be badly outnumbered and she did not have enough riders to even contemplate taking on this number of manticore. Elise glanced below and saw Jacinto's men making good progress on the demons, pushing them back onto each other. The retreat had begun and already they were disappearing into the forest. She made her decision. They would not let the elf archers fend off the manticore alone. All they had to do was delay the manticore so they could get back into the safety of the woods. With a series of arm signals the sky riders rerouted their flight into the direct path of the manticore.

Kieran and a regiment of elves had set up the temporary bridge platforms as Jacinto and his men pushed back the demons. Now he and his men had a clear route across the river. In small groups they began to cross, and Kieran kept the archers firing to give them cover as they crossed.

"Sir, the forces are in full retreat!" Darg informed the elf captain.

"Jacinto and his men are starting to ride through and across the river. Once they are through we'll get the rest of our line back to the ridge," Kieran said.

"We had better hurry! The woodland captain left us as she has another threat to deal with," the other elf captain pointed to the sky. Kieran followed Darg's direction and saw the manticore.

"Can you get a messenger to Teague to abandon the ridge? He is too easy a target and won't have a chance," Kieran asked.

"I will send one of my men. I do not know if it will do any good as he has very little chance to retreat," Darg said. Kieran knew he was right but held out hope his friend on the ridge might be able to get away.

"Go, its time we all got out of here. We are losing this fight!" Kieran muttered.

"Agreed, see you on the ridge," Darg nodded and saluted his fellow elf captain. He was gone to send off a messenger and to help assist the retreat into the woods and up the path back to safety.

Neil, Tasha and Tony ran to the edge of the trees and took stock of the situation. The retreat was now in full mode and groups of soldiers were running back into the forest and up the valley to safety, putting distance between themselves and the demon hordes. Axel and Ruskin with Thatcher appeared, covered in mud and blood but not looking any worse for the wear than anyone who had been in a fight.

"Guys, glad you could join us," Tony quipped. "Take a few of them down?"

"Aye lad we did, twas a good time, but fer now I be glad ta be gettin' th' hell outta here," Axel replied. "It be getting a tad too close fer comfort out there."

"Yer tellin me, them things a wee bit thick. Cut down three; five take their place, bloody messy!" Ruskin added.

"Will be glad ta get somewhere a wee bit quieter," Thatcher agreed.

"Head on up boys, see you at the rendezvous," Neil said.

"Aye, we will at that," Axel motioned with a swing of his axe. The three of them ran on into the woods with another group of retreating elves and the mass exodus was well under way.

"Vasilis, make sure the last line holds long enough to allow everyone back into the forest," Neil reminded him with a wink.

"We will sir, you have my word," Vasilis saluted. He was off barking orders to the third line as they took position to hold any demons that might keep advancing.

Jacinto and his own forces were over the river and as the last of them crossed they set the bridge on fire to give the demons still on the other side of the river second thoughts about on using them as an easy way to get across. Helana's forces were scattered and confused, and the southern segment was still working their way over the ridge. The giants were just beginning to get their senses together and were struggling to stand and General Vadeez was shouting to get the trolls and the other creatures back in line.

Shar came running up to Tony, Neil and Tasha, a smile on her face. "I can't think of any reason why we need to stay around here any longer, can you?"

"Good work Shar," Neil thanked her.

"I think even Malcolm would be impressed," Tasha winked. "How are you feeling?'

"I'm okay, a little tired but nothing significant. So far so good on any retaliation from Helana. We better not push our luck!"

"Good idea, time to go," Tony motioned with a wave of his hand. Together all four were off and running with the rest up the trail and onward to the rendezvous point.

Captain Elise and her fellow gryphon riders kept their speed up as they flew in on the approaching manticore, hoping the creatures would take the bait and pursue them. It would at least give the archers on the ridge time to get away. The company raced in on the monsters and swooped in close to get their attention. On her command the riders banked hard and dove for the ground, hoping at least some of the manticore would follow. To her relief, a good number of the creatures broke from the mass and came in pursuit of the gryphon riders. There were still a few that didn't come after them and instead remained on course for the retreating forces.

"All right men Captain Elise have lent us a hand! Let's make sure what she's done is not wasted! Take aim and may we send these creatures back from where they came!" Teague commanded at the top of his lungs. The archers shouted together and let their arrows fly at the manticore.

The messenger sent by Captain Darg arrived and sought out Teague. Once he found the captain, he relayed the message from below.

"Sir! We are ordered to retreat back to the rendezvous," the elf informed the captain.

"I hear you sir, but we are not retreating until all the ground forces have fallen back," Teague said.

"Aye sir. Do you need any help?" the elf offered.

"We have an empty ballista that could use a commander, are you game sir?" Teague asked.

"I can handle it sir," the elf bowed.

"Then it is all yours, make'em count!"

Helana was running out of patience and as her army floundered she decided to take matters into her own hands. This little war had gone on long enough and it was time to make this all come to an end and take as many fighters as possible out of this lackluster effort to stop her with her casting. It would be a nice 'warm' conclusion to what had started as a fog filled damp day.

"*Power of Dark I call on thee, burn this land as I command, scorch the trees, burn the grass, let all that stand in your way fall into your heat, burn up the hill burn strong burn fast, so it shall be*!"

A small spark ignited in a single blade of grass, and it slowly began to spread, jumping from one patch to another, moving up to a small bush and the flames started to fan each other from the heat it threw. The third line of defense was now in full retreat mode and was moving quickly into the forest, and all failed to notice the small fire begin to pick up speed. It stemmed from one bush to a tree, and another, and then more grass until one spark had expanded to a full fledged fire. It leapt to the trees and each flame started eating at the forest that was the escape route for the resistance forces. Helana smiled as she watched the fire take hold and grow.

Chapter Thirty

A lone freighter rode the waves of the ocean and its crew went about their duties as they would any other day. A few men tended to the deck, mopping it to get the remaining sludge from their salvage operation wiped off. A couple others stood on the platform above the steering cabin, sipping their coffee and talking about the success of the last couple of days. Nothing was out of order, until the shockwave exploded outward from the vortex created by Helana. It expanded out over the ocean and slammed into the boat knocking the coffee cups from the men's hands and throwing all of the men down to the deck! After it was over, the men stood and surveyed first each other, and then the boat. Two more men ran out from inside the cabin shouting and wondering what the hell had just happened and then one noticed the change on the horizon. Where once there had been nothing but water, there was now an island, an island that had just appeared out of nowhere.

"Where the bloody hell did that come from?" one man muttered in shock.

"An island just doesn't appear out of nowhere, get me th'maps an'do it quick!" The captain shouted.

"Look cap'n, up in the sky, ain't never seen anythin like that before!" one other crewmember pointed. Above the new island was a dark cloud mass that was swirling in a circular counter clockwise motion. Out of the vortex five creatures emerged and the boat crew stared in disbelief.

"I don't know what th'hell is goin on, but I ain't likin it," grumbled another crew member.

"I'm still waitin on th'bloody maps, bring me the thing will ya before I keep yer share of th'salvage," repeated the Captain.

"I'll get'er," one man said. He went inside and returned a few minutes later with maps in hand. The captain grabbed them and spread them out over a large box strewn on the deck. He stared at the drawings, the names and tried to determine what it was he was trying to see. Then he connected a few of the names to where they were.

"Lads, ya recall stories yer daddy would talk to ya about an island, a place where an ancient king may lay in rest?" He looked over his crew and watched them think about what he was referring to.

"Yer not meanin those old stories of that English king, what's his name? Are ya?

"I be indeed lad," the captain nodded. "That king was supposed to be laid ta rest on an island, ya recall th'name?" the captain pushed them to think.

"Bloody hell, yer talkin of Avalon aren't ya?" beamed one man.

"Now yer talking. An island appears, here," the captain pointed to the map. "In a place not all that far from Camelford. That be a name which links that king to th'island ta where it was supposed ta be."

"Can ya imagine th'reward if we find that tomb!" one crewmember shouted excitedly.

"What king?" asked one man. He was completely confused about what they were talking about.

"Yer a might young, figures ya wouldn't know it," grunted his fellow shipmate.

"Easy lads, I ain't sure what those flyin things are, but we best arm ourselves, and make way to th'island," the captain smiled. "This is a once in a lifetime opportunity."

"Which King?" the young man asked again.

"Arthur lad, King Arthur," smiled the captain. "Men, get what ya need and get the gear ready, we're goin ashore."

"Aye captain," the men agreed.

Merlin held his staff firmly and watched the wraith emerge from the vortex. The elves had set up their line of defense on the catwalks of Camelot and waited as the creatures closed in on the castle. Morgana was off with the other council members to begin the incantation to rebuild the magic that had protected Avalon all these centuries. Before he could help them he had to deal with the wraith.

Zach moved in next to Merlin, "What do we do about the vortex?"

"I'll take care of that, but I need you to help the elves fend off the wraith until I've closed the door. Once I have that accomplished I'll contend with the wraith, keep the sword near! You might need it," Merlin said. He strode off to get a better position to cast the spell needed to close the vortex and Zach turned and bolted for the catwalk to join Riane and Falon.

He joined Riane and she smiled on seeing him. "Come to join in on the fun have you?"

"Always," Zach laughed and grabbed an extra crossbow that Riane had grabbed for him.

"I got it just for you," she said with a grin, "I thought you might join us."

"Let's get rid of these things so we can get back home."

"Did you just call it, home?" she checked.

"Yeah, I did," he smiled.

The wraith flew in on Camelot and the elves greeted the monsters with a swarm of arrows, which managed to slow the dark minions a little, but they continued on despite the elves defenses. A second wave of arrows filled the sky and still the wraith flew in on the catwalk. The group flew by and grabbed a few elves with their clawed feet, tossing them off the catwalk, and using their wings to stir up a wind and offset the attack of the warriors fending the walls.

"Shoot the wings! Shoot the wings!" Riane commanded. She reloaded her crossbow and fired again, her arrow striking amidst the thick of one wing of an attacker. It buckled in flight and adjusted its path. Riane smiled, her guess was a good one, and she had found a weakness. She shouted out the orders again and the elf forces changed their strategy and keyed in on the wings of the wraith.

Zach took note of the attack pattern; they had gotten awful close to himself and Riane. They couldn't be keying on them could they? Helana would not know what they were doing or that they were even here, could she? He looked down at Excalibur and felt the warmth of the handle. Or could she? The wraith had to be her doing, was her strength so much so that it could open the doorway from the new world to this one? If that was the case, then they had to get back and the sooner the better!

He lifted his bow and let an arrow fly into the nearest wraith. It hit its mark and the creature shrieked in pain. It whirled its head to get a look and it seemed to recognize him. That couldn't be good he thought to himself.

It and another wraith changed their attack and flew in on Zach, Riane and Falon. Falon leapt off the catwalk on to the steps to avoid the attack but Zach and Riane felt the brunt of the assault as the creatures slammed into the wall, sending debris everywhere. The two wraith retreated back to alter their flight and make another pass. Zach wiped the dust off him and looked for Riane. He couldn't see her! Then he heard her shout and ran to the edge of the wall. She was hanging on to the edge and was in full sight for the returning wraith!

"Hang on Riane!" he shouted. Zach reached down and grabbed her wrists. "I've got you; I'm getting us both out of here!"

Falon ran back up to assist and fired her bow, sending her shot into the wing of the nearest wraith! It screeched and changed course, flying directly into another volley of arrows from the rest of the elf forces. Full of arrows, and unable to control its flight anymore the one wraith fell from the sky into the courtyard where it was swarmed on by armed elf guard who disposed of the menace with their spears.

Zach pulled with all his strength and slowly got Riane back up onto the ledge. The one wraith came in, even as Falon fired another arrow into its wing. The creature ignored the wound; its focus was directly on Zach. It landed on the edge of the catwalk and shrieked! Falon tried to reload but the thing knocked her sideways with a swipe of its other wing. It leaned in, its maw opened, exposing the razor teeth as it locked in on Zach.

Zach reached down and lifted Excalibur, the handle warm to his touch, he brought the blade around in defense and it cleanly cut through the neck of the beast, beheading it in one clean sweep. The head fell down off into the moat, and the body stood there momentarily and then tumbled backwards, following the severed head into the waters. Zach let out a sigh, and looked at the sword; it glowed momentarily and then returned to its normal state. He helped Riane stand, and then the two of them went over to assist Falon. Once she was up and had her bearings she pointed to Excalibur.

"Well Zach, if there was any doubt about the sword, I think you just erased it," Falon said with a smile.

"Just lucky," he replied.

Riane gave him a kiss on the cheek. "It is more than luck."

Merlin whispered the words he required, repeating them slowly and carefully to get the enchantment correct. It had been some time since he had conjured up the magic and he wanted to make sure he got it right! He saw the attack on the catwalk and was impressed with how Zach had taken care of the wraith with the help of Excalibur! If he had any doubts on the man, it was vanquished with that display of ability! Merlin only paused for a short moment and then returned to the task at hand. He finished the words for his spell and the staff he held flared to life! He thrust it forward and a white bolt shot out and skyward until it gained the vortex! It spread out then and tore at the vortex, disipating it until the opening was gone and only dark cloud remained. Satisfied, he nodded. There, one task done, now on to the next.

Two wraiths were now dead, and only three remained but those three were wreaking havoc on Camelot's walls and cutting into the elf defenders. A large number of casualities were everywhere from the carnage. Merlin directed his attention on the remaining wraith and with a few words; his staff came alive once more and in three quick shots, disintegrated the wraith in midflight. The threat was gone but it gave the wizard cause for concern. First, they had gotten through from the new world that much he did know. Second, the magic cast to open the gateway had also exposed Avalon and that now was his deepest concern. Third and the scariest of the three, that the magic ability to open the doorway between two worlds was considerable.

Zach, Riane, Fallon and the Elf General came over to him, as he stood there looking up at the sky. The wizard greeted them with a nod and a smile.

"Good work General. It has been a while for you and your men," Merlin said.

"Aye Merlin, it has. Felt well, though a little more warning would have been nice," the General smiled.

"We have not had the time to reacquaint general. It is good to see you again Vil, your son has grown into quite the commander as well," Merlin complimented.

"Indeed he has, he is somewhat more adventurous than me, but being young it is to be expected. Zach, we never had the chance to officially meet below, I am General Vil, keeper of Camelot and the protector of this island. It is an honor to meet you," General Vil bowed and then shook Zach's hand.

"Please, not so formal, we're all the same here," Zach said with a wave of his hand.

"As you wish," Vil said.

A few shouts erupted from the catwalk and an elf appeared through the gate racing in on his horse and leapt off. He came running up, and General Vil recognized him as one of the patrol guards who kept watch on the circumference of the island. The rest of his party was trailing behind as they rode into the courtyard.

"General, a boat has appeared just off shore. There is another smaller boat approaching the island," the elf informed everyone.

"They can still see the island," Vil murmured. "Take another party with you down to the shoreline, keep them there, do not let them go any further!"

"General, tell Morgana to keep working on the protection spell, I will deal with these intruders myself," Merlin said.

"Are you sure that is wise?" Vil asked.

Merlin merely smiled. "This will be more fun than anything; there is nothing they can do to harm me. Care to tag along you three?"

"Well hey, I'm not one to pass up on anything fun," Zach grinned. He handed the sword to the General for him to hold on to, but the elf refused to take it.

"Sorry sir, that is yours, I am not allowed to handle Excalibur."

"You're kidding right?"

"No sir," Vil smiled.

"There are rules Zach, if you wish, you may leave the sword back in the chamber and we can collect it later," Merlin suggested.

"Fine, be right back." Zach jogged off and disappeared into the entrance that led to the lower chamber of Arthur's resting place. He reappeared several minutes later without the sword. The group then started off for the beach to greet the latest visitors and see what it was that brought them here.

On the beach, the captain and his crew approached the sandy shoreline, anxious to set foot on a legendary island of lore. The light show they had witnessed in the sky earlier had made them somewhat apprehensive but when the storm had ceased, all was calm and their courage came back. Now that they were almost to the land, each of them was eager to be the first to set foot on it.

"Easy boys, bring'er in slow, ya might spill my coffee," the captain quipped.

"Just think of th' papers an'what they'll be sayin when we

come back with all th'treasure!" one man said the excitement evident in his voice.

The boat sailed up to the shoreline and hit the sand with a light grinding sound as it slid up. Two of the crew jumped out in waist deep water and sloshed their way up the shore, and pulled the boat up further so that everyone could get out and begin their exploration.

"There we go lads, time to go do a little diggin!" the captain shouted. He stepped on to the sand and knelt down to touch it with his fingers. "I'm livin a dream, standin an'touchin the island of Avalon. The boys back at Cardiff aren't gonna believe this."

"Then captain, we might have ta bring back a few trinkets to show'em," one man chuckled. "I plan on retirin after this one. We are gonna be so rich!"

Another voice interupted their train of thought, "Is that so, I highly doubt that will happen today. It might perhaps another day, but not today."

The captain looked up towards the trees and saw the older man wearing a long tattered cloak and holding a staff of sorts, and had two women and another man with him. Where in the world did they come from? This was his claim as far as he was concerned and these strangers weren't going to keep him from the find of the century!

"And who might you be?" the captain asked.

"No one in particular," Merlin replied.

"That not be an answer," the captain scoffed.

"You are tresspassing on private property gentlemen; I'm going to have to ask you to leave."

"Is that right," the captain chuckled. He pulled out a pistol and held it towards the four. "I don't think so mate, you see, this place is up for grabs as I see it. Since it wasn't here before but now it strangely is, well, in my book, that makes it first come first serve."

"I beg to differ sir; this island is not something you can just pillage at your discretion. This island is indeed private property, and according to law, you are the tresspasser and hence, you are the one breaking the law."

"Show me a deed showing the rightful owner of this place and I'll leave," the captain sneered. "No? Don't have one? Didn't think so. So, if you will step aside we will take a little tour of the place." He waved his gun around to emphasize his point, and his fellow shipmates did the same.

Merlin sighed. "If you insist on being stubborn, then so will I."

"And how is that?" one crew member asked curiously.

Merlin answered the question with a wave of his hand and all of the men's firearms flew from their own hands and into the water. Then he merely smiled at the men.

"I did ask nicely."

The men had no idea what to do next, and started to back away, back towards their boat. Merlin waved his right hand again and all of the men were thrown up and into the water. The wizard walked down to the edge of the water, as the men splashed frantically to swim backwards away from him.

"Enjoy your day gentlemen," Merlin said with a chuckle. He murmured a few words and all of the men vanished, along with their small boat and returned to their frigate. Merlin disappeared then and reappeared on the deck of the larger boat. All the men were looking around trying to figure out what had happened when they saw Merlin.

The Captain waved him off, trying to prevent any further surprises. "That's enough, whoever you are, we're leaving!"

"Oh yes you are, but first, you will not remember any of this, you are going to sleep now, and when you awake all you will recall is a long day at sea and a successful day of salvage. You will not remember anything but that. Sleep well," Merlin said calmly. He waved his hand once more and all of the men fell asleep where they stood. Satisfied, Merlin disappeared again, and returned to the edge of the shoreline. The wizard turned around and wandered back up to the three waiting for him at the tree line.

"What'd you do?" Zach asked.

"I merely put them to sleep. It looked like they were a little tired," Merlin joked.

"And?" he pushed for more.

Merlin sighed and chuckled. "They will wake up not remembering a thing. Now, let's get back to Camelot and get this island back under its magical shroud and hidden from any further curious passer by's. I think we've had enough excitement for one day!"

Chapter Thirty One

Elise banked her gryphon once more, and still the manticore kept close. She and her fellow gryphon riders were doing their absolute best to stay a safe distance and draw the creatures away from the rest of the ground forces. The retreat was now in full operation and now it was time to do their job and somehow rid themselves of these flying beasts! A task easier said than done. These ceatures were as determined as they were lethal.

She flashed her riders another hand signal to move into the forest itself and try to lose them, by using the trees to throw them into disarray. Elise glanced upward to the ridge, hoping Teague would be able to follow through on his own retreat with his fellow archers.

The captain of the riders led her flyers into the forest and the race to manuevre through the trees was now underway. She held on tight to her gryphon's bridle guiding her ride as best she could and at the same time relying on the gryphon's own survival instinct to aid her. An array of darts slammed into a tree near her, and she leaned in closer to the gryphon for protection from any further attempts by the manticore to kill her. She and the flyers whisked in and around the trees dogdging low branches and fallen trees. Elise saw one of her riders fall from his ride, a number of darts protruding from his back. The gryphon managed to fly a little farther before it too crashed into the foliage after the poison from the manticore's darts took effect. Elise swore under her breath, another friend was gone and she had had enough. She pushed her gryphon harder and her flyers followed suit. They all knew their rides would not last much longer without rest.

Then as quickly as they had appeared, the manticore abruptly retreated, breaking off their pursuit and flying up out of the trees and out of view. Elise and the others took notice and she decided it was time to take advantage of it and go find the retreating forces and see what was going on. She signaled them all and led the way back to the rendezvous point.

Teague watched Elise take a large portion of the flying demons with her, and was relieved but at the same time shouting orders to his archers to ready themselves for the remainder that still pushed on to the ridge. They would hold the ridge and give the rest a good chance to retreat back to the rendezvous point.

"Hold the line men! Make those arrows count and fire on my order!"

The archers lifted their bows, loaded and aimed at the remaining approaching manticore. Teague waited until they were almost on top of them and then shouted the command.

"Release!"

A rainshower of arrows bombarbed the creatures and they stopped in mid air at the ferocity of the assault. It was only a few moments before the archers had reloaded and had another slew of arrows in the air. A few manticores opted to fall back altogether rather than push on, and the remainder stayed the course. A number of the creatures flung their tails and unleashed their own attack on the elves. Some of the archers felt the blow of the stingers and fell off the ridge, already dead as they tumbled to the ground below. The manticore flew over and swung around to take another pass at the ridge.

Teague was determined to stay as long as they could. He ran along the line encouraging his men and reloading his own bow as he did. They lifted their bows once more and waited for the attack.

"Release!" the captain shouted and let his arrow go. The sky filled once more with elf arrows and they all found a target in the myriad of manticore.

The monsters backed down, opting to fight another day and flew off to their waiting master, leaving the elves to themselves. Teague was relieved but didn't want to wait around and see if they would change their minds.

"All right men! Let's get out of here! To the Rendezvous point! Move move move!" he ordered, shouting at the top of his lungs.

The elves emerged from their places and bolted for the woods, not waiting to see if the flying demons would return. They entered the woods at a full run, unaware that below in the lower treeline the fire started by Helana was now evolving into a raging inferno, eating trees so fast as though it couldn't eat them fast enough to feed its desire.

Elise landed her gryphon and ran over to meet with a few of the elf captains already at the rendezvous point. She saw no sign of Brielle, Shar, or the king and queen and looked to the captains for answers.

"Good to see you again Kieran. Any word on Shar? Or the King and Queen?"

"Not as yet, there are still forces working up through

the woods. They were one of the last groups to retreat," Kieran said.

"I don't like it, it doesn't feel right," Elise said with a shake of her head. "I'm going to go and have a look."

"You think something is wrong?" the elf captain wondered curiously.

Elise shrugged, "I don't know, but nothing has really gone right today, I just want to be sure."

"Aye, good idea, I'll get some men to go back in and make sure the rest find their way," Keiran said.

Elise nodded and ran back to her ride and as she did a couple of the surviving riders approached her.

"What is the word captain?" asked one.

"I'm going back to fly over the woods and have a look," she informed them.

"May we go with you? You might need our help," offered one elf.

"Thank you! Climb aboard riders," Elise smiled at them.

In the thick of the forest the last of the retreating forces were making their way up the ridge on the predetermined escape route once it was time to fall back. Everyone was running as fast as they could, dodging low branches and avoiding tripping over tree roots that may be sticking out of the moist ground. No one knew if the enemy was in pursuit or still a disorganized mess back on the plains, so the goal was to retreat as quickly as possible and get on the move back to Cambridge for the final stand against Helana.

Shar stopped running, and breathing hard in an effort to catch her breath, turned around to look back from whence they came. Something felt wrong, but she couldn't quite determine what it was! After a few moments she shrugged it off and ran on, putting it from her mind for the time being.

Neil, Tasha and Brielle were running next to one another as they pushed themselves to keep up. He and Tasha had to pause every so often to get their wind back, and Brielle would stop with them. She did not want to leave the pair alone; they were too easy a target for anyone, or anything.

"Remind me to take up jogging after this is all over with," Neil gasped between breaths.

"My lord, what is 'jogging'?" Brielle asked.

Neil took in several breaths and pointed to the elves running by them. "We run, like this, but to do it to get in shape."

Brielle nodded, understanding more or less what he meant. "Sir, the elves are more adept at running than you. You could 'jog' as you call for days on end, but you will never be able to keep up with us."

"Gee, thanks for giving me a reason to not jog," Neil laughed.

Tasha winked at Brielle. "He wouldn't have done it anyway."

"Hey, I would have," Neil defended with a chuckle.

"Shall we go then? We can jog up to the rendezvous point. It will get you started on the way to getting yourself in shape," Brielle said.

"I guess," Neil replied. "After you captain," he motioned for her to take the lead.

"I insist you go first, in case you fall I can help you up," she countered.

Tasha laughed at the remark and started running, "Keep up if you can my king!"

Tony and Mia ran alongside Axel and Ruskin, making sure the two didn't get lost in the underbrush, and all four were doing their best to keep up with Thatcher who showed no signs of being winded. The gnome appeared to be putting some distance between himself and the four and they weren't about to let Thatcher put them to shame.

"Move it boy, the gnome is gettin' on," Axel challenged.

"Me? You two are the ones holding me up!" Tony retorted. To emphasize the point he pushed harder and put some room between himself and the two dwarves. Mia was already getting ahead of him and closer to Thatcher.

"Move it ya slow troll!" Ruskin snorted as he passed Axel.

"Hey, get yer bloody axe outta my way!" Axel answered as he in turn passed his brother.

"Come on then!" Mia shouted, teasing as she ran alongside the gnome.

"Just keep up you three! We only got a bit o'way to go!" Thatcher bellowed as he dodged another tree root. The very same root caught Ruskin's foot and the dwarf went tumbling through a thicket. Axel fell down in a fit of laughter and Tony stopped running to get them both back on their feet and back on track to the rendezvous point.

"At this rate we'll never get out of these trees," Tony scoffed as he began to jog on after getting the two of them back up and running.

The trees caught fire with each new ember that caught a branch and exploded into flame feeding the frenzy as the inferno moved up the treeline and upwards to the retreating forces. The blaze was still some distance behind but it was gaining ground fast, preceeded by an immense amount of smoke, being thurst up the landscape by a wind that fanned the flames. It was the first thing Elise saw as she and the two other riders flew back down into the valley, the ever expanding mass of smoke filtering up from the forest below. She glanced at the other two and they nodded at her to acknowledge it. It was moving up the treeline quickly and would overrun the final retreating forces. The King and Queen were still in there! And so many more! What could she do? She thought of options and came to one quickly, and the easiest to accomplish. Elise had to find Shar; the mage would be able to help somehow!

She banked her gryphon down lower to tree level and yanked on the reins to make the creature 'bark', and hopefully attract the attention of Shar. She signaled her fellow riders to do the same and all three circled above the trees with their gryphon 'barking' to alert anyone who may be below in the forest.

Tony heard the odd screeching noises above, and stopped momentarily to listen. He shouted at Thatcher. "Hey Thatch! What's that noise?"

The gnome paused in his own running and put his ear to the sky. The screeching appeared again and he looked over at him, "Not sure lad, the gryphon perhaps? A bit odd though I must say."

"Yeah, it is," he nodded. Tony looked back, "Come on you two, pick up the pace!"

"Don't wait fer us boy," puffed Axel. He and Ruskin were sweating profusely and were stopping a bit more often to catch their breath. The run up the ridgeline was more exhausting than they had anticipated.

Elise and her riders banked around in circles, trying to cover as much forest as possible, but so far they had not illicited any response. The smoke was getting thicker and she could see flames now at the tops of the trees and it was moving quicker now, devouring each new tree to feed its hunger. She and her two other riders risked flying in lower to hopefully catch someone's attention. Elise felt she could almost reach down and grab the tops of the trees they were so close, but kept focused on locating Shar.

Shar stopped running once again, and this time listened to her surroundings. She heard it then, the gryphon bark, and looked up at the sky. She sensed another change in the landscape, and the smell of smoke was now evident. Smoke? Why would there be smoke? There was a reason the gryphon were sounding off and she thought it best to find out why. Shar lifted her left hand and cast a simple spell, seeking the source of the gryphon and immediately located Elise. Another quick incantation and her mind read Elise's mind, and told the rider where she could be found.

Elise felt the magic and the directions from Shar, and signalled her riders to follow her down into the forest. Carefully they guided the gryphon between the trees and settled down on the ground not that far from Shar. The mage and a few others ran up to see Elise, relieved to see she was all right.

"Captain, good to see you again," Neil nodded, relieved.

"Sir," she returned the nod and leapt off her ride. "Shar, we've got a new danger for everyone still retreating."

"What is it?" Shar asked.

"Fire and it is spreading fast, and moving up the treeline! You must be able to smell the smoke by now?" Elise checked. She looked at everyone and all gave her a nod.

"I was wondering about that. How big is this fire?" Neil inquired.

"It is huge, and it is almost here," Elise replied.

"There is no way everyone can outrun it," another rider informed them. "It will catch the retreat before they can reach the rendezvous."

Elise nodded. "We need to get you two out of here now! You will ride with us." She motioned for Neil and Tasha to follow her.

"That may be fine for us, but what about the rest? We can't leave them to the fire!" Tasha said.

"Take them, I will deal with the fire," Shar said.

"Don't be crazy!" Adeena piped up.

"Is that possible?" Neil wondered.

Shar let out a deep breath, "I believe so, and I have no choice but to try."

"If anyone can do this, it would be her," Brielle added.

"Maybe there is something else we can do," Neil threw the idea out there.

"Not enough time, this fire is likely Helana's doing. It will need my magic to stop it," Shar said.

Smoke was now beginning to show itself, signalling the fire was close and getting closer with each passing second. There was no time to debate, and no time for any other ideas. They would have to rely on Shar and her ability to stop it, or at the very least, slow the fire down.

"Neil, Tasha, come with us please. Go with my riders. I will stay back with Shar," Elise said, authority evident in her tone.

"See you at the rendezvous," Neil said to Shar.

"Show that witch what you can do!" Tasha added with a grin.

"Keep them safe riders," Brielle urged and she was off running back on up the hill. "Good luck Shar!" she waved.

"Thanks! And I will Tasha," Shar smiled back. "Now go, Adeena, get going before the smoke starts to affect you as well."

"Ahhhhh I can outrun any old smoke anyday anytime,"

she replied with a chuckle. Adeena then went up to Shar and gave her a hug. "See you at the top of the hill."

"Yes, you will. Now, go."

Neil and Tasha left with the other two elf riders, each taking a place on the back of the saddle as they climbed onto their respective gryphon. The elf riders guided the gryphon up through the trees and both were gone from view as they cleared the top of the treeline. Adeena was already off and flying back on up the hill, in an attempt to catch up to Tony and the dwarves she had seen earlier. Shar looked at Elise and merely gave the elf a nod of acknowledgement.

"This is now between me and Helana. Stay near as I will likely need some help after I have cast the spell."

"Aye, I shall," Elise smiled.

Shar turned around, took in several deep breaths and waited for the fire. It did not take long to show itself, as the flames appeared, consuming branch after branch. The smoke was now much thicker, and making it difficult to breathe. Shar thought of the magic she needed and began to whisper the words. Each phrase took form, and she lifted her hands to send the magic forth into the fire. As she spoke the final sentence a wind began to take form and swept around the elf and the mage, pushing all the smoke back into the fire. The magic formed and Shar released it, sending a shock wave with the wind into the inferno. Magic met magic and a rumble reverberated throughout the surrounding landscape. The wind slammed into the fire and acted like a wall as the fire stopped dead in its tracks.

Shar knew that would not be enough and called on more magic to get the wind to push the fire back unto itself. She sent another wave of magic with more wind and it threw the fire backwards to where the flames were now consuming it and all at once Shar's magic and Helana's erupted skyward hurling a giant wave of flame into the sky and then it extinguished in a big burst of wind. Shar was breathing heavily and fell to her knees as the magic faded. Elise ran to her aid and helped her stand.

"Is it over?" the elf asked.

"Yes, it is done," Shar whispered.

"Then we must go, in case the witch decides to relight the fire," Elise said. She assisted Shar to her gryphon and got the mage settled into the saddle. The elf captain took her own position and grabbed the reins. With a command they were airborn and lifting up through the trees. In short order they were skimming over the trees and on their way to the rendezvous point where they would all regroup and consider their next course of action.

Helana watched the fire explode in the sky and cursed under her breath. This new nemesis was a worthy opponent indeed! For a moment she thought about reigniting the fire but opted to let it go. There would be a time she could use her magic for a more worthwhile cause. To expend energy as she pleased would exhaust her before she could reach Kildare, and that she would not allow. Malcolm and the elves would feel her full potential and she wanted to be sure they knew they were defeated.

A look below at her own scattered army made her even more frustrated. This new magical individual had thrown a wrench into her own counterattack. That was a mistake she would not make twice. She cast her magic and vanished in a whirl of blue light and wind, and reappeared near General Vadeez who was trying to reorganize the trolls into an orderly line.

"Problems General?" she asked.

Vadeez turned to face her and frowned. "These creatures are not worth the time my queen, we are better off without them!"

"They clear the path for the rest of the army; we will still need them, at least for the time being."

"As you wish. What is our course of action now my queen?" he wondered.

"Move up the hill. Get them," she pointed to the trolls, "to clear the debris out of the way. Go directly to Kildare. March them there. I want to pay a visit to my future home before we move on to Cambridge and finally rid ourselves of the elves, and Malcolm! "

"It will be done," nodded Vadeez.

"One other thing," Helana started as an idea came to mind. "Put a group of the demons with the giants, and a few trolls, for good measure. I'm going to give our little fighters something else to contend with."

Vadeez did as he was told and with the help of a few other officers of his dead army, he got a good sized group herded together and Helana strode over to survey the horde. They were but a small piece of a much larger entourage, but it would be enough to give the elves some grief.

"Shortly you are going to appear in a forest. Find the elves, and any others who may be hiding in there and kill them all!" She ordered, her voice oozing venom as she spoke.

"With honor my queen," snorted one demon lifting its axe, the blade blood stained and chipped.

"Have fun," she smiled and cast the incantation. Her hands casted the magic and the group vanished in a whirl of blue light and wind. Satisfied, Helana returned to face General Vadeez.

"Get the rest of this mess organized; have them all ready to march again within a day. I've given you some more time to regroup. That excuse of an army hiding up there on the hill will be busy enough now," Helana said. A wide smile slowly adorned her face.

Chapter Thirty Two

Zach touched the door that guarded King Arthur's tomb and ran his hand along the wood work, settling on the latch that kept the door closed. How in the world was he the descendant of this legendary king? That same question kept reoccuring in his mind and each time he couldn't think of a proper answer. So he merely put it aside, only to have it pop up again everytime he wasn't thinking of something else.

"Curious?" Merlin asked as he entered the chamber.

"About? Him? Wouldn't you be?" Zach chuckled.

"From your standpoint I guess I would be," Merlin said as he sauntered over. He touched the door himself and looked at Zach. "Would you like to go in?"

"Am I allowed?"

"For this particular occasion, I think it will be fine. Besides, I'm with you," Merlin grinned. He tapped the latch lock and the door opened. "No one has entered his tomb since we placed him within, not even I have stepped in this room. There are too many memories and it can be painful when it comes to thinking about the past."

"I know what you mean," Zach nodded. "Are you sure it's okay?"

"In you go," Merlin motioned with his right hand. "After you."

Zach stepped into the room and watched as a couple torches lit up as they entered. In the center was a coffin, with a shield draped over it. The coffin was a dark wood, and had a gold edging along its sides. It wasn't quite what he was expecting, but Merlin answered that question.

"He was a man who never thought of himself above any other, the gold lining along the edges are the only markings that would extinguish itself from any other man's final resting place. Arthur would have never allowed us to do anything more."

"His shield I assume," Zach said. He stood next to the coffin but was scared to touch it.

"Yes, it was," Merlin answered quietly.

Zach reached out and touched the coffin. He let out a sigh, and then tapped the handle of Excalibur that rested at his side in its casing. He glanced over at Merlin who seemed to be lost in his own thoughts, no doubt reliving old memories of long ago. Zach closed his eyes and tried to comprehend all of what had happened to him in the last few days.

"I will do my best to uphold Excalibur, and you sir," he whispered.

"I'm sure he knows that Zach," Merlin said quietly. "Shall we go? We still have a boat ride ahead of us."

"Yes, I'm good," Zach nodded in reply. Together they left the tomb and the door closed behind them. Merlin replaced the latch and they made their way up the stairs to the courtyard above. Riane, Falon and the council were waiting for them.

"Are we leaving now?" Falon asked.

"Yes, we are. A short visit to the shop and then we'll be

off to where we need to cross over to the new world," Merlin answered.

"It will be nice to go home," Riane said as she lifted up her backpack and tossed it over her shoulder.

"Once we take care of a few things back in London, we can get on our way and to putting an end to this witch's insanity," Merlin said.

"I would like to accompany you my friend, my daughter may have need of my assistance," Oberon said. He didn't ask it as a question, but more as a request.

"Of course, I will call on you once we have arrived at our crossover," Merlin replied.

Morgana floated over to the wizard and faced him. "Take care old friend, and do not wait several hundred years to pay a visit."

"I will keep that in mind Morgana, I am sure I will be back soon enough," Merlin smiled.

Two other elves emerged from the group and Zach recognized them immediately. Though, the first time he met them, they did not look like elves.

"Rachel? Christina?" Zach chuckled. "You are both elves?"

"Of course, much like Riane, the magic to hide who we are isn't that difficult," Rachel said.

"I had to be sure you found your way over to my shop somehow. They gladly accepted the task of pushing, if you will, in the right direction," Merlin snickered. "Of course, they had no idea who they were waiting for, even I wasn't sure. I knew where you would arrive, but who you were, well, even magic can't have all the answers."

"Unbelievable," Zach sighed.

"We are ready as well for the trek sir," Christina said.

"Excellent, then let us depart and be on our way," Merlin piped up and nodded to the rest of the council. "I will let you all know how it turns out, or not, depending on the outcome."

"Be careful Merlin, this is magic even you have not encountered," the Lady of the Lake warned.

"I shall," Merlin assured her.

The group, Merlin, Zach, Riane and Falon, and accompanied by Rachel and Christina, made their way out of Camelot's courtyard and down the path to the shoreline of Avalon where their boat awaited.

"And you two are coming along because?" Zach finally asked, deciding it might be a long time before Merlin offered the information.

"We are your protector's sir, as Arthur's heir and carrier of Excalibur, we are to stay at your side until this ordeal is over," Rachel replied.

"Oh, really, well, there's something you don't hear every day," Zach cracked. The two elves failed to catch on to his little joke and he didn't bother to explain it. He was too tired to try.

The boat trip back was quiet and uneventful, and after all that the group had been through in the last number of days, the serenity was welcome. The sky darkened and the stars lit the way back to England. Zach, Riane and Falon sat on the deck and watched the water go by. No one talked much and opted instead for a few drinks to keep the coolness of night at bay. At the cove, where they had picked up their boat earlier, no one was seen. Apparently it was abandoned for the day upon their arrival. The boat was docked, secured and together wandered back to the small shop to a waiting taxi.

"You th'ones who called fer a cab?" the driver asked.

"Yes, we are. Thank you for waiting sir," Merlin thanked the man with a handshake and a group of bills.

"Hell, I'd wait all night fer a fair this big," the man

chuckled. "Gonna be a tight fit in th'back there, didn't know there were six of ya."

"We'll be fine. Off to London, as fast as you can drive," Merlin instructed.

"Aye sir, London she is." The driver put the car into gear once the group had settled in and drove off down the narrow road that would eventually get them into the busy streets of London.

The cab driver did enough talking for the entire group the whole ride back, and at one point even Merlin got tired of his bantering and waved his hand to silence him. Zach chuckled and sat back to watch the starlit sky go by and the odd light marking the yard of some small country home. Exalibur rested on his lap, wrapped in cloth, to hide it from any curious eyes. Riane was sitting next to him and was fast asleep; her head resting on his shoulder and Falon was talking quietly with Merlin in the front. Christina and Rachel hardly said a word, merely looking at the passing countryside, much like Zach was doing. All in all much like the boat trek back, it was quiet once Merlin had cast his spell on the cabbie to keep him silent. On arriving back in London, they were dropped off back at the tea shop and the cab driver had his 'spell' lifted and Merlin paid the man, with a tip.

"Well sir, if ya ever need a ride again, ya call anytime," the driver said.

"I will keep that in mind. Thank you and have a good night," Merlin nodded. The driver motored off to his next fare and the group went on in to the tea shop.

"I will brew up a fresh batch of tea for us," Falon said.

"Good idea, we can all use a pick me up. Don't get too comfortable everyone, we won't be staying long," Merlin informed them.

"Where are we off to next?" Zach yawned.

"To the only place that will get us back to the new world. I have no doubt that the witch has put magic in place to keep us from returning. This one portal will be the only way back," Merlin explained.

"And where the hell is that?" Zach asked.

"Why Stone Henge of course," Merlin replied matter of factly. "I have one errand to attend to, I will be back momentarily." With that the wizard left the shop and instantly vanished.

"He's good," Zach murmured. "Wait a second! Did he say Stone Henge?"

"Yes he did. Zach, sit down, relax and I will have that tea ready in a few minutes," Falon replied.

"Make mine a coffee, I'm losin my energy here," Zach yawned again. He sat down at the nearest table and made himself comfortable.

Riane sat down next to him and laid her head down over her arms on the table. "I am exhausted; all this traveling has worn me out."

Zach chuckled. "Well, we're almost done here. I promise, once we get through this we can come back here and tour around on a more casual pace."

"I would like that," Riane smiled. She leaned up and gave him a kiss.

"Tea is ready!" Falon piped up. "Your coffee is nearly ready Zach." She brought over several cups and placed the pot on the table. Everyone helped themselves to the tea and Zach yawned a few more times.

Merlin reappeared then, quite abruptly and caught the group by surprise. He chuckled and motioned to Falon. "Sorry all, I did not mean to startle you. Have a cup ready for me Falon when I return."

"You just did sir," Fallon replied, a little confused at her teacher's comment.

"Yes, but I have to leave again, and Zach is coming with me," Merlin further explained.

"I am? Now where?"

"Just a quick jaunt! We won't be long."

Zach stood up and stretched. "Keep the coffee warm."

Christina and Rachel stood to accompany them as well, but Merlin waved them off.

"No need ladies. We will be quite safe. Stay, and enjoy your tea."

Merlin and Zach left the shop and started down the pathway.

"So, where are we off to?"

"We are already here," Merlin smiled. Zach looked around and noticed they weren't on the path anymore but in a building standing in a hallway. He glanced around trying to figure out where he was and couldn't recognize it immediately.

"And where is here?" he asked.

"Look around again, see if it looks familiar," the wizard urged.

Zach took another look and at first didn't see anything in particular that stood out, but then he recognized a painting, and then another and then a few other odd and ends and looked back at Merlin.

"I've been here, earlier, on a guided tour," Zach murmured.

"Yes, I recall you mentioning that, but what is the name of this place?" Merlin pushed him.

"This is where the royal family lives – Buckingham, palace," he whispered.

Merlin watched him for a moment and smiled. "Feels like something else though, doesn't it?"

"Sorta like, home," he paused, recognizing what he had

felt earlier when he and Riane had been on the tour. “Like home,” he looked at Merlin.

“Indeed,” Merlin said. “There is someone who would like to meet you.”

“Meet me?”

“Yes, an old friend. I made a promise to all who have sat on the throne, and I am glad to finally deliver on it.”

“What promise is that?” Zach wondered, his curiousity now getting the best of him.

“A promise that if I ever found Arthur’s heir, I would introduce that person to them,” Merlin replied.

“Okay,” Zach nodded. “Wait a second, who are you referring to? The royal family?”

“Only the one who sits on the throne.”

“You are kidding right?”

Merlin laughed lightly, “No, I am not.”

“They know you exist?”

“Yes, she does, and as I said earlier, only the one who sits on the throne. I have always, and will always, serve those who sit on the royal throne. Another promise I made to Arthur long long ago.”

“Are there any other surprises?” Zach asked.

“A few,” Merlin hinted and motioned to a door at the end of the hall. “She is waiting for us, shall we?”

“I guess, no idea what I’ll say,” Zach shrugged.

“You might surprise yourself,” Merlin said with a chuckle.

The two wandered down the hall and the wizard knocked quietly on the door. A quiet female voice echoed out from behind it, “Yes, do come in.”

Merlin pulled the door open and bowed on entering. An elderly lady sat in a chair, next to a desk, with a lamp lit to cast a dim light throughout the room. The lady stood and bowed back to Merlin and walked over to shake his hand.

"My dear friend, thank you for coming by. Two visits in one night, I am quite lucky," she smiled.

"It is I who is lucky my lady, I have brought someone for you to meet," Merlin stood aside and motioned to Zach. Zach in turn nodded to the woman.

"Is this?" the woman looked at Merlin.

"Yes, he is. The magic of Excalibur says it is so," Merlin assured her with simple nod and smile.

The woman moved around Merlin and held out her hand for Zach. He reached out and shook her hand, and bowed somewhat awkwardly. She laughed lightly and nodded to him.

"This is an honor, I never would have thought I'd meet someone such as you," Zach said as he stood straight.

"No my young man, the pleasure is mine. To meet the heir of Arthur has long been awaited by many. I feel very lucky to have that honor bestowed upon me. For a long long time the myth has been passed on from generation to generation. This is a day I will remember for the rest of my days, knowing that Arthur's heir does indeed exist," the woman motioned to the desk and an awaiting pair of chairs. "Join me for a cup of tea? And we can talk for a time."

"Yes, sure, I could use a cup. It's been a hectic few days," Zach replied. He followed her over to the desk and sat down at the chair she pointed to. She sat down as well and Merlin poured the two each a full cup of tea.

"Join us won't you Merlin? It would be nice to visit with you as well," she urged.

"How can I refuse such an offer," Merlin agreed with a smile. "It would be my pleasure."

Merlin, Zach and the older lady, one Queen Elizabeth the 2nd sipped their tea and talked casually about Zach's life - who he was, and what he did for a living, among other things. The conversation was light and strayed from Zach to the Queen herself, and her family. There was even some light discussion on Merlin, who as usual was vague in his answers. The sitting was enjoyable and a second cup was poured without question. The visit lasted into the early hours of the morning and when Zach left Buckingham Palace with Merlin, he truly felt like he was leaving home. He sighed as the dawn of the new day had begun to show itself with a brightening sky and the sounds of birds breaking the silence.

"I sure didn't see that coming," Zach said.

Merlin snickered, "Well, our business is done here Zach. Shall we gather the others?"

"I guess it's that time huh," Zach nodded.

"Yes it is. We have a door to open and a bridge to cross. It is time to pay a visit and show this witch the power of Excalibur!"

Chapter Thirty Three

Tony, Mia and Thatcher emerged from the woods and stopped to catch their breath. A few moments later both Axel and Ruskin followed and looked as though they had been playing in the dirt and were sweating profusely. Both collapsed to the ground in front of them, breathing as though air was hard to come by and they wanted to get as much in as they could. Tony couldn't help but laugh at the two and Thatcher eventually gave in to the laughter as well.

"You two really need to use your legs a wee bit more, an'a bit less of th'horse," Thatcher mocked.

"You," Axel gasped, "Never," he took in another gulp of air, "Mind ya gnome."

Tony fell to his knees in a fit of laughter and shook his head. "Pick yourselves up before anybody else sees you."

"Don't," puffed Ruskin, "care."

"Oh, I think you might," Tony quipped as he saw Adeena approach.

"Well now, a little bit of a run and you two are wallowing in the dirt, so why does that not surprise me?" Adeena said shooting the insult right at the two dwarves.

"Drat, ya go fly off an' be a demon's lunch won't ya?" Axel growled as he sat up, still breathing a bit hard.

"Has everyone made it up the hill?" Tony asked.

"Almost, we're waiting for a few stragglers," Adeena replied. She looked back at the dwarves and stuck her tongue out at them.

"Oh that'll scare th'likes of no one," Ruskin snorted.

"Where's Neil and Tasha?" Tony wondered as he looked around.

"Not here yet, but they're just about, Brielle is with them and a few other elf guards," Adeena said.

"What about the other captains?" he inquired further.

"Teague and his archers haven't arrived yet, but Shar says they are on their way," Adeena said.

"Good," Tony stood up and looked around. He noticed the groups were re-organizing and getting their forces realigned. The march back to Cambridge may run into the odd roadblock so the group wanted to be prepared, just in case.

Neil, Tasha with Brielle and a few other elves appeared from the woods and waved to the rest as they wandered over. The ranks had thinned considerably but they were still a fairly large size force, but no match for what waited below in the valley. Darg, Riss, Taith and Kieran along with Elise approached the group and nodded to one another.

"Good to see you all. Any word on Teague?" Neil asked.

"On his way," Riss replied.

"How bad is it?" Neil pushed for more answers.

"Over half of my regiment is gone," Darg muttered.

"I have only five riders left," Elise said, struggling to get the words out. "Two of the gryphons are hurt badly as well, leaving us with three in total."

"Where is Shar?" Tasha asked.

"Resting, by the gryphon," Elise assured her. "She is fine."

"We can't stay long everyone. They may be disorganized in the valley but they'll be on the march within the next day. We have to put some distance between ourselves and them and rejoin the rest at Cambridge," Brielle spoke, the urgency evident in her voice.

The trees began to shake and the sound of branches snapping reverberated out from the forest, and all turned to listen to the new sounds echoing with ever strengthening fervor. Something was approaching and it wasn't a part of their group of that much they were certain. The captains broke off running in different directions shouting orders as they did to get their forces set up and ready for whatever was moving in on them. The trees were literally being thrown aside and and three enormous figures were the first to step out of the forest. The giants had found them.

Shar stood up and leaned against the gryphon for support; the animal looked down at her and acknowledged the mage's presence with a snort and bob of its head. She stared up at the giants as they stopped their forward progress and looked around to see where they were. Elise came running up and put her arms around Shar to lend her support.

"How are you?" the elf asked, a look of concern on her face.

Shar waved her off, "I am fine, and I am strong enough to stand on my own, thank you though."

Elise backed off and nodded to her. "Are you sure?"

"Yes, yes, I'm fine."

Shar went back to the giants and began to think of options of a defence against them. She sensed the magic Helana had used to get them here, and there were others, other creatures waiting in the forest. The mage felt their presence and shouted to warn the rest.

"Watch the forest! There are more hiding in amidst the trees!" Shar was walking towards the forest's edge and drew her cloak in closer.

"Shar!" Elise shouted. The elf was confused. Did she go after her? Or leave her to her own agenda? Elise swore under her breath and opted to go assist the other captains in their efforts to organize the fighters. She bolted off to give Darg and Riss some aid to get their battered group together.

"Where did they come from?" Neil asked as he ran on to regroup with the rest.

"My guess is this would be Helana's work," Tasha said.

Shar ran by them going directly towards the giants and caught the two completely off guard.

"Shar?" Tasha checked as she stopped. Neil took her by the arm, and beckoned her to stay with him.

"Leave her! She is more than capable of taking of herself. We need to get back and get some distance between them and us," Neil said.

Tony, Mia and Thatcher, with Axel and Ruskin were also bolting to get behind the elf lines and give some sort of distance between themselves and the giants. As they got in behind Kieran and his men, a swarm of demons launched themselves out of the woods and only paused momentarily before charging the forces. The groups were still trying to get organized but a few lines had regrouped and were ready.

"Archers! Fire at will!" shouted Kieran.

A slew of arrows were let loose at the demons, which only slowed them briefly. The horde rushed on, eager to tear into the unprepared forces. Shar strode closer to the enemy and she could hear the others shouting at her to get out of there but she paid no attention to them. If Helana was determined to show off her abilities, then she would fire back at the witch and show her she had another mage with which to contend.

The demons were almost on top of her, but she was already voicing the incantation she needed and brought it to bear on all the demons as they nearly overwhelmed her. Shar flung her hands out and let the magic go! The creatures stopped dead in their tracks as though hitting an invisible brick wall, and then in one giant wave as though it were splashing in towards a shoreline, Shar impelled them backwards and into the trees. She did not stop there! Weaving her hands in a circular motion she aimed her magic at two enormous trees and tore them from the ground and heaved them through the air and at the three giants. The massive creatures were unprepared for the attack and were no match for tree clubs that battered them relentlessly. They fell to the ground, beaten and bloodied. The demons reappeared from the trees and Shar brought forth one last stream of magic and aimed it at the earth. The ground swelled and then burst upward, and then the land collapsed down, creating a cavity of sorts. The giants, the demons and anything near them were pitched into the fissure and with one final sweep of her hands; Shar closed the earth once more. With an enormous shudder it was over and the minions of Helana were buried.

Shar was breathing hard, and fell to her knees, completely drained from exerting all of the magic. Brielle and Elise were the first to catch her just as she fainted from exhaustion and the rest caught up to assist them carry the mage to a place where she could rest.

"We can't stay here! Helana may send more of her army after us," Tony said.

"We stay with our plan to keep moving. We can rest back at the river upstream where we crossed before. Once we get on the other side we can set up camp for the night and get some rest for a time," Neil said.

"We'll be on our own for a time, Shar won't be able to help us for a while now," Tasha added.

"She's done more than we could have ever asked of her. I think we can get by until we get back to Cambridge," Neil smiled.

"I'll get everyone moving. Captains, to your ranks, get them on the move," Kieran motioned.

"Aye, I've had my fill of demons fer a time," grunted Axel. He ambled off to collect his horse and Ruskin trailed right behind him.

Helana drew her cloak in close to hide her face; she had felt another surge of pain as her features twisted further to the demon side. It was almost too much to bear but the after effect of her strengthening magic made the pain worthwhile. She detected a surge in magic brought on in the distance and nodded in appreciation of her new foe. This person was starting to turn into a worthy adversary after all. Only time would tell who this individual was, but she wasn't too concerned. After all, by the time she reached the elf border her magic would be too strong to stop. She smiled at the thought and turned to look at her legions, nearly reorganized after the delay at the falls. Her pets for the sky had been decimated and she had replenished them with more, brought forth from the depths of the void that had kept her prisoner until her escape. Now, they would outnumber anything the elves or any other force could defend against. The manticore would be unstoppable the next time they would meet!

She whispered and let her words flow on the wind, to the one person for whom she intended them.

"Kill the queen! Your opportunity will be while the mage in your midst rests. Kill her tonight."

Up past the ridge, through the trees, the words wound their way, riding the wind, until they came to the ears of Helana's spy.

He listened and nodded. "It shall be done."

That night the combined forces set up camp just over the river upstream a ways from the valley and they hoped, some distance from Helana's demons. The strategy was to rest until dawn and then begin moving again, and attempt to stay just ahead of Helana's horde. They were counting on her taking a detour to visit Kildare, Neil citing her desire to sit on that throne too strong to not do so. That would give them the required time to get back to Cambridge and rejoin the full force that would be awaiting her arrival at the boundaries of the elf lands.

"I see no point trying to stop her any further. We need to get back to Cambridge, and together we will put up our final line of defense," Kieran stated. The torches, lit to provide light, threw shadows over his face but everyone knew the elf spoke with authority.

"Well, the usual doesn't seem to be working. Anyone have any other ideas?" Neil asked curiously. No one spoke. "Anyone?"

"I agree with Kieran. We make for Cambridge and avoid any more losses," Riss nodded towards Kieran.

"Then am I to assume we are all in agreement on this?" Neil checked with a look around the room. He was greeted with a nod from each captain and everyone else attending the meeting.

"We ain't got th'bodies ta do much more sir, we best get back an'plan to hold'er at th'elves," Axel said.

"There will be a solid group of dwarves and gnomes

already on their way to Cambridge to join us. Our best hopes lie there," added Jacinto.

"May I add something?" Captain Elise asked.

"Go ahead," Neil urged.

"Even if my father brings our entire sky rider force, we will still be undermatched for any more of those flying things the witch has. We will be vulnerable from the sky, we will only be able to do so much before even we will be overwhelmed," Elise said. "We may have the speed, but they have the numbers, and the gryphon will tire long before we can stop them."

"Then we hope Helana hasn't got many more of them left either," Tasha sighed.

Shar entered the gathering at that point, still obviously tired, but well enough to say her piece. "She has more, I can feel her using her magic, and there will be many."

"We'll have to figure out how to stop those things," Neil started.

"Manticore," Shar interrupted. "Creatures of myth, but where evil lives, so must they."

"We could use one other option in fighting them," Tony spoke up.

"Oh, what's that? Spit at'em?" Ruskin snorted.

"Be quiet, let him talk," Adeena hushed him.

"The Dragons. They could give those things a run for their money," Tony suggested.

"The Dragons? Tis only been a short time since we last got into it with'em, ya think they're really up fer helpin us?" Thatcher muttered. He had his doubts, but he had to admit the idea had merit.

"We don't have the time to ride out to them, there's the problem, even though I do like the idea," Neil said.

"I agree with Neil, there just isn't enough time, even if

we ride day and night, we would not get to them in time to do us any good," Mia concurred.

"See, even th'tracker has sense ta her," Axel said.

"I could send someone there, that would give us the time to see if they can help," Shar offered.

"Shar, you just used a lot of magic back there, you won't have the strength," Tasha said.

"I can do this, I've been resting all afternoon, I might not get you right into the ravine, but at least close enough that you can go in the rest of the way," Shar reaffirmed her statement.

"It's too risky," Brielle piped up.

"I'll take the risk, with Mia and Adeena, since she's the only one who can speak dragon," Tony pointed to the fairie.

"Tony, no, I won't let anyone risk their lives with the dragons, we don't know if they'll even let you speak to them," Neil said.

"We have to do this. Shar, send me to the dragons and I'll bring them back. You have my word," Tony pleaded. "Neil, she can do this, and so can I. We have to give it a shot."

Neil sighed, and looked around the room; no one knew what to say. He thought about it and Tasha pulled him back, and the two whispered amongst themselves.

"I think she can do this, there's something about her magic, it's different somehow," Tasha spoke into his ear.

"Different? How?"

"I can't explain it, but I really think she can do this, we have to give it a try," she added and looked into his eyes. He smiled at her and nodded.

"Okay."

He faced the group and nodded to Shar. "All right Shar,

since the dragons really do have as much as the rest of us to lose, we'll let you do this."

"Good, when morning breaks we'll reconvene before we depart." Shar looked over at Tony and Mia. "Pack light, and only what you need. I won't be sure as to how close I can get you, so the lighter you pack, the better off you'll be."

"Gotcha," Tony replied.

"Then that's it everybody, we leave for Cambridge at daybreak, and Shar will do her thing with Tony and Mia. Stay alert tonight! We don't know what surprises may await us out there," Neil warned. The group broke off, going their separate ways.

"I'm going back to our tent. Coming soon?" Tasha asked.

"Yes, I'll be right behind you," Neil smiled and gave her a kiss. "I'm going to talk with Tony for a bit and then I'll join you."

"Don't keep him out too late," Tasha teased and Tony chuckled.

"I'll try not to," he replied.

Tasha ventured off and Neil, Tony and a few others hung around to talk about his latest quest.

"I still don't like it," Neil said.

"Well, it'll get us some much needed reinforcements for the air," Tony retorted. "Besides, I'm getting kinda bored."

"Bored are ya? Boy, ya wanna die again?" Axel cracked.

"Once is enough, for a long long time," Tony jested. "Maybe bored was a bit strong of a word."

"Ya think?" Thatcher joked with a laugh.

The elves were congregating in groups, standing around small fires to keep warm and keep the light to a minimum from the flames. Tasha nodded to each group as she passed and slowly made her way towards her tent, unaware that she was being watched. A lone figure stepped away from a group and began to follow.

Brielle and Elise fed the gryphon and made sure the animals were well secured for the night.

"I am sorry about your fallen riders. They will be missed," Brielle said quietly. "They were good elves."

"Aye, they were," Elise added. She patted her gryphon and gave it a quick kiss on the cheek. "Be good tonight, okay?" she winked at her ride.

The gryphon winked back and settled itself down on the ground to rest for the night. Both elves wandered over to a nearby fire and took notice of one of their missing brethren.

"Where did Cael go to?" Elise asked.

"He went off that way," motioned one elf.

Brielle looked in the general direction and thought about it for a moment. She looked over at Elise.

"Isn't that where Neil and Tasha's tent is?"

"Yes, why?" Elise wondered.

Brielle had a bad feeling and started off in the same direction. "She went off to her tent by herself did she not?"

Elise started to follow, "Yes, but why?"

"She is unprotected," Brielle said, panic starting to rise within her. Elise realized what she was getting at and both elves broke into a run.

"Cael, what are you doing here?"

"Nothing Captain, just going for a walk," replied Cael.

"Be on your way," the Captain pointed.

"Aye," Cael bowed and turned to leave. He never had the chance to defend himself as the blade drove into his back, and through his heart, killing him instantly.

Tasha thought she had heard voices outside and looked towards the entrance to her tent. It was a large enough canopy that a large group could gather inside and not be crowded, and was intended to be a meeting tent but was instead used as theirs for this particular night.

"Neil?" she spoke loud enough that anyone outside would hear her. No answer. She shrugged it off and went back about getting herself ready for bed. The queen heard footsteps on the gravel and thought it might be Neil this time.

A figure entered the tent and Tasha turned to see who it was. She barely had enough time to lift her arms in defense as the man lunged at her, knife drawn. Tasha grabbed the man's arms and twisted him to the side, the speed of his attack carried him into the cots that were set up and Tasha fell backward to the ground. She looked at her attacker and went wide eyed with shock.

"Captain?"

The Captain gathered himself and threw the cots aside and began to close in on the queen once more. Tasha pushed herself back away from the man and as he dove at her again and she lifted her feet and kicked him back once more. She let out a scream and tried to find something to use against this assassin. Tasha grabbed a small bag of supplies and threw it at him. He dodged it easy enough and took a swipe at the queen, the blade just grazed her arm as she jumped back, and Tasha realized her charm given to her my Malcolm was not having any affect! It should be able to protect her but it was doing no such thing!

Another scream echoed through the camp and Neil heard it this time and he knew Tasha's voice. He was running at full speed with Tony, Thatcher and the dwarf's right behind him. A surge of absolute panic went through him and Neil swore at himself for letting her go off by herself.

He could never forgive himself if something were to happen to her. He ran harder, trying to breathe in as much air as his lungs would let him as he pushed on.

Brielle and Elise ran into Mia going in the same direction, all three did not have to say anything but kept going on a full run to get to the queen before it was too late! All three had their weapons drawn as the tent came into view.

Tasha fell back against the ground, her arms holding the assasin's arm with the blade just inches away from her chest, and she felt her strength begin to give way, and slowly the knife neared.

"Why," she gasped, struggling to hold him off.

"My queen asks, and I obey," he hissed.

Tasha saw his eyes then, now red, and what had been elf was now demon. She cried as the assassin smiled an evil smile as he pushed the knife down closer to killing her. Then the tent front was whipped open and Brielle, Elise and Mia entered. Mia saw the knife almost at Tasha's chest and dove at him, pushing him off and sending the knife flying in a different direction.

"Vasilis!" Brielle shouted.

Vasilis stood up and sneered at the two elves. "What do you want elf?"

"What are you?" Brielle said confused at what she was seeing.

"I am becoming what I have always wanted! Stronger than any elf!" he replied with a shout, taunting her.

"You betray your own kind," Elise snapped back.

Vasilis laughed. "She will rule this world and the old; there is nothing you can do to stop her!" At that he bolted from the tent and all three went to Tasha's aid.

"I am fine," Tasha said, on the verge of crying. She had been a fraction of an inch from death and could not control her emotions.

Neil ran into the tent and saw Tasha on the ground, Mia holding her and he dashed over and knelt down in front of her.

"Are you okay?"

Tasha nodded and fell into his arms, weeping uncontrollably. He looked at the three women, wanting answers.

"It was Vasilis! He tried to kill her," Brielle said.

"What? Vasilis?" he asked in disbelief.

"He ran off. He'll likely try and go back to Helana," Elise said.

"Your not making any sense," Neil said, his voice on the verge of anger.

"Vasilis was turning into a demon, or he always was one. He serves Helana," Mia said calmly trying to keep Neil from losing his control.

"Find him! Don't let that son of a bitch get away," he ordered.

Brielle nodded and was off running to get the troups alerted and on patrol. Tony and Mia with Ruskin and Axel right behind went after Vasilis in the direction Mia had seen him go.

Thatcher and Elise stayed with Neil and Tasha, in case the assassin should try and finish the job he had nearly completed. Elise kept watch and Thatcher stayed near the couple as Tasha cried into Neil's shoulder, unable to stop her tears. Neil held her tight, thankful Vasilis had been unable to finish the task.

The night went by and no patrol was able to find Vasilis. Even Mia and Tony lost his trail after a short time and reported back with no results. Finding the former trusted captain was put on hold as the suns started to show themselves and the day was set to begin. As the camp stirred, Teague and the surviving archers appeared, much to the relief of the rest and were welcomed openly. Of course the elf captain complained rather jokingly and loudly that he and the others had to run that much farther since they had been abandoned back at the ridge. He was brought up to speed on the situation regarding Vasilis but reported he had not seen the elf at all on their trek back to them. Neil was angry and vowed he'd find the traitor, but for now, he was about to send another friend off on another quest and still did not like the idea.

"Are you sure about this?" Neil asked again.

"Yeah, I'm good. You just keep Tasha safe and I promise I'll bring back some more reinforcements for us. Every little body, or dragon in this case, will help," Tony smiled confidently.

Shar had rested through the short night and was rested enough to attempt the transportation incantation and send Tony, Mia and Adeena to the dragon's ravine. She stood tall and drew her cloak in tight.

"Stay close while I cast the magic, I'll do the best I can but depending on my strength, you may have a bit of a walk on your hands," she managed to crack a smile.

"We'll be fine. Do the best you can," Mia said.

Adeena gave Shar a big hug and the fairie saluted her. "See you at Cambridge my friend."

"Say hi to Blinky for me," Shar replied.

"I will. He should be pretty big by now," Adeena said.

"I hope he remembers us at least," Tony quipped.

"All right, together," motioned Shar.

The three stood close as Shar closed her eyes and visioned where she wanted to send them. The memories of six months ago were drawn on and her lips began to speak the words to bring about the magic to transport them. Her hands opened and a white ball of light began to form. It then left her hands and expanded in size and then encompassed all three. The magic began to circulate and in a flash all three were gone. Shar opened her eyes and fell to her knees.

Brielle and Elise moved in quickly and helped the mage stand. Shar was limp and could barely move. Finally she closed her eyes and fainted. Both elves carried her over to a waiting wagon and placed the exhausted woman inside.

"She was more tired than she let on," Tasha sighed, shaking her head.

"Will she be all right?" Neil wondered.

"In time," Tasha assured him. "She spent a lot of magic in a short time, and she needs sleep a lot of it."

"Let's hope it worked," Neil said.

"Bloody right, or I don't wanna know where they ended up," Axel scoffed.

Chapter Thirty Four

Tony, Mia and Adeena reappeared abruptly on a rocky crag of flat stone and hit the surface rather hard, after materlizing just inches above it. All three rolled over the stone until coming to rest against the mountain wall that stretched up as far as the eye could see. The top of the mountain was hidden by a thick fog. Tony groaned and sat up slowly, trying to get his bearings as to their location. He looked around the landscape, and it did not take long for him to realize where they were.

"We're in the valley where we fought the dark dragon," he murmured.

"That would make sense. She would've drawn on her memories to get us here," Mia said as she slowly stood to stretch and rub her aching legs.

"A bit of a rough ride though," Adeena grumbled shaking herself to get the dust off.

"We're here or at least close to where we need to be. As good a place as any to get started," Tony commented as he stood up and wandered over to the edge of the rock slab.

"That way," Mia pointed with a smile, knowing Tony was looking for the easiest route down.

Tony motioned for her to take the lead, "after you."

Adeena transformed to her fairie size and flew off down the canyon wall and waited for them to work their way down to level ground again. Once all three were reuinted, they moved off in the direction of the Dragon's Ravine. Adeena took the lead and flew ahead to scout for any sudden surprises that might not usually reveal themselves. It was a relatively quiet walk, and as they passed the ruins of what had been Rakia's fortress, they could not help but to stop and take a long look.

"Nothing but broken rock and ash," Tony mumbled.

"What had been, is no more," Mia added. She looked at Tony, "have you heard anything about Rakia since?"

Tony shook his head and shrugged, "not a word. Malcolm never brings it up and no one has really thought about her much, not even Shar."

"At least not publicly with any of us, but I'd think Shar would be wondering about her every so often," Mia said.

"Oh likely. It is her sister after all!"

Adeena flew up and changed back from her fairie form. She stood there and crossed her arms. "Are you two going to stand there all day? We do have some dragons to find."

"Are you my mother?" Tony quipped.

"No, and if I was, I'd be more stern," the fairie frowned.

Mia and Tony chuckled and started walking again. The fairie flashed back into her true form and once again, flew on ahead to look for an easy path to take into the Ravine. It did not take her long to find a way and waited patiently for Tony and Mia to work their away across the valley floor. Together all three started up the path and on towards the Dragon's Ravine, hoping the creatures were in a friendly mood and not so ready to burn or perhaps even eat them!

As they trudged on the heat in the mountains incremently

grew and Tony and Mia were sweating freely after only a short walk deeper into the mountains. There were active geysers as they proceeded, spouting off steam and in some cases a small pit of molten lava was bubbling, spitting out drops of searing melted rock and ash. The stench of the geysers and lava pits was unbearable, the hot acidic air was difficult to take and Tony and Mia both covered their faces with their cloaks to make it easier on their lungs.

"Up here you two!" Adeena beckoned. "The air isn't so hot!"

"Awesome," Tony coughed. He didn't need any further encouragement and Mia was following right behind him as they scampered up the rocky slope to another trail of sorts the faerie had discovered.

Sure enough the air was much more breathable and both shoved their cloaks back into their packs and continued on their trek. The heat was still evident, but at least they weren't walking amidst the steam. The group came to a narrow ledge that ran alongside another mountain and took a good look at the landscape below. There were no signs of any dragons as yet, but they had to be getting near. A roar in the distance confirmed their thoughts. The Ravine was close at hand.

"So any idea on what you're going to ask them?" Mia wondered as they plodded along, climbing over all the boulders and rocks strewn over their chosen path.

"Not a clue," Tony replied with snicker. "I'm wingin this as we go."

"Wingin?" Mia asked curiously. "Another Zach term?"

Tony laughed at the remark, and shrugged. "I guess so, but a lot of people use that term on occasion."

"It does sound a lot like something Zach would say," Mia puffed as she jumped over a large boulder, following close behind Tony. "Think he's okay back where you came from?"

"Oh yeah, he'll be fine, I'm sure we'll see him again soon enough," Tony replied.

Another roar, followed by another in the distance brought them to a stop for a moment to listen but after a minute they continued walking. A short walk later they saw shadows flying through the clouded sky and hid under some cover to wait and see what would emerge. The first sighting brought nothing into view, the second shadow produced a dragon as it dropped from the clouds and flew low over the mountains, as though it was looking for intruders in their home.

"Didn't you mention the last time you came through here you had to deal with brownies?" Tony asked. "Are they around here?"

"They were on the other side of the ravine," Mia pointed. "We didn't see any on this side after we had gone through."

"Good, not in the mood to deal with anything else but the dragons right now," he said with a sigh of relief.

As they got out from behind the cover of their rocky hiding spot, they came face to face with a good sized dragon sitting on the ledge staring straight down at them, his head hovering just above them.

"Oh shit," Tony muttered in shock.

The dragon looked at them with squinted eyes, snarled and then arced its neck lower and put its winged arms down on the ground and smelled the trio. It growled even louder and its mouth began to open.

"Blinky, you behave," Adeena took on her full sized form and scolded the dragon.

The dragon was a little taken aback by the response and glared at the faeire. For a moment it did not move and then it seemed to recognize her. To emphasize that, the dragon stuck out its tongue and licked the faeire. Adeena was now suddenly covered in slime and she screamed in disgust. The dragon blinked its eyes and did it again, thinking the faerie liked it.

"Ohhh so disgusting! Blinky stop that!" Adeena shouted. She was sputtering the words in the dragon's language and both Tony and Mia could only assume she was telling the dragon to quit what it was doing. They couldn't help but laugh at the sight.

"Nice Adeena," Tony winked.

"Oh shut up," Adeena snorted angrily. She faced the dragon once more and shot off a few more words in 'dragon' and 'Blinky' seemed to grasp what she was saying. The dragon stood tall and let out a roar and then lifted itself off the ground and flew off back towards the ravine that housed the rest of the dragons.

"How did you know that was, um, your dragon friend?" Tony asked, not knowing how to word the question.

"His color, and he's still not full grown, not hard if you know what you're looking for," Adeena replied matter of factly. She wiped some more slime off herself and swore under her breath at the aroma of the dragon's spit.

"They all look alike to me, for the most part," Tony shrugged.

"Look at them closely, you'll see different colors, spikes, sizes, they are different in many ways. I'm impressed she was able to figure out who that dragon was," Mia smiled with a nod to Adeena.

"I could use some help here! This stuff isn't exactly what I want to wear," Adeena grunted. She scraped off some more slime and tossed it to the ground.

"We need to find you some sort of pond, spring, so you

can wash off," Tony said. "Maybe, Blinky was it, can find you one?"

"Just give me your cloak, that'll do," Adeena retorted.

"Mine? Just go roll around in the dirt," Tony replied.

"Give me your cloak," Adeena scowled. She held out her hands and wasn't going to take 'no' for an answer. Tony sighed and gave in. He dug out his cloak from his pack and handed it over to the faerie. She wasted no time in using it to wipe off the rest of the remaining dragon spit and once she was done handed it back to Tony.

"You can keep it," Tony waved her off. Adeena crumpled it up into a ball and started off walking again.

"Keep up you two, he's gone off to tell the rest we're coming, we don't want to keep them waiting," she said.

"You could've said that!" Tony said as he and Mia moved to follow her.

"You didn't ask," she merely retorted.

"That's not the point!" he exclaimed.

"She is right though, we didn't ask," Mia reminded him.

Tony gave up on the argument knowing full well he wouldn't win and sighed.

"Fine, let's get moving; we don't want to keep the dragons waiting."

The three strolled along the pathway and the Dragon's ravine began to loom large and the path itself came to an end at a ledge overlooking an enormous canyon that was the home of the dragons. Mia was taken aback by the sight! The last time she was this way she had led the group including Zach and the two dwarves along the outer edges of the ravine and not through the home itself. Seeing the nesting area was phenomenal! There were so many dragons, and all three felt like they were mere bugs to be squashed by the dragons.

There were ledges with dragons lined along each side by side, as far as the eye could see! Enormous nests had eggs in a few, and below along the floor of the ravine, steam rose steadily hiding whatever may be below. All of the dragons were looking up towards them, as if wondering why they dared tread on their territory.

"Oh geez, look at them all," Tony murmured.

"I hope you know what you are going to say," Mia whispered.

"I'll think of something," he looked at her and winked.

One dragon rose above the rest, lifting away from the pack and flew towards them. 'Blinky' was next to reappear, moving up and away from another herd of dragons and followed the larger beast up to the ledge. The trio moved back from the edge as the two dragons closed in and set down just in front of them. The larger dragon set its wings back as it took several steps forward. It growled in its native dragon tongue and Adeena nodded after it finished.

She looked at the other two. "They want to know why we've come here, why we've promised to stay away and yet, here we are, again."

Tony took in a deep breath of the stagnant hot air, and looked at the dragon. "Tell him we aren't here to do any harm to them," which he thought sounded kind of stupid considering there were only three of them. "Tell him we're here to ask for their help."

Adeena shrugged, "I don't think he's going to like that but I'll tell him anyways."

"Then remind him we've kept our promise to protect them from any hunters, and will continue to do so."

Adeena nodded and spoke the dragon words to make the beast understand what Tony had just said. It listened intently and looked at Tony after the faerie had finished speaking. It growled out some more words and Adeena faced Tony to translate.

"He knows about our promise. He made it with the king, not you," Adeena informed him.

"Let him know I'm the one who enforces that law. He needs to listen to me, we need their help," Tony motioned for her to speak to him.

Adeena spoke the dragon tongue, and the large dragon, after listening to her moved in closer to the group and lowered its head to stare directly at Tony.

"Why, should we help you?" it asked. Adeena translated.

Tony took in another deep breath. He had its attention at last. "There is a witch that is wreaking havoc everywhere, stirring up things, destroying everything on her way to the elves." Adeena continued to translate while Tony spoke. The dragon said nothing but listened to all that Tony had to say.

"She has the demons at her command! They're everywhere, and anything that is evil is out of their cage and loose on Avalon. We need your help to fight the flying things, we only have so much help at our disposal and they're starting to win. If you could help us, it will help yourselves as well because if she wins this, she'll be coming after you next."

The dragon remained quiet for a time and then spoke, with Adeena translating the language.

"We know there is something evil amidst us; we can sense it, now we know what. Understand, we are grateful for your law to stay away from us and there are many of us who would like to see you leave but if this witch is bound to destroy, then we will be hunted again."

After Adeena's translation Tony nodded to the dragon and added. "We are asking a lot of you I know, but if it wasn't important, I promise you, we would have left you alone. We face something more powerful than there has ever been before; I ask on behalf of the king and remind you of your promise to lend assistance if we should ask. We need your help desperately."

Blinky snorted a few dragon words and Adeena tried to hush him with a wave of her hand. The larger dragon turned to look at the smaller and snorted its own warning of quiet to Blinky. Blinky settled back on his hind quarters and waited patiently. The one dragon returned to face Tony and Mia.

"I will talk with the others. Wait here until we return," the dragon instructed as per Adeena's translation.

Both the larger one and Blinky lifted off and flew back into the ravine to convey Tony's message to the rest of the dragons. Tony had to admire the creatures and their abilities and thought they weren't too different than the rest of them. They discussed things in committee, and made decisions based on what was best for the group. It was strange how despite different creatures and their lifestyles, they all still were very much, alike.

"Hopefully this won't take too long," Tony commented as wandered back to the edge of the crevice that formed the Dragon's Ravine.

"Don't count on it," Adeena sighed. She ambled over to a rock and sat herself down and tried to make herself as comfortable as she could.

"I'm hungry so we may as well eat while we wait," Mia said. She dropped her pack down on the ground and dug through it to find some rations that they could chew on to satisfy their appetite.

After some bread and dried meat, Tony found a spot on the ground and leaned up against the mountain wall. It wasn't all that filling of a meal and the stone he was sitting on hurt after a short time but he might as well catch some sleep while they waited for the final decision. Mia walked back and forth, unable to sit, too anxious to get the word on whether the dragons would help or not. She heard Tony snoring, and chuckled, amazed at how he could just fall asleep at a moment's notice on some rock no less. Her nervous nature prevented her from ever dozing that easily, so she opted to pace instead.

The three had no idea how much time passed by, but Mia eventually gave in to sleep and settled in close to Tony and leaned on him for some comfort against the mountain. Adeena even passed out at some point from boredom more than anything and was the first to stir when she heard movement on the ledge. The faerie sat up and saw 'Blinky' sitting there, his head lowered, apparently waiting. She wondered for what and got her answer a moment later when the larger dragon reappeared and settled in next to her smaller friend.

"Wake up you two, they're back," Adeena piped up. She tossed a few pebbles at them to get their attention and both woke, groggily to her stone throwing.

"All right, I'm awake, stop that," Tony said as another pebble bounced off his head.

"They're here," Adeena pointed. Tony sat up quickly and saw the two dragons sitting on the ledge once more. He and Mia both stood and walked several steps forward. Adeena jumped up and took her spot next to them.

"What is your answer?" Tony asked. Adeena translated.

"The answer, is no, from most, but myself and several others will go with you to help if we can. We cannot make any promises our presence will be helpful," answered the dragon. Tony scratched his cheek on hearing the translation.

"I understand, and you have our thanks to those of

you who will help us. Anything is better than nothing," he nodded in appreciaton.

"Do you have a name?" Mia asked.

"I am Drayler. I spoke with your king and made our promise to him," the dragon replied with a bow of his head.

"Thought he looked familiar," Tony said quietly. He shook his head at Adeena so she wouldn't translate. "Ask them when they will come?"

Adeena did so and waited for the response and translated it back to Tony. "In a day. They will find us on the trail back and come with us then."

"A day, well, that's cutting it pretty close but I'm not about to be picky," Tony commented. "Okay, we will see you in a day."

Adeena passed the message on and the dragon nodded once more. It lifted off the ledge and flew back on down into the ravine, leaving 'Blinky' there by himself. The smaller dragon spoke and Adeena wandered over and patted him on the side of the head.

"It's okay Blinky, as soon as you get older you can fight with the rest of them," she smiled.

"I'm guessing they won't let him come along?" Tony checked.

"No, he wants to but they won't let him." Adeena gave 'Blinky' a little kiss on his scaly cheek and stepped back as the dragon dropped off the ledge and spread its wings to catch the wind's updraft, and coasted from view back into the mists.

"We got what we came for, at least a little bit. We better start back. We've got a bit of a run ahead of us," Tony muttered. He threw his pack over his shoulder and looked at the other two.

"Hey, I'm not worried - you two just try and keep up,"

Adeena grinned, flashed into her true faerie form and was off flying seconds later.

“You heard her,” Mia teased. The two started jogging along the trail, following their little faerie friend as fast as they dared. It was a long walk back to Cambridge, and they were going to have to pace themselves.

Chapter Thirty Five

Zach, and his entourage walked down a path as the sun began to rise for the new day. Merlin was leading the way but Zach had no idea where. They had driven for a time and after getting dropped off at a certain point by the cab driver they had gone the rest of the way on foot. There was a lot of fog this particular morning and so they couldn't see a whole lot of the landscape around them. Merlin walked on confidently, apparently knowing exactly where he was going. There was very little conversation and Zach just followed along thinking the guy had to know what he was doing, and where he was going.

"Are we there yet?" he quipped.

Merlin stopped and turned with a very annoyed look on his face. "Almost, and please don't use that ridiculous question again!"

Zach chuckled and nodded. "Sure, couldn't help myself though. It was there."

"I could write a book on how many times I've heard that question," Merlin sighed and even got a chuckle out as he said the sentence. "So far twice from you. At this rate I'll be rich."

"Let's just wait and see," Riane urged Zach as she took his hand and squeezed it.

"Okay, okay, I'll be quiet," he replied.

They trudged on through the mist until they came to a chain link fence, approximately eight feet high and Zach looked at it curiously. How in the world were they going to get around this? He had to shake his head after thinking about it because he realized he only had a wizard and a wizard in training, in the group. It should be easy to get through!

"I'm going to take a kick at the can here, and say we need to be over on the other side someplace?" Zach asked.

"Kick at the can?" Rachel asked curiously.

"One of his sayings, just don't pay attention to it," Riane snickered.

"Good deduction though Zach, yes, we need to be on the other side and here, at the gate we will proceed to go through," Merlin cracked. He stopped and opened the gate, passing his hand over the lock, and watched it drop to the ground harmlessly.

"Well that was a bit of a letdown, was expecting something grand," Zach kidded.

"I'll do my best to do something more extravagant, just for you, next go around," Merlin teased. He stood at the gate and motioned everyone to pass on through. He followed behind and closed the gate after himself once everyone passed. The group waited for him to take the lead once more and they continued to follow him through the fog for a short distance. When he came to a stop Merlin looked around and nodded.

"There has been some excavation work apparently on the fence. As always. I'm trying to figure out why this exists! Quite humorous I must say but, we're here."

"Where?" Zach asked.

"Stonehenge my boy, stonehenge," he murmured. He moved his staff through the air and the fog lifted enough for the group to see the stones, standing quietly on the Salisbury Plain in the English county of Wiltshire. The sun was barely visible through the mists and the morning air was damp, the dew glistening on the stones as the weak sun's rays hit them.

"I never would have believed it if I wasn't looking at it," Zach muttered.

"This is where we all crossed the very first time. This is the only portal left on this world that I can open back to the new world. The witch has closed off every other point of entry, so we had no choice but to come here, where the magic is at its strongest," Merlin explained.

"Will it work?" Riane wondered.

"It should, even her magic will have its limits, especially on this world," Merlin answered confidently. "Time has not been kind to the stones, quite worn down I see."

"So, is there a switch or something you turn on?" Zach said jokingly. He was so tired and wanted nothing more than to get it all over with and get back to business on Avalon.

"My my aren't we full of funny words today," Merlin retorted. "Relax Zach, we will be leaving shortly. First, we need to call on Oberon. He is coming with us."

"Sorry, I'm just tired, and I tend to be a little less serious when I am." Zach yawned and wandered over to stand next to one of the stones. He looked around and took in the formation, and had to think about the history these large rocks had seen over time. It was almost uncomprehensible. He ran his hand over the smooth surface and then stepped back to take it all in.

Merlin strode up to one particular stone, and tapped it with his staff and spoke several words that none of them could make out. A new mist formed around the stone and the king of faerie appeared out of the mist, seemingly from the stone itself and bowed to Merlin.

"I've been waiting, thought you may have left without me," the king smiled.

"Never old friend," Merlin bowed in return. "Are we all ready to go then?" he surveyed the group and each nodded in response.

"Anytime," Zach nodded.

"Into the middle of the formation everyone, when the gate opens it will be quick," Merlin beckoned anxiously. He was just as excited as the rest! He had not seen the new world since he had opened the door the very first time and was curious to see it again.

In the center of the formation the group gathered and Merlin looked towards the sky, lifting his staff to call on the magic. It had been centuries since he had drawn on the magic to open the door and use Stone Henge. As he spoke the words it all came back to him as though it was only yesterday, and the magic began to form.

It started with his staff, and a bolt of white light shot out to connect with the first stone in the formation and encircled it, then moved on to the next stone and the next until the entire circle was engulfed in the magic. Merlin spoke the final phrase and the vortex began to form

"Stay together everyone!" Merlin shouted the reminder.

The vortex took on its full form, the fog seemingly being swallowed by it as the wind rushed in. Merlin guided Christina to it and she stepped into the magic that swept her up into the gateway. Rachel went next followed by Oberon, and then Riane. Each disappearing into the magic in a flash, and Merlin motioned to Zach. He nodded and ran on in, and was swept up in an instant. This trip was somewhat different than the prior trek he and Riane had experienced! It was surprisingly smooth and was as though he was walking along a path and stepped out onto lush green grass in just a few moments, leaving the pulsating bright lights behind and was greeted by a grey sky. He saw the others just a short distance away and then Merlin appeared beside him. Zach looked back to witness the vortex shrink and then vanish in a flash of white light. The doorway had worked.

Merlin took in a deep breath and let it out slow. "It is nice to be back."

Helana felt the immense use of magic immediately the vortex opened and she felt her anger begin to boil. Somehow someone had managed to reopen the door back to this world. She was surprised at the strength of the magic used to break through her barrier and was curious to know its origin. That would have to wait for now. Her minions, after getting reorganized had been on the march now for almost a full day and would arrive on the outskirts of Kildare castle in the very near future. The throne she wanted would soon be hers and she was curious to see her future home.

Helana watched her army march from the top of a hill, and she smiled again, despite the drawback in the valley and the numbers lost, they were still more than a match for whatever the elves could muster. Unlike them, she could replenish her forces from the depths of the void. There were more than enough demons wanting out to ravage the land. Her power was still gaining strength and by the time she reached the borderlands of the elves, she would be near full strength and would enjoy every moment as her horde annihilated the races.

The outline of Kildare castle came into view as she transported herself just ahead of her army, and the home of the monarchy stood out against the evening sky, the shadow of it cast upon the land around it. Helana grinned and closed her cloak in tight around herself and with a wave of her hand vanished again. She rematerialized in the courtyard and looked around at the ramparts. The building was abandoned. It was what she had expected.

"No one to welcome your new queen?" she shouted out. Her voice echoed through the courtyard and into the empty halls. Helana laughed and cackled in glee and she strutted up to the top of the rampart to watch her forces arrive where she would reign over Avalon.

The earth vibrated as the mass approached slowly, appearing at first over the outlying hills and then onward covering every inch of land as they moved in closer to Kildare Castle. The throng stopped at the edge of the moat surrounding the castle and looked up at Helana, waiting patiently for them above on the catwalk. There were so many, and from her vantage point, with no obstructions or divided forces, as one whole entity they stretched for as far as she could see. The flying demons, the manticore, flew in above and landed all across the catwalk of the castle and there was barely room enough for all. The stench of it all would have made any other person pass out, but to Helana it was like a bouquet of flowers.

"Welcome to your new home!" She shouted to the masses. Helana was greeted by screeches and howls loud enough to drown out a stadium crowd.

"We march on the elves as soon as the suns go down! We should be there by dawn!" she bellowed out. Again, they howled in response. "By tomorrow night, WE WILL RULE AVALON!" Once more the mob screeched. Helana turned and started down the steps, whispering so that only she would hear, "And on to the old world, where I will rule without anyone to stop me."

Neil rode with Tasha straddled in behind him on their horse, with Brielle, Shar, Tony and a number of others beside to protect them from any further threats. There had been no sign of Vasillis at all during the day as they rode on, retreating back to the elves at Cambridge. Neil had scouts looking for the renegade elf steadily. When one scout would return another would take his place in the hunt. The remaining few sky riders were looking for the elf captain in an expanded search area but still the assassin was not found. Tasha was still in shock, and had said very little since the attack. After Tony had been transported she had been virtually silent after the shock of the night's events began to sink in.

"How long til we get ta Cambridge?" Axel asked. He moved his horse in closer to Neil and tugged at his beard nervously.

"By tonight," Neil simply replied. He wasn't in a conversational mood and Axel picked up on that right away and left the answer at that without any further prodding.

A scout rode up; looking exhausted after a long ride and nodded to Neil.

"Sir, as you thought, the horde has gone north, straight towards Kildare."

"Good, that'll buy us some time. Thank you, go see Kieran and get some rest. He'll send out your replacement," Neil pointed to the back of the caravan.

"Aye sir," the scout nodded. He turned his horse and trotted back to find the elf captain.

Tasha sat up and gave him a tighter hug. "It's okay Neil, I'm fine."

"I can't stop thinking about Vasilis, his treachery, and that you were nearly killed."

"I know," she whispered. "I know, but don't get obsessed, we'll find him eventually."

Neil closed his eyes and let out a sigh. "I'll try."

Vasilis stood on a distant hill and watched the retreat back towards Cambridge. He swore at himself again for failing to fulfill his task. He could not bear to face Helana as a failure. She would not take it well to find out the queen was still alive. He would not return to his own queen until his task was done but he would take it one step further now, he would kill both the queen, and the king. With them out of the way, and both Malcolm and the elves about to fall, Avalon would have no one to lead any sort of resistance to Helana. The puzzle would be complete, and he would surely be rewarded.

Merlin looked the landscape over and smiled at the sights around him. Despite the graying sky it felt as fresh as it did the first day he had walked amidst the grasses and walked among the trees. His smile did not last overly long once he felt the oppressive dark magic loose on the world. He was amazed at the strength of it all, and realized they were in a war that had no definite outcome.

"We have arrived in time I would say. Much longer and even that doorway may have been unable to bring us here," Merlin said.

"It is quite beautiful," Falon observed as she brushed her hair out of her eyes.

Merlin sighed, "Yes, it is. If these clouds were not blocking the sky you would be even more amazed my dear student. Now, Zach, Riane, which way do we go to find the elves?"

Riane had surveyed their surroundings and did not take long in recognizing where they were. She promptly pointed to the south.

"We are north of Cambridge, just past Vanier Lake. We have a few hours of hike ahead of us," the elf replied.

"We are?" Zach asked. He looked around, and finally

began to recognize the area. "Oh yeah, been a while since I rode this way." He looked at the distant mountains. "I remember now. You said we couldn't go over there," Zach pointed, "something about sacred ground for the elves."

"Aye, it is my love. Perhaps one day I will show you," Riane smiled, leaned in and gave him a quick kiss.

"I'm going to hold you to that," Zach said.

"Since I do not exactly know where it is we are going, we will have to walk, which is a good thing. I would rather the witch not know my abilities just yet," Merlin piped up.

"That portal would have alerted her," Oberon said as he started walking.

"Oh yes, she knows someone is here, she just does not know who yet!" Merlin smiled.

Chapter Thirty Six

Tony, Mia and Adeena continued to jog along the mountain path but were finding it slow and were taking far too long in making any progress in getting closer to Cambridge. Mia suggested they work their way out of the mountains back down to the grasslands. Out there they would be able to move faster and have fewer obstructions. It was still a long way back to the elves and at their present rate they would not be able to make it back to assist in the defence against Helana. So the trio altered course and moved eastward down through the mountains and soon enough found themselves free of rock and narrow pathways and stepped out into the openness of the Rathgar Plains.

"Good idea! This will definitely make the running easier," Tony puffed as he stepped out into the tall grass.

"We're never going to get back to help on time," Adeena whined.

"You can always go on ahead without us! We'll just meet you there," Tony said.

"And leave you two to fend for yourselves? I don't think so," the faerie replied. "I'll stick around at least until we get to the end of the mountains."

"Thanks Adeena, we will enjoy the company," Mia commented with a smile.

"Well gang, let's get movin," Tony sighed as the brisk evening air of the prairie brushed up against his face.

"It is going to be a cool night," Mia said adjusting her pack.

"Good, then running won't be so bad," Tony chuckled.

The three broke into a run then, well two did, Adeena transformed back to faerie form and flew on ahead trying her best to keep the other two within view. As evening began to fade to darkness the group found a place to rest under a series of rocks next to the mountain. They looked as though they had fallen off in several chunks at one time, but would serve nicely as a hiding place until they were ready to continue.

"Do we risk the run at night?" Tony asked, wiping sweat off his forehead.

"We don't have a choice, if we are to get to Cambridge before Helana we'll have to keep moving," Mia said.

"I can light the way, well, to a point," Adeena offered.

"Thanks, we're going to need it. At least you won't be as obvious as a torch would," Tony commented.

"Then we go on?" Mia checked.

"Yes, just give me a second to catch my wind. I ain't in very good shape," Tony gasped.

"Use your horse less then," Mia teased. She stood up and vanished from sight as she started out again.

"Smart ass," Tony muttered. Adeena laughed and flashed into form once more and her 'lighted' faerie form guided the two as they jogged along on the Rathgar Plains.

General Vadeez walked with Helana as they toured the empty Kildare castle. Neither said much but chose to merely acknowledge each other's presence. As they entered the throne chamber, the witch paused as she saw the two seats occupied by Neil and Tasha. She raised her hand and one burst into flames and vanished.

"There will be no need for two," she looked at Vadeez who nodded his agreement.

Helana walked up the few steps to the remaining chair and stopped in front of it. General Vadeez stayed where he was and waited for her to finish whatever it was she wanted to do. Helana walked around the remaining throne chair and then slowly took her seat.

"What do you think general? Does it fit me?" she smiled.

"Yes my queen, it is a nice fit," he bowed.

"I think so too. It is long overdue," Helana murmured. She ran her hands over the arm rests, savoring the touch and sat back.

"My queen, I would have thought you would have wanted to create your own throne?"

"Oh I will, one that is more suited to what I want. I intend to rip this castle apart and remake it to meet my standards!"

"Will we continue our march in the morning then?" the general wondered.

"No," she answered quickly. "We go on as planned. We march all night. I want to be there on the last sunrise any of them will ever see," Helana flashed an evil grin and stood once more.

The two of them left the room and as they did Helana stopped and turned, taking one last look. She raised both her hands and shouted several words and then the room began to rip apart. Rock, wood and mortar crumbled and began to burn and one large column crashed from the ceiling, obliterating the last throne. Satisfied the magic was at work they left and emerged into the courtyard as the towers of Kildare exploded sending debris in every direction. Walls crumbled and fire burst forth, devouring each stick of lumber. Every painting that hung on the walls turned to ash, every curtain, and every inch of carpet and flooring cracked and disintegrated into the fires. Nothing was spared as the dark magic tore at what had been the monarchy's home since their arrival on the new world. Vadeez and Helana walked over the drawbridge and rejoined the horde that waited. Behind them the fire and destruction raged on, consuming Kildare stone by stone.

"WE MARCH ON TO THE ELVES!" Vadeez shouted.

The throng screeched in glee and all of the generals from the risen dead began to push the minions in the direction of the elves castle. No more waiting! The final push was now under way to get to the border of the elf domain. Helana and General Vadeez, among others, watched as Kildare castle burned, and crumbled to the ground. All that remained untouched was the front entry gate, and the drawbridge.

Helana stared at the burning remnants of the monarchy, "I will rebuild it with the ashes of the elves and all of the rest who stood in our way. It will make for a nice reminder of their failure at trying to imprison me."

"I cannot wait to see it all," General Vadeez growled. "That will be a great day indeed."

Neil reigned in his horse as another scout rode up to the front of the caravan. He was looking as exhausted as those before him and the elf bowed to Neil.

"Sir, there are reports from a few other scouts that there is smoke rising to the sky from the general direction of Kildare."

Neil felt Tasha hug him tighter on hearing the words. He nodded at the scout.

"Thanks, go get some rest." The rider got his ride turned around and trotted back to the rear of the lines.

Tasha let out a deep sigh. "Kildare is gone isn't it?"

"That would be my guess," Neil said quietly.

"My home, our home, gone," she forced out the words. Tasha buried her head in his back and cried again.

"We'll rebuild after this is all done, I promise," Neil assured her. "Thatcher," he tried to change the topic. "How much further do you think it is until we get to the border river?"

"Not long m'boy, we'll get there just as night should fall," the gnome smiled.

"Sounds good, I think we all need some rest," Neil returned the smile.

"Aye sir, that yer right on," Thatcher nodded.

Zach and company crested a hill and finally saw the tall towers of Cambridge castle. It was sight he was glad to see again! He thought he'd never be back to see the elves home but after what felt like weeks they were back. The flags of the elf nation fluttered on each of the corners atop the towers. He did notice one difference though. Instead of the one flag's emblem, there were several now. A different one on each corner, and the one emblem of Cambridge hung from the center structure instead. He looked to Riane for an answer and she was already anticipating his question.

"All of the elf nations, together," she said answering his thoughts.

"Oh, I see."

"They have built a magnificent home," Merlin observed. "Who is the king now?"

"My father, Xanthus," Riane replied.

"Your father?" Merlin questioned curiously.

"Yeah, that was kinda what I said when I found out the first time," Zach quipped.

"Yes, I am a third generation elf on this world, grand daughter of Kemal," Riane said.

"Kemal was a good elf. One I could always trust," Merlin bowed to her. "Princess Riane, grand daughter of Kemal, would you care to take us to your home?"

"It would be an honor sir," she smiled back at the wizard.

As the group moved down the hill and past the tall tree tops that had obscured the area around Cambridge, they noticed then the phenomenal number of tents all around the castle. They were scattered for almost as far as the eye could see and Riane had to stop and take in the sight. The rest did the same, trying to comprehend what it was they were seeing.

"They have all come to fight Helana," Riane grinned. She was overwhelmed with joy and gave Zach a big hug.

"That's impressive," Zach commented with a whistle.

"Amazing," Merlin whispered. He moved on first and the rest followed behind. It did not take long for them to make their way out of the trees and out onto the lower lands surrounding Cambridge. The first rows of tents were just a stone's throw away and a number of elf guards on watch came running to find out who they were.

"Identify!" shouted one guard.

Riane stepped forward. "I am Riane, daughter of king Xanthus, I suggest you let us pass."

"Riane!" another voice echoed in from the tents. Another elf emerged and came running.

"Uncle Ledal!" Riane shouted back. She ran over to him and both elves hugged the other.

"I heard you were off someplace. Welcome back!" Ledal

beamed. He gave his niece another hug and motioned for the guards to lower their spears.

The company wandered over and Riane did the introductions. "This is Oberon, Christina, Rachel, Falon, Zach and.."

"And an old friend," Merlin interrupted.

"No name for you?" Ledal joked.

Merlin chuckled. "I do have a name, I am Ambrosius."

"Welcome then to all of you. Come with me and I shall bring you into the castle. My brother will be glad to see you!" Ledal urged them to follow and they did. He stopped and looked over at Oberon. "You are faerie?"

"I am! Very observant Ledal. I have come to lend my help to the faerie."

"They need some sir. Apparently they are not well off at the moment," Ledal said.

"Oh, how is that?" Oberon was curious.

"My brother can tell you more. I just arrived a day ago myself." He led them on and the group followed close behind.

Zach leaned in close to Merlin. "Why the name change?"

"I didn't change anything, that is my name," Merlin replied with a chuckle.

"What?" Zach expressed his disbelief. "Is there anything else you want to tell us?"

Merlin shrugged, "No, I don't think so."

Zach shook his head and rubbed his temples. He felt a headache coming on and wanted something to dull the pain he knew was about to hit him.

They traversed and meandered through the assorted tents and elf races until they finally reached the common path used by everyone to enter the castle. It was well worn from the looks of things; the grass was brown and the ground well packed and dusty. Dust clouds filtered up as they strode on to the road and over the drawbridge leading into Cambridge. Ledal had sent one of the guards on ahead to alert Xanthus and Malcolm that they were coming and both were waiting in the courtyard for them.

Malcolm had an enormous look of relief on his face as he saw the group and almost ran over to greet them with open arms. He gave Riane a hug first and shook Zach's hand enthusiastically. Riane did introductions once more and as she came to Merlin, she paused. The elder wizard stepped around Christina and Rachel and shook Malcolm's hand without saying a word.

Malcolm stared at him and began to realize who the man was. "My word."

"Malcolm is it, Schredrick's successor, it is an honor to meet you sir," Merlin bowed.

Malcolm bowed back to his fellow wizard.

"This, Malcolm, Xanthus, is Merlin," Zach finally introduced.

Xanthus and Malcolm were speechless and Ledal looked at Merlin with a look of surprise as well.

"Merlin?" Ledal checked.

"Yes, I was a bit misleading back at the woods, I'm sure you can understand," Merlin said.

"Of course, yes," Ledal nodded.

Xanthus was beaming and held out his hand for Merlin. "Welcome to Cambridge sir."

"Thank you Xanthus. I like your choice of names for your home, this world. You chose well," Merlin said.

"We are all honored you have come to help us," Malcolm said with a smile. He looked at Oberon and had to think for a moment and then came to another realization. "Oberon, my apologies. I did not recognize you at first!"

"Why would you. We have never met," Oberon chuckled.

Malcolm laughed, "True sir, but I should have known the name. It is an honor to meet you. The king of faerie on this world is a gift to all of us."

"Tut tut, I am here to see how my daughter is fairing! Ledal made mention on the walk down that the faerie are not well. Is this true?"

Malcolm and Xanthus expressions turned sad and both looked at the other, neither sure on how to break the news.

"There is much that has happened recently. Your daughter is well and recovering nicely. She will be thrilled that you are here!" Xanthus said.

"I see there is much to talk about," Oberon sighed, concerned that there was more to it than they were willing to talk about at that moment.

"Yes, there is," Malcolm nodded. "Welcome once again, to all of you."

"I am glad to be here," Merlin let out a sigh. "Now, we need to talk and see where we stand at this time. Is there someplace we can go for some privacy?"

"Yes, we can go the council chamber. We've been sorting out strategies there," Xanthus pointed.

"I will take you up," Malcolm offered.

"Lead on," Merlin motioned. He and Oberon followed the wizard and the others stayed behind.

"I will be there momentarily," Xanthus said. He turned back to Riane and gave his daughter a large hug. "Welcome home."

"It is nice to be back father," Riane replied. She looked at Ledal. "Did Elise come with all the rest that are out there?"

"She did, she came earlier and was part of the advance group that came to lend a hand," Ledal answered.

"Hand with what?" Zach asked.

"We launched an early surprise attack on Helana's army, at the falls. We're still waiting on word from those forces," Xanthus informed.

"Elise was in that group?" Riane asked.

"Yes, her and Brielle," Xanthus replied.

"Brielle is here too!" Riane exclaimed.

"I hope we hear something soon. It has been too long," Ledal muttered. "That in itself is not good."

"I have scouts patrolling the river in case they should show, we will hear something soon," Xanthus assured his brother.

"So I guess we've missed a bit since we've been gone?" Zach asked matter of factly.

"Yes, we will be having a meeting later tonight to go over things. You will be brought up to do date then," Xanthus said. "I will take my leave then and see you all again later."

"I am off to the river with a few of the other generals. One more survey before the witch arrives," Ledal bowed and departed.

Zach, Riane and the others hung back in the courtyard for a moment.

"So who are this Elise, and Brielle?" Zach asked.

"They are my cousin, and my sister. Elise is my cousin and Brielle is my younger sister," Riane answered with a smile.

"Well then, isn't this day full of surprises," Zach sighed.

As evening turned to night and all light faded, Adeena's 'light' was barely enough to keep Tony and Mia from running blindly into a tree, or whatever else might get in their way. It was at some point just after dark had settled in that the three began to hear some unusual sounds from the sky. Finally the group stopped when the noise started to repeat itself.

"There's something hunting us," Mia whispered.

"What? Shit, we better find someplace for cover!" Tony said, a bit of panic in his tone.

"This way, there was some shrubs near the rocks," Adeena beckoned. She hastily led them to the area; it was small, but adequate for their purpose. All three crawled under the shrubs and did their best to conceal their whereabouts.

Whatever it was that was hunting was getting closer and something hit the ground hard, and began to claw at the dirt and grass. The dark of night hid whatever it was and none of them breathed, too scared to give away their hiding spot. The creature in question was obviously looking for something, and was having some difficulty in finding it. Then the noise stopped and they heard it sniffing, smelling, and realized it would find their scent! A low guttural growl filtered over as the thing began to move again.

"I know that growl," Adeena muttered. She jumped up and disappeard into the blackness.

"What the? Adeena get back here!" Tony whispered urgently.

"Blinky! Stop making so much noise!"

Mia couldn't help herself but giggled at the remark. "I think we know what's out there now."

"I'm going to kill that dragon," Tony muttered, "not really, well, you know what I mean."

"Come on out you two! It's safe!" Adeena yelled.

Tony and Mia walked up to see Adeena standing in front of the dragon Blinky, and the beast looked at them curiously. It growled again and Adeena translated.

"He says he's coming to help us."

"Wait a second; didn't the other one say he couldn't?" Tony checked.

"He's going with us anyway, and so are a few others," Adeena said.

"Really, so where are the rest?" Tony wondered.

"Waiting up on the ridge," Adeena pointed up behind them.

Tony tossed out another question, "How's that going to sit with that Drayler dragon, and the others?"

Adeena asked Blinky and the dragon snorted out some of his own language and Adeena in turned gave Tony the answer.

"They don't know, but they want to help anyways."

"Well," Tony scratched his head, "nothing we can do about it I guess."

Another howl in the sky caught their attention and Tony looked at Mia while shrugging his shoulders.

"Now what?"

"Another dragon," Adeena answered for her. "I think it might be one of the adults."

"Huh? Are you kidding me?" Tony exclaimed.

The faerie shook her head. "It sounded like it from that howl." Blinky growled and Adeena nodded her head. "Yup, I was right. Blinky just said so."

"Thanks Blinky," Mia smiled at the dragon. Adeena translated and the dragon bobbed its head.

In a few moments, Drayler appeared and landed behind Blinky, sending a cloud of dust up as he hit the ground. The considerably larger dragon towered above the smaller one and looked as enraged as some parent might be on finding out their kid had been sneaking out to go to an all night party. Blinky cowered and slunk low to the ground.

Adeena was spouting off some dragonspeak to do her part in easing the situation and it seemed to have some sort of effect on the elder dragon and the two became engaged in quite the conversation. Tony and Mia stood there, dumbfounded, and wondering what in the world the two were possibly talking about. The smaller, youthful dragon even seemed to perk up and was soon standing tall once more. After several minutes Adeena turned to Tony and Mia.

"Drayler has agreed to let the younger dragons help, to a point," she began. "They won't fight unless they have to, and we will be able to use them as a scout, at least I think that's what he said."

"Really? Good work Adeena," Tony complimented.

The faerie did a little curtsy, "You are welcome sir."

Mia giggled. "Is there any chance they might be up for giving us a ride back to Cambrdige?"

Adeena was all smiles. "Yes, they are! I already asked them. The rest of the dragons are on their way and once they get here we'll all go at once."

"This night has suddenly gotten pretty good," Tony said all smiles on hearing the news.

Ledal and his patrol trotted along the Norcross River, finalizing locations for all the weaponry that was already on its way to the banks in preparation on the witch's arrival. As they surveyed, a shout from one of the patrols on the far side of the river alerted them to another party approaching.

"Who is it?" Ledal shouted back.

The elf general got his answer as a gryphon appeared out of the darkened sky and landed a short distance from them. The elf piloting the animal jumped off and ran over, and Ledal recognized his daughter immediately.

"Elise!"

"Hello Father!" she replied running up. Ledal leapt off his horse and greeted his daughter with an enormous hug. He was so relieved to see her alive and well that he almost couldn't contain himself.

"You have had us all worried," Ledal said.

"The rest of the forces are not far off, they should be at the river's edge anytime now," she informed him.

"You heard her! Get the rafts ready! We have company on the way!" The general ordered. All the elves on the patrol went to work preparing the many rafts that waited on the banks for just this reason. They were skimming across the water as quickly as they got them into the water. The wait wasn't long as the first of the resistant fighters appeared with Neil and Tasha in the lead. The rafts ferried everyone over and as more arrived on the opposite side one elf would grab another raft and start back with the other until every raft was in operation and the transfer from one side to the other was far more expedient.

"You are the new king and queen I take it, my congratulations on your nuptials, and my apologies for being unable to attend," Ledal said bowing to both Neil and Tasha.

"We understand, you are Ledal, leader of the woodland elves. Your daughter has told us a lot about you," Tasha smiled as she shook the elf's hand.

"Well I don't hear that very often. Usually she has nothing to say about me!" Ledal quipped as he winked at Elise.

"Thanks for coming to help out in all this," Neil added.

"Gladly, we all have a lot to lose if the witch has her way," Ledal commented. "Was your attack on her at the falls successful?"

"To a point, yes, but she knew we were coming so we didn't quite have the impact we were hoping for. If it wasn't for our friend Shar we might have lost more than we did," Neil explained.

"I've heard a lot about her the last few days! Quite gifted

I understand. We are having a meeting later this evening to go over everything and set up our final plans," Ledal said.

"Good. Once our other friends Zach and Tony get back we'll hopefully have all the pieces together," Neil added.

"Zach? A Zach showed up earlier this evening with a few others," Ledal smiled. "I do not know about any Tony, but the other is back from wherever it was he went."

"That's fantastic news!" Tasha exclaimed.

"You two go on with the rest; I'll make sure the last of the forces get over the river. I've been stuck inside plotting strategy! It is nice to finally be out! I will see you again back at Cambridge!" Ledal moved off at that point, stopping to give his daughter one more hug and then was off to shout further instructions.

"Let's go, I want to see how Zach faired," Neil urged impatiently.

"It would be faster if we took our horse," Tasha laughed as she stood next to their ride. Neil was already starting to run and realized he wasn't thinking clearly.

"I knew that," he replied walking back to the horse.

Elise was laughing with Tasha. "I will see you both back at the castle." She jogged off still laughing and Neil climbed up on the horse with Tasha jumping up to sit behind him.

"Now we can go," she teased.

"Yeah yeah."

Chapter Thirty Seven

Zach placed Excalibur down on his bed and kept it covered in the cloth that had kept it hidden ever since they left Camelot. He stared at the package for a moment and then wandered over to his window to look outside and get another look at all the campfires surrounding the castle. It was a sight to see, first the tents, and now the fires themselves dotted the entire landscape like Christmas lights on a tree. A light tapping on his door diverted his attention away from the fires.

"It's open."

Merlin stepped in to the room and wandered over to stand next to Zach at the window.

"Quite the sight I must say. Amazing what one thing can do to ally those who haven't spoken to one another in some time!"

"Yeah, I didn't realize how many different races of elves there are, grey, dark, woodland, ice? Any others out there?" Zach wondered.

"Maybe one or two, but they are so misplaced in the eastland or northland areas that they may not even know what is going on over here," Merlin replied.

"So, you've had a chance to talk with Malcolm?"

"Yes, albeit briefly, but I have an idea as to what is going on. I will be talking further with him after the meeting. It is you I need to talk to for a time," Merlin said. He left the window and took a seat on the bed.

Zach turned to face him. "What for?"

"There are a few phrases I need to teach you, for when you use the sword," Merlin explained.

"Okay, shoot," Zach stood up straight and crossed his arms to listen.

"It is not that easy, I suggest you take a seat," Merlin motioned to a chair that suddenly appeared in front of him.

Zach blinked to make sure he wasn't seeing things and finally settled into the chair. He stared at Merlin wondering what exactly it was he had to say that required him to take a seat.

"Repeat these words," Merlin began. *"All olle est malum shall die, all olle est opacus ero brought in liburnica."*

Zach tried to say the words but bungled the pronunciation horribly. Merlin sat up straight, and focused his gaze on Zach. "It means all that is evil must die, all that is dark shall be brought into light. You must pronounce the words in that language, otherwise the magic will not work."

"Why?" Zach asked.

"It is an old language of elves and faerie, the faerie no longer use the language and the elfish has changed over time. It was used in the creation of Excalibur. So then, try this phrase, '*sicuti hic blade est purus of heart, tam shall thee imus ad it.*' It means blade pure of heart so thee will fall to it."

Zach took in a deep breath and tried to repeat the phrase and failed miserably. Merlin looked at him and wondered how he could ever teach these words to the man!

"And this final one, '*malum testamentum non imus atquin imus cata Excalibur's will, tam it must ero*'. Go on, try," Merlin urged.

Once more Zach spoke and despite his best efforts to get it out right, he could not say the words. He stood up frustrated and swore a few choice words to vent. Merlin sat there, trying to figure out how to teach the language but it might take days to get it right and that was a luxury they didn't have and he could not use magic to further Zach along because the one who spoke the words had to do so without his interference. He went to stand and his hand touched Excalibur on the bed. The wizard looked at the cloth and an idea came to him.

"Try holding the sword as you say the words," Merlin said.

"So I can screw it up all over again?" Zach muttered.

"Just do as I ask," Merlin repeated, in a firm voice. Zach looked at him and knew the man was serious. He walked over and pulled the cloth off. Grasping the handle firmly he held up Excalibur.

"Say the words," Merlin instructed. *"All olle est malum shall die, all olle est opacus ero brought in liburnica."*

Zach breathed in deep and began to say the phrase. *"All olle est malum shall die, all olle est opacus ero brought in liburnica."*

He had no difficulty and he looked at Merlin curiously. "What the?"

"Go on," Merlin urged.

"sicuti hic blade est purus of heart, tam shall thee imus ad it. Malum testamentum non imus atquin imus cata Excalibur's will, tam it must ero."

Zach felt the handle of Excalibur warm to his touch and he stared at Merlin. "What just happened?"

"Like you saw the words on the blade before, this time

the blade itself has helped you say the words," Merlin smiled. "You are truly Arthur's heir after all."

"Do me a favor. Don't tell anyone else. I asked Riane to keep it a secret to, and she promised she will. Nobody needs to know right now."

Merlin nodded. "As you wish. So it will be!"

Another knock, a quite enthusiastic knock on the door caused both to turn.

"Zach! You decent in there?" Neil joked from the other side. Merlin stepped back into the shadows as Zach walked over to the door. He opened it up and Neil walked in all smiles and overjoyed at seeing his friend.

"Hey there," Zach chuckled.

"Great to see you again! So, how was the trip? Did Riordan help much? Come on talk!" Neil nagged. It was then he saw the other man standing off to the side of the room. "Oh, sorry, I didn't know you had company."

"No big deal, someone you should meet anyways," Zach beckoned for him to come in to the room further.

Neil stepped into the center of the room and Zach motioned for the other man to join them. The elder gentlemen stepped into the light, holding his staff and Neil had no idea who it was.

"Neil, this is, well, a man of legend. The one I was sent to find, Neil meet," he paused and looked at Neil. "Merlin."

Neil's gaze went from Zach to the man, then back to Zach and then back to the man. The name echoed in his head and he was having a hard time accepting it. Finally he looked at Zach.

"Merlin?" he whispered.

"Yes, this is Merlin. The one you've read about, and Merlin, this is Neil, my friend and.."

"King of Avalon, a part of the new monarchy," Merlin

smiled and held out his hand. Neil accepted it and shook it nervously.

"It is an honor to meet you sir, and Neil is just fine," Neil said with a smile.

"Ah yes, uncomfortable with the title, I've seen a few of those in my day," Merlin snickered. "It is a pleasure to meet you Neil, I've heard a lot about you and the others these last few days."

"Zach tends to exaggerate a bit," Neil cracked. He was still shaking Merlin's hand and the wizard looked at him, wondering if he was going to get his hand back.

"Oh, sorry," Neil apologized as he let go. "I just never, ever, thought I would ever meet, well, a myth."

"As you can see he's no myth, well, aren't we supposed to go to some meeting right away?" Zach asked as he tried to change the subject.

Neil looked back at Zach, "Yes, one of the other reasons I came up to see you. Nice sword," he pointed at Exalibur in Zach's hands.

"Thanks," Zach simply replied. He put the sword aside and placed it back in the cloth on the bed.

"Bring it with you Zach," Merlin winked. "They need to know about it."

"If you say so."

"The sword?" Neil was curious now. He looked at the cloth wrapped package as Zach picked it up.

"You'll see soon enough," Zach teased. "Oh yeah, before I forget," Zach reached into his bag on the bed. He withdrew two chocolate bars and tossed them to Neil.

"You actually remembered them," Neil laughed. "I'm going to save these for after this is all over with."

Zach chuckled, "You do that." He adjusted Excalibur and tucked it in close to his side and along with Merlin and Neil on either side, the trio left his room and proceeded down the hall to the others anxiously awaiting in the council chamber.

Oberon sat on the bed, next to his daughter Leasha and held her hand while she slept. She had not stirred at all since his arrival and the king of faerie was growing concerned despite the healers assuring him she was merely sleeping so that she may heal within. He had no concept of time and was surprised when Xanthus and Malcolm appeared next to him.

"It is time for our meeting sir; would you like to join us?" Malcolm asked.

"I would, but I wish I could say the same of my daughter," Oberon replied.

"You may remain here if you wish," Xanthus suggested.

"No, she is still sleeping and I am told she won't wake at least until sunrise. Let us go and see if all are ready for the storm ahead," Oberon stood and covered up his daughter with her blanket. "I will see to it they pay for the destruction of Tir Nan Og," he murmured.

"How was your visit with the other faerie?" Malcolm wondered as they began to walk.

"Good, they are happy to be alive, sad on losing their home but that is to be expected. Maybe when this is over I may go into Tir Nan Og and see if I can restore it, it cannot hurt to try," Oberon said.

"We will do what we can to help," Xanthus offered.

"Music to my ears sir, your father would be proud of you, you have quite the kingdom on this world," Oberon complimented the elf king.

"I am glad you approve. How are the realms back on the old world?" Xanthus inquired.

"Surviving, but I am told things will change in the not

too far off future, but that is for another day's talk, let us see if we are ready for the witch!" Oberon piped up as he slapped Xanthus across the back and put his arms around both wizard and king. "It is good to be here!"

The air was cool as they rode below the clouds, almost so close that Tony felt he could reach out and touch them. Though he was scared if he did so he might just lose his already perilous grip on the dragon that carried him! Mia was escorted on her own dragon as well and Adeena flew with Blinky because the two seemed to share a special bond that they had developed back when he was but a small hatchling. Once all the dragons that were willing to help against the witch had shown up the entire company had departed for Cambridge, with the three of them carried on three of the younger dragons.

The ride was exhilarating and Tony got a great view of the landscape below. The lights of Fairview were dim in the distance, and the mountains became hills as they distanced themselves from the dragon's home. The dragons flew in formation and the elders kept the younger brood in line and on course. Every time one would try and venture off the elder would quickly push him back in place!

It wasn't long before the view of Cambridge came up, a dark shadow as the suns descended on the day, and the towers were lit up like towers at an airfield to guide in airplanes. The flickering lights around the castle were even more fantastic to see! There were so many, and Tony saw Mia look at him with a huge grin. He gave her a thumb up and she looked at him, a little confused. He'd have to explain that signal when they were back on the ground. Before they had departed the mountains Tony had instructed Adeena to tell the dragons where to land, so as to avoid any unnecessary panic.

The castle grew in size as they approached the dragons changed their flight and were going where they had been instructed to land. Once they were back on the ground Tony, Mia and Adeena would go to the castle and explain what was going on before the dragons would show themselves. The flight came to an end far too soon for his liking and they were landing in a meadow back of the woods. All the dragons drew in close as Tony dismounted. He, Mia and Adeena joined up and Drayler spoke a few words that Adeena translated.

"He says they will not go any further until called upon," Adeena said.

"Good. Tell him thanks again and let's get back to the castle," he said, anxious to get back to Cambridge and see what was going on.

Adeena spoke to the dragon and waved as the three of them ran off into the woods, and back to the haven of Cambridge castle to give them the good news on their latest alliance against the witch Helana. The dragons sat back and kept watch, waiting for their call to fly into action and assist the only king who had ever promised to keep them safe.

All of the generals, both elf and human, dwarf and gnome, captains and any other important to the defenses was there to get in any final ideas or strategies that may work against the witch. It was a full room and everyone was talking amongst themselves as they waited for those to lead the meeting to enter. As Zach stepped into the room with Neil and Merlin, the room went quiet, most wondering who the newest stranger was in their midst. Tasha worked her way through the crowd to take her place next to Neil and he smiled on seeing her.

"Who is our guest?" Tasha wondered.

"Introductions are coming. You're going to love this!" he beamed. "Are Malcolm and Xanthus around?"

"Both will be here shortly. They went to find someone," Tasha said.

Tony, Mia and Adeena were ushered into the room by a few elf guards and Tony went all smiles on seeing Zach standing next to Neil. He moved up and shook his friend's hand as enthusiastically as Neil had earlier.

"When did you get back?" Tony asked.

"Just this evening I heard you went off to see the dragons?" Zach queried.

"How did that go?" Neil asked before Tony could reply.

Tony smiled and gave him a thumb up. "Good, to a point anyways, we've got some help, not a lot but I think enough to give us a fighting chance."

"Where are they?" Tasha wondered.

"We set down just off in the woods, a ways off so as to not alarm anyone. They'll stay out of sight until I go get them," Tony said.

"Great news! I'm beginning to think this stand against Helana has got a good chance now," Neil smiled.

Malcolm, Xanthus and Oberon entered the room and all went quiet. Malcolm and Xanthus walked to the front of the council table and faced the entire group. Oberon went to stand beside Merlin and both winked at the other. All the leaders of the races, captains and generals of the troups camped outside, waited to hear what had to be said on the eve of the encounter with the witch.

"Everyone, thank you first and foremost for being here and I wish we could have gathered on a more joyous occasion, but sadly that is not to be the case. This fight that has come to the elfland border will determine whether this world and even our old home world will survive the onslaught of this evil. To that end we have asked all of you for your help, and you have all answered the call, for that, myself and Xanthus once again would like to thank you for your support. We would not be able to do this without your assistance. I have also sought out help from the old world, and I would like to introduce to you two who have offered to aid us in our time of need. First, the king of faerie, Oberon," Malcolm motioned for him to step up and Oberon stepped forward and bowed.

There were hushed whispers throughout the room and the faerie king stepped back to his place beside Merlin. Malcom spoke once more.

"And one who had helped so long ago to find this home for us, and who has offered his assistance once more, and for that I am truly grateful, may I introduce, the wizard Merlin." Malcolm nodded to the legendary man and the mage smiled and stepped forward. There were gasps, and even more whispers throughout the room. More from disbelief than anything. They had all heard stories passed on from generation to generation, but to see the man in person was uncomprehensible.

Tony went wide eyed and looked at Zach who just cracked a grin and winked back at the younger man. Tasha stared at Neil and he had a smile that looked like it was fixated there permanently.

"You knew and didn't tell me?" she whispered.

He leaned in, "I just found out myself."

Merlin spoke and the room went silent once more. "Hello to one and all, it has been some time since I visited this world and I am glad to see it doing well. When Mr.Thomas came calling on me and explained the situation I could not turn my back on those who needed me. It is an honor to be here amongst you, all fighting for the same common cause." On that he stepped back again and Malcolm spoke up.

"We are indeed lucky to have you here sir, furthermore, I am going to hand the floor over to Merlin who will explain what it is we must do, if you will," Malcolm bowed.

"Thank you Malcolm." Merlin moved up to the table and pointed to the roughly etched diagram on the map. "The fight is only one piece of what we must do to stop this witch. Her evil has suprassed all boundaries with her mergence with the demon; this is all new territory to even me. I have never encountered this, ever, so we are all learning at the same time. I have brought with me a weapon, forged long ago by elf, faerie, and others to combat such darkness. It strikes at evil directly, and therefore, must be used on the witch herself. The war against her legions is only a small part of this, and without the witch being struck down, make no mistake we will lose this. She need only open the gate into the void to replenish those we cut down, and so, she must be stopped. This weapon has been entrusted to young Mister Thomas behind me, and only he can carry it. No other," Merlin said as he looked around the room. "We will need him to get to the witch. If she does not die, then we all will."

"It will not be easy for him to get near her, she will be well protected," Ledal spoke up.

"I, Malcolm, my apprentice Falon and the mage Shar will be doing our best to keep her occupied. You and your armies will need to keep hers occupied, we will have to get him through the lines and to her; both Malcolm and I have discussed this and have come up with the best option. A group will move through it all," Malcolm pointed with his staff to the map on the table and Merlin continued. "As the fighting goes on and will work their way up to her. At that point, Mister Thomas will have to decide how it is he will strike at her; we will do our part to keep the witch busy to allow him this opportunity."

"Who will be in the group?" Darg asked curiously.

"Anyone who wishes to be," Merlin replied.

"There are a few who have already commited to this," Malcolm added. "This is something we must do, as Merlin says, if Helana is not stopped then we will very well lose this war."

"Why is he the only one who can carry this weapon?" Kieran wondered.

"He was the one chosen by the council who forged the sword. The magic will not work if he is not wielding the blade," Merlin answered. "Zach, come forward, show everyone the sword."

Zach took a few steps up to the table and carefully laid the cloth covered blade on it. He removed the covering, and everyone got a good look at the weapon, the sword. The leader of the Dark Elves stepped up to the table and pointed to the sword.

"A mere blade, this is what will kill the witch?" Peresca snorted.

"This is no ordinary blade general, this is Excalibur," Merlin replied as he pointed his staff at the sword that lay on the table.

"Excalibur?" Escalan, general of the sand elves said aloud.

"Thee Excalibur," Merlin nodded.

Neil gasped, amazed at what he was hearing. All of his old history classes were coming back to him in flashes and to bear witness to it all in front of him was unbelievable!

Peresca bowed to Merlin. "I now understand! My apologies."

Merlin waved her off. "No need to apologize general. I would be asking the same question if I were you."

Malcolm spoke up to change the subject albeit, just

slightly. "With that strategy in place, how are the rest of the forces lined up?"

Each general took their turn to explain their defense plan and how it would be executed on the field. As each phase was guided through in detail, everyone got to understand how the stand at the river would play out. At the end of it all, there was a general knowledge of the battle plan throughout the room. Now it was all a matter of following through. The Elves, humans led by Jacinto and his captains, a number of gnomes and dwarves that had made the trek to assist in the fight all had their place in the forthcoming battle. The key in it all was the group that had to fight their way through to Helana so that Zach could use the sword Excalibur and hopefully end it once and for all. Or in the end, the dark clouds that hung over the world of Avalon would never allow the light of day to be seen, ever again.

"Everyone, thank you for everything, there is a good chance some of us may never see one another again after this, understand that all of your efforts are recognized by me, Malcolm, Xanthus and to all who participate in this fight. This is a war we could not win without you, all of you. I do hope at the end of it all, we can all be here to toast to our victory and to an end of this evil. Be safe," Merlin finished his speech and a general murmur echoed throughout the room.

Malcolm walked over to Merlin as the group talked amongst themselves for a time, discussing the situation. Malcolm leaned in close.

"May we talk in private?"

"Of course, shall we adjourn to your study?" Merlin suggested.

"That will be fine," Malcolm replied. Both wizards left the room and slowly the meeting filtered out into the hallways as each went off in their separate groups.

Axel and Ruskin came up to Zach as he wrapped up Excalibur in its cloth wrapping once more.

"Ya know we're comin with ya, ya ain't goin up against no witch without us," Axel grunted.

"Aye, someone got ta keep ya outta trouble," Ruskin added with a chuckle.

"I'd be glad to have you along," Zach smiled back at them both.

Neil moved in beside him. "I think we gotta talk some more about this trip of yours, I'll get us some ale and we can shoot the breeze for a bit."

"Sounds good, hey Tony, up for ale?" Zach asked.

"Bring it on," Tony agreed.

Malcolm and Merlin strolled into the study, or library that Malcolm kept at Cambridge. Here he did most of his work, and kept everything stored in various texts on the assorted shelves that lined the room. It was here the text Merlin had sent with his teacher Schredrick was kept as well. On seeing the book sitting on the stand in the corner of the room, Merlin wandered over and opened its pages to have a look.

"It has been a long time since I made this book," he sighed.

"We have done our best to maintain it over time," Malcolm said.

"I can see that. Thank you." Merlin smiled at his fellow wizarding brethren. "You want to talk more about the incantation that Zach will use with Excalibur?"

"Yes, I do. I have found a companion spell that will assure us that Helana will not only die, but be split apart from the demon with which she has merged."

Merlin looked at him closely. "I know of the spell you talk about Malcolm. It has a high price, a very high price."

"I am aware of that, but it is the only way to assure the sword will destroy what she has become," Malcolm said.

"You ask a lot of yourself Malcolm, and of your young apprentice Shar," Merlin said quietly. "Is your apprentice ready for what you are asking of her?"

"She is ready," Malcolm nodded. "I can teach her nothing more at this point. She is more than capable of learning what she needs on her own, over time."

"I am not going to convince you either way, but all I will say is, are you sure this is what you want?"

Malcolm nodded slowly. "Yes, I have thought about it for some time. It is time, and as long as Zach is able to get to Helana, it will assure us of success."

"I understand," Merlin sighed. "I am envious of you that way; I hope one day I will have that choice to make."

"I am sure you will," Malcolm smiled. "No one is to know of this, just you and I."

"Of course," Merlin agreed. "I have one secret of you as well my friend, but first, I think we should have some tea and sit for a time."

"I agree," Malcolm said. The two wizards sat at the small table in the room as Malcolm brewed up some fresh tea. They sat for a time, merely talking, and sharing stories as though they had been friends for a great many years.

A scout galloped into the courtyard of Cambridge castle and jumped off his ride. Two other elves attended to the horse while he went in search of someone to give them news he had to share. He found Xanthus talking with a few of the other elf leaders and bowed to them as he approached.

"Yes?" Xanthus asked.

"I have news sir; we have seen the front lines of the witch's army in the distance. They will be here at the river by dawn."

Chapter Thirty Eight

Dark clouds moved across the sky, thickening and rolling as they neared the elf border. Thunder and lightening that boomed and flashed, warning that there was a storm on the horizon, a dark demon onslaught. The lightening lit the sky for a brief moment before darkness returned and then it would flash again, providing a brief spark of daylight once again and then back to darkness. It looked like rain in the distance and the air turned cold as the wind brushed over the landscape. Those who waited at the border felt the chill from the wind and their breath exhaled as mist while they waited. It would not be long before the storm arrived.

Helana's army stomped onward and as the sight of the Norcross River came into view the horde let out a loud howl that could be heard echoing over the land. They moved even faster as their goal was almost attained and would soon cross over into the long forbidden elf lands. Each demon that walked or crawled, every monster that slithered or flew, and all of the things that moved in this throng salivilated at the thought of destroying the elves! They could not contain their desire for achieving such an accomplishment!

Helana herself watched on the hill overlooking the

Norcross River and smiled at those who waited to greet her. Malcolm had done an admirable job in recruiting others to fight back against her, but it would only make her savor her victory that much more. Her legions marched on and the ground shook as they moved, and she hoped it would send a shiver through the spines of each and every elf, human, dwarf, and gnome that waited on the other side of the river. They would fall to her and she would be sure to stomp out the life force of each one.

"We will wait for your order to cross the river," General Vadeez said as he stepped up beside her.

"I will clear a way through the water. You will have no difficulty crossing," she assured him.

"Is your old teacher waiting there for you?" he asked.

"Yes, he is and by the looks of it, he has called on all the elf races for some help. There is more magic here than I expected. Whoever came over from the old world has some magic at their disposal. This will be more fun than I had anticipated!"

"Interesting, will they pose a threat to us?" Vadeez was curious now.

"Not at all, but it will be more of a challenge," Helana smiled. "Let's go say hello."

"Archers to your positions!" bellowed Teague. "Taith, keep the left flank in line, don't let them back up. They need to keep the demons from coming in behind. The same goes for you Darg, keep the right flank in place."

"Aye it will be done, we will do our part, I challenge you to do the same," Darg, captain of the grey elves replied.

"We'll be front and center in it all captain. See you in the courtyard for drinks after!" Teague saluted his fellow dwarf.

"I'll bring the brandy!" Darg laughed.

"And I'll bring the mugs! Cheers captains! Good fighting!" Taith yelled as he jogged off to lead his contingent.

Zach stood at the back of the combined forces with Neil and Tony as they watched Helana's army start their march down towards the Norcross River and for the first time all three had a good look at what they were up against. They had seen her army the first time at Livina, and then the dragons at Rakia's keep but none compared to what they were seeing now. There were so many it! It was as if they were crawling over each other to get to them. To find Helana and get to her was beginning to feel like an insurmountable task.

"Look at them," Tony whispered.

"Just numbers! We have the skills, in the end that will make the difference," Neil said.

"I hope your right," Zach mumbled.

"Well I'm off to the dragons with Mia. Send Adeena when you need us," Tony instructed.

"We will. Good luck," Neil smiled and shook Tony's hand.

"Don't worry. We'll see each other at the end of all this," Tony spoke confidently. "We've still got a lot of exploring to do."

"Aye, we do," Zach grunted in his best Axel impersonation.

The three laughed lightly and Tony departed, to do his part in the defence of Avalon. Zach pulled his cloak in tight, feeling the weight of Excalibur strapped to his back, hidden from view from any curious onlookers. Neil put his hand on Zach's shoulder.

"Are you sure you're up for this?" he checked.

"I don't have much of a choice! I just hope we can get to Helana," Zach replied quietly.

"I Wish I could say I knew what you were going through.

To a point I kind of do, but I don't have a lot to compare it to," Neil said with a chuckle, trying to lighten to mood.

"We'll figure it out," Zach smiled.

Riane, Tasha, Shar, the dwarves and Thatcher all sidled up and the group stood there watching the advancing army of evil as it thundered down the hills towards the river. The entire defence contigent waiting on the elf side of the river were nervous and anxious to shoot first, but all were under direct order to not fire until instructed to do so.

"Who gets to go with me?" Zach asked curiously.

"We all are ya fool, we ain't lettin ya get ta have all th'fun," Axel grunted.

"And a few others, as well as a number of the elf soldiers. You're going to have more than enough company along for the fun," Riane added.

"Aye, we all know what be at stake lad, we'll be there ta help ya through," Thatcher said with nod.

"Malcolm, Merlin, Falon and I have our own tasks to keep Helana occupied. Between us we should be able to allow you to get near her without detection," Shar assured him. "Magic against magic will cloud Excalibur's presence," she finished.

"Where are they anyway?" Neil wondered.

"They are on their way," Shar said.

"Forgive me for asking this again, but are you sure of what you wish to do Malcolm?" Merlin asked, hoping to hear a different answer.

Malcolm nodded certain of the incantation they were to use with the power of Excalibur. "It is. She will not have another chance to strike, this time she must be stopped."

"Very well," Merlin smiled. He turned to speak to Falon who was waiting patiently on the other side of the council chamber. "Falon, we are ready now. Are you versed well enough on your tasks?"

"Yes sir! I am looking forward to practicing what you have taught me," she acknowledged.

"I am sure you are! Then, let's not keep the witch waiting. She is almost here," Merlin said. The three of them left the room together and walked on down the hall to join the rest of the company waiting on the field already. All three vanished and reappeared behind Neil, Zach and the rest a moment later.

"I see the enemy is near," Merlin commented, catching them off guard.

"You could cough or something to let us know you're here," Zach muttered.

"Nervous?" Merlin teased. "I will remember to do that next time."

"She is coming well prepared I see," Malcolm observed. "She is near her full strength; I can feel the darkness like it was next to me."

"Like a weight pushing against you," Shar said enchancing the description.

"She is here, hiding amidst the demons," Malcolm muttered. "We have got our work cut out for us."

"Nothing is ever easy when we want it. We'll just have to be creative to get her to show herself," Merlin said.

The horde rushed on to the river's edge and as it neared the entire mob slowed and came to a standstill at the water, waiting for the chance to cross into elf land and into the waiting armies on the other side. Helana stood among her minions, disguising her location to allow for confusion on Malcolm's part and the other mage that she had encountered at the falls. She wanted nothing more than to torment them both, to make them suffer for as long as possible.

Helana spoke, her voice echoing over the land, reverberating in every direction to hide her further.

"***I am here to claim what is mine! Bow down to me as your queen and we will avoid this unnecessary slaughter***!"

"*We will never bow down to you Helana, or to your demon! We will fight you with everything at our disposal*!" Malcolm shot back, taunting her.

"***Then you and everyone else will die, I will have my throne and this world, and after I am finished with you I will cross over to the old world and destroy all who refuse to worship me!"*** Helana retorted.

"You will have to go through us to accomplish that, and we will not stand aside!" Malcolm answered her threat.

"***You think you can stop me***!" Helana shrieked, and laughed, "***Then you are a bigger fool than I thought.***"

Merlin spoke up, "We will not allow you any further! This ends right here and now witch; this is how it will be!"

Helana did not recognize the voice, and was curious as to who would be so bold! "***Just words, words I will make you eat***!"

"You can try, but I don't think so, not this day!" Merlin shot back.

"***So be it***!" Helana roared. "***Throw this water aside, gone it will be, dry as sand it will turn, do as I command and so it will be***!"

"*Generals, captains, when they move into the riverbed you may fire at your discretion, good fight to you all*," Merlin whispered, his words flowing over air and into the ears of those who needed to hear them. All acknowledged his command with a nod and each waited for the onslaught to begin.

As Helana's words reverberated over the land the

Norcross River began to evaporate, the water shooting straight up into the clouds and within a matter of minutes the river was gone, replaced by a small valley where water once ran. The mud slowly dried as the magic took hold and as it solidified the horde stood ready.

"All Archers forward!" Kieran bellowed. His order echoed down the lines by each elf holding a bow. Both right and left flanks moved to face forward and aimed their arrows.

The demons couldn't wait any longer, and they pushed the trolls in front of their own lines into the hollowed earth that had been the river. The surge was on.

The Dead generals resurrected by Helana moved quickly to get the creatures in line and orderly before they lost control. They moved to the front of their divisions and shouted orders, using their mace's to crush any demon's skull that did not stay in line. The monsters learned quickly to obey and the borderline mass hysteria was kept at bay, this time. They followed the trolls into the breach and the enormous army that was Helana's began to cross into elf territory.

"Wait!" Darg shouted, "Wait for your orders!" He watched the mass move closer and even he felt the overwhelming sense of impossibility on seeing such a display of numbers. He kept his calm and kept the rest doing the same, "Wait!"

The minions of darkness led by the trolls reached the half way mark across the breach and the elves lifted their bows, awaiting their signal to open fire. Each of the captains watched, and waited, and when they finally decided they had ventured far enough into the river, the word was given.

"Reeeeeleaaaaase!" Keiran hollered at the top his lungs. Each archer aimed their bow and let loose the initial volley of arrows. They rained down on the demons like a rainshower, but for each one that fell, five were there to replace the fallen.

"Reeeeelease!" Teague shouted and let his own arrow fly. Wave on wave of arrows cut into the enemy and the dead began to pile up and even slowed the push of Helana's army. The trolls were the hardest to fell by the arrows and the beasts kept trudging on, doing as they were told, pushed by the witch's own commanders. Most of them knew there was no defying the witch so there was no escape from the madness. Driven, they let the arrows strike, and walked until they could walk no more. As one troll would collapse, the demons in every shape and form would merely walk over top.

The screeching and howling was almost deafening as Helana's monsters closed the gap between them and the defenders along the elf border. The archers were reloading and shooting as fast as their abilites allowed them but they could only do so much, it was time to go into the second phase of the defence and the infantry elves stood ready.

Riss, captain of the Dark elves, shouted orders as he lifted his own elven sword, ready to step into the brink of darkness itself.

"First line advance!"

The elves marched ahead, swords held ready as the enemy approached and as the elves stepped off into the river's breach, the war began in earnest as swords swung fast and with precision, cutting down the demons, and dark creatures with skill. As the hand to hand combat began, Merlin watched and nodded to his fellow mage's.

"I will cast the first spell, then all of you begin immediately after! Be sure to be random in your targeting! We need to get her attention!" Merlin instructed. He lifted his staff and sent a wave of magic into a line of demons, crushing them to dust. The wizard smiled, knowing he would have just given his ability away but it would draw the witch out.

Helana saw the magic, and felt it. She was surprised at its strength but the demon side of her recognized the power of the magic. Helana twisted her head to the side to stave off the pain shooting through her as the demon Valgor began to dominate what was left of her human side. His mind had merged with hers and his thoughts became hers.

"Merlin," Helana whispered as the demon mind started to dominate. Helana thought back on the stories of old, of a master wizard who had found this world and had brought them here to save those who were of magical origin or who practiced the art. Valgor knew more, he had faced Merlin once, long long ago and that memory surfaced the moment Merlin had cast his magic.

Valgor's words echoed in her mind, "*He is a strong wizard, if he is here then it was he who came over from the old world and he might have brought something else, a weapon of magic.*"

"A weapon? What kind of weapon?" Helana whispered in response to the demon's words.

"*Powerful, and dangerous! Do not underestimate him*!"

"Will he have the weapon?"

"*No, he is not allowed to use it; it is ancient, forged by the faerie! Only a chosen one can carry the blade*!"

"Then there is someone here who is likely carrying it," Helana snarled.

"*He will be after, us*," the voice echoed.

More magic flared throughout the battlefield, as demons either burst into flame, or were swept up by a wind that threw them for great distances, or even turned on each other killing themselves in the process. Helana sensed the incantations and the degrees of strength varied, so she assumed there had to be several casting including Merlin,

Malcolm, Malcolm's own student perhaps and even one other. The witch watched as her army was held fast in the riverbed, the elf infantry holding their own with their blades as the demons lacked the skill to fight. If she bore magic they would find her, but she had no choice, and she was confident her ability easily surpassed those who defied her, or dared to stop her, even Merlin.

"Vadeez! Push them in harder, I will give them skills to fight," Helana whispered, the words finding the ears of her general. "***Vox of atrum reperio qui pugna per thee, tribuo lemma solers pugno ut elf, sic mote is exsisto***" Helana cast her magic and smiled. "My flying pets," she murmured as she looked to the sky, "time to show and do my bidding."

The demons abruptly began to fight with a new zest that the elves found disturbing and now faced a foe that appeared to be as evenly matched as they were. The tide began to turn in favor of the dark army and the elves slowly began to lose ground.

"It is time to ride!" Jacinto shouted.

"Aye sir!" Riley nodded. He gave his horse a kick and began to shout orders as he galloped along the line of riders. Their fighters shouted enthusiastically and lifted their own swords, ready to move as soon as the word was given.

"In the sky," pointed Escalan, elf general of the Sand elves. "We have more to contend with!"

The demon manticore appeared out of the clouds and Ledal was already signaling his own woodland elves. Led by Elise, the woodland sky riders lifted off from their own resting place near the back of the lines, waiting for their turn to get into the fray. They rose to meet the manticore as another war in the sky was about to erupt.

Merlin watched, and waited and when Helana threw out her magic to the demons, he got a vague idea of where she might be. It was time to test that theory. He lifted his staff and took aim at the horde.

Helana sensed the magic a moment too late and it struck near, causing her guard to go up automatically. She quickly withdrew the magic to avoid detection and snorted in disgust. She was angrier at herself than at the magic thrown at her, for being so careless, and vowed it would not happen again.

Merlin smiled and looked at the others. "We have her!"

"Be sure to direct magic away from Helana! We have to keep her thinking she is in control!" Malcolm reminded Shar and Falon. He turned to Adeena who had been waiting patiently near. "You may go to Tony and Mia now, let them know we need their help."

Adeena smiled. "Thanks Malcolm. I'll tell them right away."

"Take care little one," Malcolm gave her a smile and a wink then returned his focus to the task at hand.

Adeena flew off and found the remark from Malcolm a little odd but shrugged it off. She had to get to Tony fast; there was no time to waste. The gryphon could only outlast the manticore for a period of time. Eventually the flying demons would wear down the riders.

Elise and her riders banked hard in every direction, as fast as the gryphon would allow, to offset the manticore's attack and to confuse them. The goal was simple, to keep them from finding a simple target for their spiked tails and the poison darts they hurled. It had worked to some success back at the falls so it was logical to do it once more. Then they could gang up on the creatures in their pre-assigned groups and slowly and methodically take out as many as they could.

She signaled her regiment and they were off! Her team flew in close and drew one of the manticore away from the herd. She was the bait and lured it in and then her team surrounded the beast and with precise shots from their bows attacked it until it fell from the sky. As her group turned to return to the thick of the battle, they saw the manticore doing their own gang tackle on a group of sky riders and within moments all five in the group were tumbling towards the ground, dead from the poison inflicted darts.

Elise winced at the sight, and realized this was a fight they were going to lose if they weren't able to take out a few more manticore in each attack. One at a time wasn't going to work. She signaled her team again with her arms and once more they were flying at breakneck speed into the fury.

Malcolm and Merlin approached Zach and his entourage. Zach knew what was coming and smiled nervously at both. Both had a look of absolute seriousness about them so he swallowed in a big gulp of air and waited to hear what they had to say.

"Zach, we know where she is, at least an area. You and your group will move in that direction, and when you see her, do what you have to get near her," Merlin reminded.

"We will use more magic on our end to enhance what you will do to assure her defeat," Malcolm added. He reached over and put his right hand on Zach's shoulder. "Just be your creative self and it will all work out in the end."

"Thanks for the confidence Malcolm, remind me to pour you a cup of ale when this is over with," Zach said with a light chuckle.

"Perhaps," Malcolm smiled in return. Zach thought that was a bit strange on his part to say but shrugged it off as Malcolm just being Malcolm.

"Remember, Zach must get near enough to the witch in

order to use Excalibur, give him the help, and the protection he needs," Merlin instructed one final time as he glanced at Riane.

Riane smiled and nodded, understanding fully what had to be done. "We will make sure he gets to her."

Malcolm grabbed Tasha by the arm. "My lady, I will not allow you to go on this one."

"But," Tasha started and then Malcolm gave her a stern look that even made her cringe and she decided to obey, "Very well."

"Please reconsider yourself Neil?" Malcolm looked at him next.

Neil merely shook his head. "I will not leave my friend to do this alone; I will be there with him."

"I will watch him closely," Brielle assured Malcolm.

"Indeed," Malcolm sighed. "Keep your charm around your neck. It will give some measure of safety, but be wary regardless."

"You can count on it! See you for that ale afterwards," Neil winked.

Malcolm nodded and he along with Tasha returned to their positions beside Falon and Shar. Merlin faced the group and lifted his staff, and a small white light encircled the end of it.

"Here is where the witch waits," he said. The light left the staff and went from each person touching their forehead and then moving on to the next. At the last person, Zach, it touched his forehead and then vanished.

"Good luck," Merlin said. He left them then to stand next to Malcolm and the others, and the group gathered in a circle.

Amongst the company there was Axel, Ruskin, Thatcher, Brielle, Riane, Neil, Christina, Rachel, a few other elf guards from all the races of elf and of course Zach.

"We follow Jacinto and his riders first, after that we will have a few lines of elf infantry to assist us, after that, we will be on our own," Christina said.

"Stick together, avoid getting separated or we are lost," Rachel added. "Keep Excalibur hidden until the last possible moment Zach, she will detect it if it is drawn too early."

"Got it! Let's go already before I get sick," Zach muttered.

"Send word to Jacinto," Neil pointed to an elf guard. The elf nodded and was gone to deliver the message.

Jacinto chewed on a stick, anxious to get into the melee and take out a few demonkind. He wasn't much for sitting around and when he saw the elf guard running towards him a big smile adorned his face. Finally!

"Yes?" Jacinto grunted.

"You have the word to proceed sir!" the elf stated.

"Good," Jacinto moved his horse to stand front and center of his line of men. "Ride fast, Ride hard men! Take as many with ya as ya can!" His shout echoed down the line and each man cheered sending a rousing chorus over the melee. Jacinto drew his sword and led the charge!

"Onward men! For Avalon!" he bellowed. With one kick they were off stampeding down into the fracas and as if on cue, the elf infantry stood aside to let them pass. Jacinto looked for the direction to proceed and Merlin gave him the direction, and as the words sounded in his head spoken by the mage, he changed course and his men followed. They rode full stride into the midst of the rabble!

The grey clouds hung low, almost feeling as though they were right above those fighting on the ground and for those in the air it was like flying through a consistent mist that did not give way. Tony wiped his face, removing the moisture that clung to him and began to drip into his eyes. He held on tight to the reins constructed by Mia and Adeena so that they could be secure in riding the dragons and to guide them properly.

Once Adeena had brought them their message to go airborne they were quick to get organized and with Adeena's translations they had a plan of attack in place and were off. They rode the wind and stayed in the clouds for as long as they could and when they viewed the manticore below and the gryphons trying to outrun them Tony gave Blinky a kick and the dragon dove. The rest of the herd followed and Drayler was quick to overtake and take the lead.

The remainder of the elder dragons followed Drayler and was upon the manticore before the flying demons knew what was happening. The dragons tore into the creatures, grabbing them with their claws and crushing them, and dropping them to the ground. They were quick to manuevre and the manticores were no match! Their spikes hurled by their tails had no effect since they could not penetrate the scales of the dragons. They were defenceless.

Elise smiled on seeing the dragons join the fight, and felt her spirits rise. She signaled her team and they all regrouped with the rest of the surviving sky riders to use a different tactic and draw the manticore away from their groups to make it easier for the dragons. Her hand signals were understood and they went right to work! In their own packs they moved in and about the manticore to draw them apart and the creatures took the bait. As they separated Drayler and his fellow dragons attacked, grabbing them, ripping them to shreds or crushing them. In a matter of a short time frame the manticore were nearly obliterated.

Helana watched the war in the air and was astounded to see the dragons appear and virtually decimate her flying arsenal. Her anger grew to a rage, and she could not resist but to strike back at the creatures that dare join forces with the elves and the rest. She muttered a number of phrases and lifted her hands to the sky, sending a bolt of lightening into the sky and into the nearest dragon that was within reach. The bolt slammed into the dragon's underbelly, ripping it apart, killing it instantly. The corpse dropped from the sky and collided into the ground amidst the demons. Helana howled in frustration, and sent one more bolt into the sky and then stopped, realizing she had given her exact location away to her nemesis.

"She has let her guard down," Malcolm grinned at Merlin.

"Evil always does. Anger always clouds ones thoughts," the wizard said. Merlin looked to Zach and his company and everyone nodded in response. They knew where to key in on now.

"Let's go," Neil said withdrawing his sword. "Watch yourselves everybody!"

The company started forward then, and with Jacinto and his men ripping into the enemy with zeal, and the elf ground units holding their ground solidly against the horde, they had a course to follow. Each had their weapons drawn as they neared the melee and waited nervously for the first demon to break through and strike.

Chapter Thirty Nine

Zach pulled out his own regular sword, keeping Excalibur hidden underneath his cloak and sheathed. As they ran on and got near the elf soldiers fighting with the demons and whatever else was amidst the dark army the stench was horrifying in itself and he wondered how he could keep from retching! Between the smell and his nerves he was stunned he hadn't passed out yet! The rest of the company was on edge as the battle went on around them, as the elf lines were thus far holding the enemy back!

"I hate all this sneakin! I need ta give those demons a taste of dwarf steel!" Axel growled as he held his axe ready.

He got his wish a moment later when the first demon to break through the ranks landed next to the company and lifted some sort of weapon that looked like a pole-axe and began swinging it wildly. Axel and Ruskin moved in quickly and almost pushed each other into the thing. The creature was grotesque and misshapen, standing nearly eight feet tall and looked like an imp with beady black eyes and matted fur along its back and horns protruding all over its body. As each dwarf tried to get closest to the monster an arrow slammed into its skull and it fell backward to the ground.

Axel and Ruskin looked back at their group and Rachel was holding her bow.

"What'd ya do that fer! That one was mine!" Axel shouted.

"Yers! Was mine!" Ruskin retorted.

"Next time just kill it," Rachel replied. She reloaded her bow and the group moved on again.

As they entered the throng of the battle, the space to move was less and less and Jacinto's men had hit a wall of demons that were too overwhelming. The path to Helana was suddenly blocked.

"Push on men! Push!" Jacinto shouted. A number of demons launched themselves at the giant man and grabbed the neck of his horse, pulling it down to the ground and the big man tumbled to the dirt.

"Archers! Fire in the center zone! Fire at will! Cut a path for them!" shouted Kieran. He and his archers reloaded and fired as quick as possible, and slowly the effect of the swarm of arrows took its toll on the demonkind.

"Reload! Keep it going!" Kieran ordered.

Jacinto regained his senses and quickly stood up with his sword. The nearest demon saw him stand and moved in to strike. The large man held his ground and the two fought it out with blades swinging until Jacinto brought up his free hand with another hidden blade he had withdrawn and drove it into the creature's jaw and up into its skull. It fell down, dead.

"Good one sir! Are ya needin some help?" Terry asked as he rode up.

"Keep the men movin Mister Baker. If they stand still they'll end up on the ground like me! Go on!" Jacinto ordered.

"Aye sir!" Terry nodded and galloped off shouting.

"Keep movin men! Don't stand around unless ya have to! Move! Move! Move!"

"I'm with you now," Jacinto shouted to Neil as he cut down another demon with his sword.

"Behind you!" bellowed Axel. The dwarf was off and running with Ruskin behind him. The dwarf dove right into a group of three demons moving in on Jacinto and then four more swarmed on top of the dwarf with their blades drawn and digging to get at the dwarf.

"Axel!" Ruskin hollered. He ran up with his axe swinging and cut down two demons instantly. Another group of four monsters charged and the dwarf turned to fend them off, leaving his brother to fend for himself.

Jacinto got into the scrap, but wound up getting knocked over by some sort of lizard demon that had appeared out of the thick. The two of them rolled on the ground, struggling to get the upper hand. The demon tore at his chest and his claws gouged deep, and blood soon covered Jacinto's body. The large man grabbed the thing around the neck and squeezed with all his strength and then abruptly twisted the demon's head, snapping its neck. It fell off of him and to the ground. Jacinto slowly got to his feet, using his sword to stand and looked around. The company with Neil and Zach were nowhere to be seen.

Ruskin was near, fighting for his life and Axel was still underneath a pack of demons, likely gone at this point. He let out a loud bellow and ran past several elf soldiers who were trying to reform a line and cut down a demon moving in on Ruskin. He would not let both of his friends die.

The company kept trudging on, fighting the horde as they progressed and then they could go no further. The elf lines were too thin and were falling quickly now. Jacinto's men were now scattered, trying to keep the elf lines that were still holding from collapsing any further. Axel, Ruskin and Jacinto had been there and then vanished amidst the fighting. Now, it felt like they were surrounded by a dark mass that was closing in on them.

"We have to help them," Malcolm said as he watched.

"All of you, strike at the demons around them. Do it carefully, without getting too close to the company! The witch cannot know they are there!" Merlin instructed.

"We need to do more," Shar urged.

Xanthus had joined them and was watching the war unfold. "There are no more elves to help! We are spread out as is, and they are on their own now."

Shar frowned. "Refocus the archers then. Use them more!"

"We are doing what we can, the dark army is already moving in behind us," Xanthus shook his head. "If the left and right flanks fall, then we are finished."

"Shar, I understand your concern, but do as Merlin has asked. We can do our part to get Zach to Helana," Malcolm urged calmly. "He will find a way."

Tony watched the fighting below as he and Mia, and Adeena had stayed back with the younger dragons to assist if needed. The elder dragons and the woodland sky riders together had virtually eliminated the manticore and some of the riders were already going back to the castle to rest their rides. This fight was far from over and they would still be needed. Elise rode up with her gryphon and held her ride steady alongside 'Blinky' and Tony.

"We are losing the fight below!" Elise shouted.

"I can see that, what about Zach and Neil?" he asked.

"From what I've seen they are stuck somewhere in the mess," Elise informed and shook her head. "It is not looking good."

"No! We can't let that happen! Any of your riders still up for some fighting?" he checked.

The elf captain nodded positively. "What did you have in mind?"

"Hold the line! Hold it!" Taith barked, trying to encourage his unit to stay the course and keep the demon swarm from breaking through. The right flank was feeling the pressure from the extreme numbers of Helana's army and was beginning to thin out.

Shar sent a surge of magic into the throng to aid as best she could be but for every dozen or so creatures she eliminated, they were quickly replaced by twice as many. The demons were actually overwhelming their magic. She watched helplessly as the elves fought with determination to stave off the evil.

"Archers, reload, take aim at the back of the mass, maybe we can slow them that way," Taith ordered. He lifted his bow and shot as often and as fast as his skill allowed, and the other archers did the same. Wave on wave of arrows continued to rain on the horde and still they came, unrelentless, unweilding.

Riley, Keller and Terry rode their horses as fast as they were able, cutting down demons as they galloped and doing what they could to keep the weakening elf lines from complete collapse. Still, they and the other riders were tiring, and so were their horses. A spear flew out from the mass of demons and impaled Riley's horse, and both rider and horse fell to the ground.

"Are ya all right?" Terry shouted.

Riley stood up with his sword drawn and looked around the battle surrounding them, "I'll be fine, go on and keep the men in order! I'll catch up with you later!"

"We ain't leavin ya!" Keller yelled back. He leaned over, his hand outstretched for his friend. "Get your ass on this horse!"

Before Riley could move one step forward another spear flew out from the mass and this one struck Keller in the chest and the man collapsed to the ground. Riley shouted in shock and Terry pulled out his crossbow and took a quick shot at the one demon that was moving in on them carrying several more spears. The creature stood above them, it was at least seven feet tall and had two arms on each of its sides, three were carrying the spears and covered in dark matted hair with eyes that looked like they belonged on a common honeybee.The arrow from his bow hit its target directly in the neck and the creature gagged and fell to its knees. Riley in his rage ran over and swung his sword around and cleanly cut the monster in half with all the strength he could muster. The next second he was turning and running back to his friend.

Terry was off his horse now and had picked Keller up, and tried to pull the spear out but it was lodged in too far. He shook his head as Riley ran up.

"No use, it ain't comin out," Terry said.

Riley knelt down. "You fool, you shoulda listened to me."

Keller coughed up some blood and smiled at his friend. "Never do," he coughed. "Been a good ride though! It be my time, don't let them win."

"Not as long as I live," Riley assured him. He grabbed his friends remaining hand as Keller began to shake, and then he went still and let out one last breath. Riley lowered his head in sadness, in disbelief that his friend was suddenly gone.

"We got to keep moving Riley," Terry urged.

"First we get Keller out of here, I won't leave him here!"

Riley stated. Terry nodded and both men put the man over his horse and Riley climbed up. Terry remounted his own horse and amidst the fighting weaved their way to the back of the lines where the archers were situated and gave the body over to a few elf guards who followed Riley's instructions on where to put Keller's body. A moment later both Riley and Terry were galloping back into the melee.

Tony and Mia led the younger dragons, who were more than eager to get in on some of the action, down on the fracas below with Elise and a number of gryphon riders following. They flew low and fast, with both dragon and gryphon using their talons or claws to grab a number of demons and toss them to the side. It gave the forces fighting on the ground another shot of confidence and they renewed their fight with more enthusiasm!

Tony smiled as Drayler and the elder dragons joined in and tore at the demons, sending them scattering in all directions. They wouldn't make much of a difference in making a large dent in the numbers of Helana's army, but they could confuse them and give their own defences a better chance.

Neil looked up and watched as the dragons, and woodland elf gryphon riders were doing their part to assist the ground attack after the threat from the air was extinguished. He felt they might just be able to pull this off yet. A warning shout from Brielle caused him to turn, sword raised and just in time. Neil fended off a blow from another sword, and then he saw his opponent.

"Ready to die king?" Vasillis sneered.

"Not yet you traitor," Neil shot back.

"We'll see," Vasillis retorted. He lunged at Neil and

the two clashed swords, with the elf now turning demon pushing him hard!

Brielle saw the confrontation and could nothing about it; she was preoccupied by a couple other creatures that were preventing her from getting close to Neil. She fought back and saw around her chaos within the entire company. Christina and Rachel were standing near Zach, protecting him and fighting off the monsters that were a part of Helana's army. She could not see the dwarves anywhere, and the gnome Thatcher was fighting alongside Riane against some of the undead men who would just not go down! She could sense her sister's frustration and Brielle in turn was frustrated by the demons that appeared from everywhere just when it seemed they were making some headway! She drove her sword into one of the things and then refocused her attack on the second one that stood in her way.

"Hang on Neil I'll be right there!" Brielle shouted as she engaged the other demon.

Tasha stood by Malcolm and the rest, watching helplessly at the carnage before her. Her desire to be near Neil and fight with him was pulling at her relentlessly and she saw her chance to sneak away when all of them were preoccupied trying to distract Helana. She quietly stepped back and away and found a horse just a short way off. She checked for a sword and found one strapped to the saddle along with a bow and arrows. Tasha climbed up on the horse and gave it a kick! In moments she was riding at full gallop into the battle below and Malcolm saw her too late.

"My lady!" he shouted and cursed under his breath as she vanished into the mix.

"She will fine," Shar assured him.

"I do hope you are right," Malcolm replied with a nod and weak smile.

"Hold the line! Hold the line!" Darg bellowed. He swung his sword around and decapitated one imp cleanly and moved in on another.

"There are too many!" one elf shouted back.

"You hold that line and don't you let any of them pass! We only need a little longer!" Darg answered back, hoping he was speaking the truth. The line was on the verge of collapse and soon they would be overrun. The dark army was like one giant mass that seemed to have no end and the entire defence was beginning to wane.

Tony and the remainder of the flying armada kept up a relentless pace of attacking Helana's army and the plan to confuse was working, albeit only slighty. He felt completely helpless wishing he could do more as the horde pushed on, and he could see the elves, dwarves, and humans losing ground as the gap between lines continued to narrow. Despite the strikes from Merlin and Malcolm, the power of Helana's magic was beginning to show itself. Then he saw Helana, standing by herself, surrounded by a contingent of demons who stood guard. He pulled on his reigns and guided 'Blinky' around and towards Zach and his company.

He made the dragon fly low and shouted to get Zach's attention. "Zach!" He waved frantically.

Zach heard the shouting and looked up as Tony neared on the dragon, so low he thought he might be able to reach up and touch the dragon's belly.

"That way! She is just over on that hill to your right!" Tony barked as he flew by pointing. He and his dragon flew on and up to make another pass and had to readjust their flight as an array of spears were hurled in their direction. Tony swore under his breath, it was too risky to make another pass that low. He hoped Zach had heard him.

Zach had heard him clearly and shouted to the rest. "This way, we need to go this way!" He was pointing earnestly.

Riane nodded in acknowledgement and swung her blade around to cut down another of the men resurrected by Helana. Finally, the thing lay still on the ground.

"Helana's work, they're being kept alive by magic," Thatcher coughed as he wiped the dirt from his beard. "The bloody things just don't die!"

"Aye, come on then Thatch," Riane beckoned. She started running over to get to Zach and then a shout from Neil brought her around. She saw him engaged in battle with Vasillis and would have gone to aid him except Thatcher cut her off.

"Nay lady, I'll go an'give the lad a hand! You stay with Zach!" Thatcher said and pointed to Zach. "He be needin yer help more."

Riane smiled and nodded. "Be careful," and ran off towards Zach.

"Always am," Thatcher chuckled. He was off to aid Neil and saw Brielle fighting off three demons now and had to risk aiding her before he could get to Neil. She was badly outnumbered!

Thatcher ran up on the scene and cut off one demon at its knees and the creature turned to look to see what had just happened. Thatcher whirled his blade around and the creature's head tumbled to the ground, and the body followed suit, collapsing in a heap.

Brielle nodded her thanks and kept on fighting the two that were still engaging her. More demons broke through the ranks of the elf infantry and Thatcher was soon fighting off an imp, and completely cut off from Neil now as well.

Neil swung hard and felt his blade connect with Vasilli's and still the elf did not give ground. The once trusted elf merely smiled and glared at him with his eyes now red and lunged once more at the king. Neil stepped back to defend the blow and nearly lost his balance in doing so. The elf attacked with a renewed fury when he saw him trip and Neil kept moving back to give himself some room to regroup. The elf kept pushing, his sword slamming down on Neil's and then he fell backwards onto the ground and propelled himself backwards with his legs as Vasilli's sword crashed into the ground where he had just been.

"I will enjoy this king, and then killing your queen will be even more to my liking, killing her and her unborn child!" Vasillis drove his sword down again and Neil rolled to the side to avoid the strike.

Neil lifted his sword and fended off another strike but the force of the blow sent his sword flying out of his hands. Vasillis stood there, smiling, his teeth now sharp, and razor edged. His transformation to demonkind was nearing completion. Neil got a good look at his assassin then, the skin on the elf's face beginning to peel off like a snake shedding its skin. The elf's hair was turning black and growing longer and the eyebrows turning pitch black to match the hair. Neil pushed himself backwards along the ground as the Vasillis struck again and again, each time his sword was getting closer to its target.

Brielle watched helplessly while fighting off another imp and cutting it down then two more replaced it and even Thatcher who had come to her aid had been beset by creatures of darkness and was beginning to show signs of fatigue. Both could do nothing to aid Neil, he was on his own.

The dragon's continued flying in and around the horde, with the woodland riders doing the same, taking chunks of the demons out with their clawed talons and doing their best to avoid arrows and spears launched skyward by Helana's army. Elise and her riders were beginning to drain, and she knew the dragons had to be weakening as well. A series of spears shot upward and Elise did her best to guide her gryphon through them but one spear found the wing of her ride and the creature tumbled to the ground. The gryphon was wounded but managed to land well enough to avoid a complete collision with the surface. They landed amidst the cluster of creatures and they were as shocked as Elise was to be amidst them. She had her bow up and firing arrows within seconds when the demons realized they were the enemy. The array of Helana's army closed in quickly while Elise did her best to take as many down as she could before they swarmed. Even her gryphon used its talons to tear apart a demon or two that had gotten too close.

To her shock, several of her riders landed next to her, crushing and killing the demons nearest as they did, and moments later Tony and Mia landed with their dragon rides. Tony, and Mia and the rest of the riders jumped off while the gryphons and the dragons, which had never gotten along together, formed a circle around the riders.

"Didn't want you to face them alone!" Tony shouted.

Elise wanted to cry on seeing them all, and jumped off her wounded ride, and hugged Mia. "Thank you."

"We weren't going to leave you," Mia smiled back.

"We can't stay long!" shouted one woodland rider as he lifted his bow.

"We have to stay as long as we can, we can help our lines from here, help divide the demons!" Tony said.

"They will overtake us in short order," the rider said.

"If we can't get Zach to the witch, it won't matter if we live," Tony commented. "Are we in agreement?"

Everyone nodded in unison. Tony smiled and lifted a bow. "Good, now let's take a few of them with us and give our guys on the other side of this mass some help!"

Neil rolled to the side once more and Vasilli's sword sliced into the ground. The elf lifted his blade and circled around the fallen king, trying to determine the fastest way to kill the man.

"My queen will reward me well for this! Ready to die now king?" Vasillis taunted once more. He lifted his sword for the death blow that would put an end to one half of the monarchy.

"Not yet," Neil barked back and withdrew a knife he had hidden in the side of boot and heaved it into Vasilli's knee. The elf screamed and fell to his remaining good knee.

"I will cut you into pieces for that!" Vasillis snarled. He ripped out the knife and tossed it aside. He stood once more and lifted his sword, then moved in on Neil.

Tasha galloped through the fighting around her, trying desparately to locate Neil. She rode on in the general direction she thought the company had gone and came across Jacinto and Ruskin fighting with a troll and saw Brielle fighting some kind of creature with some assistance from Thatcher and the elf in turn saw her. Riane's sister pointed frantically at something and Tasha looked to see Neil rolling to avoid a strike from Vasillis. She rode past Brielle then and without her horse even stopping, leapt from it, with her sword drawn as the traitor closed in on Neil. She ran, ignoring everything around her as the only thing she locked in on was Vasillis.

Neil looked up at the elf, now almost demon, and shook his head. "You don't have to follow her; you can fight against her with the rest of us!"

Vasillis laughed and motioned around the battlefield. "And lose like you are? I don't think so! Time is up king," Vasillis sneered and lifted his sword. Neil had no energy left to run, or crawl. The assassin had him at last.

Vasillis screamed in agony then and his sword fell to the ground. The elf whirled to see Tasha standing behind him, her sword embedded in his back. Vasillis staggered backwards and fell to one knee, gagging and spitting blood. Neil could not believe what he was seeing and was never so happy to see Tasha! He found some strength then and grabbed a sword off the battlefield and walked over to Vasillis.

The elf looked at him, with pure hatred in his eyes, and spat out some more blood at him. "Damn you all."

"Not this time Vasillis! For the traitor you are I hereby sentence you to death," Neil muttered. "You can go back to your own hell." He swung the sword around and cleanly cut Vasilli's head off. The decapitated body slowly tumbled to the ground and Neil fell to his knees, exhausted from the fight. Tasha ran up and held him up by putting her arms around him.

"I'm glad you don't listen to me," he smiled at her.

"So am I," Tasha replied. Brielle and Thatcher ran up to them and took defensive stances against any further attackers.

"Are you all right?" Thatcher checked.

Neil nodded back, "Yes, but I'm too damn tired to go any further."

"We can rest for a moment, and then we can go find Zach," Tasha said.

"Yeah," Neil puffed, "a few minutes and then we'll go.

Zach knocked down one demon with his sword and drove it through the monster's skull. For every step forward he was had to take two back to fight off more of Helana's army. He felt the tide turning in the witch's favor and knew he had little time left to find her and do what he had to do. The elf guards around him were beginning to thin and soon it might just be him and Riane to find the witch. He turned to seek her out and saw her take down an imp and then out of the mass a troll emerged and moved in on her. Zach went wide eyed and shouted a warning! He turned and ran to her aid and arrived at her side just as the troll got there.

Riane shot an arrow into the behemoth's neck and then drew on her sword. She saw Zach next to her and gave him a wink. The elf moved quickly and dodged the first strike from the troll who carried a giant flail, two large poles joined by a chain that had spikes sticking out from the one piece. The weapon slammed into the dirt, scattering debris and Zach stepped back a few steps to get a clearer view. He barely had time to step aside from the second strike as the flail swung by and just missed his head. Zach tumbled backwards and lost his sword as he did. It tumbled away from him and he quickly scrambled to his feet and ran off to avoid the third swing from the troll. Riane had encircled the creature and had leapt onto its back and drove her sword deep into the monster's back. It reached back and just got a piece of her cloak, and threw her off! Riane rolled onto the ground, coughing as the wind got knocked out of her.

The troll moved up and lifted its foot to crush her. Zach saw it and without thinking, reached back and withdrew Excalibur. He ran in and in one quick motion cut the troll's leg off as it lifted. The sliced leg fell to the ground and rolled in the dirt, the troll in the meantime howled at the top of its lungs at the pain inflicted on it. A number of elf archers ran up and unloaded arrow after arrow into the thing and soon it succumbed to the fight and fell to the ground dead.

Zach looked at Excalibur and remembered the warning from Merlin; he quickly shoved the sword back into its sheath, hoping it was not too late!

Merlin felt the sword getting drawn and whispered to himself, "No!"

Helana sensed the magic of the sword once it was free of

its sheath and she grinned wickedly. The weapon did exist, and was used foolishly! Finally, she had a key target. The one threat that could stop her! Then as quick as it was there, it vanished again, and she became infruriated. No matter, she knew how to find the sword and its bearer now! She knew the magic it bore, and the one who carried it would have the same magic within them.

Helana spoke the words of the incantation she needed in which to call on a demon she knew could find the sword bearer. A demon that lived off souls and this demon would be perfect to find the soul of the one who wielded the weapon of magic.

"***Ex depths ego dico in thee , orior oriri ortus ego scisco, reperio animus quisnam wields veneficus amidst nos totus a animus vos mos take , animus quisnam portatus is veneficus ego tribuo ut thee , teneo veneficus , peto is sicco , attero somes , permissum is non ago quod animus est vestri , sic mote is be'***

The words of the spell she repeated again, "*Out of the depths i call on thee, rise i ask, find the soul who wields magic amidst us all, a soul you will take, the soul who carries this magic i give to thee, know the magic, seek it out, destroy the body, let it not live and the soul is yours, so mote it be'*

A crack in the earth opened and a shadow filtered upward, slowly taking shape amidst the dark mist. A cloaked wraith formed, ink black in color and its shape hidden beneath it as it floated above the ground. The crack sealed and Helana faced the demon. The demon shifted in and out, appearing and disappearing for a moment at a time. It did not show itself but stayed within the cloak and black mist that encircled it.

"This is the soul you seek," Helana whispered and lifted her hand towards it. The creature reached out and touched her fingertips. A brief flash of blue light and then the demon nodded that it understood.

"Kill this person and its soul is yours to keep as promised," Helana stated.

A whispered voice barely audible replied, "It shall be done."

"Go," Helana ordered. The wraith vanished for a moment and then reappeared as it began its search amidst the carnage for the soul it was instructed to find. Slowly it slithered its way over the ground, smelling, looking for the bearer of Excalibur.

Merlin thought it was an error on his part at first. He sensed a casting of magic and thought it was merely more of the same by the witch but then the dark magic formed completely, he looked up at the war below and muttered words he thought he would ever say out loud.

"A Bodach."

Chapter Forty

The demon hunting Zach stayed low to the ground, sniffing, seeking out the magic his soul would have in order to wield the sword Excalibur. It would not stop until it had found the soul it wanted, and the body that contained it was dead. The Bodach vanished at times for a few seconds then it would reappear again in a different location as it hunted, yearning to taste the soul of its victim.

"A Bodach?" Malcolm asked, checking to see if he was hearing Merlin correctly.

"Yes, A Bodach, it will not stop until it has killed the one it wants and I believe it is hunting Zach," Merlin replied. The wizard was concerned now; there was no stopping a Bodach by magic alone.

"We use our magic on it, the amulets," Shar suggested.

"No, it is not of our world. It is a different demon. This one is not corporal; it is of the spirit world, like a ghost. Magic will not work on it," Merlin replied.

"Then what do we do?" Shar asked, beginning to panic. "How do you know it's after Zach?"

"He took Excalibur out of its sheath! She will know of

its existence now!" Merlin snapped. He was as scared as she was. He was at a loss as to what to do.

"It will be after the one who carries the sword," Malcolm said. "He has to be warned, he might be able to fight it off with Excalibur."

"Good, very good Malcolm, he might just be able to do that," Merlin said. He patted Malcolm on the shoulder and looked at Shar. "My lady, sorry for my rather abrupt reply, but I am as concerned as you are."

Shar waved him off. "Is there anything else we can do?"

"You and Falon keep doing what you are doing, help the others as best you can, we need more time for Zach to get to the witch," Merlin instructed.

"Gladly sir," Falon nodded. She and Shar both went back to casting magic into the horde with more zest, not caring if the witch knew what was going on or not. They had to buy their forces more time.

Merlin faced the battleground, and quietly spoke words that floated over the wind, and on towards Zach and Riane. They found Riane's ears first and the elf stopped to listen.

"There is another demon coming towards you, a Bodach, it is a spirit looking for the soul of the one who carries Excalibur! Use the sword on it if you have to. Our magic cannot be used against it! Watch for it carefully, it will phase in and out, and will be hunting near the ground!"

Zach heard it then and looked at Riane. "A what?"

"A Bodach. It is looking for you because you used Excalibur! Helana knows it exists now," Riane said.

"How am I supposed to kill something that comes and goes?" he asked.

Riane shook her head, not having an answer to that question. "We will have to try with Excalibur."

"Fine," Zach muttered. He withdrew Excalibur

and looked around the battle. "You want it? Come and get it then!" he shouted out the challenge as he held the sword high.

Helana felt the magic again, and for an instant felt fear. More so the demon side of her, than what was left of her humanity. Then the fear subsided as she watched her army begin to crush those who dared stand against her. The forces of elf dwarf, human, gnome and others were beginning to get pushed back and soon her soul hunter would be rid of the one weapon that could kill her and it would all end shortly thereafter. Helana began to think about whom she would destroy first. Malcolm? Xanthus? Or kill them all at once? Perhaps she would begin with the new monarchy and finally finish with the last daughter of a king she had despised ever since she was a child. A memory flashed into her mind of a time when Tasha's father had forbade Tasha from playing with her as a small girl. The words he had spoken still burned to this very day 'we do not play with peasants'. Ever since that day she had wanted nothing but to destroy that family. Now she would finally finish a task she had started over a year and a half ago.

Riane grabbed Zach's arm and he lowered the sword. "Put it away, don't pull it out until you need to," she warned.

"I guess," he replied. He shoved the sword back into its sheath and both waited, and watched for any sign of this Bodach creature.

"Stay alert!" Christina shouted as she cut down another creature. Then an arrow struck her in the chest, and then another. The elf guard fell backwards and Rachel caught her.

"No!" Rachel shouted. She held her friend up and tried to get the arrows out of her.

"Watch Zach, keep him safe," Christina urged. She screamed as the pain surged through her.

"They aren't in too badly, you are going to live," Rachel said with encouragement as she yanked out one arrow and then the other.

"It hurts," Christina gasped, trying to stay alert.

"Get her out of here!" Riane ordered.

"We will not leave you!" Rachel countered. "We are sworn to protect Zach!"

"I will protect him," Riane kneeled down. "Take her to get some help, or she will die from her wounds. Go, I will protect Zach."

Rachel nodded and with the help of a couple other elf guards they carried Christina off the field of battle. Riane, Zach and a few other elf guards are all who remained of the initial company. Everyone was now scattered throughout and they had no idea who was still alive or who was dead. Riane watched the melee, looking for any signs of the Bodach that hunted Zach. Then she saw it, only for a moment, but she saw it. She looked over at Zach and he showed no indication that he had seen what she had. Riane moved in close to Zach to stand right next to him.

Ruskin cut down two more imp like creatures and paused to catch his breath. Jacinto finished off the horned monster he had been fighting with and the two stood together watching all the fighting around them. They could tell they were starting to lose the fight and both shook their heads in recognition of the fact. The pile of demons that had jumped on Axel was still there, and finally the two of them ran over to get rid of the lot. To their surprise the creatures were pushed upward and an axe blade came about cutting the group cleanly and efficiently. All of the demons collapsed to the ground in a heap, and there stood Axel, bloodied and battered, but still alive, with a stupid grin on his face.

"Brother! You are still alive!" Ruskin bellowed in joy.

"Aye, I am! Take more than a mess o'demons ta kill me off," Axel spat out some blood and pulled a knife from his shoulder.

Jacinto laughed as he rubbed the little man on the head. "You are one stubborn dwarf!"

"Never ya mind, where be Zach? We're gettin a bit beat up out here! We gotta get'em to th'witch!" Axel said, wincing as he began to wrap the wound from the knife.

"Back this way, I think," Jacinto shouted. The trio ran on to find their friend amidst the rabble and to lend a hand if needed.

Riane watched and then saw the Bodach again, this time much closer. It was on Zach's trail now and the creature paused to assure itself of where it had to go. Then it was gone again, and Riane watched closely, noticing the dirt would move aside as the demon shuffled along in its hunt. She knew where it would come out next. The elf looked at Zach for a moment and then made a decision. Riane reached under Zach's cloak and pulled out Excalibur. She ran away from him, holding the blade in front of her as she approached the Bodach.

Zach felt the sword get lifted off his back and he turned to see Riane running away form him. "Riane! What are you doing?" He started after her and then he saw the Bodach appear.

The soul stealing spirit appeared in front of Riane; floating high above her and the elf looked up at the demon and did not waver before it. "Here I am! I am the bearer of the sword Excalibur! I am the one you want!"

The Bodach stared at her, as though thinking, and then in a flash its black cloak wrapped around the elf and lifted her high up off the ground! The elf was twisted around by the cloak and the spirit's magic and felt every bone in her body getting crushed by the demon. She screamed from the agony and she let go of Excalibur as the bones in her arms and hands shattered and was unable to hold the blade any longer. It fell to the ground as the Bodach continued to do as it was told, kill the bearer of the sword. Riane was tossed around in the air by the cloak and mist that encircled it and she screamed from all of the pain inflicted on her. The Bodach wrapped her completely within the cloak, and she vanished from sight.

Zach was so stunned with the events unfolding before him it wasn't until she vanished that he ran as fast as he could to help her, but he knew it was already too late. He picked up Excalibur and looked up at the Bodach.

"Let her go!" he shouted. The Bodach looked down at him and then the cloak opened and Riane fell to the ground in a heap, and still within the foldings of the cloak Zach could see a shadow of Riane. It was her spirit, her soul, gone from her body and taken by the Bodach.

"Noooo!" Zach screamed in horror and threw Excalibur with all his might. The sword flew through the air and struck the demon full center within the cloak. The demon lurched and howled in anguish! A howl that caused everything to stop and listen!

The spirit of Riane was tossed away from the cloak and Zach watched as the soul of Riane came down and paused by her body, but did nothing more. The spirit looked at him, smiled and blew him a kiss and then vanished, and he heard the words 'thank you' echo in his ears as it disappeared. He looked up at the Bodach and watched as the demon fell to the ground, the cloak falling off of it, exposing a skeletal old man, which slowly deteriorated into dust before him. The Bodach was dead as the cloak vanished with the mist that had harbored it. Excalibur lay on the ground but Zach ignored it. He ran to Riane and ever so carefully lifted her in his arms as he sat next to her.

Tears were welling up in his eyes as he held her. To his shock, she opened her eyes and ever so weakly, smiled at him. She winced, and tears flowed freely as she could not bear the pain that shot through her entire body. Zach could feel something was wrong, her body was twisted and bloodied and seemed to be soft all over. He could feel the bones in her arms were shattered and who knows what else the demon had done to her.

"I wish I could do something to ease your pain," he whispered, barely able to talk as he cried.

"There is! Do as I say," she gasped.

"What?"

"Repeat after me," Riane wheezed.

"Okay," Zach nodded.

"Hold my hand," she urged. Zach took her hand, and felt no bones within it. "***take poena ego sentio quod peniculus is absentis , sentio haud magis tamen tripudium , quod tribuo meus substantia ut unus iacio me , vivo porro quod solvo , sic mote is exsist.***"

Zach repeated the words with her, to his surprise; he found no difficulty in saying them. As they finished the phrase, a blue light formed around their hands and moved on to his. He stared and watched as it faded on his hand and he thought about what she had made him do, the words translating in his mind. "Take the pain i feel and brush it away, feel no more but joy, and give my essence to one casting with me, to live long and free, so mote it be."

"What did we just do?" he asked.

Riane smiled, "taken my pain away and I give to you a gift from me. Be well Zach, my love."

Zach cradled her close and let the tears flow. "I love you Riane, my love."

Riane let out one last breath and Zach felt her body go limp within his arms. He cried, not caring who saw, or what was going on around him. A part of him just felt like it had been torn away, ripped from his body, leaving a big empty void that could never be filled again. There was so much ache in his chest that he felt he could not breathe, that everything was a big blur all around. There was nothing he wanted now but to see Riane recover and walk back to Cambridge with him but he knew that would never happen, ever again. He sat there, with her in his arms as Jacinto, and the dwarves walked up, and Neil with Tasha appeared along with Brielle, who saw Riane in Zach's arms and fell to her knees at the sight.

"Riane?" Brielle whispered. "Riane?"

Zach looked up at them all, and shook his head, tears clouding his view. "She's gone."

Brielle looked at him in shock, "No, no, it, it can't be, she's my big sister, and she can't be gone."

Neil knelt next to Zach. "What do we do now?"

Zach shook his head, refusing to let go of Riane. "I don't care."

Brielle was now sitting on the ground, crying with her head in her hands. Around them the fighting continued, the surviving elf guards doing their best to keep the horde at bay but they were closing in quickly.

"Then Helana has won," Neil muttered. "We retreat back to Cambridge; maybe we can hold them there."

Tasha nodded. "Yes, that is the best option."

Zach looked down at Riane, his heart was shattered, and

the pain was overwhelming. He ran his hand over her cheek and then looked back up at the group. "No, we go on."

"Are ya daft? We can't get through this?" Axel snorted.

Jacinto snorted in reply, "Aye, I'm with Zach. We go on!" Jacinto looked around the battleground and saw who he wanted. He waved over Riley and Terry and both men galloped over to see their leader.

"Gather the men; we make a run at'em, now!" Jacinto ordered.

"Aye sir, consider it done," Riley bowed.

"Mister Baker, get the lads with the spears up front and center, we'll use them to cut our way through now! One good push ought ta do it!" Jacinto barked.

"Yes sir!" Baker saluted. Both he and Riley kicked their horses on and they began to rally the last of their men to make one last rush on Helana.

"Any word on Tony?" Neil asked.

"Nothing for a bit now. They're out there somewhere though," Thatcher said.

Zach looked at Brielle, "Can you take care of your sister, until I get back?"

Brielle moved over to sit next to Zach and took over holding her. "I will keep her safe until you return, I promise."

"I know you will," Zach smiled. He leaned in and gave her a kiss on the cheek. Zach stood up, the anger within him swelling. He sought out Excalibur and found it where he had left it on the ground. Zach grabbed it and held it high.

Helana felt the magic of Excalibur surge again, and she thought it odd that the weapon was still possessed of its magic. Maybe the Bodach had failed? Could that be possible? The witch shouted orders at her guard and looked at Vadeez.

"Make the final push on the elves; crush them once and for all!"

"Yes my queen," Vadeez bowed and disappeared into the horde.

Zach looked at the group, his face covered in dirt and tear stained, the streaks leaving trails on the dust that stuck to his cheeks. Now he was more determined than ever to put a stop to all of this, the loss of Riane was too much to bear and he used that grief to fuel his anger.

"Axel, Ruskin, Jacinto, get those elf guards in front and have them kill everything in the way. We don't stop until we get to that witch. Once we get to her, deal with anything that she has as protection. I'll take care of her."

Neil smiled, "Gladly my friend. Let's go finish her off!"

"You, you five, stay with Brielle and watch over her! Nothing gets by you, understand?" Zach shouted.

The elf guard acknowledged their orders with a bow and formed a circle around Brielle and the fallen Riane. They stood ready, waiting for anything to dare try and get by them.

Riley and Baker rode up leading a group of fellow riders. They were a small group, but would suffice for what they needed. They formed a line on Riley's orders and waited for the order to ride.

Jacinto looked at Zach and he looked down at Excalibur. "Tell them to ride, and ride hard."

"Ride men! Onward!" Jacinto bellowed. Riley took the lead with Baker at his side and the group of riders charged on, yelling as they rode, spears drawn to deal with the demons that stood in their way. They thundered on, pushing aside all the creatures that got in their path until they hit the thick of the pack. They drove into the rabble with spears drawn and shoved the monsters back in one enormous push. The elf guard moved in behind to work on the remainder! Another group of dwarves ran in to lend a hand and soon there was a path cut through the thick of the mass as swords and axes spared nothing that got in their way!

Zach drew his cloak in tight and sheathed Excalibur. He pulled the hood of his cloak over his head and motioned for the group to move forward. Zach grabbed a sword off the dirt and moved to follow the group in the back. He had to be unseen and by trailing behind would give him the best shot at Helana.

The group moved forward carefully into the midst of the attack and fended off anything that got close. Riley and Baker along with the riders dismounted and drew their swords to take care of the fighting on the ground. Then Zach saw the witch, Helana, standing there, looking out over the fighting.

He came in next to Neil, and pointed. "There she is, do anything you can to distract her, I only need a second," Zach said.

"We'll take care of it. You just do what you need to!" Neil replied with a nod. He motioned for everyone to pick a spot and the group moved in on the demons that surrounded Helana. As a whole they engaged the protectors and made every effort to keep them occupied.

Merlin watched and waited, and knew their time was near its end. The witch had nearly decimated the right and left flanks, and there was no one to take the place of the fallen. They were now beginning to retreat and both flanks were nearly closed in on one another. He had detected Excalibur and then it was gone again. He was curious to know what was going on out there! There had been no word on anything that was transpiring on the battleground and for all he knew, the company could have failed! Still, he kept faith in Zach, and hoped that the man could fulfill the job he had to do.

"Keep up your magic! Just a little longer!" He shouted in encouragement and lashed out at the dark army with a bolt of lightening, taking a line of demons out in the process.

Tony, Mia and Elise fought hard with the other riders and with the gryphons and dragons doing their best to keep the enemy at bay, they were managing to hold on, but Tony did not know for how much longer! Even the dragons were showing fatigue! Demons were able to launch themselves onto the dragons and claw at them vivaciously until the dragons were able to shake them off. It wasn't looking good.

Zach stayed back, waiting for the moment to rush the witch, his grief for losing Riane welling up inside more and more each second he stood there. He would make her pay for what she had done! Then Jacinto cut down a demon and in a quick thought heaved his sword at the witch! Helana turned and caught the blade with ease and it turned to dust in her hands. There, there was his opening! Zach bolted forward and shoved an elf to the side so he could get around him and continued on, waiting for the last possible moment to withdraw Excalibur! Helana had her back turned to him and was completely unaware of the threat as Zach moved in closer and she turned around just as Zach was a mere few steps away from her. She stared at this man who was running at her and she started to laugh. Zach reached behind himself as he threw his cloak back and withdrew Excalibur!

Helana sensed the magic immediately and thought it impossible! Before she could bring her hands up to stop Zach he thrust the sword forward and drove it into the midsection of the witch. Helana screamed as the pain was unbelievably unbearable! She looked up at Zach and he stared back at her, and she saw the determination in his eyes. This man was the true bearer of this weapon and her Bodach demon had failed her. Then Zach began to speak words, words she recognized, and her demon entity within her also recognized the words.

"***All olle est malum shall die, all olle est opacus ero brought in liburnica.***" Zach did not pause and continued with the next phrase.

"S***icuti hic blade est purus of heart, tam shall thee imus ad it."*** And then the last phrase, ***"Malum testamentum non imus atquin imus cata Excalibur's will, tam it must ero."***

Merlin detected the magic immediately and beckoned to the rest. "Zach has invoked the magic! He has found Helana! Quickly, beside me!"

The three of them, without Xanthus, moved in next to the wizard and all four vanished in a flash. They reappeared moments later and Merlin put his hands on Zach. He looked at Merlin and wondered what he was doing there? Merlin merely gave Zach a small smile and then placed his right hand on the witch's shoulder. In a flash Merlin was speaking another series of words and Malcolm was repeating them as he moved to grab Excalibur's handle, his hands holding Zach's to the handle. Zach glanced at Malcolm with a question burning in his mind, '*what are you doing*?' To Zach's amazement, Malcolm answered him in his thoughts.

'*Do not fear what we are doing Zach, this is to assure that Helana's time will come to an end.*'

Helana looked at all of them, fear evident in her eyes as she felt her life beginning to leave her and the demon inside screaming to be set free but she knew that it was dying too. As Merlin and Malcolm spoke the incantation Helana realized what they were doing and grabbed the sword's blade to try and remove it, but to no avail, Zach held firm and stared at her, with hatred and revenge glaring back at the witch. The magic of Merlin spread from his hand onto the witch, down the blade of Excalibur and onto Malcolm. All three gleamed in a white pulsating light and Helana let out a shriek that cascaded over the countryside! Every demon, every fighter stopped and listened.

The white vibrating light leapt onto Shar and encased her. The mage felt strange warmth all over, and Malcolm's voice whispered in her mind, easing her anxiety as to what was happening.

'*We are putting an end to Helana forever Shar, you have been my brightest and sharpest student ever, and going forward I know you will exceed even your own expectations! Be ever aware of what goes on around you, and never fail to listen, it will take you further than you may imagine, I entrust to you the amulets their keeper and guardian, be well Shar!*"

Merlin finalized the magic, "***Unus animus pro alius , bonus quod nocens vitualamen una ut terminus una sic is ero ut decretum me".*** Zach heard the words and understood its meaning and turned to look at Malcolm just as the wizard began to fade. "*One soul for another, good and bad sacrificed together to end together so it will be as decreed by me.*" Malcolm gave Zach a wink and nodded and then was gone within the light that pulsated around them. Then the magic ended.

The white light dissipated and Helana let out another shriek as her body convulsed uncontrollably. Zach held steady, keeping Excalibur embedded in her, not letting go until he was sure the witch was dead. Helana threw her head back and a dark image began to pull away from her body and form next to her. The demon Valgor whom she had merged with was ripping itself free of the woman, and as it did, Merlin moved to stand with his staff ready.

Valgor took shape, collapsing to its knees as it did, and looked up at Merlin. The demon sneered, even though it was dying, not wanting to give the wizard the satisfaction of seeing him defeated.

"There will be another to replace me," Valgor spat.

"As always Valgor, I would expect no less from your kind," Merlin retorted. "You escaped once, but not this time." He held his staff out and a string of currents shot out, slicing through the demon, burning it to ash. Valgor was dead.

Helana now in her full human form fell to her knees as she grasped the blade of Excalibur. Zach knelt with her, holding the sword steady. Blood dripped from the sides of her mouth, her life near its end. Helana looked to Merlin, and acknowledged the man with a bow. Merlin shook his head in disgust and drew his cloak in close and waited.

"You," she coughed, "it has been an honor, and I," she spat out a mouthful of blood, "was a fool to my ambitions."

"At least you have learned something then," Merlin sighed. "Perhaps you will find peace in death."

"Perhaps," Helana replied. She coughed uncontrollably and the blood ran from her mouth. As her life faded Helana stared up at Zach and smiled. "Well done, Zach."

"How do you know who I am?" Zach asked while his teeth gritted in anger.

"Enjoy the gift from the elf," Helana coughed and then let out her last gasp and fell over onto Zach, dead. Zach pushed her up and the lifeless body slid off the blade and tumbled to the ground. Helana was finished, forever.

All over the battlefield, as Helana died, the demons she had called forth began to burst into flame. Everyone moved away from the creatures as the earth opened up and the darkness began to pull the burning demonkind back down into the void from whence they had come. The monsters fought back against the darkness but each failed as one by one they were swallowed up by the ground and the dirt closed over top leaving no sign they had ever been there in the first place. The surviving trolls dropped their weapons and sat down where they were, offering no resistance. Elf guards took control and ever so slowly began to herd the trolls together. The men resurrected by Helana began to dissolve, and crumbled to the ground in heaps of ash, dead once more. Piece by piece those that were any part of the dark army, were taken into custody by the elves. With the demons gone there was only a small portion to bring under submission. The war was over!

Neil ran up and helped Zach stand. "You okay?"

Zach nodded and handed the sword to Neil. "Hold this."

Merlin said nothing, but watched as Zach turned and slowly walked down the hill. No one got in his way as he wandered back over to Brielle who was carefully holding Riane in her arms. She looked up at Zach and he smiled at her and then knelt down.

Tony, Mia and Elise ran over then and saw the scene unfold. Tony shook his head in sadness on seeing the fallen Riane. Mia began to cry and put her arms around Tony and he held her close. Elise walked over and helped Brielle stand, and did her best to try and comfort her fellow elf, and cousin. Shar saw for the first time her friend, that Riane was gone, and had to turn away as she felt the tears begin.

Zach carefully held Riane in his arms as he stood and the tears began once more. He began to walk back towards Cambridge, oblivious to everything around him. The only thing he wanted to do was take her home.

Shar looked around then, wondering where Malcolm had gone. In her left hand she realized she held the staff that contained the amulets and her curiousity was getting the best of her now. Malcolm's words were still echoing in her mind. She went over to Merlin and the wizard looked at her, knowing she was full of questions.

"Where is Malcolm?" she asked.

"He has moved on Shar, that staff belongs to you now," Merlin answered quietly. "It was his choice and his way to assure Helana's defeat."

"He, he's, gone?" Shar spoke the words, finding it extremely difficult to say them. Malcolm couldn't be gone!

"Yes, he has left you in charge as guardian now," Merlin smiled. He patted her on the shoulder. "Understand he would not have done this if he did not think you were ready."

"But I'm not!" Shar replied, tears welling up in her eyes. She was just absorbing the thought of losing Riane, but Malcolm to. It was just too much! Shar staggered in circles and Falon rushed over to help her stand. Shar began to cry and Falon looked to Merlin.

"Take her to the castle, help her to her room and keep her company," Merlin suggested. Falon spoke the words and both she and Shar vanished in a flash.

"We won, but the price," Neil faltered, trying to keep his own composure. "The price was too high."

"Yes, indeed," Merlin sighed and lowered his head in sadness. They had paid dearly.

Axel, Ruskin, Thatcher with Jacinto lending a hand, shouted at everyone to stand aside and to let Zach pass. The four kept the pathway clear as Zach ever so carefully walked back towards Cambridge over the battleground with Riane in his arms. Elf soldiers from all the races bowed as he passed, but Zach did not see them, only Riane mattered and getting her home was all that counted. Brielle and the others trailed behind, as the walk was quiet and full of grief for all that had fallen this day. As Zach made his way over the field, Xanthus, Riane's father walked down to meet him.

The elf king stopped in front of Zach and he looked up at the king. Xanthus had tears streaming down his face as he brushed the cheek of his daughter. Brielle ran up to her father, Xanthus and she hugged her tightly while they cried for the sister, the daughter they had lost.

"May I take her home sir," Zach forced the words out as he tried to speak clearly in his grief.

Xanthus smiled. "Yes, you may."

"Thank you," Zach managed to smile his appreciation.

With his friends leading the way Zach wound his way over the landscape until he arrived at Cambridge castle some time later. Adeena, Oberon and the faerie kind greeted them and on hearing the news, expressed their condolences with great sadness on the losses. Zach found his way up to Riane's room and Tasha opened the door for him. He walked in and turned back to his friends.

"I'll be okay, I will see you later," Zach murmured.

"If you need us just shout," Tony said.

"We'll be near," Neil added.

"Sure," Zach smiled back faintly. Tasha closed the door and then gave Neil a hug as she began to cry.

"Let's go get some rest," Neil said, trying to comfort her. "See you all later."

"Yes," Tony nodded. The group broke off and went their separate ways, some to their rooms, others to the catwalk to take in the air and to put the day to rest. Ever so slowly the forces began to arrive back to their camps outside Cambridge, to rest and begin the process of healing.

Zach laid Riane down on her bed, and had sat down

next to the bed to be alongside her. She lay there quietly, in peace and Zach thought of all they had been through since he had arrived on this world and everything they had done back on his world. He wished they could have done more together and the thought that she was gone, finally struck home. Zach put his head in his hands and wept.

Chapter Forty One

Two days after the battle against Helana, the funeral was held for Riane and for the wizard Malcolm. Both were to be enshrined at the elves mausoleum that was located in the mountains to the north of Cambridge castle. There was to be a funeral procession with a contigent of elf soldiers carrying the body of Riane, wrapped in cloth and in her casket at the front of the line. Malcolm's casket was to be pulled behind her in a wagon and those entrusted with his safe keeping on the walk to the mountains was none other than Tony, Mia, Jacinto, Axel and Ruskin, Thatcher and a few select Elf captains that included Elise, and Kieran. Walking behind the two groups would be the king of the elves, Xanthus, his daughter Brielle with Neil, Tasha, Zach and Shar. Oberon and the fairie Adeena along with the other elf generals would be in the next cluster and then anyone else who wished to partake in the procession would follow.

Shar was having a difficult time accepting that both her friend Riane and her teacher Malcolm were gone. The thought of having the guardianship of Avalon thrust upon her without notice was overwhelming and her fear of being unable to do such a task weighed on her mind every waking moment. It was a visit from Merlin on the night before the funeral that helped ease her anxiety, albeit only slightly.

"May I come in?" Merlin inquired as he stood at her door.

"Of course sir, have a seat," Shar replied pointing to a chair that stood across from her as she sat at her room's window.

"You look deep in thought," Merlin observed as he took his seat in the chair.

"A lot on my mind. May I ask, why did Malcolm not talk to me about what he was going to do?" Shar was curious, and wanted some answers to her questions.

"You know him better than I," Merlin sat back. "If I were to wager a guess, I would say he knew you were capable of assuming his role and thought it best that you not know. Tell me Shar, if you discovered he was about to sacrifice his life to assure the witch's demise, would you have done anything to stop him?"

"I would have probably done something, it is in my nature," Shar sighed. "Still, it is unfair of him to ask this of me. I am not ready for this responsibility."

"My lady," Merlin smiled, "none of us are ever ready to take on such drastic changes to our lives. In a lot of circumstances we never plan how our lives will unfold, that is what makes life so unique. There are many turns in a road, many paths we may take but it is how we react to these changes that make us who we are. Even I have had many surprises, and will likely still face a surprise or two before my time comes to an end."

"I am not sure I can do this," Shar repeated her fears. She looked at the staff that had been Malcolm's and the wizard followed her gaze.

Merlin leaned over and took the staff with the amulets in his grasp. "I remember giving this to Schredrick long long ago, and he was just a young man at the time, perhaps even younger than you are and he to questioned his ability to take charge of such a task. Especially leading the races on to a new world where no one had a place to call home. He adapted, and so will you Shar. I can feel the magic flow through you and I can tell you that your skills surpass Malcolm's, and his. You have a very strong gift that even you do not know of what you are capable. Malcolm knew this, and thought you were the one person who could be guardian. You my lady, will do well, and I will be here on occasion to help you in the transition. There will times you will need my guidance and I promise I will be here to help."

"There are more changes coming?" she asked curiously.

"Oh my yes! If there is one constant in magic, it is that there is always change."

"Thank you Merlin. I'm sure I'll need your help at some point," Shar gave him a small smile of appreciation.

"I will be here when you need me most," he assured her. "Now, how about some tea to refresh ourselves and we can talk of other things?"

"I would like that," Shar said.

Merlin put the amulet staff aside and went about making some tea for them. He found what he needed on the small table against the far wall and in no time had a fresh pot brewed. After he had poured them each a cup, they sat by the window and talked about the world of Avalon, and the races that called it home.

Zach had kept to himself in the days leading up to the funeral, having food brought up to his room when needed and only allowed Neil and Tony to visit. Their drop-ins were usually very short, and the conversation was almost non exsistant. Both friends did what they could to try and ease the pain he was going through but Zach felt more at peace when he was alone. He appreciated their concern but this was something he had to deal with and the only way he knew how was to stay away from everyone. Zach had never experienced this kind of loss, ever. He had lost a grandmother when he was just a teenager but that was nothing compared to this. The emptiness inside his chest was unbearable and though he had food brought up, he barely ate. On the day of the funeral he had dressed and thrown on his cloak, but remained in a daze even as Neil and Tony came knocking at his door.

"Are you ready Zach?" Neil checked.

"I'm good, let's go," Zach motioned for them to lead on.

"I understand we walk quite the ways up to the mountains, past the lake," Tony said, trying to make conversation.

"Yeah," Zach nodded, "Riane had said it was a sacred area, but I had no idea it was there," he tried but couldn't get the words out.

"We get what your saying Zach. Its okay," Neil assured him. He gave Zach a pat on the back and Zach nodded.

The procession began at Cambridge Castle and once it began, every elf that had journeyed to fight Helana had stayed for the funeral and followed behind. Zach had no idea how long the walk was, and when he looked around on occasion he saw Shar had the same expressionless face as his own. She looked at him once and smiled. She knew what he was going through and in turn he understood what she was feeling. They marched on, quietly, as no one said a word while they walked. They passed by Vanier Lake, and then more fields and slowly the trees began to establish themselves. When the mountains came into view Shar took his hand in hers and together they followed behind Neil and Tasha as they came upon the doors to elf mausoleum.

The doors were enormous, reaching nearly twenty or so feet in the height and it took a large number of the elf guard to draw them open. Malcolm's casket was removed from the wagon and carried by the chosen pallbearers. The procession then moved inside and was greeted by an even vaster hall that had been carved out of the mountain. The roof of the mausoleum was rounded out, and the grey stone smooth as though polished. A number of great columns were located in key locations to keep the hall intact and hold the mountain from collapsing in. The floor was a smooth white stone, which shone as the torches inside were lit one by one. Riane's casket was placed next to another that rested near the back wall. Malcolm's was taken over to a location left of Riane and placed down beside another. Merlin moved to stand at the center of the hall and looked at everyone there. The hall was full to capacity and he bowed to all. Xanthus had asked him to lead the proceedings due to his own loss and thought he would be unable to carry it out. Merlin had accepted and was honored by the request.

"We are here this day to pay homage to those we care dearly about. I am honored to be here amongst you all and it is with great sadness that we gather here today. Two who have done so much, and in turn to whom we owe a great debt, will be remembered for their sacrifices. Riane, daughter, sister, and captain will always be in our hearts, in our memories as she leaves us far too soon. Malcolm, guardian, teacher and friend will never be forgotten and will, like Riane, be in our thoughts forever. Two souls, who have moved on, in peace, have come to their final resting place and here they will stay in serenity and solitude. We will remember them both, always and forever."

Merlin bowed to the gathering and then both Xanthus

and Brielle came forward. The elf king placed a rose on his daughters wrapped body and Brielle placed her sister's sword next to her. Xanthus walked over to Kieran then and took from him, a crossbow. He went over to Zach and held the bow up. Zach looked at him, somewhat stunned, and the elf king put his mind at ease.

"She would want you to have this honor Zach."

"Thank you sir," Zach replied. He took the crossbow and walked over to Riane. He stood there for a moment, looking down at her and his tears slid down his face and tumbled onto her. Ever so carefully he placed the crossbow on her arms and leaned in close to her.

"Sleep well my love, I will never forget you." He began to sob and tried to regain his composure but could not. Neil and Tony both ran up to him and lended their assistance in helping him stand and slowly they made their way back to the rest. Shar gave him a hug and together they cried. Neil and Tony took one of Malcolm's cloaks and favorite texts and placed them in his casket.

A plaque was carried over to Riane's resting place first and placed on the pillar that stood at the foot of her grave. Then a second plaque was taken over to Malcolm's grave and put on the pillar in front of his resting place. Merlin walked over to each one, first Riane's, then Malcolm's and engraved words on each with his magic.

"A Life gone too soon, a life always remembered, their next journey begins and may they find peace wherever it is the road may lead them"

Merlin faced the crowd once more. "Thank you all for coming. In closing, I would just like to say something I had an old acquaintance say to me once, 'death, the last sleep? No, it is the final awakening'. I have come to understand what Walter meant by that comment as the years have passed by and I believe it is so true for each of our loved ones who have left us far too soon. Remember to cherish each day, each moment, and each breath you take as we travel down life's road. Thank you once again for sharing this day and to all, have a safe journey home."

Everyone slowly exited the hall and once it was empty, the elf guard began to close the doors. When they shut and the sound of the stone grating on stone came to an end, Zach stared at the mountain for a few moments and then turned away; the pain of it all was too much to bear. On the trek back to Cambridge no one said anything, the mood was somber and no one really felt like talking. The night was quiet too, as those camped around Cambridge were not in a mood for a lot of celebrating their victory over the witch just yet.

Neil joined Tasha on the catwalk and together they both stared out over the grounds below. The faerie were seen off on the one side doing some sort of dance thing with Oberon's laughter breaking the silence. At least some were in a better frame of mind.

"So, why didn't you tell me you were pregnant?" Neil asked. He had been putting off the question for some time but he could not wait any longer.

Tasha looked at him, "Excuse me?"

"I know you're expecting," Neil smiled. "Vasillis said so when we were fighting."

"Well, I was hoping to find the right time to tell you but that just never seemed to happen."

Neil took her hand in his, "You risked a lot more by not telling me."

"I knew you wouldn't let me leave Cambridge if you knew, and I was not going to let you go off alone," Tasha said, defending her silence.

"Likely, but still, you should have told me sooner," he repeated himself.

Tasha sighed. "You're right, I should have. I'm sorry."

Neil leaned in and gave her a kiss. "I'll forgive you, this time," he smiled. "Don't let it happen again."

Tony and Mia showed up then, climbing up the stairs to the rampart and Tony pointed to the woods off to the side of the castle.

"The dragons would like to talk to you before they leave," Tony said.

"Oh, sure, let's go see them. I need to thank them anyways," Neil replied.

The company found their way over to the dragons waiting patiently at the edge of the woods. Adeena was waiting there too, sitting on 'Blinky' and rubbing the dragon's neck.

"Hi guys," Adeena waved.

"Hey Adeena, give the dragons my greeting to," Neil said.

Adeena translated as requested and she in turn translated Drayler's reponse. "He would like to thank you for keeping your word against hunting them."

"Tell him I will always keep that in effect, and tell him I appreciate his and the others help against Helana. It means a lot to me and Tasha."

Adeena translated and Drayler bowed to them. Adeena translated the dragon's words.

"You may call on us if you ever need our aid. Like you, we will keep our word," Drayler replied.

"Safe journey home friend, if I may call you friend?" Neil asked.

Drayler nodded. "Yes, friend."

On that, Drayler and his fellow dragons lifted themselves into the air and slowly disappeared into the night sky, mere shadows against a star filled horizon. Blinky was the last to go and Adeena gave her friend a big hug.

"See you soon, be good now," Adeena waved her finger

at him. The dragon smiled and bobbed its head as though saying 'okay' and spread its wings as he lifted and took flight to catch up to his brethren. Soon he and the dragons were out of sight and the company adjourned back to the castle and came across the dwarves Axel and Ruskin in the courtyard carrying a mug of ale each.

"Hiya sir, care ta join us for a mug or two?" Axel chortled.

"You know, don't mind if I do," Neil answered. "How about it crew?"

"Good a plan as any," Tony agreed.

"Follow us, we're sittin over this way," pointed Ruskin. The two dwarves led them to a campfire just outside the castle where Thatcher, Falon, Jacinto and a few of his men were enjoying some spirited talk and some ale from a nearby keg.

"Sir Neil, Lady Tasha, Mister Tony, ya'all come sit, enjoy the warmth of the fire!" Thatcher beckoned to them.

They all found a seat around the fire, and Thatcher handed out mugs to each of them and then the two dwarves went about pouring the ale in good proportions. The fire was stoked by Riley and Baker, each taking turns to throw a log on to keep the flames high. After what they had all been through, each felt at ease for the first time in a while. It had been a sad day but now the mood was beginning to lighten, the fire and the ale helping that along just a tad.

"Any idea how Zach be doin?" Axel asked.

"Tired, he's up resting in his room," Neil replied quietly. "I wish I could do more for him."

"Shar has been quiet all day as well," Falon added.

"Give th'man time. He's lost a great deal, an' her too," Riley piped up. "We all have. A toast friends, to a good man Keller, may he find peace wherever it is he be."

"Aye, to Keller, and to all who fell," Jacinto added.

The company clanked their mugs together in the toast and the rest of the night was spent enjoying the ale and talking about their plans for down the road. It was late at night before they retired for the night. Adeena returned to her fellow faerie in their tents, the dwarves to their own campsite and likewise for Jacinto and his men. Thatcher ventured off to see his fellow gnomes who had set up camp and the rest made their way back to the castle. On entering the courtyard, Neil and Tony noticed Zach was standing on the catwalk, staring out over the darkened landscape. Tasha, Mia and Falon went off to check on Shar while the two men strolled up the steps to see how Zach was coping.

"Hey, how are you doing?" Tony wondered.

Zach turned to see them and smiled back. "I'll be okay guys. Don't worry I ain't gonna jump off into the moat."

Neil and Tony laughed lightly, glad to see Zach's sense of humor had returned in some lighter form.

"Well good, I'd hate to jump in after you! I've had too much ale," Neil burped.

"It's just hard to believe she's gone. I keep thinking I'm going to see her pop up around some corner," Zach murmured.

"Yeah, and I keep expecting Malcolm to appear and offer me some advice on something. I'll miss him, a lot," Neil said.

"Shar's guardian now then?" Zach asked.

"That's what Merlin said. Malcolm left his staff in Shar's care now. Notice her hair and how blonde it's got?" Neil checked.

"Yeah, looks weird on her," Tony commented.

"Guys, I've been thinking about something all day and I've made a decision," Zach started.

"Oh, what would that be?" Neil inquired.

Zach looked at them. “I’m going to go home, back to our world.”

Neil and Tony stared at Zach expecting a punch line but nothing came.

“Seriously?” Tony wondered.

“Yeah, seriously. I need to get away from here for a time,” Zach took in a deep breath of the night air, as he tried to keep his composure. “I can’t be here as long as Riane is still in here,” he pointed to his head and then his chest. “The pain is too much. If I go back maybe it’ll help me. I know I can’t stay here right now.”

“I don’t want to see you go my friend, but if it’s what you need to do, then you do what you have to,” Neil said. He put his left hand on Zach’s shoulder. “You do what you feel is right.”

“Thanks,” Zach nodded.

“Any idea how long you’ll be gone?” Tony was curious. He didn’t like how it sounded and had a bad feeling about it.

Zach shook his head, “No, I don’t.”

“It won’t be the same around here without you, but hey, I get it,” Tony said.

“Yeah, you’ll be missed,” Neil added. “Especially Axe and Ruskin, they’ll have nobody to drink or play poker with.”

The three men chuckled lightly and Zach let a few tears escape and trickle down his face. Neil shook his hand and gave him a hug and Tony did likewise. The three men said nothing for a time, opting to stand there and watch the stars flicker in the sky and the campfires in the fields slowly fade. It was near daybreak when the three adjourned to their rooms with a simple nod to the other as they disappeared behind each door.

A few days went by and slowly the mood to celebrate their victory over Helana surfaced. A number of huge bonfires were lit each night and every different elf race held a gathering to toast their victory and to remember those who had lost their lives in the war. It was a celebration that lasted several days and once the party mood had run its course the camps began to disband and each tribe started on its way back to their homeland. The exception of course being the faerie that had no home to return to anymore. Oberon was planning on staying for a time to help heal Tir Nan Og and do what he could for his daughter Leasha, who was improving nicely. Xanthus promised to do what he could with any elf magic the faerie needed.

The gnome kingdom had been destroyed and thus the gnomes began to think of places where they might resettle. In a gesture of goodwill the dwarves offered their home as a base from which they could work out of until they were able to determine where it was they wanted to settle. Jacinto offered assistance to the gnomes as well, offering to help guide scouting parties as they explored all their options. The war had brought all the races together and Merlin was impressed by it all. He had plans to go home soon and he was at peace knowing that they were all in good hands with a monarchy that cared and by a new guardian that had a lot to offer.

Shar was still uneasy in taking on the role of guardian but felt reassured by Merlin's offer to be there when she needed him. She heard of Zach's desire to leave and felt saddened at the thought but knew that Zach needed to leave. She would be busy with Neil and Tasha for a time, helping them rebuild their own home and to assure that Tasha's pregnancy went well. There were other matters of course, and she hoped she was up for the tasks ahead.

"Where do we even begin with Kildare? Maybe we

should start fresh and build from scratch?" Neil suggested as he walked with Tasha and Shar in the courtyard of Cambridge.

"I like that idea, a new beginning," Tasha smiled as she held his hand.

"You have a lot of work ahead of you then, don't expect me to use too much magic," Shar teased.

"We wouldn't expect that from you Shar," Neil replied. "You know we never had an official ceremony making you guardian. Maybe we should?"

Shar shook her head. "No, that is not what Malcolm would have wanted. I am quite happy without one."

Tasha gave her friend a hug. "Then let us make it official."

Both she and Neil stopped and faced Shar. The mage stood there, holding the staff with the amulets.

"As your king and queen, you are hereby given the title of guardian of Avalon, keeper of the amulets and watcher of this land and its races," Tasha said.

"Do you accept this?" Neil asked.

Shar looked at the staff and then gave them a smile. "I will do my best to uphold what is required of me, and to protect this world and its races as asked."

A set of hands clapping made all three turn to look and Merlin stood there, with Falon at his side. The wizard was clapping and smiling and Falon followed suit.

"Well said, I could not have put it better myself," Merlin said.

"Thank you sir," Shar replied.

"You are welcome," Merlin bowed. He looked at Neil and Tasha. "I wanted to let you know that I'll be leaving in the morning, but my young apprentice here would like to stay on for a time, if that is okay by you?"

"Of course! She's more than welcome to stay as long as she likes!" Tasha said.

"Zach going with you?" Neil asked.

Merlin gave a small nod, "yes, he is. Not to worry, I will keep an eye on him for you. I will be by on occasion to check in on young Shar here and relay anything you may wish to pass on to Zach and likewise from him."

"That would be great, thank you," Neil said.

"It is the least I can do."

The wind blew across his face as he stood in the meadow and it felt warm on his skin. The tall grass rustled around him and brushed against his legs. He noticed a cabin nearby and began to walk through the tall grass towards it. A voice called out to him and he turned to see a woman. He recognized her and waited for her to catch up.

"Malcolm!" Riane said as she ran up. She gave him a hug and he returned her affection.

"Hi my dear, how are you?"

"I am good. Where are we?" she wondered.

"I have an idea, and I think the answer we seek is at that cabin. Shall we go see?" he suggested.

Riane nodded and took his hand in hers. Together they walked through the meadow enjoying the sunshine and the serenity around them. At the cabin a man stepped out the door and waved to them. Malcolm recognized his old teacher immediately and smiled. It had been so long since he had seen Schredrick! He and Riane strolled up and Schredrick shook Malcolm's hand enthusiastically and then gave the elf a huge hug.

"Welcome, both of you," Schredrick said.

"Where are we sir?" Riane asked curiously.

"We are somewhere that is a resting place before you go

on, if you will," Schredrick commented. "There is someone here to see you my lady. He's been waiting anxiously."

"Oh?" Riane was curious. Another elf appeared from around the cabin and held his arms out for her. "Grandfather!" Riane ran up to Kemal and gave him a huge embrace.

"It is nice to see you again, though I had hoped for not some time yet, but still, I am glad to see you Riane." Kemal took her hand, "come, let us go down by the lake, Schredrick has quite the garden these days."

The two elves wandered off, leaving Schredrick and Malcolm to themselves. Schredrick led Malcolm as they walked, and let out a deep sigh.

"I am happy to see you Malcolm, so you felt it was time did you?"

"Yes, I did. My student is ready to take over from me, and I had to be sure that the foe we were facing was destroyed."

"Good for you, it is not easy to accept that our time is at an end. I felt the same when I left you to assume the guardianship, but it has been a pleasant time here. I always have a visit from Kemal, and others, but it will be nice to move on. It is your time now Malcolm, to once again take over from me here."

"And what of Riane?" Malcolm looked over towards the elf.

"I will see to her safe arrival, and I will stop by on occasion to visit so be ready to always have the tea on," Schredrick chuckled.

"I will be sure," Malcolm laughed. He looked around and smiled. "I will miss the others though."

"You can always check in on them on occasion. Be sure to ask for permission first. They frown on that if you don't," Schredrick winked.

"Thank you for the advice," Malcolm nodded. "How is the garden?"

"Doing well. I left it in good shape for you," Schredrick said as he patted Malcolm on the back.

Riane and Kemal strolled over to rejoin them and Riane looked at Malcolm.

"Will Zach be okay?" she wondered.

"He will be fine, in time my lady, he will be just fine," Malcolm assured her. "It was a nice gesture on your part to give him your gift."

"I thought he should have it, he has a great task ahead as a future king," Riane gave him a big smile and then hugged Malcolm.

"Indeed he has," Malcolm said.

"He will see you again in time my lady. To you it will be like you were never apart," Schredrick commented. He looked up at the sun and then back at them all. "Kemal, shall we escort our guest?"

"I think we should, her grandmother is eager to see her, and Riane, Your mother waits too."

Riane beamed, "Mother? It will be nice to see her again, and Grandmother as well!"

"Malcolm, I will see you soon for tea," Kemal shook the wizard's hand.

"I look forward to it," Malcolm answered with a grin.

"Then I shall take my leave of you. Keep things in order as you see fit. This is your home now," Schredrick motioned around the landscape.

"I will. I look forward to your visit. Safe journey Riane. I hope to see you soon as well," Malcolm said as he gave her one last hug.

"Of course, take care my friend," Riane hugged him back and then stepped back with Kemal and Schredrick. The three of them turned around and started to walk off, and slowly vanished, leaving Malcolm standing by himself. He let out a deep sigh and took a look around. Well, what to do first?

"I think a cup of tea is in order, and then perhaps, a little tending to the flowers."

The morning of Merlin and Zach's departure came soon enough and everyone was there to see them off! Zach entered the council chamber of Cambridge castle and was a bit taken aback at all of the faces there to greet him. No one wanted to miss it and the chamber was full! He shook hands with everyone who approached him, from the elf captains Kieran and Elise to Terry Baker who he had just met recently and wished them well as they did likewise to him. Once he had worked his way through the crowd he came to the front of the room and faced all his good friends.

"Sure you want to do this?" Neil checked, just to make sure.

"Yeah, I do. After all that's happened, I need a break," Zach replied with a nod.

"Keep in touch, and come back when your ready, I'll take care of your horse til then," Tony said with a grin. Both men shook Zach's hand once again and gave him a quick hug. Shar threw her arms around him and held him tightly.

"I'll let you know how things are going back here every once in a while," she said.

"Thanks, I'd like that," Zach reiterated his appreciation.

Mia gave him a hug and a kiss on the cheek, "I'll keep Tony out of trouble until you get back."

"Good, he's going to need the help," Zach quipped.

Tasha took her turn to hug him. "See you soon."

Zach smiled and gave her a kiss on the cheek. "You ever need me, you call, and I'll be back in a flash."

"I'll hold you to that," Neil cracked.

Adeena flew up and hugged him tightly and then tweaked his nose and laughed. "For good luck."

"Thanks, I think," Zach snickered.

"We'll keep the ale fresh for ya m'boy, an'a mug ta pour it in," Axel stated.

"Aye, an'lots of it," Ruskin chortled.

"Stay well my friend," Thatcher said.

"Save some of your tobacco for when I get back, and we'll see who can puff bigger smoke rings," Zach teased. Thatcher laughed and shook Zach's hand vigorously.

"Are you ready Zach?" Merlin checked.

Zach adjusted his backpack and looked around the room at everyone once more. "I'm ready."

Merlin faced the room and bowed. "Thank you for having myself, Rachel, Christina and Falon as your guests. It has been a true joy to come back. I hope to do it more often going forward, take care everyone."

Falon gave Zach a hug and looked at Merlin. "See you soon sir."

"That you will Fallon. Do let me know when Rachel and Christina are ready to come home as well. Well, shall we go Zach?"

"Anytime," Zach replied.

Merlin cast the magic he needed and a vortex took shape on the wall in front of them. The doorway was opened and it waited for them to enter. Merlin gave a final wave and then stepped in, vanishing. Zach looked over to Tony and Neil and gave them a thumb up.

"Good luck everyone. Keep in touch!" Zach walked into the vortex and disappeared. The magic faded slowly and soon dissipated leaving a room of people staring at an empty wall. The group broke up and everyone went about their normal business once again, whether it was packing to return to their home or preparing their horses, readying food or just the joy of visiting with one another. The day was young and there was still much to do!

The war of magic's was over, and a new beginning for the races was now underway. Those who had drifted apart had become close once more; those who had mistrusted now had restored faith in one another. Together they had stopped a formidable foe and going forward no one doubted that they could conquer any road block they may face or any challenge thrown their way. Unified, the new world of Avalon was about to embark on an entirely new path, the road less traveled.

Seven months after returning to the 'old world' Zach had settled down in London England. He discovered that the services for a private detective were quite in demand so rather than go back to Seattle he stayed on there. He was able to find a suitable place to live and had plenty of work to keep his bank account and himself, happy. Zach kept himself occupied with a lot of work and that in turn helped in his healing from the death of Riane. It was nice day, without rain for a change and he was busy shooting pictures for a client when he got a surprise visit that day.

He turned the camera on, and let it do the work, shooting automatically while he sat at his table at the tea shop. Zach was sipping another new tea he was trying when he looked up and there in front of him, sitting at his table was Merlin.

"Do you always have to do that?" he asked.

"I find it amusing to see the look on your face each time I do it," Merlin grinned.

"Yeah yeah, well I haven't seen you in a while," Zach scoffed.

"I've been busy, tending to my shop, visiting Shar and assisting her but I am always around Zach. I am sworn to watch over you," Merlin said. "Now that Rachel and Christina are finally back, they will be looking in on you which will free me up for other things."

"Uh huh, I know. So what's new back on Avalon?" he asked curiously.

"Neil and Tasha have had their baby, a girl; they've named her 'Brandy'. A tribute to Riane's favorite drink I understand," Merlin answered. He watched for Zach's reaction and noticed that he didn't flinch this time on hearing Riane's name. Perhaps he was beginning to move on.

"Good for them, nice name too," Zach said quietly. "And Tony?"

"Off in the woods somewhere with his lady Mia, likely watching the unicorns as usual. May I ask Zach, do you still have a hole inside, as you put it, from Riane's passing? Merlin inquired, his curiousity getting the best of him.

"I don't think that will ever go away. Something felt like it died with her that day, I can't explain it."

"Do you ever wonder about the gift Riane gave you?"

Zach looked up from his tea cup. "I'd forgotten about that, I remember her saying that, and then Helana said that too? What the hell kinda gift?"

"Do you really want to know?"

"Hey, you opened the door, no chance your closing it now," Zach retorted.

Merlin laughed and sat up as the waitress wandered over. "Would you like anything?"

"Cup of regular tea, thank you," Merlin said. She left

and Merlin looked back at Zach. "Very well, recall the words Riane used in her spell?"

"Vaguely, get to the point. What is this gift?"

"She has given you her life force, the elf life force," Merlin answered.

Zach sat there for a second, thinking about what he had just said. "Her life force?"

"Yes, her life's energy, an elf's life energy."

"And?"

"Think about it, how long does an elf usually live?"

"Well, a long time."

The waitress came back with Merlin's tea and he thanked her and then smiled at Zach.

"Exactly."

"So, uh, what? I'm going to live a long time?"

Merlin winked. "Jackpot, as you would say."

Zach sat back in his chair trying to get a grasp of this new information. He was going to live a long time? How long was a long time? Zach looked back at Merlin.

"How long am I going to live?"

Merlin shrugged, "no idea."

"That's bullshit."

"Really, I have no idea. That was her gift to you, so now you get to live a little longer than usual," Merlin said.

"Great! So now I can hurt that much longer," Zach groaned. He took another sip of tea and shook his head.

"Time is the one thing that heals all wounds Zach, even this. In time you may find love again."

"I don't think so."

Merlin shrugged. "In time, you may, love can appear when you least expect it."

"Sure sure." A voice of recognition shouted out from behind and made Zach turn. There stood a familiar face he thought he'd never see again.

"Zach Thomas! What are you doing here in London?"

"Michelle?" Zach sat up. He turned back to Merlin but the wizard was gone. "Figures."

"What are you doing here in London?" Michelle Bruce repeated. She ambled over to his table, and both were rather shocked at seeing the other.

"I could ask you the same question," he said.

"I'm working here now; remember back in Seattle I was packing to leave? Well, this was where I was going. I work at the Museum of London."

"Well, isn't it a small world?"

"Isn't it though? Can I join you?" she checked, as she pointed to the empty seat.

"Have a chair, so, how is work?"

"I'm loving it! Nice to be working at a place that I get to focus on the field I enjoy, medieval histories."

"I remember," Zach chuckled.

Shar sat up in bed abruptly and tried to breathe; she pulled at her shirt and ripped it away from her neck and then rolled off the bed and collapsed to the floor. Finally the air came through and she gasped it in big gulps, refilling her lungs. Tears streamed down her face as she sat up, drained from the experience. The dream was so vivid that it still haunted her vision. Shar cried as she tried to wipe the tears from her face, still breathing hard to calm herself. She had never experienced anything like that before and she was scared because of it. Off on the far side of the room a figure stepped out of the shadows and Shar raised her hands instinctively in defense and then recognized her visitor.

Merlin came into the light cast by the candle by her bed and knelt next to the mage. He put his hand on her shoulder and spoke to her calmly. Slowly Shar got herself under control.

"Are you better now?" he asked.

"Yes," she nodded, "what just happened?"

"You had a dream, correct?"

"It was like I was there," Shar gasped, wiping the sweat from her forehead. She realized she was drenched from the experience.

"It is always hardest the first time. Once you are able to master your dreams, then it will not hurt quite as much."

"What?" Shar looked at him, confused.

"There will be more dreams; they allow you to see things you might not otherwise see. A part of your abilities my lady that are just beginning to show themselves."

"The pain, unbearable," Shar murmured as she got herself under control.

"I'm here to help Shar, like I said I would be, breathe deeply, and sit back," he encouraged.

Shar stared up at the ceiling and then back at him. "How do I understand them?"

"You will need to remember what it was you saw, and take those images and piece them together. You will never have a complete answer but it will give you insight."

"What I saw, was, something, someone, coming from the, east, yes, who has a lot of hatred," Shar muttered as she tried to visualize what she had dreamt.

"Yes, I know what you are talking about," Merlin sighed.

Shar looked at him. "You do?"

"Oh my yes, I have had this same dream. Someone wants retribution, and one day they will show themselves. They will be coming here looking for it."

A SNEAK PEAK AT 'TRIO BOOK FOUR: RETRIBUTION'

The elf looked over the man, and then back to his fellow council members. He stood and pointed to their council leader, motioning for him to take his seat with the rest of them.

"I prefer to stand; it was I who organized this council in the first place so you will listen to me and what I have to say. I bring this man to us because he can aid us in our goal to make our prescence known in the west. Kildare is rebuilt and is as it was before, but the races are working in unison. There are no more petty wars or arguments over land, the witch did the one thing she did not want to do, unite them all. It is up to us to divide them once more if we are to succeed in taking control of this world!"

"And how is this man going to help us? He is nothing more than a woodsman, living in a cabin and foraging for berries," the elf snorted.

"Careful what you say Trian, he is not what he appears to be," the man said. "Even all of us together can not take on the guardian, she is far too powerful. He has the ability we need to break down her strength and get the races fighting with one another as before!"

"We have stayed away, hidden here in the east, as you suggested and now you want to stray off our goal to do something that will take even longer to attain? How is that a benefit to us?" Trian questioned.

"This man," he pointed, "can make it happen a lot sooner than you may think."

"And how is that going to be accomplished?" Trian muttered. His faith in what he was saying was virtually non-existant.

“I can speak for myself,” the stranger said, speaking up for the first time.

“Then talk,” Trian urged.

“I have done it in the past, and I can do it now. I have a gift to bargain with one and make promises to another, as each is broken with the other, the trust is lost and therefore, you cause chaos. It will not be as difficult as you may think.”

“Is that so, and how is it you have such confidence in yourself?” Trian pushed for answers.

“I was a part of a great war, caused by my betrayals and lies, and all of my kind were killed cept me. I tricked my way here, and have stayed here ever since. I gave the witch some ideas and she failed to use them well, but my strength is returning and I can give you what you want so badly and all I ask in return is to be a part of your council.”

“You want to be on the council? You? And just who are you?” Trian asked.

“Who am I? I am,” he looked at all the council members and smiled a wicked grin, “I am Loki.”

CPSIA information can be obtained at www.ICGtesting.com
Printed in the USA
BVOW012211071011

273075BV00001B/1/P